SUMMER SQUALLS

SUMMER SQUALLS

Murder and Intrigue
in Rehoboth Beach

TOM DONNELLY

Charleston, SC
www.PalmettoPublishing.com

Summer Squalls
Copyright © 2022 by Tom Donnelly

First Edition

Hardcover: (DJ) 979-8-8229-0323-4
Paperback: 979-8-8229-0324-1
eBook: 979-8-8229-0325-8

"To my wife Joan and my granddaughter Claire."

CHAPTER ONE

Havana Harbor

On the morning of 13 September 1677, six treasure-laden Spanish galleons and eighteen escort vessels lay at anchor in Havana Harbor. After four months of interminable delays, Admiral Jose Estevan Alcazar's fleet was finally prepared to sail for Spain. Alcazar had pushed for a mid-July departure, but shipments of silver reales from the mints in Mexico City and Lima and gold escudos from Cuzco, Mexico City, and Bogotá were weeks late in arriving.

By the mid-1600s, Spanish authorities had restricted the amount of gold and silver each ship carried to limit loss in the event of capture or sinking, but a series of European wars had left Spain's treasury bare. Each galleon in the Alcazar fleet would carry almost one and a half times the "authorized" limit.

As the sun rose over the ramparts of Morro Castle, Alcazar was preparing to meet in the Castillo de la Real Fuerza with the governor general and the captains and masters of his fleet's ships. He finished putting on his uniform, clasped his saber to the sash around his waist, and walked to the French doors opening onto the balcony. Alcazar threw open the drapes and stepped out to look over the harbor. Boats moved throughout the anchored ships, bringing sailors and supplies to the treasure fleet.

A soft knock on the door momentarily diverted Alcazar's attention away from the harbor.

"Enter."

Pablo Garcia, Alcazar's personal valet, entered the room carrying a large silver tray.

"Excellency, I am so sorry to bother you, but I thought you might enjoy some breakfast before your big day."

"That is very kind of you, Pablo." Alcazar motioned for Pablo to sit. "What will you do when I leave today?"

"Well, sir, I'm sure the governor general will find another assignment for me. Otherwise, I will return to my family and farm our land."

"Would you consider returning to Spain with me? I know you have a family here, but arrangements could be made to have them follow you in the next convoy. You have served me faithfully the last four months, and I assure you that you will be treated well."

Pablo looked down sadly. "It has been an honor to serve Your Excellency, but I could never leave my wife and children. Besides, Havana has been my home for almost thirty years."

"I understand and thought that might be your answer. I have something for you." Alcazar handed Pablo a rather large envelope. "I want you to have this, and I hope it will help provide you and your family a little better life. It's likely that I will be returning to Havana in a year or two, and I expect you to return to my service."

"It would be my honor, and thank you for your generous gift. I will be at the docks to see you off." Pablo bowed and left the room.

This morning could not end soon enough, Alcazar thought; he ached to be at sea and, soon, to see his family again.

Alcazar was a strict naval commander who had distinguished himself in the Anglo-Spanish War as a young ensign and, most recently, in the Franco-Dutch War as a captain of the fleet. Despite his lineage, he'd risen rapidly through the ranks based entirely on merit rather than family influence and money.

The room fell silent as Alcazar rose from his chair to the left of the governor general and approached the dais. He looked out at the assembled captains and sailing masters, cleared his throat, and began to read the fleet's sailing orders.

"The fleet will consist of six galleons: *Santa Ana*, *Nuestra Señora de la Purification*, *Santiago*, *La Concepción*, *San Juan Baptista*, and the *Magdalena*. Seven corvettes, seven frigates, and four caravels will sail as protection for the fleet. The galleons will sail in a one-two-two-one formation ringed by the heavily armed escort vessels. Each ship will maintain visual contact during daylight and utilize fore and aft running lanterns at night."

Alcazar briefed the captains on major storm activity in the southeastern Caribbean as reported by recently arrived ship captains. He directed that, after rounding the Florida peninsula, the fleet would sail in a north-north-easterly direction through the Bahama passage rather than the usual east-northeast trade route to Spain. Alcazar accepted the risk of running into English corsairs but postulated that it was less likely that the fleet would run into violent weather hugging the east coast of the continent until they could safely turn east to Spain. But he was dead wrong.

Admiral Alcazar's authority was absolute; he took no questions as he turned to leave.

The governor general rose from his chair behind Alcazar, the room jumped to attention with a rattling of sabers and squeaking of wooden chairs on the marble floor. Not a voice was heard until Alcazar and the governor general had exited the hall. It was time for the blessing of the fleet.

At precisely 1030 hours, the bells of the many Catholic churches in Havana began to ring throughout the city, beckoning the citizens to the harbor for the blessing of the fleet. From every quarter of the city, men and women from all walks of life emerged from their homes, shops, and inns in their finest garments. Thousands ringed the harbor, peered out from shop windows along the docks, or sought out the highest elevation from which to watch the Mass and following celebration.

The assembled mass of ships' captains and masters followed Alcazar and the governor general at a respectful distance out of the hall and down the stairs to the courtyard. By midmorning, the temperature had risen to over ninety degrees. Alcazar and his entourage descended the stone steps from the courtyard to the central dock.

As was custom, an ornately decorated marble-topped altar was placed on a wooden platform facing the harbor, entirely draped in red-and-yellow fabric. A large golden crucifix sat in the middle of the altar, and three three-foot-tall gold candleholders were placed on each side.

Three ornately carved high-back wooden chairs with red velvet cushions were placed eight feet behind the altar for the governor general, Admiral Alcazar, and the archbishop of Havana, His Holy Eminence Luis Manuel Fernandez de Aragon. Ten feet behind the three red-velvet-cushioned chairs were sixty simple wooden chairs arranged in three perfectly spaced rows for the fleet's captains, masters, and Havana's government officials of lesser rank.

At 1100, the dignitaries, with military precision, ascended the steps to the platform and took their designated seats.

Bishop Diaz led a procession of priests and acolytes along the harbor road to the ornate platform. As the bishop climbed the steps to the altar, followed by two black-robed priests swinging smoking silver globes of incense, nearly a hundred priests from throughout the island moved into position, ringing the altar platform.

This was Catholic pageantry at its finest, and the bishop had no intention of missing his opportunity to perform for the assembled masses. He turned and bowed, acknowledging the governor general, Admiral Alcazar, and Havana's archbishop. He then turned to the altar facing the harbor and the assembled congregation.

Alcazar fumed silently as the bishop droned on for almost an hour in both Spanish and Latin, the language of the Catholic Mass. Recognizing Alcazar's growing impatience, the governor general whispered, "At least for you this will be over soon—unless you'd like to take him with you."

Alcazar smiled knowingly and shook his head in the negative. "Sorry, Excellency, he's needed here."

At last, the bishop turned to face the gathered dignitaries, beckoning them to come forward and receive the Eucharist.

After Communion and a final benediction, the bishop turned toward the harbor, raised his hands to the heavens, and made the sign of the cross, blessing the fleet and thus signaling the Mass was finally over.

From La Punta and Morro Castle, cannons roared a final salute to the fleet, and cheers erupted throughout the harbor.

The governor general accompanied Admiral Alcazar to the end of the dock, wished him Godspeed, and continued to watch as the admiral was rowed out to his flagship, the *Magdalena*.

CHAPTER TWO

Javier Vega watched the Mass and festivities from the forecastle of the *La Concepción*. As sailing master of the ship, Vega could and probably should have attended Admiral Alcazar's briefing and the blessing of the fleet. Instead, he contended to Captain Martinez that preparations to sail were behind schedule, so it would be more beneficial if he remained on board to ensure that provisioning was completed and the ship was prepared to weigh anchor at the appointed hour. *La Concepción* had been Vega's home since he first signed on as an apprentice seaman at the age of fifteen; he had always been more comfortable at sea than on dry land.

He moved to the main deck and watched as the crew completed preparations to sail. The nearly two-month delay had taken its toll on the ship's crew. Many experienced members of the crew had signed on with other ships sailing for Spain and other ports throughout the Spanish realm. Others, weary of the dangers and hardships of life at sea, had decided to settle in and around Havana.

Vega had never sailed with such an inexperienced crew. If the voyage proved uneventful, the handful of experienced sailors could train the new crew sufficiently for a successful voyage, but he knew that severe weather or attack could spell disaster for the *La Concepción*.

As he watched the captain's launch approach, he moved to the main deck to greet Martinez, brief the captain on preparations, and receive his orders.

Captain Juan Martinez, son of Charles II's cousin, of the House of Hapsburg, was the least experienced of the fleet's captains. Fortunately, Martinez knew well his limitations and, in effect, relinquished command of the galleon to Vega. Vega greeted Martinez with respect, and the two retired to the captain's cabin to discuss the fleet's orders and preparations to sail.

On the high tide, the ships began to weigh anchor and move out of Havana's harbor to the open ocean. First the armed escort vessels moved out of the harbor and took up their designated positions in the formation. Finally, the galleons exited the harbor to join the fleet. By midafternoon, the fleet was under sail and headed for the open Atlantic. A steady breeze out of the southwest filled their sails, and a few clouds dotted the horizon; otherwise, the ocean was relatively calm, and the sky was clear in all directions.

As the sun set on the fourth day out, the fleet was off the Carolinas, hugging the Atlantic coast. The winds had stiffened and were now blowing at twelve to fifteen knots out of the east-southeast. To further complicate matters, the fleet was also sailing into a thick fog bank. Heavy gray clouds could now be seen to the southeast. Within minutes, Vega lost visual contact with the rest of the fleet. Being the trailing galleon on the starboard side of the formation, to avoid a possible collision, he turned the ship three degrees to starboard, knowing that the escort vessels were well to his east.

For over eight hours, the fleet sailed through a thick fog, and then, suddenly and without warning, the *La Concepción* shuddered. Vega rushed down from the aftcastle, shoved the helmsman aside, and grabbed the wheel—there was no response. The ship was rudderless, and the winds were blowing the ship back to port. It was now critical that the ship's sails be stowed and anchors dropped.

This was the type of emergency that Vega feared. Remarkably, under the direction of the veterans, the novice crew responded as well as could be expected. Vega additionally ordered that their situation be signaled to the fleet; however, given the conditions, he did not hold much hope that the message would be received. After several minutes, no response was forthcoming—they were now alone and dead in the water.

Martinez emerged from his cabin. It was the first time the crew had seen their captain since leaving Havana Harbor. He looked at Vega questioningly. Vega explained what he feared had happened; Martinez mumbled something to Vega and retreated to his cabin.

Vega ordered the carpenter's crew over the side to examine the sternpost-mounted rudder from the waterline and another to check the steering and pulley mechanism under the aftcastle deck. The crew examining the pulley system returned within a short time to report that the steering cables had snapped but could be repaired in a couple of hours.

Vega continued pacing the deck until the ship's carpenter and his assistant pulled themselves over the railing, soaked and trembling from the cold. The news was not good; they reported that the upper and lower gudgeons had snapped and both pintles were gone. The middle pintle and gudgeon were intact but would never be able to control the rudder system under full sail. The carpenter believed that extra pintles and gudgeons were on board; if so, repairs could be accomplished in approximately three to four hours. If new pintles and gudgeons had to be forged, it could take at least twelve hours to repair the rudder system.

After nearly an hour, the carpenter and his assistant emerged carrying the spare pintles and gudgeons. Vega drew a sigh of relief, which quickly faded when he saw the carpenter's face. The carpenter informed Vega that, due to the worsening conditions, it would likely take closer to six hours to repair the rudder.

By midmorning, the carpenter reported that the repairs to the rudder were completed. However, looking to the east and south, Vega realized that the delay had cost them dearly. He sent for the captain.

Within minutes, Martinez joined Vega on the main deck. Vega gestured for Martinez to follow him to the aftcastle railing. The ocean was rolling with six-to-eight-foot troughs but no whitecaps. Vega explained he had only seen this phenomenon once, preceding a massive hurricane. He feared that within a few hours they would be fighting fifteen-to-twenty-foot swells. Martinez believed their only hope was to attempt to outrun the hurricane at full sail, and Vega agreed. The outer bands of the storm were now visible in the southeastern sky, and the winds had picked up to thirty knots out of the southeast.

By noon, *La Concepción* was under full sail heading east-northeast. Vega retreated to the captain's cabin to examine the charts and maps and determine a plan to save the ship from the impending storm. Martinez believed that the Dutch and English were still at war, and Spain was a Dutch ally. Therefore, sailing into the Chesapeake estuary for refuge was not an option. Vega recalled a Dutch settlement, Swanendael, farther north and another small harbor between the Chesapeake and Delaware estuary. They agreed that their only reasonable option was to turn back to the northwest, hug the coast, and try to reach the Dutch settlement in the Delaware estuary or the smaller bay to its south.

La Concepción sailed into the early evening hours before disaster struck. Vega was at the wheel when the rudder system again failed. The winds out of the east had reached hurricane strength hours ago. Suddenly the mainmast snapped and fell to the port side with sails and rigging now trapping several crew members beneath. Rudderless, the ship was now corkscrewing in the twenty-foot swells. Vega knew the ship was doomed. Men were being swept overboard by the enormous waves, and the ship was now taking on water at an alarming rate.

Vega scrambled across the pitching deck and headed for the captain's cabin below. He burst through the door and found Martinez on the floor. With the storm raging, Vega had not heard the shot. The back of Martinez's skull was gone. Vega knew his time was running out. He grabbed the ship's log off the table, wrapped it in an oil-cloth, and tucked it into his waistband.

As he exited the cabin, the ship lurched to starboard, and he was slammed against the bulkhead. He reached the main deck and quickly recognized that the only escape was over the port rail. The entire forecastle and two-thirds of the main deck were now below water. He started to climb over the rail as a huge wave slammed into the starboard side and washed him overboard. He was now disoriented and fifteen to twenty feet below the ocean surface. He expelled air from his lungs and kicked and clawed, racing the air bubbles to the surface.

Vega surfaced into a watery hell. *La Concepción* was gone; sails, rigging, and parts of the ship littered the ocean. Vega swam toward a cargo hatch cover twenty feet away, grabbed hold, and pulled himself on top. After over an hour of plunging into the troughs of waves and riding their crests, Vega heard the sound of pounding surf above the roar of the wind.

CHAPTER THREE

Vega lay in the wet sand, his left arm and leg extended, his right arm and leg pulled in, and his body half buried in sand. With great effort, he rolled onto his back, pulled the oilskin-wrapped ship's log from his waistband, and tossed it onto the sand next to him. It had miraculously survived the sinking and its aftermath.

Pain pulsed through his body as he tried to get to his knees. He gingerly touched his forehead and winced in pain; the left side of his face and his entire forehead were severely abraded. His whole body ached, and his first deep breath caused a sharp pain in his right side. Vega rose to his feet, turned toward the ocean, and tried to walk. He stumbled drunkenly in the loose sand but within a few steps regained his balance and footing.

The ocean was as calm as he had ever seen it. The surface of the water resembled a mirror lying flat on the ground, and the sun's reflection off the water momentarily blinded him. Wreckage and a few bodies floated eerily on the surface and near the beach; small waves lapped at the shoreline. He surveyed the beach to the north and south; if anyone else had survived, they were nowhere in sight.

As Vega walked toward the shoreline, he suddenly noticed that his feet were cut and bleeding.

A large body floated facedown at the shoreline; Vega did not need to see the face to know it was the Moroccan merchant, Tarek. Better known to the crew as *El Cerdo*, "the pig," the Moroccan had purchased passage on the *La Concepción* by virtue of his friendship with Captain Martinez. Vega despised the man, and given the chance, any member of the crew would have gladly ended the Moroccan's voyage.

Vega reached down and pulled the leather half boots off El Cerdo and threw them onto the beach. They would be large for him, but he would need them if he were to make it to the Dutch trading post to the north. With considerable effort, he rolled the huge Moroccan onto his back and unclasped the large gold-linked money chain from around his waist. It was relatively common for wealthy merchants to wear these chains around their waists. Each thick chain link was roughly the equivalent of two escudos. Once a price was agreed upon for an item, the merchant would simply twist off the number of links required for the purchase. He knew the Moroccan also carried a money purse, and, after some searching, he found the leather pouch half filled with gold and silver coins. Vega tucked it into his front pocket.

He walked up the beach several yards and quickly found the cargo hatch cover that had carried him to safety, half buried in the sand. He stood the hatch cover on end and rolled the square mahogany cover to the water's edge. He collected the leather boots, money chain, and two casks of rum floating on the surf and placed them on the hatch cover.

Vega's plan was to float the hatch cover across the entrance to the small bay and head north along the beach on foot to the safety of the Dutch settlement. He estimated, based on the map, that the Dutch settlement was no more than a day's journey to the north. He pulled the makeshift raft into the water and began swimming the raft and his newfound belongings the four hundred yards' distance to the north shore. The current was swift, and it took Vega the better part of two hours to reach the far shore. Exhausted and cold, he pulled the hatch cover onto the beach and unloaded it. He headed toward the dunes and quickly found what he was searching for—a rock the size of a large man's fist. Returning to the raft, he grabbed one of the casks and smashed the rock into its top. The wooden lid broke inward. Vega raised the cask of rum and drank. The liquid warmed him inside, and he lay back on the sandy beach to rest, exhausted.

As the sun reached its zenith in the late summer sky, Vega got to his feet and pulled on the merchant's boots. He wrapped the gold money chain around his waist and picked up the unopened cask of rum.

Vega turned and headed north to an uncertain fate, not knowing that the English now controlled the Dutch settlement.

CHAPTER FOUR

Henlopen Estates, Rehoboth Beach, Delaware

Dr. Michael Finley stared at the heavily insured Brink's envelope and smiled. He did not have to open it to know its contents: it held the culmination of a twenty-seven-year search.

He only wished that Sarah had lived to share his joy at completing his quest. He thought back to their anniversary trip to Hawaii, where they'd fallen in love all over again, not just with each other but with the islands.

Finley, a world-renowned cardiologist, had been absorbed in his work during the early years of their marriage. Consequently, he'd had little time for Sarah, much less a family. Eventually, he could see how his work and long hours away from her had been tearing at the fabric of their marriage, and he had been determined to make it right.

Early in their marriage, she had accompanied him on one of his lecture appearances at an American Medical Association convention in Honolulu, but for Sarah it was as if she were on the trip alone. He never left the hotel, with his endless committee meetings and lectures.

She toured Oahu extensively on her own: Pearl Harbor, Iolani Palace, the Punchbowl National Cemetery, and the Bishop Museum. She fell in love with Hawaii, and it was not lost on Michael.

A couple of weeks before their thirtieth anniversary, he surprised her with his anniversary gift, a month-long trip to Hawaii, longer if she liked. It would be just the two of them—no work, no schedules. He told her to pack light, that they would buy anything and everything they needed when they got there, and by the way, they were leaving tomorrow. He now fondly remembered her child-like glee as she joyfully screamed and jumped into his arms.

Over the years, the islands became their special place, and they returned almost every year. They immersed themselves in the history and culture. She collected feather leis, Niihau necklaces, quilts, and virtually everything Hawaiian. Sarah decorated their new home in Henlopen Estates almost entirely with Hawaiian decor. She called it "East of the Islands"; it was their East Coast paradise.

Finley collected the finest specimen of every postage stamp issued by the Kingdom of Hawaii from 1851 through the Republic of Hawaii issues in 1898. Until today, he had all but one, the Missionary Stamp, Scott Catalogue Number 1. It was one of the rarest stamps in the world; only a few existed, and only one was known to be in mint condition. He commissioned Rawlings and Kempler out of San Francisco to find him that stamp. It cost him more than half a million dollars, but tonight he owned it. The last hole in his magnificent collection was now filled. He would take it to the safety deposit box in the morning.

He thought of Sarah and that tragic night he got the call.

"Dr. Finley, this is Chief J. R. Johnson. There has been an accident. Sarah was involved; she's being transported to Cape Henlopen Medical Center. I am sending over a patrol car to pick you up, and I'll be at the hospital when you arrive."

When Finley arrived, Chief Johnson informed him that Sarah had sustained head and neck injuries and was currently being prepped for surgery to relieve the pressure on her brain.

Sarah was returning from volunteering at a homeless shelter in Milton when her car had been struck by a drunk driver running a red light on Delaware's Route 1. The driver was a nineteen-year-old recent high school graduate from Maryland on beach week. The boy sustained a broken nose, three broken ribs, and minor lacerations. His passenger, an eighteen-year-old local girl, had been pronounced dead at the scene.

After six hours, neurologist Dr. Arthur Goldman, a friend and former colleague, entered the waiting room. Goldman was stoic and urged Finley to sit down. Finley remembered every word as if it were yesterday.

"The next twenty-four hours are critical. If she survives, we'll be better able to evaluate her chances of recovery."

She didn't.

The next few days and weeks after her death were a blur. Several friends and neighbors volunteered to help with the arrangements, but most of it only he could do. He soon realized how woefully unprepared he had been for the death of his spouse.

Before he met her, Sarah had served as an army nurse in Vietnam, and she was buried with full military honors at St. Peter's by the Sea Episcopal Cemetery in nearby Lewes.

Finley shook his head as if to return to the present. He picked up the envelope, crossed the kitchen, and walked down the hallway to his office. He pushed aside the framed map of the Hawaiian Islands and, with three practiced turns of the dial, opened the wall safe and placed the envelope inside. He thought, *How cliché; what self-respecting burglar won't look for a wall safe?* Finley locked the safe and walked back down the hall toward the great room when the doorbell rang.

Who the hell would be out on a night like this?

For the past three days, a nor'easter had settled in over the Delmarva Peninsula, causing considerable destruction along the coast from Cape Henlopen to Ocean City. The rains and gale-force winds were as bad tonight as he could remember.

Finley walked to the door and looked up at the security camera. The grainy black-and-white screen showed a young girl standing in the wind and rain, apparently soaked to the skin, her long blond hair hanging straight to her shoulders.

He opened the door and motioned her into the foyer.

"I am so sorry to bother you, but your house had the only lights on in the entire neighborhood. My car broke down on Ocean Drive, and I was hoping I could use your phone to call AAA." She anticipated his question before he opened his mouth. "My cell phone is dead; I am really sorry to impose upon you."

"It's no problem. Let me get a couple of towels. You can hang your coat on the rack in the corner."

Finley locked the front door and turned away. "Follow me, the phone is in the kitchen." As he turned toward the kitchen, she inconspicuously unlocked the front door and then followed him through the great room and down the hall to the kitchen.

Entering the kitchen, she explained, "I was babysitting for a family in North Shores, and when I started up the car to leave, the lights seemed dimmer than usual. As I drove onto Ocean Drive, the 'check gauges' light started flashing on the dashboard. The headlights and dashboard lights got dimmer and dimmer, and finally the car just quit."

"It sounds like your alternator is gone. Unfortunately, your car will have to be towed. The phone is on the wall next to the refrigerator, and the phone book is in the top drawer. Help yourself."

"That's OK, I have the number." She took her wallet out of her purse and searched for the card.

"Would you like something warm to drink? I was just about to brew some tea."

"No, thank you. You've been too kind already. I'll just get AAA and return to my car. Again, I am so sorry for the intrusion."

She pulled a card out of her wallet and appeared to dial the number on the back.

"This is Pamela Quinn. My car broke down on Ocean Drive in Rehoboth Beach across from the Henlopen Estates Beach Club. I think it's the alternator." She nodded at Finley, and he smiled in acknowledgment. "Thirty minutes? That's great, thank you so much."

Finley failed to notice that Pamela's finger was on the receiver the entire time.

"Let's go into the family room. You can wait here until the tow truck arrives." Finley preceded her down the hall and stopped short in his tracks. A stranger stood in the middle of the living room, rain dripping from his bucket hat and raincoat. He tossed the hat next to the chair and sat down.

"What the hell? Who are you, and how did you get into my house?"

"Doctor, please sit down. We have some business to attend to," the stranger replied.

"Get out of my house now before I call the police." Finley could feel the rage building inside him as he menacingly stepped toward the stranger.

"Doctor, turn slowly to your left and please sit down so we can talk."

Finley turned to his left and found himself staring into the barrel of a .38-caliber Smith and Wesson revolver. It seemed to dwarf the petite girl holding it to his head. He slowly sat down in the chair indicated for him by the intruder.

"Thank you, Doctor. We have no intention of harming you, but we will if necessary. I need a couple of favors from you, for which you will be generously compensated."

Finley surreptitiously glanced over his left shoulder. *Could I wrestle the gun away from the girl?* he wondered. The stranger didn't appear to be armed.

The girl, sensing a possible move by the doctor, stepped back and moved to his front.

"Dr. Finley, look at me," the stranger instructed. "I need your undivided attention. First, I need your home for the next six to nine months. You will be relocated to a very comfortable oceanfront residence south of here. It's well appointed and stocked with everything that you will need, including all types of entertainment. The only caveat is that you will have no contact with the outside, and you will be guarded and monitored at all times."

Finley knew he was being fed a crock of shit.

The stranger leaned back in his chair and waited for Finley to respond.

"This is outrageous; I won't stand for it," Finley replied.

"Doctor, please don't make this any more difficult. You really have no choice. Under the circumstances, I think I'm being quite generous."

The stranger pulled an envelope from his jacket pocket and produced three letters.

"I need you to sign these three letters. The first one is a letter from you to me, your 'nephew,' requesting that I come to Rehoboth as soon as possible to manage your affairs while you attend to your sister—my aunt's—last wish, to die in her own home in Florida. We are such a loving family, don't you agree?" The stranger stifled a laugh but smirked at Finley instead.

"The second letter is from you to the town manager informing him that your nephew will be managing your household affairs in your absence, and the third is your power of attorney granted to me, your nephew."

The stranger got up, walked across the room, and placed the three letters on the coffee table in front of Finley's chair. He handed Finley a pen and said, "Sign."

Finley again looked at the girl and heard the trigger cock. In total defeat, he picked up the pen and signed the letters.

"What now?" Finley asked.

No sooner had he leaned back in his chair than he felt the needle enter his neck and the warm liquid course through his veins as the girl pushed home the plunger.

"That should put him out for at least three hours, enough time for you to get him out of here." The young girl broke the needle off and placed the plunger in her pocket.

"Change of plans, darling. Randy should be arriving any minute. He will take care of the good doctor. Sammy and the others should arrive by morning from North Carolina. I'll carry him down to the drive-through. In the meantime, why don't you fluff up the pillows and we'll take my new 'boudoir' for a test drive."

Finley's home, like many other seaside homes, was built up on pilings. The ground level provided room for parking, storage, and a utility enclosure. Stairs off the kitchen led down to a large cinder-block-enclosed utility room and workshop. From there, a door opened onto the reinforced concrete slab under the house.

The stranger picked up the limp body of Dr. Finley and effortlessly threw him over his shoulder. He walked down the hall to the kitchen, and the girl opened the door leading to the ground level. The stranger realized immediately that the stairs were too steep to carry the body down to the utility room. He turned and placed Finley's body on the kitchen floor, grabbed his feet, and slowly dragged the body down the stairs. Finley's head bounced up and down the steps as the stranger pulled his legs down the stairs.

At the bottom of the stairs, he flicked on the light switch, and the twenty-by-twenty-foot room was bathed in bright white light from four large fluorescent fixtures mounted in the ceiling. He sat on the bottom steps and examined the room. Straight ahead was an eight-foot-long workbench and chair with a large assortment of tools artfully arranged on pegboard hung on the wall behind. To his right, about twelve feet away, was a metal door leading to the drive-through under the house. Behind him on the opposite facing wall was a chest freezer.

He settled in to wait for Randy to arrive. He would dispose of the good doctor where he would not be found.

CHAPTER FIVE

Delaware Route 1 near Indian River Inlet

Randall Crockett drove north on Delaware Route 1, hunched over the steering wheel of the top-heavy van and trying to follow the lane markers in the late winter storm. At full speed, the wipers worked in vain to keep the pounding rain off the windshield as the gale-force winds buffeted the large van. He reduced his speed to thirty miles per hour and turned on his emergency flashers.

The ringing cell phone broke his concentration. He slowed, reached across the dashboard, picked up the phone, and looked at the caller ID. It was Malone, as he expected, probably wondering where he was and what was taking him so long.

He pressed answer. "What do you need, Malone? This is not a good time."

"Where the hell are you? You should have been here over an hour ago," Malone replied.

"Yeah, well, you try driving this piece of shit for four hours through this fucking storm."

"All right, when will you be here? I've got important things to do."

Yeah, like screwing that little bitch Pamela, he thought enviously.

"I'm fifteen miles south of Rehoboth on Route 1. I should be there in thirty minutes if it doesn't get any worse."

The phone went dead, and Crockett angrily threw it on the front passenger seat.

Crockett drove slowly into Henlopen Estates. He passed darkened houses on both sides of the street; it was like a ghost town, only with multimillion-dollar homes rather than run-down wooden shacks. He came to a T in the road and turned right toward the ocean. The storm was letting up some, and he could now make out the seemingly vacant homes on both sides of the road, each sitting the requisite distance from the street's centerline.

He drove slowly down the street and saw a house on the left with a few lights on. *This must be the place*, he thought. Although he couldn't make out the street number, it was as Malone had described it: a two-story Southern plantation–style house sitting ten feet above the ground on wooden pilings. A porch ringed the front and sides of the house on the first level, and latticework hid the stark pilings from view.

Crockett pulled into the driveway and turned off the van's lights. Malone suddenly appeared from under the house and guided him in with a flashlight. He backed the van under the house and turned off the engine. Crockett was exhausted and collapsed back into the bucket seat.

Malone banged on the driver's side window. Crockett opened his eyes and glared back through the tinted glass. He slowly opened the door and climbed down.

"This is your new chariot, sire," Crockett said mockingly. "It's fully equipped for a wheelchair-bound gentleman such as yourself." He didn't give Malone a chance to respond. "The front driver's seat comes out, and the motorized wheelchair in the back slides in and is clamped in place by pushing the lever on each side forward until it clicks into place. Pull the levers out and up and the wheelchair is disengaged. The accelerator and brake can be controlled with the levers on the back of the steering wheel. It's easier to operate than it looks; trust me."

Crockett motioned Malone to follow him to the sliding door on the right side. "This door slides open, and the remote control allows you to activate the wheelchair lift." He pulled the remote from the right pocket of his jeans and demonstrated.

"It would appear that you've thought of everything," Malone grudgingly replied.

"I'm not done. If you're going to pull this handicapped act off, you'll need to be extremely convincing. There are two wheelchairs in the back of the van. One is motorized and can be charged by simply plugging the charging mechanism into the outlet next to the elevator over there." He motioned to the elevator shaft in the far rear corner of the drive-through. "There's also a manual wheelchair for use in the house."

"Where did you get the van, and can it be traced?"

"Let's just say it's from a friend who has no further need of it, and I have taken great care to ensure that it cannot be traced. Now, where's the package you want me to dispose of?"

"That's been taken care of. I need you to go to the warehouse and wait for Sammy and the others to arrive. You can take Pamela's car, which is behind the house next door."

"Sure. I get to drive that piece of shit, and she gets to motor around town in a brand-new white Mercedes."

"How many out-of-work former cops do you know that drive around in new Mercedes, and how many successful real estate agents drive beat-up Toyota Corollas? Look, if we're going to pull this operation off, we're all going to have to stay in character—all of us, understood?"

Crockett grudgingly nodded.

"All right. Getting back to business, the warehouse is located on Love Creek about twenty minutes from here. Go back to Route 1 and head north to Route 24. Turn left onto Route 24 and drive about two and a half miles southeast. Cross over Love Creek and take your first left. It's a gravel road barely wide enough for two cars to pass. You'll see a large sign for Hazelwood Iron Works. That's the place."

Malone pulled a key from his right pants pocket and handed it to Crockett. "This opens the chain on the front gate. Don't forget to lock it once you're inside. It also opens the front door to the warehouse. It's well stocked with food and supplies. The beds and bathroom are on the second floor. Sammy and the others should arrive no later than midafternoon tomorrow. I'll call you if they are delayed. The first delivery is scheduled for next Friday at approximately 3:00 p.m. You'll rendezvous with the Columbian freighter *Niño de Christo* at channel marker thirteen. Here are the GPS coordinates." Malone handed Crockett a folded three-by-five card.

"There's a fifty-foot oyster boat tied up under the warehouse. It's not fast but shouldn't raise any suspicions. The key is labeled and on the desk in the office. The money is waiting to be deposited into an offshore account. Once you've verified the shipment, call me on the satellite phone in the console and I will complete the deposit. It will probably take only a few minutes for them to verify receipt."

Crockett turned to leave, but Malone stopped him.

"What about the job interview?" Malone asked.

"I got a call yesterday; I've got an interview with the chief of police next Monday morning."

"Don't blow it; we need you on the inside. And your cover story?" Malone asked.

"I used my cousin in Louisiana as a reference. He's an assistant chief with the Slidell Police Department and has agreed to verify my extensive law enforcement résumé."

"Did you include your five-year stint in the Alabama State Penitentiary on your résumé?"

"Fuck you, Malone." Crockett shook his head in disgust and left.

Malone walked through the utility room and climbed the stairs to the kitchen. He walked through the kitchen to the hallway and entered the spacious bedroom on his left.

Pamela sat up in bed. "What took you so long?" she asked.

"The good doctor has been disposed of, and I have my new wheels. I'm not looking forward to it, but tomorrow, I become a paraplegic and Finley's nephew, and you go back to your 'successful' real estate career."

"I'll be glad when we can finish this job and get the hell out of here." Pamela beckoned Malone to bed.

"You've got a long wait, honey. This job and the operation at the warehouse will take several months, maybe longer."

Malone disrobed, turned off the light, and climbed into the bed next to Pamela's warm, naked body.

CHAPTER SIX

FBI Headquarters, Washington, DC

Jack Scanlon took the last award plaque off the wall and read the inscription: *The Federal Bureau of Investigation Presents Its Distinguished Service Award to John W. Scanlon in Recognition of Ten Years of Outstanding and Dedicated Service to the Bureau and in Appreciation of Exceptional Leadership, Loyalty, and Character.*

He placed the plaque in the cardboard file box and moved the box to the chair next to the door. He pulled a small tube from his pocket and dabbed a bead of toothpaste into the hole left by the picture hook. He moved to the window, leaned back against the desk, and looked out onto Pennsylvania Avenue one last time. It was early May and Washington, DC, was in full bloom. It was almost noon, and hundreds of federal workers from offices up and down the avenue were spilling out onto the National Mall to enjoy the first real taste of spring.

He looked left toward the Capitol and thought back to January 20, 1981, the inauguration of President Ronald Reagan. Scanlon was ten years old when his father, Lieutenant General William T. Scanlon, had brought him and his older brother, William Jr., to witness the swearing in of the new president. Earlier in the week, it was announced that, after 444 days, the American hostages in Iran would be released. The hostage crisis had virtually guaranteed the defeat of the incumbent, President Jimmy Carter. It had been a blustery winter day, but Washington was in a celebratory mood.

At the time, Jack had no inkling of his father's status among the Washington elite, but he knew their seats and the attention and deference paid to his father indicated that he was someone very important. Three and a half years later, his father, mother, and older brother would be dead, killed by a drunk driver on their way home from his brother's high school graduation. If it hadn't been for a broken leg and wrist, he would have been with them. Instead, he had remained at home that evening with his aunt Ellen.

All of the memories of that tragic night and the days that followed came flooding back and engulfed him with an acute sense of loneliness, even after more than twenty-eight years.

He remembered that the doorbell had rung around 10:30 p.m. He and Aunt Ellen had been watching an old movie that evening, her favorite, *Casablanca*, starring Humphrey Bogart and Ingrid Bergman. Ellen, nearly asleep, got up from the couch to answer it.

Jack heard voices in the entrance hall and then a muffled scream and sobbing from his aunt. He quickly grabbed his crutches from the floor, balanced himself on the arm of the chair, stood, and hobbled out of the family room and down the hall to the front door to see what was wrong. Ellen was propped against the wall, breathing rapidly, with a Virginia state trooper supporting her by the elbow and waist. The door was open, and an infantry captain and army chaplain in dress blues stood on the threshold. The chaplain, with a Bible in his hand, looked befuddled and ill prepared to administer to the grief-stricken.

The days and weeks ahead seemed like a blur. He remembered the military funeral attended by hundreds of mourners, including the secretary of defense and the vice president. Oddly enough, it provided a welcome distraction to the unknown of what might lie ahead for an orphaned thirteen-year-old.

A knock on the open office door brought him back to the present.

"Sir, the deputy director would like to see you in his office as soon as possible," his young secretary said.

"Thanks, Mindy. Do you know what it's about?"

"No, sir. He personally called, not Marilyn, and I didn't have the courage to question him about it."

"Smart thinking. He can get a bit prickly about staff's 'need to know.'"

Jack followed Mindy out the door and down the hall to the central bank of elevators. He pushed the button and waited. After a few seconds, the elevator doors behind him opened. He turned, entered the elevator, and pushed the button for the top floor.

When the doors opened, he stepped out into the plush mahogany-paneled hallway leading to the suite of executive offices and conference rooms. He turned right and walked down the hall to the deputy director's suite. The frosted double glass door bore an inscription in gold lettering: *James G. Rankin, Deputy Director.*

Rankin had come to Washington almost forty years ago as a young aide to Montana Congressman William "Wild Bill" Buchanan. His great-aunt, a staunch pacifist, was the first woman elected to Congress and was one of fifty-six members of Congress who voted against entry into World War I in 1917. She was the only member of Congress to vote against declaring war on Japan after the Pearl Harbor attack on December 7, 1941.

When George Herbert Walker Bush was elected president in 1988, Buchanan, now a first-term senator, became a major power player in the Senate by virtue of his close friendship with the newly elected president. As young representatives, Bush and Buchanan had served together in the House and became the closest of friends, akin to brothers. Rankin sought a senior position in the White House, and Buchanan procured it for him. He soon parlayed it into an appointment as assistant director of the FBI for legislative affairs. From there it was a short hop, skip, and a jump to deputy director.

Rankin was not a political hack. He was brilliant, with all the quality traits of a born leader.

Jack opened the double doors and walked toward the desk belonging to Marilyn, Rankin's executive assistant.

"Go right in. He's been waiting for you." Marilyn pointed over her right shoulder to the double doors.

The door was open, and Jack leaned his head inside. Rankin looked up from the papers he was poring over and motioned Jack to one of the overstuffed chairs facing his desk.

"So, Scanlon, what's this crap about you retiring from the bureau?" Rankin bellowed, his gravelly voice reverberating throughout the room.

"Well, sir, I've come into a considerable sum of money and thought this would be a good time to retire and try something different," Jack stated uneasily.

"I know all that shit." Rankin paused and leaned back in his chair. "First, Jack, you can't retire until I sign your application to retire." Rankin held up Jack's unsigned application. "Second, you're too young to retire, it's a resignation, and third, I don't think you've thought this through. More importantly, the bureau needs you. Therefore, I'm offering you another option."

Jack was about to argue the point but thought better of it, deciding to hear Rankin out.

"I am offering you an eighteen-month sabbatical. During that time, I want you to write a manual or manuals on forensic principles and procedures for use by our bureau agents in the field, a sort of 'Forensics for Dummies,' if you will."

"Sir, forensic science is an enormous field of study with a myriad of subsets. There's forensic medicine, pathology, psychology, crime scene evidence, geology—and that doesn't even scratch the surface. What you're asking would take years, not to mention that the science is changing constantly."

"Well, we're not going to pay you to lay on the beach and drink strawberry daiquiris for the next eighteen months," Rankin quipped.

"Pay me?"

"Yes, pay you. Under this agreement, you will continue to be a bureau employee at your current pay grade and with your current title. You'll enjoy all the benefits and privileges to which you are currently entitled. I will, however, need to appoint someone to serve as acting division chief, and I would like you to recommend someone."

Jack didn't hesitate. "That's easy. Jacqueline Nguyen. She's the best we have, and she is very organized. You'd be a fool to select anyone else."

Rankin raised one eyebrow and stared across the desk at Scanlon.

"Ah, let me put that another way," Jack quickly said. "What I meant to say was she's superbly qualified, and there is no one better in the bureau to handle the job."

"Nice recovery. Look, Jack, getting back to the scope of this assignment, what we need is a reference guide in layman's terms that our agents in the field can learn from and apply to the cases they're assigned, nothing more. We're too understaffed and swamped with case work to always depend on your people in headquarters to get back to them. Can you do that?"

"Yes, sir, I believe I can."

"So you're accepting my offer?"

Jack hesitated. "Yes, sir, I am. It's a very generous offer, and I won't let you down."

"I know you won't," Rankin told him. "Listen, Jack, if after eighteen months you still want to resign, I won't stand in your way, but know that the bureau—no, *I* will do everything in my power to keep you here for years to come."

Rankin picked Jack's retirement application off his desk and, with great flare, tore it in two.

"Sir, what about my office? Do I still need to clear it out?"

Rankin thought for a minute. "No, I'll find another office for Ms. Nguyen. You can keep your office. Now get the hell out of here. I have important matters to discuss with the boss."

Jack offered his hand, and Rankin rose to shake it.

"Understand, Scanlon, we don't do this for everyone."

"I understand quite well and appreciate what you're doing for me. You may well have saved me from making an impetuous decision that I would likely regret for the rest of my life."

Jack turned and headed out of Rankin's office with a little livelier step than when he entered.

Marilyn turned as Jack came out. She smiled. "Well, did you finally come to your senses?"

Jack also smiled. "Yes, I did." He waved over his shoulder and headed for the elevators.

CHAPTER SEVEN

J ack heard the knock and turned toward the open door to his office to see the grinning expression on the face of his closest friend, Micah Cruise.

"Well, welcome back to the bureau's newest superstar," Jack exclaimed as he crossed the room, greeting his friend with a handshake and a bear hug. "So you finally got the son of a bitch?"

"Yes, we did, and we couldn't have done it without your hunch, or should I say wild-ass guess," Micah teased. Throwing the file box on the floor, he plopped down in the chair and kicked his size twelve loafers up onto Jack's desk.

For the past five months, Cruise and his team of agents had been trying to solve a series of murders along the I-10 corridor from El Paso to Los Angeles. Over a period of two years, seven women ranging in age from seventeen to thirty-two had been found buried nude in shallow graves only yards from the interstate. Each of the victims had been raped and strangled to death. Jack's team in Washington identified six of the seven victims from missing-person reports, dental records, and, in two cases, DNA samples. Five of the women were under the age of twenty and either runaways or prostitutes. After the discovery of the fourth victim in the desert outside Phoenix, local authorities from three jurisdictions decided to call in the FBI.

After examining the files and evidence sent to Washington for analysis, Jack suggested to Micah and his team that they might want to consider the possibility that the unknown subject, or unsub in bureau-speak, might be a long-haul trucker.

"How did you take him down?" Jack asked as he sat down in the chair opposite Cruise.

"For several weeks, Lisa posed as a runaway at a truck stop outside of Chandler; you remember her, she looks like she's fifteen. Anyway, one night, this truck driver had been watching her for about an hour before he came over to her table, sat down, and offered to buy her something to eat. She politely declined. He then asked her where she was going. Lisa told him it didn't matter, since we didn't really know which direction he was heading. He told her he could take her as far as Los Angeles, and they got up and left. She was wired, so we heard the entire conversation. It was almost midnight when they left the diner. When he pulled out, we had a car in front of his rig and two trailing it at a distance. We followed them for almost an hour before he pulled off the interstate onto a dirt road. He got out and walked around to the passenger side and ordered Lisa to get out. He then pulled a knife and made her climb into the sleeper cab. On Lisa's signal, we surrounded the cab and called him out. He didn't even resist; it's almost like he wanted to get caught."

"Sounds like an episode of that new TV series *Criminal Minds*," Jack interjected.

"The forensic team searched the rig from top to bottom and found seven pairs of women's panties in the cab. The results aren't in yet, but we're confident that the DNA will be a match for the seven bodies found along I-10."

"You and your team did a great job on this one," Jack congratulated him. "What's your status? Are you back in town for a while?"

"I have to clean up a few loose ends, and then I'm taking a few weeks off. I'm going home to visit the family. My father's health is failing, and my mother's not sure she can take care of him in the long term, so there are some decisions to be made. After I return, I've been assigned as an instructor for at least nine months at the academy at Quantico. Oh, by the way, what's this I hear about you retiring?" Micah suddenly remembered the purpose of his visit.

"There's been a change of plans. Director Rankin just offered me another option, and I accepted. Why don't I fill you in over a few beers? I'm buying."

"Sounds good. I've got to file my report, but that shouldn't take more than an hour or so. I'll meet you at the Old Ebbitt Grill at five thirty. Oh, and while you're at it, why don't you call Duffy, Matt, and Doc and invite them to join us?"

"Consider it done."

CHAPTER EIGHT

Rehoboth Beach, Delaware

Kate Simpson watched her eleven-year-old son bound down the front steps, cross the gravel drive, and push his way through the newly planted juniper trees. He emerged onto Ocean Drive just as the school bus rolled to a stop.

Kate waved to the bus driver, and she returned Kate's greeting with a crisp military-style salute. It had been their regular routine for several years.

Polly Beckwith was a legend in the Cape Henlopen school system. She had driven school buses for the district for close to twenty-five years. She was a no-nonsense breast cancer survivor whose husband had run off with his twenty-eight-year-old secretary two years earlier. Through it all, Polly kept her head down and pressed on ahead with her life. Her children, as she referred to the students who rode her bus, loved and respected her, and in return she took great care to deliver them safely to and from school each day.

Kate hated Monday mornings. She grabbed a coffee mug from the cabinet above the kitchen counter, placed a K-cup in the Keurig, and pushed the button. The coffee maker groaned into action; the sound reminded her of a foghorn out at sea. Within seconds, the hot coffee began to fill the mug.

Kate hugged the warm mug with both hands against her chest and inhaled the aroma of the coffee. She sighed; somehow the morning had gotten away from her.

She took her cell phone off the charger and dialed her office. The phone rang twice, and a nasally woman's voice answered.

"Sussex County Women's Center, Julia speaking."

"Good morning, Julia. It's Kate. I just wanted to let you know that I'll be going directly to my ten o'clock with Mr. DiLano, so I won't be in the office until around eleven thirty. Are there any additions to my calendar for today?"

"No, ma'am. You have a meeting with the architect at 1:00 p.m. to review the plans for the new building and a budget and finance committee conference call at 2:00 p.m."

"Thanks, Julia. I have all that on my schedule, and I'll be there in plenty of time. If you need me, call me on my cell."

"Yes, ma'am."

Kate placed the iPhone back in its charging cradle. She put the mug in the sink, crossed the family room, and walked down the hall to the master bath off her bedroom. She hung her robe on the hook behind the door and let her silk nightgown fall to the floor. She stood and stared for a second at her image in the mirror. *Not bad for a thirty-seven-year-old*, she thought. She turned, walked into the oversized shower, and turned the water on. Adjusting the knobs until the water temperature was as hot as she could stand it, she stepped back, closed her eyes, and let the hot water pulsate onto her neck and back. Her day was starting to improve.

As Kate pulled out of the driveway, she noticed a moving van in front of the house next door. The house had been vacant since her neighbor, Ellen McCarthy, died of a heart attack in early February. Kate liked Ellen a lot and was heartbroken when she learned of her death. She and Timmy had been in Florida visiting her parents when Ellen died; she had barely gotten back in time for the memorial service. Ellen had more energy and zest for life than anyone she knew. Always the life of the party, she seldom missed an opportunity to be with her enormous circle of friends and neighbors. She was known throughout Sussex County for her philanthropic endeavors and fundraising abilities. The year before she died, Ellen was invited to the state capitol, where the governor named her Delaware's Woman of the Year.

For ten years prior to her death, Ellen had shared her home with her partner and longtime companion, Missy. Where Ellen was outgoing and extroverted, Missy was the exact opposite. One day, as Ellen later explained it, Missy just packed up and left with no explanation. Ellen was devastated and withdrew into her shell. Some of her friends were convinced that she ultimately died of a broken heart.

Kate now wondered who her new neighbors would be.

CHAPTER NINE

Kate pulled into the parking space marked "Goodwin Industries—Guest Parking." She walked up the steps to the double glass doors and pushed the dime-sized white button. The guard at the desk buzzed her in.

"Good morning, miss. Who are you here to see?"

"I have a ten o'clock appointment with Mr. DiLano."

The guard pushed a book across the counter and asked that she sign in. He dialed four numbers on the phone and waited. After Kate finished signing in, the guard turned the book around. "Ms. Miller, this is Arthur at the front desk. I have a Katherine Simpson here to see Mr. DiLano." He listened for a moment and then said, "Yes, I'll send her right up." He hung up the phone, grabbed a clip-on visitor badge from the shoebox on the desk, and handed it to her. "Take the elevator to the fourth floor. His office will be down the hall to the right."

"Thank you, Arthur, and have a great day." Kate smiled and walked down the hall to the elevator.

Something seemed odd to Kate as she walked down the hall to DiLano's office. This was a good-sized four-story building, and yet the only person she had seen so far was the guard at the front desk. Come to think of it, there were only a handful of cars in the sizable parking lot.

DiLano's administrative assistant looked up as Kate entered the office. "Good morning, Ms. Simpson. Mr. DiLano is just wrapping up a conference call with his construction supervisors. He'll be with you shortly."

Goodwin Industries was the largest construction conglomerate on the Delmarva Peninsula. The company had been in existence since the early '50s and, over the past sixty-plus years, had built most of the high-rise hotels and condominiums from Ocean City to Bethany Beach. Over the past five years, however, under DiLano's leadership, the company was changing direction, buying up large tracts of land within a fifty-mile radius of Rehoboth Beach for the development of planned communities.

Kate had read that the move was highly controversial for a host of reasons, not the least of which was the financial impact it was having on Goodwin Industries' bottom line. Newspapers throughout the region had questioned the speculative nature of DiLano's direction, and a recent *Wall Street Journal* article had sent the company's stock into a tailspin. Regardless, Goodwin Industries was the first on her list of potential big-money donors to help fund her latest dream, a state-of-the-art regional facility for battered and abused women.

After close to twenty minutes, DiLano's assistant rose from her desk and opened the door to his office. "Ms. Simpson, Mr. DiLano will see you now."

The office was very sterile; glass and polished steel dominated the decor. A laptop and printer sat on a credenza behind the desk. Except for an artist's rendering of what appeared to be Goodwin Industries' latest venture, the room was devoid of decorations.

DiLano rose to greet her. They shook hands, and he motioned toward two chairs directly in front of his desk. DiLano was a handsome man, Kate thought, in a swarthy sort of way. He was a little over six feet tall and appeared to be in great physical shape. He reminded her of Al Pacino in *The Godfather,* except taller.

"It's a pleasure to meet you, Ms. Simpson. My assistant tells me you're here to discuss a sponsorship opportunity."

Kate sat back in the chair, crossed her left leg over her right, and leaned slightly forward. "As you know, I'm the director of the Sussex County's Women's Center in Lewes. I am also the executive director of the Delmarva Women's Center Foundation. The foundation's goal over the next five years is to build three state-of-the-art regional facilities for women who have been either beaten or abused. The regional centers will provide room and board and counseling for these women until they can get back on their feet. The first regional center is planned for Sussex County and will be built in Lewes. While Sussex County will provide the foundation with a grant, that will only cover a small fraction of the $2.2 million price tag. We are looking to finance half of the remainder and raise the other half through contributions and sponsorships."

DiLano leaned forward. "So what's the bottom line as it applies to Goodwin Industries?"

"Well, the foundation's board was hoping that Goodwin Industries would become our founding sponsor at $500,000."

Delano sat back in his chair and looked up at the ceiling for a second or two. "Let me ask you this, Ms. Simpson—who will build these regional facilities?"

Kate started to answer, but DiLano interrupted her. "Let me cut to the chase. If Goodwin Industries is hired to build the regional facilities, I will write you that check right now."

Kate shifted uncomfortably in her chair. "Mr. DiLano, believe me, I would love to say yes, but our charter and bylaws require that we seek competitive bids on all contracts over $10,000."

"Then that presents us with a problem, but I'll tell you what we'll do. If you can raise $500,000 by July 1, Goodwin Industries will match it."

The offer caught Kate off guard. "Ah, that's a tall order, Mr. DiLano. You're giving us a little over six weeks to raise a half a million dollars in a down economy."

Kate sensed that DiLano's temperament had changed dramatically. His friendly demeanor was now gone.

"Under the circumstances, that's the best I can offer."

"Can I get that in writing?"

DiLano rose from his seat, and Kate followed suit.

"What, my word isn't enough for you, Ms. Simpson?"

"It's not that. I'd call it the lawyer in me, but the foundation's board requires we get all offers in writing."

"Very bureaucratic of the foundation, don't you agree?"

47

"I suppose so, but I'm simply an employee."

"I will have a signed offer letter for you in the morning. Now, unfortunately, I have a conference call with my board of directors, so I'll have to see you out."

Kate frowned to herself. It was one those "don't let the door slam you in the ass on the way out" moments.

CHAPTER TEN

Kate pulled out of the parking lot and turned left at the light onto Route 1 North. It was Monday at 11:00 a.m., and yet traffic was at a standstill. She inched along for twenty minutes, past the myriad of outlets and strip malls, until, finally, she could exit toward Lewes and her office. She pulled into the parking space reserved for "DIRECTOR, Sussex County Women's Center," turned off the car, and grabbed her briefcase off the front passenger seat.

Julia didn't own a car, but there was a rusted-out, beat-up Chevy Monte Carlo parked in the visitor's space next to her. Kate opened the door to the center's reception area, and Julia looked up from her keyboard.

"Good morning, ma'am." Julia tilted her head to the right, and Kate turned to see a young woman curled up on the sofa in the far corner. "Ms. Ramsey is here to see you."

"Please, Ms. Ramsey, why don't we go into my office? It's more comfortable and private. Can we get you anything to drink?"

The young girl shook her head and reluctantly rose from the sofa. She turned her face away from Kate's gaze and preceded her into the office. Kate judged her to be in her early twenties, maybe five feet, four inches tall, no more than 110 pounds, with shoulder-length brown hair.

Kate motioned her to the two armchairs in the corner. "Please sit down. Let's talk."

The girl sat down in the overstuffed chair, pulled her knees up, and hugged them to her chest. Again, she turned her head to the right, away from Kate's direct line of sight.

"What's your first name, Ms. Ramsey?"

"It's Tina."

"Do you mind if I call you Tina?"

"No, but I really shouldn't be here. I'm sorry for bothering you." She started to get up, but Kate gently placed her right hand on the girl's arm.

"Please don't leave. Let's talk. Could I ask you how you got the bruise on your right cheek?" Kate grossly understated the visual evidence of a severe beating.

The two sat in silence for several minutes before the girl finally said, "It was my boyfriend. He came home late from work and was terribly upset that I didn't have dinner ready for him. It was all my fault. I was late getting home from work, and we had no food, so I went to the grocery store to get something for dinner. I got home only five minutes before him."

"Tina, it wasn't your fault. Get that out of your head. Do you understand me?" Kate's tone was firmer now.

"I guess."

Kate eased forward in her chair and again placed a reassuring hand on the girl's forearm. "What did he do to you?"

Tina sighed. "He hit me with his beer bottle on the forehead and punched me in the face." She pulled her hair away from her face to show Kate the bruise. The gash on her forehead was two inches wide and deep. The blood had coagulated and matted her hair. The punch to the face was less severe but would easily leave her right eye black and blue.

"Have you seen a doctor?" Kate asked, knowing the answer.

"No. I don't want to make a big deal out of this."

Kate backed off, sensing the fear and agitation in Tina's voice. "OK, let me make a suggestion. It sounds to me like you and your boyfriend need a little space, some time to cool off. I would recommend that you stay here with us tonight, and we can reassess your situation in the morning. We have a great facility here with everything you will need in the near term. What do you say?"

"I guess that will work. He probably needs some time to cool down." Tina tried to bury herself in the over-stuffed chair.

"All right, let me take you upstairs and get you settled in. Did you bring anything with you? If not, no worries."

Seeming more relieved, Tina got up and followed Kate to the elevator. They exited the elevator on the second floor into a suite of three rooms. A young black girl sat at a desk in the corner working on a laptop.

"Good morning, Crystal," Kate said as the girl looked up from her laptop.

"Good afternoon, Ms. Simpson," the girl replied with a playful smile on her face.

Kate looked at her watch and, with a shrug of her shoulders, acknowledged that it was, in fact, no longer morning. "Crystal, I want you to meet Tina Ramsey. She'll be staying with us overnight."

The two girls acknowledged each other, and Kate motioned for them to join her on the L-shaped couch in the center of the room. Kate turned to address Tina. "Crystal came to us about ten days ago under circumstances similar to yours. Since then, we've found Crystal a good job with Wexler Lumber Company, and at the beginning of July, she will be moving into her own apartment."

Kate turned and pointed over her right shoulder. "Crystal's room is on the right, and your room will be across the hall. There is a shared bathroom between the two rooms, with a lock. Please remember to unlock the door when you are through using the bathroom. You can stay with us for as little or as long as you like. Do you have a job?"

Tina nodded. "I work as a cashier at Walmart, but my next shift isn't until Wednesday afternoon."

Kate opened her portfolio and handed Tina her card. "This card has my cell phone number on it. Don't hesitate to call me if you need anything. In the meantime, I'm going to leave you in Crystal's capable hands. There is a self-service sundry shop on the first floor. Crystal will take you down and give you the door code. Pick out anything you will need. On the counter there is a clipboard. Check off the items that you take so we can replenish. There's no charge for anything in the shop."

Kate rose to leave. "Oh, by the way, I would like to have a nurse stop by this afternoon and take a look at your injuries. If you're OK with that, I'll set it up for around 4:00 p.m." She looked questioningly at Tina.

"Yes, I'd appreciate that, thank you."

Kate was pleased that Tina was finally beginning to communicate. "All right, I'll see you around four."

Kate's day continued to improve. The architect's plans for the new women's center were spectacular beyond her wildest expectations, but she continued to fear her fundraising efforts would doom the project.

Her conference call with the foundation's budget and finance committee went equally well. She briefed them on her meeting with DiLano. They dismissed her concerns about being able to raise the necessary funding to get the project off the ground. She didn't share their optimism, but it made her feel a little less stressed.

The rest of Kate's week flew by. While several appointments with community businesses did not net her that big-money sponsor, they did get her $80,000 closer to the half million-dollar match. However, the clock was ticking, and Kate was running out of viable prospects.

Crystal and Tina had hit it off immediately, and when they weren't each working, they were virtually inseparable. Kate felt a little better about life as she prepared to head home for a restful and relaxing weekend. Tonight, she would take the love of her life out for sushi. Timmy was the best thing in her life, the only good thing that had come out of an abusive marriage.

CHAPTER ELEVEN

He was a little over six feet tall and ruggedly handsome. He pulled Kate close and gently kissed her on the lips. Suddenly he lifted her off her feet and into his arms. He carried her up the beach and laid her down on the blanket they had used earlier for their romantic dinner. She looked up at him as he bent down to kiss her and slowly unbutton her blouse.

Kate bolted upright as her alarm buzzed her awake. "Damn, where is he?" she asked herself. *It was so real.* She sat on the edge of the bed for a moment getting her bearings. Her perspiration-soaked body trembled as she grudgingly accepted that it was only a dream. She stared down at her jogging shoes sitting on the floor next to the bed, reminding her that today was her day to run. Religiously, she did weight training on Monday, Wednesday, and Friday and ran the days in between. Sunday was her day off. She glanced over at the clock; it was 6:13 a.m. The five-mile course she ran would take her about forty-five minutes, so she should be back at the house in plenty of time to cook Timmy breakfast before she took him to tennis practice at nine thirty.

She got dressed, went to the kitchen for a bottle of water, and headed for the front door when "Fight Song" by Rachel Platten announced an incoming call on her iPhone. She stared at the phone for a moment, trying to decide whether to answer it. She didn't recognize the number. Finally, she lifted the phone from the charging cradle and pushed "answer."

"Is this Katherine Simpson?"

"Yes, it is. Who's this?" she asked with a hint of irritation in her voice.

"This is Dr. Rosenbaum at Cape Henlopen Medical Center. I'm sorry to bother you at this early hour, but we just admitted a severely beaten young woman to the ICU. I thought you'd want to know."

"Doctor, I'm a bit confused. Why are you calling me?"

"I'm sorry, I failed to mention that she had your business card clutched tightly in her left hand when the ambulance brought her to the emergency room a few hours ago."

Kate felt her knees go weak as she grabbed onto the granite countertop for support. Her first thought was *Please don't let it be Tina.*

"Ms. Simpson, are you still there?"

"Yes, I'm sorry. Is the woman's name Tina Ramsey?"

"We don't know. She had no identification on her when the ambulance brought her in, and they didn't find any at the scene. According to the officer in charge, she was found by a passing motorist around 3:00 a.m. in a ditch along Route 9 just south of Cape Henlopen High School."

"Is she a little over one hundred pounds with shoulder-length brown hair, maybe five foot three or four?"

"Yes, that description fits her pretty well."

"I believe she's a girl from our women's center. I'll be there in about thirty minutes."

"Thank you. I'll meet you in the ICU on the second floor. Ask for Dr. Stephen Rosenbaum when you get to the nurses' station."

Kate pressed the "hang up" icon and took a deep breath, trying to collect her thoughts. *Why didn't Crystal call me?* she asked herself. She thought about calling her and decided it wouldn't serve any purpose at this point.

It was too early to wake Timmy. She would leave him a note and ask her friend Roberta to take him to tennis practice at the club. She changed into a pair of jeans and a white long-sleeve blouse. In less than three minutes, she was back in the kitchen searching for pen and paper to write Timmy a note. That done, she picked up her purse and cell phone and headed for the front door, dialing Roberta as she hustled down the front steps to her ten-year-old Jeep Wrangler in the driveway.

Kate walked past the reception desk in the hospital's front lobby entrance and headed for the bank of elevators down the hall. The sterile smell of the recently cleaned linoleum floors sent a mild burning sensation up Kate's nose. She pushed the silver button indicating up and waited for the next elevator to chime its arrival. When the doors opened, two nurses exited the elevator laughing and talking about their plans for the weekend. Kate entered, pushed the button for the second floor, and waited as the elevator doors slowly closed.

The doors opened at the second floor, and she headed for the double sliding glass doors marked "ICU." The doors opened automatically. Inside, three nurses were examining charts and busily writing notes in patients' records as she approached the nurses' station and stopped at the counter.

"Excuse me, could you tell me where I can find Dr. Rosenbaum?" She sensed that the nurse at the desk was about to get snippy, so she added, "He told me to ask that he be paged when I arrived."

Before the nurse could reach for the intercom button, a voice behind Kate said, "I'm Dr. Rosenbaum. You must be Ms. Simpson."

She turned and extended her hand. "I'm Kate Simpson."

"Thank you for coming so quickly. I sincerely hope this is not who you think it might be," Rosenbaum replied.

Despite the tragic situation at hand, Kate couldn't help noticing how incredibly handsome Dr. Stephen Rosenbaum was; she tried to push the thought out of her mind as they shook hands. *Be professional*, she thought to herself. He seemed to hold her hand longer than she thought necessary, and she sensed that the three nurses behind the desk thought the same.

Rosenbaum was at least six feet two with wavy black hair, perfectly styled. He stood erect, and, despite the white smock, she surmised that underneath he had the body of an athlete. She guessed he was a few years younger than she, most likely in his early to midthirties.

Rosenbaum turned toward the nurses glaring at Kate. "Would you hand me the chart for the patient in 116?"

The nurse seated at the desk pulled a chart out of the metal file holder affixed to the wall, smiling a sickly-sweet smile while handing the clipboard to Rosenbaum. The other two were still glaring at Kate.

"She's down the hall, Ms. Simpson. Follow me."

"Please, Doctor, call me Kate."

"Only if you call me Steve."

Kate looked over her shoulder and smiled at the three nurses as she turned to follow Rosenbaum down the hall. He stopped at the door marked "116," with the name-plate under the room number indicating the patient's name as "Jane Doe" in black Sharpie.

"She's in here." He held the door open and motioned for her to precede him into the room.

Kate recoiled at the sight of the young girl in the bed. "My god, how could anyone do such a thing to another human being?"

The girl's head was almost totally wrapped in gauze bandages. Only her closed eyes, nose, and one ear were visible. An oxygen tube was clipped to her nostril, and bags of some sort of solutions were being fed into her left arm intravenously.

"We had to shave portions of her head; it took over a hundred stitches to close the wounds to her head. We did extensive X-rays, and they show three fractured ribs on her left side, a broken right wrist, likely a defensive wound, and extensive bruising all over her body."

"I can't believe this is real," Kate said softly. "I've never seen a woman beaten this badly."

"That's not the worst part. This poor girl has several broken bones that have fully or partially healed. It's my opinion that she's been used as a human punching bag for some time."

Kate leaned forward to steady herself on the bed and took a deep breath.

"Are you all right? I think you should sit down. Can I get you some water?"

Before she could answer, Rosenbaum raised her up by one arm and led her to an uncomfortable-looking chair in the corner of the room. "Take a minute, Kate."

"Thanks, I'm fine. I just didn't expect anything like this. Will she be all right?"

"Her vital signs are as good as can be expected, given the injuries. She's heavily sedated, and we're feeding her through a tube in her stomach. I don't believe her head injuries will result in any permanent damage."

Kate looked at him quizzically. "But...?"

"I'm sorry, I guess I danced around your question. Doctors tend to do that when put on the spot. It's too early to say, but strictly between you and me, I think she'll recover physically, and I emphasize *physically*."

Kate gave him a weak smile. "Strictly between you and me, thank you."

"Don't mention it. Now, more to the point of you being here in the first place, is this the girl you suspected it was?"

"I think so—same height and build—but I can't say positively it's her. But I know someone who possibly can help. Have you taken fingerprints or checked dental records?"

"The police took her fingerprints, but if she's not in the system, it's a dead end. As far as dental records are concerned, what do we compare them with? You see the problem here? If we can identify her, we might be able to find out if she has any preexisting conditions that could complicate her treatment and recovery."

Kate stood up. "I need to talk to someone about this. How can I reach you?"

Rosenbaum rooted through his lab coat without success and finally pulled a beat-up business card out of his pants pocket. He tried to straighten out the card, gave up, and reluctantly handed it to her.

"Sorry about the card; doctors seldom carry business cards on them. This is an old card from…well, here, it has my cell phone number on the front."

Kate tucked the card into the pocket of her jeans. "Thanks. I'll call you as soon as I know something." It was time to find Crystal.

Kate glanced up at the clock on the wall over the reception desk. It was almost 10:00 a.m. The sliding doors parted, and she was surprised at the temperature as she exited the main entrance. It was unusually hot for late May. She pulled her cell phone out of her purse, entered her code, and scrolled through her contacts. She tapped the name "Julia Wilson" and then the number. After a few seconds, the phone began to ring.

"Hello, this is Julia."

"Julia, it's Kate. Would you do me a favor? Can you check to see if Crystal is in her room?"

"Ah, ma'am, it's Saturday, and I'm at the beach with my boyfriend."

"I am so sorry; this has been a crazy morning. Can you tell me the last time you saw Crystal?"

"Hold on, let me get someplace where I can hear you better."

Kate waited a minute or two before the girl came back on.

"Ms. Simpson, can you hear me?"

"Yes."

"That's better. Well, she got back from work yesterday around 4:00 p.m. and went directly upstairs to her room. Around 5:30 p.m., I went back to restock the sundry room and upstairs to see if they needed anything. Crystal and Tina were in the game room watching TV. I told them I was leaving, they waved, and I locked up and left. Is there something wrong?"

"No, there's nothing wrong. I just need to talk with her. Do you know if she's working today?"

"Yes, but her shift doesn't start until noon. You should be able to catch her before she leaves for work."

"Great. Thank you and enjoy your weekend. Again, I'm sorry to have bothered you."

"No problem. See you Monday."

Kate ended the call and dropped the cell phone back into her purse. She unlocked the beat-up Wrangler, hopped in, and quickly unzipped the front windows on each side. The air conditioner had long since died, and she saw no reason to have it replaced or repaired. She reached across to the passenger side and pulled down on the top latch and then did the same on the driver's side. She got out and unzipped the rear side curtains on each side and threw them in the back. *It is time to go topless*, she thought as she pulled back the canvas top and secured it in the back.

She exited the parking lot, turned right onto Savannah Road, and drove the mile and a half to the women's center. She drove around to the back of the building, parked, and searched for the key fob in her purse. Kate climbed the back stairs to the suite of rooms on the second floor. Crystal looked up from her laptop as Kate walked in.

"Ms. Simpson, what are you doing here? It's Saturday. Has something happened?"

"If you mean to Tina, we're not sure yet. However, you need to tell me everything that happened from the time you got back from work yesterday."

"I should have done something to make her stay," Crystal moaned.

"Calm down, tell me everything that happened." Kate sat next to Crystal on the couch.

"I got home around four. When I got here, Tina was sitting in the chair over there, and I could tell she'd been crying. I asked her what was wrong, and she said her boyfriend had come to her work and begged her to come back home. She told him no, and he cursed her and stormed out of the store. Around six thirty, he started calling her on her cell phone. After about the fifth or sixth time, she turned off her phone and suggested we leave and get something to eat. We drove to Stripper Bits, ate dinner, and got back here a little after eight. We both went to bed around ten. I woke up around one thirty and heard Tina talking to someone on her phone. She was crying and then yelling and then crying; it went on that way for about twenty minutes. Finally, she hung up. I tried to get back to sleep but couldn't. Then around three, I heard her door open, and she walked down the hall to the back stairs. I got up and followed her. When I got to the door, I saw her get into a black Ford F-150. I know because my dad used to have one. I tried to get a license plate number as they pulled away, but the angle was bad. However, it was a New Jersey plate, and the first three letters were ZLM followed by four numbers. Has something happened to Tina?"

"We don't know, but there's a girl in the hospital, badly beaten, who, as far as we can tell, closely resembles Tina."

"Does she have a blue butterfly tattoo on her butt?"

"What?"

"Tina has a blue butterfly tattoo on her left butt cheek."

"Excuse me, I've got to make a call." Kate walked to the window, pulled the rumpled card out of her jeans, and dialed the number. It immediately went to voice mail. "This is Kate. Check and see if the girl in 116 has a blue butterfly tattoo on her left buttocks and call me back ASAP."

Kate joined Crystal on the couch.

"Is the girl in the hospital going to be all right?" Crystal asked.

"She's been badly beaten, but the doctor seems to believe she'll pull through."

"If it's Tina, can I see her? We've become good friends in the short time she's been here, and I feel responsible."

"Get that out of your head; you're not responsible. If it is Tina, she won't be having visitors for some time. The girl in the hospital is in a medically induced coma."

Kate's phone rang. She quickly picked it off the coffee table and tapped the receive symbol.

"Kate, this is Steve; she's your girl. I'm so sorry; please know I'll do everything in my power to pull her through this. In the meantime, let's get this son of a bitch."

"Thanks, Steve. I'll be back in touch as soon as I know anything more."

Kate sank back into the end of the couch. They sat there in silence for several minutes until Kate said, "Crystal, I want you to think hard. Did Tina ever mention her boyfriend's name, where they lived together, or anything that might help us identify him?"

"I tried a couple of times to quiz her about her boyfriend, but she shut down every time I asked. I've been trying to think of anything that might help, but I'm drawing a blank."

"If you think of anything, and I mean anything, give me a call regardless of what time it is. You have my number?"

"Yes, I have your card in my room."

"OK then, I will see you on Monday. Don't forget you have a late shift starting at noon."

"Thanks, I won't."

Kate got halfway down the hall when Crystal yelled, "Ms. Simpson, wait! I just thought of something that might help."

Kate turned around and walked back toward Crystal.

"I think she's from around Philadelphia. She was surfing through the channels one night and stopped on the Phillies game. She said her dad used to take her to the games before he got too sick to go. That might also jive with the plates on the truck. Maybe they were both from the same area. Does that help?"

"That helps a lot. You've made the haystack a little smaller. Again, if you think of anything else, call me."

Kate called out for Timmy as she entered the foyer. Hearing no response, she decided to call Roberta.

"Robbi, where are you guys? Is everything all right?"

"Relax, Kate. Timmy and I are having an early lunch at the club. We're just about to leave. His lesson went well; he's getting very good. In fact, the pro suggested he enter the twelve-and-under tennis tournament next Saturday, and if it's all right with you, I'll sign him up."

"That's fine. Look, take your time. I've had a bad morning. I'll fill you in later. I'm going out for a long run to clear my head. Are we still on for tennis in the morning?"

"Yes, we have a court from ten until noon. I'll pick you up around nine thirty and you can fill me in."

"I'd better drive separately. I've got several stops to make before and after. See you at ten."

CHAPTER TWELVE

Jack opened the sliding glass door to the deck and stood there taking in the magnificent view. The late afternoon temperature was in the mideighties with a gentle breeze blowing up the coast and not a cloud in the sky. He stepped back inside, picked up his laptop, a legal pad, and a pen off the counter and returned to the deck. He sat down at the picnic table, adjusted the umbrella, and opened the laptop. It was time to get to work.

He had written a textbook on forensics two years earlier and surmised it would provide a good outline for the manual. He opened his laptop and clicked on the folder icon marked "Forensic Science, Pathology and Standard Methods."

Winston ambled through the sliding glass door, wagging his tail, and curled up at his feet. He reached down and scratched the dog's head. Winston reflexively rolled onto his back, looking forward to his afternoon tummy rub. Jack pushed back his chair and got down on his hands and knees next to his sixty-pound ball of fur. Winston was much more than Jack's dog; he was his soulmate. Over the past year and a half, he had gotten Jack through a difficult period in his life.

Jack hopped back up, grabbed the pen and legal pad, and began to jot down some notes. *How much does a field agent really need to know about forensics?* he asked himself. He started to compile bullet points:

- secure the crime scene
- protect the crime scene from contamination
- properly collect and catalog evidence
- establish the chain of custody

Jack stopped writing, sensing he was no longer alone.

"Permission to come aboard, sir."

Jack looked up to see a young boy standing on the top step of the stairs leading down to the beach. He looked to be about eleven or twelve years old, with a full head of wavy red hair. He wore a red bathing suit, sandals, and a blue T-shirt with "Remember Pearl Harbor" on top of a print of the USS *Arizona* Memorial. In his left hand, he held a manila folder stuffed with loose-leaf papers and a notepad.

Jack smiled. "Permission granted."

The boy walked over and extended his hand. "I'm Tim Simpson, and I live next door." He pointed over his shoulder. "Are you our new neighbor?"

"Yes, I guess I am. I moved in last week. I'm Jack Scanlon. Would you like to sit down?" Jack motioned to the table. The boy laid the folder and pad on the table, knelt down next to Winston, and held out the back of his hand for the dog to sniff. Winston licked the boy's hand and rolled onto his back.

"What's his name?"

"He's Winston."

The boy rubbed the dog's head and ears. "His hair is softer and silkier than any dog I know. What kind of dog is he?"

"I don't really know for sure. My vet seems to think he's a Portuguese water dog and poodle mix, clearly more water dog than poodle."

"How old is he?"

"Again, not really sure of that either. The vet says he's no younger than four and no older than six."

The boy stood up.

"It's getting hot. Would you like some lemonade or a Coke?" Jack asked.

The boy nodded. "Coke please."

"I'll be right back."

Jack returned with two Cokes and a plate full of cookies. "So are your parents in the navy?" Jack asked, pointing to the boy's T-shirt.

"No, my grandfather is a retired navy admiral. He took us to Hawaii last year for Christmas vacation, and we got an admiral's tour of Pearl Harbor and the *Arizona* Memorial. It's amazing. Have you ever seen it?"

"I have. I was never stationed there but was on TDY—temporary duty—training in Hawaii."

"So you were in the military?"

"Yes, I was in the navy for a little over eight years. For the last six, I was a Navy SEAL. We did HALO training in Hawaii."

"What's HALO?"

"It stands for high altitude, low opening. You jump out of a plane, sometimes as high as twenty-five thousand feet above sea level, glide to a very low altitude, and open your chute."

"Sounds like fun. Were you an officer?"

"Yes. When I got out, I was a lieutenant." Jack pointed to the folder and pad on the table. "So what's all that?"

"It's my research on a Spanish galleon that went down in a hurricane off the Delaware coast in 1677."

"I've read quite a bit about shipwrecks off the mid-Atlantic coast and never heard any mention of a Spanish galleon. I'm not doubting you, but tell me more about your research."

"Well, I was doing a paper for history class on the Spanish conquest of Mexico and Central America. I couldn't find much in the library or online. At least not what I wanted to write about. So I tried the Spanish archives, *Archivo Histórico Nacional*, and found a ship's log. It was from the Spanish galleon *La Concepción*, which sailed with a treasure fleet out of Havana and never reached Spain. Only one sailor survived the sinking. He was the ship's master, a man named Vega. He rescued the ship's log, and it also became a chronicle of his trek back to his home in San Sebastian. It took him almost five years."

"Just out of curiosity, what grade are you in?"

"I'm in sixth grade at Caesar Rodney Elementary."

"This seems like a very complex project for sixth grade. When I was in sixth grade, we learned about the history of Virginia. I'm not sure I even knew that the Spanish had conquered Mexico and Central America at that point. Anyway, tell me more about this treasure ship.

Wasn't the ship's log written in Spanish? How did you get it translated into English?"

"That's what's so cool about this website. There are certain documents on the website that can be translated into English, French, or German with the click of your mouse, and this was one of them." The boy picked up the folder and rummaged through several sheets of paper until he found the one he was looking for. "Here, read this. It's the last log entry."

Jack took the paper and read the entry out loud: "Eighteenth of September 1677, 2340 hrs. Sailing north-northwest under full sail, seeking refuge from severe storm, winds from the south-southeast at fifty knots. No sign of fleet."

"Based upon earlier entries, the ship should have been off the coast of Delaware somewhere between Fenwick Island and Cape Henlopen. There is no evidence that *La Concepción* ever reached the safety of the Delaware estuary. Also, there is a mention earlier in the log of a harbor somewhere between the Chesapeake and Delaware Bays, but there is no such harbor."

Jack leaned back in his chair and folded his arms across his chest. "OK, you've convinced me that a Spanish galleon—the *La Concepción*—went down in a hurricane somewhere off the Atlantic coast, but why not off the coast of New Jersey or farther north? Maybe the ship was forced out to sea by the storm and sank in deeper water."

"Two things. First, it doesn't fit with the journal kept by Vega of the sinking and his attempt to reach the Dutch settlement of Swanendael, or what's now called Lewes."

The boy pulled out several more pages from the folder. "You can have this; it's the full translation of the ship's log and Vega's journal. I've got another copy on my computer. Second, the October issue of *Delaware Today* had a story about a man from Bethany who found two gold doubloons on the beach just north of the Indian River inlet in the state park. That stretch of beach is now called Treasure Beach. Where else would those doubloons come from other than *La Concepción*? Also, how could Vega have survived a sinking miles out at sea, in a hurricane?"

"OK, once again, you've convinced me." Jack started to say something when he heard someone scream "Timmy!" from the beach. A woman was running toward the deck, and she didn't look happy.

"That's my mom."

Tim waved, and Jack started to stand when the woman screamed, "Timmy, get down here right now!" She glared at Jack with eyes that could have killed.

"I'm sorry, I've got to go. Thanks for the Coke." Tim quickly got up, grabbed the folder, and raced for the stairs. At the bottom of the stairs, the mother grabbed him by the arm and hustled him next door, up the stairs, and into the house.

What the hell was that all about? He glanced at the table, and suddenly a bell went off in his head. Strange man and young boy having a Coke and cookies on the man's deck. So much for making a good first impression on the neighbors.

Jack gathered up his laptop and legal pad and headed back inside. It was getting late, and he had a dinner date with his Realtor, Pamela Quinn, who had managed the property while it was going through probate. She'd facilitated his move and asked him out to dinner as a thank-you for letting her represent him. She had tried to get him to list the house for sale but backed off when he told her he wanted to see if Rehoboth worked for him.

CHAPTER THIRTEEN

Rehoboth Beach Country Club, Delaware

Roberta looked at her watch for the fourth time in five minutes. It wasn't like Kate to be late for anything, much less tennis. She impatiently bounced the tennis ball off the clay surface. About to check her watch again, she looked up to see Kate's beat-up Jeep Wrangler speed into the parking lot and come to a sliding stop against the log arresting barrier. Kate jumped out, grabbed her tennis bag out of the back seat, and slammed the door. She sprinted toward the court as if she could make up the lost twenty minutes of court time.

"I'm sorry to be so late. This has been a nightmare of a weekend. I'll explain later. Maybe I can get some frustrations out on the court." Kate pulled her racket out of the bag and tossed the bag under the bench.

"Ready to warm up?" Roberta asked.

"No, let's just play."

"OK, you call it." Roberta spun the racket handle in her hand and glanced at the butt end.

"Heads," Kate responded.

"The P's up. You win." Roberta tapped three balls to Kate with her racket.

Kate tucked one under the elastic waistband of her "bundies" and walked to the baseline. She tossed one of the two remaining balls in the air, coiled, and smashed the ball to Roberta's forecourt. The ball cleared the net by four feet and whizzed by Roberta's left ear.

"A little adrenaline rush?" Roberta exclaimed.

Kate ignored the comment, tossed the second ball in the air, and hit it equally hard. Again, the ball cleared the net by several feet and sped toward Roberta's midsection. Roberta sidestepped the shot and stared back at Kate in disbelief.

"Zero serving fifteen," Kate muttered almost apologetically.

Kate moved to the opposite side of the baseline, tossed the ball into the air, and again smashed it toward Roberta. This time the ball hit the net and dropped harmlessly to the court.

"Enough!" Roberta yelled. She pointed to Kate. "You, over here, now!" Roberta headed toward the tables next to the pro shop and restaurant. She motioned toward the waitress. "Vicky, two Bloody Marys, and make them stiff."

Vicky nodded and headed toward the bar.

Roberta said, "Now, do you mind telling me what the hell's wrong with you? Is it the girl in the hospital?"

"That's part of it." Kate had briefly explained the situation with the badly beaten girl but had left out the grisly details. "You wouldn't believe how savagely beaten

74

this young girl is; no one should be allowed to do that to another human being. I feel responsible; I should have done more to prevent this from happening."

"Don't be absurd. What more could you have done? You provided her a safe environment to live in with a companion who was helping her get through her problems, and it happened in the middle of the night. How's that your fault?"

Vicky returned with the two Bloody Marys and placed them on the table. Kate stirred the drink with the celery stick garnish and took a sip.

"Wow." Kate's eyes widened, and she took a deep breath.

"Hey, I told her to make them stiff."

"They're stiff all right." Kate smiled. "I may have to take a taxi home."

Roberta sat back in her chair and kicked off her tennis shoes. "Sorry, they were starting to pinch. So how's the girl doing?"

"I called the hospital on the way over. She's still in a medically induced coma, but her doctor said her vital signs are improving. He thinks she'll be conscious by the end of the week, and maybe then we can get some answers. Oh, did I tell you that her doctor is a real hunk?" Kate giggled.

"That's better." Roberta laughed and took another sip of her drink.

Kate's smile disappeared as she dropped her head and turned away.

"I sense there's something else bothering you," Roberta said.

"Yes, I made a total ass of myself yesterday afternoon in front of my new neighbor." Kate related the incident to Roberta, as well as Timmy's angry reaction.

"So you overreacted. That's no big deal. Just apologize. He should understand, and if he doesn't, that's on him."

"So what do I do? Knock on his door and say, 'This is your crazy neighbor, and I've come by to apologize for thinking you're a pedophile'?"

"Of course not. He must leave the house. Look for an opportunity to bump into him."

"Well, he does walk his dog on the beach in the evening."

"Perfect. That's your opportunity to 'accidentally' bump into him." Roberta put her tennis shoes back on and stood up. "We've still got an hour of court time left. How about some more tennis? Only this time I'll serve first."

CHAPTER FOURTEEN

It was almost seven thirty and still no sign of her neighbor and his dog. Kate watched anxiously from her kitchen window that overlooked her neighbor's back deck. She finally decided to go outside and wait on the deck. The sun was starting to get low in the western horizon, and, correspondingly, it was getting noticeably cooler. Kate grabbed her hoodie off the hook behind the front closet door and walked down the hall to check on Timmy. He was busily studying for a science final. Summer vacation was only a few days away.

"Sorry to interrupt. How's the studying going?"

Timmy leaned back in his chair and stretched out. "I'm just about done."

"I just wanted to tell you that I'm going out for a few minutes. Do you need anything before I get back?"

"No, I'm good. I'll grab a snack when I'm finished, and I plan on being in bed early."

Kate pulled the hoodie over her head and headed for the deck.

Jack dog-eared the page of the book he was reading and put it down on the coffee table. He picked up Winston's leash off the kitchen counter.

"Time for a walk, buddy. Let's go."

Winston got out of his bed slowly, stretched out his rear legs one at a time, and waited for Jack to hook him up to the leash. Jack opened the sliding glass door to the deck, and he and Winston headed for the stairs down to the dunes and the beach. Halfway down the stairs, he heard someone call out his name.

"Mr. Scanlon, could I speak with you?"

Winston froze; Jack looked up and across to his neighbor's house. It was the mad mother.

"Let's go, Winston. It's time to face the music," he said softly as he prodded the dog down the stairs.

Kate stood up and walked down the stairs. "Mr. Scanlon, I'm Kate Simpson, and I want to apologize to you for my rude tirade yesterday afternoon. There's no excuse for my behavior, and I'm really sorry. It's just…I'm a little overprotective of Timmy, and I badly misread the situation. Please forgive me."

"First of all, call me Jack, and second, if I was in the same situation, I'm not sure I wouldn't have reacted in the same manner." Jack extended his hand.

Kate smiled, reached out, and shook it.

Winston uncharacteristically barked at Kate. Jack shrugged his shoulders and smiled at Kate. "I think he's telling me he's ready for his evening stroll."

Kate smiled at Jack and dropped to one knee in front of Winston. "So who's this handsome boy?" She reached out to pet the dog, and Winston dropped to the sand and rolled over onto his back. Kate laughed and proceeded to vigorously rub his stomach.

"I think he likes you."

"Timmy said he was a great dog. How long have you had him?"

"Almost two years. He's a rescue. I was just about to take him for a walk on the beach." Jack hesitated for a moment and asked, "Would you like to join us?"

Kate got up and brushed the sand off her sweatpants. "Thank you for asking. I'd like that."

They had walked for several minutes without talking when Kate decided to try and break the ice. "So is there a Mrs. Scanlon, and when will I get to meet her?" She instantly cringed. *What a stupid question to ask someone you barely know*, she thought.

Jack hesitated for a moment and then said, "No, I'm no longer married."

"I'm sorry. I'm also divorced."

Jack wasn't sure how to respond. It wasn't a topic he particularly wanted to talk about. "Actually, Kate, I'm a widower."

"Oh god, I'm so sorry; I assumed, given our ages…It seems I can't help sticking my foot in my mouth lately."

Jack laughed. "Don't beat yourself up. I would have assumed the same thing."

"How far do you usually walk with your dog in the evening?" Kate was anxious to change the subject.

"His name is Winston, and we usually walk down to the north end of the boardwalk on the beach and back to the house on the street."

"Does a walk this early in the evening get him through the night?"

"No, this is his evening exercise. I take him out just before we go to bed, usually around eleven."

They had walked for another few minutes when Jack suddenly stopped and tore his sweatshirt off. He handed Kate Winston's leash. Kate instinctively took the leash as Jack kicked off his running shoes and pulled down his sweatpants, tossing them aside.

Kate instinctively stepped backward. "What are you doing?"

"Do you have your cell phone with you?

"Yes, why?"

Jack yelled back over his shoulder as he ran toward the water, "Call 911 and have them send an ambulance to this location!"

Kate watched as Jack took two long strides into the ocean and dove into an incoming wave. He momentarily disappeared from sight but soon resurfaced and with several powerful strokes raced toward the end of the jetty. Kate picked up Jack's shoes and clothing and moved closer to the water. Suddenly, she remembered what Jack had asked her to do. She fished her cell phone out of the right front pocket of her sweatpants, turned on the phone, and dialed 911.

"What's your name and your emergency?" the voice on the other end of the phone asked.

"This is Kate Simpson; I think there's been a drowning or something. Please send an ambulance to Deauville Beach—actually, to the beach parking lot off Ocean Drive. We're at the second jetty north of the boardwalk."

"The ambulance is on its way. It should be there in less than five minutes."

Kate looked up to see Jack at the end of the jetty. He appeared to have his right arm wrapped around someone or something in the water and was swimming and kicking toward the beach. Several minutes later he reached the shoreline, exhausted and cold. Kate started to move toward him.

"Don't come any closer, Kate. I'll come to you."

Jack dragged the body of what appeared to be a woman out of the water and about twenty feet up onto the beach. He turned and stumbled toward Kate and Winston waiting up the beach.

They could hear the sirens getting louder.

"Is she…?" Kate started to ask.

"Yes, she's dead. I believe she's been in the water for some time. Her body is beginning to decompose."

Kate cringed and handed Jack his clothes. "You better get into your clothes as soon as possible. Your lips are purple, and I think I hear your teeth chattering."

"Thanks." Jack tried to dry off with the outside of his sweatshirt and then pulled it over his head. He turned toward Kate. "Would you turn around for a second so I can get out of these briefs?"

Kate turned her back but couldn't resist the schoolgirl urge to peek. *Very impressive*, she thought, *particularly after spending over ten minutes in the cold ocean.* She quickly chastised herself. *What am I thinking of at a time like this?* She looked down at Winston, who seemed to be staring up at her disapprovingly. "What are you looking at, furball?"

"I'm sorry, Kate. What did you say?" Jack asked.

"Oh, nothing, I was just telling Winston what a good dog he is."

The sirens stopped. Through the scrub pines, they could see the flashing red and blue lights. Suddenly, two EMTs came running down the beach path between the dunes and onto the beach. They were struggling with a collapsible stretcher. Jack lifted his arms in a signaling gesture, and the EMTs stopped running.

"What did you just do?" Kate asked.

"I signaled them that this was a recovery, not a rescue."

Trailing about thirty yards behind the EMTs was another individual. He was wearing a uniform with a wide black belt, gun, and holster. He was rather tall and appeared to be slightly overweight.

Jack turned to Kate. "Who's that?"

"It's getting dark, but I think it's Chief Johnson. He's the chief of police for Rehoboth Beach."

Johnson moved purposefully toward the body lying on the sand. He knelt down beside the young woman and appeared to be examining her. However, Jack found it odd that he never touched the body.

Johnson stood up and for the first time acknowledged the presence of Kate and Jack. "So who discovered the body?"

"I guess that would be me," Jack replied. "I saw something I thought was a person floating in the water out near the end of the jetty, so I swam out and brought the body to shore. I dragged her up onto the beach, and we waited for the emergency squad to get here."

"Did you administer CPR?"

"No," Jack answered incredulously.

"Why not? It's standard procedure in a drowning."

"Because she was dead."

"And you know this how?"

Jack was starting to get annoyed. "I suppose it was the blunt force trauma to the back of her head that fractured her skull that provided my first clue. If you looked, you would see that you can actually put your fist into the wound. Personally, I think she was murdered and dumped in the ocean."

"Murdered!" Johnson scoffed. "Isn't it more likely that she drowned, and the wave action slammed the back of her head into the rocks or against the pilings?"

"I suppose that's possible, but unlikely given the wound."

"By the way, who the hell are you anyway?"

"I'm Jack Scanlon. I live up the beach."

By the tone of Jack's voice and Johnson's reaction, Kate sensed a major-league pissing contest was about to break out. She tried to settle things down a bit. "Chief, I don't know if you remember me. I'm Kate Simpson. We worked together on the first responders' charity event last fall."

"Ms. Simpson, I apologize. I didn't recognize you. Please forgive me. What are you doing here?"

"I was walking on the beach with Mr. Scanlon and his dog when he spotted the body floating in the water. He jumped into the ocean to attempt a rescue, and I called 911."

Johnson turned toward Scanlon. "All right, Scanlon, let's say, for the time being, we agree to disagree how the victim died. The medical examiner will have to do an autopsy anyway, and we'll get our answers then. In the meantime, I have a few loose ends to tie up here, but I'd like to talk to the both of you later tonight."

Kate interrupted, "Chief, Mr. Scanlon lives next door to me. Could you talk to us at my house? It's 48 Ocean Drive." She turned to Jack. "Does that work for you?"

Jack nodded.

"I'll be done here in about forty-five minutes," the chief informed them. "How does 9:30 work? That's a little over an hour from now."

"We'll see you then," Kate responded.

Kate, Jack, and Winston were almost back to their houses before anyone spoke.

"I don't like him," Jack suddenly said.

"He's really a nice guy. I've worked with him on some fundraisers, and I've seen him handle some difficult local political flare-ups with considerable tact. Give him a chance. He may surprise you."

"What do you think he wants to talk to us about? It's pretty obvious what happened. We discovered the body, recovered it, and called the police and EMTs. What else is there?"

"I don't know. Maybe he likes you and wants to spend more quality time getting to know you." Kate smiled and gave Jack a playful shove.

"Cute. You're really enjoying this, aren't you?"

"Not really. I sensed it was getting a little tense between you two back there, and I wanted to make sure two good guys didn't get off on the wrong foot. Does that make sense?"

"Yes. I promise I'll behave. Now, I need to take a shower and clean up before I come over. It shouldn't take me more than twenty minutes."

"That's fine. I'll leave the sliding door on the deck ajar. Just come in. I'll likely be in the kitchen."

CHAPTER FIFTEEN

J ack tapped on the sliding door, and Kate waved him in.

"Wow, Kate, this is a beautiful home."

"Thank you, it was my parents'. They inherited the lot when my grandmother passed away twelve years ago, and they built this home after my father retired from the navy. Three years ago, they moved to Pensacola and deeded the house to me. My mother was having health issues, and Dad wanted to be closer to a naval hospital and other facilities. There's a strong navy support network there, and being a retired admiral, he's sort of a big deal."

"Sounds like a win-win. How are they doing?"

"We visited them earlier in the year, and my mother is doing much better. They've both made dozens of friends. Can I get you something to drink?"

"Ordinarily, I would have red wine, but I think the sheriff might think that unmanly, so I'll have a beer."

"He's not the sheriff. He's the chief of police."

"OK, chief of police."

"I've got Dogfish Head 60 Minute IPA, Heineken, and Budweiser, and do you want a glass?"

"I'd better have the Budweiser. It's a more manly beer, and no glass for the same reason."

Kate sighed. "All right, I wasn't going to say anything, but you two 'manly men' were only minutes away from a dick-measuring contest tonight. I'm just saying you might want to take the testosterone level down a notch or two, and I'm sorry for being so crude."

"I'm sorry too, and I have a hunch. After he's been here for a while, offer him a beer…no glass. I'll give you the high sign."

Kate turned to refill her wineglass as the door chime rang. "Let the games begin," she muttered to herself as she opened the front door.

As expected, Chief Johnson stood at the front door. "Good evening, Ms. Simpson. Is this a good time?"

"It's Kate, and, yes, Jack is in the kitchen."

Johnson followed Kate to the kitchen. Jack got up from the stool and extended his hand. Johnson shook it, and they both sat down around the center island. "It's Scanlon, right?"

"I prefer Jack."

Johnson pulled out a spiral notebook and pen. "I just wanted to ask a few questions. This shouldn't take long. Neither of you is under suspicion regarding the girl's death."

Jack gritted his teeth and glanced at Kate. Kate nodded as if to say, *Steady*.

"OK, let's start from the beginning. So you two decided to take the dog for a walk around seven, is that correct?"

"It was closer to seven thirty," Jack said.

Kate raised her hand. "Chief, let me provide a little background. Jack is my new neighbor. He moved in a few days ago, and we met for the first time this evening. He invited me to join him and Winston for a walk on the beach."

"So who's this Winston character?

Jack knew Johnson was aware of exactly who Winston was but was jerking his chain. He didn't take the bait. "Oh, I'm sorry, Winston is my dog."

Johnson nodded. "I see. So what happened next?"

Jack continued, "When we got near the second jetty north of the boardwalk, I saw something that I thought was a person floundering in the water. I took off my sweats and running shoes and ran into the surf to attempt a rescue."

"You stripped down to your boxers in front of Ms. Simpson on your first date?"

In unison, Jack and Kate exclaimed, "It wasn't a date!"

Jack angrily interjected, "Have you ever tried to swim in sweats and running shoes? I don't recommend it."

Without a cue from Jack, Kate asked, "Chief, please excuse me for being so rude—can I offer you a beer?"

The offer caught Johnson by surprise. "Would you excuse me for a moment?" Johnson got up and walked to the front foyer. He keyed the mic on his epaulet. "This is Hobo Six, over."

A staticky voice answered, "Hobo Six, this is Eagle's Nest, over."

"Sara, this is Hobo Six. If anyone needs me, have them call my cell. I'll see you in the morning, out."

Johnson walked back into the kitchen. "If that beer is still available, I'd love one. It's been a long day."

Kate turned toward the refrigerator. "I've got—"

Johnson looked at Jack. "I'll have the same as him, Budweiser. OK, where were we?"

"I was out for an evening swim in my skivvies."

"Cute, Scanlon. I guess I deserved that." Johnson tilted the neck of the beer bottle toward Jack. Scanlon reached across the island and clicked bottles. "In all seriousness, let me ask you this: Why are you so sure this is a homicide?"

"First, the wound in the back of her head was massive, likely the result of being hit with a blunt object. Second, I would estimate that she was in the water no less than twenty-four hours and no more than forty-eight hours. Over the past three days, the ocean has been relatively calm, no wave action strong enough to cause that kind of wound."

"You're winning me over to your theory, but the medical examiner will have the final word." Johnson emptied his beer and rose to leave. "Kate, thank you for the beer, and thank you both for your cooperation." Johnson smiled mischievously. "I'll let myself out. You two get on with your date."

"Would you like another beer?" Kate asked Jack.

"Thank you, but I'd better get back to my buddy and take him out one more time."

"Jack, if you don't mind me asking, do you run for exercise?"

"Not recently. I used to run quite regularly, but work got in the way."

"I run every other day and would love to have a partner to run with. Are you game?"

"How far?"

"I run up to the end of the boardwalk and back. It's about three and a half miles."

"I'm game. What time and when?"

"I'll meet you in front of your house Tuesday morning at seven."

"I'll see you Tuesday morning, and thanks again."

CHAPTER SIXTEEN

The digital clock on the nightstand read 6:30 in large bright red numerals. Scanlon rose, walked to the bathroom, brushed his teeth, and ran a comb through his hair. Running had sounded like a better idea Sunday evening after a couple of beers. He grabbed a pair of socks, shorts, and running shoes and headed to the kitchen for a glass of water. He walked out onto the deck and looked out at the ocean as the sun was rising behind some distant clouds. He would have preferred to have a leisurely breakfast on the deck. Instead, he sat down and pulled on his running shoes, which hadn't got much use over the last four years. He felt lucky to have found them in all the unpacked boxes in the bedroom and family room. Jack walked back into the kitchen and glanced up at the clock over the kitchen sink. It was five minutes until seven. It was time to make the best of a questionable decision.

Jack opened the front door and saw Kate stretching at the bottom of the stairs.

Kate smiled. "I wasn't sure you were going to show."

Jack held up his watch as if to show her the time. "It's not even seven o'clock yet."

"Yes, but as my father used to say, if you're ten minutes early, you're late. Are you going to stretch?"

"No, I'm ready. Let's go. You lead the way."

Kate set an easy pace as they ran down the driveway and turned left onto Ocean Drive. The street was virtually devoid of traffic, so they ran side by side.

Kate spoke first. "Given the circumstances, we didn't get much of a chance to get acquainted the other night. Tell me about yourself."

Jack laughed. "You first."

"OK, I'm a navy brat. I was born at Tripler Army Hospital on Oahu. When I was born, my father was a navy lieutenant. He was the executive officer on the guided missile cruiser USS *Halsey* based out of Pearl Harbor. He was a fleet officer who spent much of his navy career at sea. In addition to Pearl, we were stationed in San Diego, Okinawa, and Norfolk. When he was promoted to admiral, he was assigned to the Pentagon, and we moved to Northern Virginia. I graduated from Langley High School in McLean and went to Princeton on a soccer scholarship. After Princeton, I graduated from Penn Law where, unfortunately, I met my former husband. We divorced, and Timmy and I moved in with my parents, in the house where we currently live. After my father retired, they built the house on a lot that Dad inherited from his parents. Shortly after we moved in, my mother was diagnosed with multiple sclerosis. The closest specially equipped military hospital was in DC, so they decided to move to Pensacola, where she would be close to the naval hospital and not have to endure the cold winters in Delaware. But you know all that. I'm beginning to re-peat myself—a bad sign. I got a job as the director of the women's center, and that's my life in a nutshell. Now, it's your turn."

They turned left on Surf Avenue and headed for the boardwalk.

"Believe it or not, I'm an army brat. Not only that, when my father retired from the army, he was a three-star general. How's that for coincidence? We both have flag-rank fathers. We'll have to watch the next Army–Navy game together. I grew up in Northern Virginia, but prob-ably not at the same time you lived there. I was thirteen when my father, mother, and older brother were killed."

"*What?*" Kate stopped running. "How?"

Jack was thankful for an opportunity to catch his breath. "They were hit head-on by a drunk driver. I was home sick with my aunt Ellen when it happened. She ended up raising me. In any event, I graduated from St. Stephens in Alexandria. Aunt Ellen wanted me to go to her alma mater, the University of Virginia. Much to her dismay, I chose the US Naval Academy. After graduation, I was assigned to the Naval Information Warfare Systems Command in San Diego. As a new ensign, I was the office gopher. I had a boring job at the command, and I had so much time on my hands that I started working on a mas-ter's degree. San Diego State offered a master's degree in forensic science on base. Eighteen months later I graduat-ed. In the interim, I applied for SEAL school and was ac-cepted. After I completed SEAL training, I joined SEAL Team 2 and did three six-month combat deployments.

The FBI approached me after I returned from my third deployment and made me an offer I couldn't refuse. After I completed the FBI Academy training at Quantico, they wanted to send me to the University of Tennessee for a PhD in forensic science. I jumped at the opportunity. I'm currently on sabbatical from the bureau, and that's pretty much it."

Kate was going to ask about his wife but thought she'd better leave that alone. "OK, we're at the beginning of the boardwalk. It's exactly a mile long, so a total of two miles down and back. In case you're curious how far you've gone or got left to go, the distance is marked in white on each side on the boardwalk in eighth-of-a-mile segments."

Kate picked up the pace a notch. Jack shook his head and fell in behind her. He thought the boardwalk was incredibly crowded for a few minutes after seven o'clock in the morning. Hundreds of runners, walkers, and bicyclists wove in and out of each other. The sunrise watchers were returning to their hotels for breakfast, and the early beachgoers were moving in to stake out their turf for their day in the sun.

"Is it always this crowded this early in the morning?" Jack asked.

"It's pretty much like this all summer."

Just past the post office, the boardwalk narrowed. They were back to single file, dodging strollers and senior citizens walking two and three abreast, seemingly unwilling to give the joggers and bicyclists room to squeeze by. At the end of the boardwalk, Kate slowed down, tapped the rail, and turned around to head back north. Jack didn't know why, but he also tapped the rail.

From behind, Jack could tell that Kate's running style was extremely efficient; there was no wasted motion or energy. Jack's thighs were beginning to burn, and his lungs were on fire. He struggled down the boardwalk past Funland, suspecting most parents would question the accuracy of the name. He passed a myriad of stores selling everything from saltwater taffy to buckets of french fries. The smell of fried bacon caught Jack's attention as he passed Victoria's. Only his pride and a wallet prevented him from stopping for breakfast.

Unknowingly, Kate was starting to pull away. Jack reluctantly picked up the pace in an effort to catch up. As Kate turned right onto Ocean Drive and the home stretch, Jack had again fallen about twenty yards behind. At the bottom of the hill, Kate turned and yelled something over her shoulder that Jack didn't quite catch. He thought she said, "If you can catch me, you can have me." He knew that couldn't be right. He looked up and Kate had again kicked it into another gear. She was sprinting for home at a pace that, even if he were rested, he couldn't match.

Jack turned into his driveway, stopped, bent over, and placed his hands on his knees. After he caught his breath, he looked up to see Kate sitting on his front steps. His legs were still burning as he walked up the driveway. He plopped down rather than sat next to Kate.

"You yelled something at me back there as you turned the corner. I didn't quite catch it."

"Oh, I said, 'I'm heading for home. See if you can catch me.'" Kate leaned back against the stairs and turned toward Jack. "Look, I apologize. I was showing off. I don't know what got into me back there. I'd like to say I'm sorry by taking you to breakfast tomorrow. Have you ever heard of or been to Royal Treat?"

"No. Remember, I'm the new kid in town."

"If you're not busy tomorrow morning, I'll pick you up for a breakfast you'll never forget. Does seven work?"

"It's a date." Jack struggled to stand up. "I need to get my body under a hot shower and get something to eat. Thanks for the running lesson."

Kate smiled. "Might you join me again on Thursday?"

"The jury's still out on that. Let's talk tomorrow."

"See you at seven."

Winston met Jack at the door. "I'm sorry, buddy. I'll get your food, and then we can take a walk on the beach." Winston followed Jack to the kitchen and sat patiently while he poured the dog food into his bowl. "After your walk, I'm going to clean up, eat breakfast, and then we're going shopping for a fishing boat. I saw this in the paper yesterday." He turned the page toward Winston. Winston yawned, turned around, and headed for the door. "Yes, I can see you're thrilled." Jack took the leash off the hook next to the sliding glass door to the deck. "Let's go for a walk…a short walk."

CHAPTER SEVENTEEN

Jack opened the passenger side door of the Jeep Grand Cherokee. Winston jumped in and curled up in the bucket seat. He drove into town and headed south on Route 1 through Dewey Beach. His Garmin on the dashboard indicated it was 6.2 miles to the marina. Winston put his head on the console, and Jack reached over and stroked and scratched the back of his head. He wondered what his life would be like today if he hadn't rescued Winston.

Winston sat up as Jack pulled off the highway into the marina. He followed the road past the RV park to the Indian River Inlet Marina's main office. He grabbed the leash off the floor and hooked Winston up. Winston was more than ready to stretch his legs and explore his new surroundings. Jack opened the office door and ushered Winston in. The young girl at the counter looked down disapprovingly at Winston.

"Excuse me. I'm here to inquire about the boat advertised in Friday's *Cape Gazette*." Jack pulled the ad out of his right front pocket and placed it on the counter. The girl examined the ad and stood up.

"I'll get the manager. He can help you with this."

Jack examined the pictures on the walls of various yachts and sport fishing boats. He turned as the manager stepped into the reception area.

The manager was in his midforties with a thinning hairline and a beer belly in training. "I'm Tony Russo, the marina manager. I understand you're interested in the Hatteras GT45 sport fishing boat we advertised last week. Full disclosure, the boat is bank owned, and I'm acting as the selling agent for the bank. The original owner was a doctor from Baltimore who came out on the wrong end of a malpractice lawsuit. The bank repossessed it in March."

"I'm very interested. Would it be possible to see it?"

"I'll do you one better. Let's take it out for a short spin in the bay. Let me get the keys. I'll be back in a minute."

"Hear that, Winston? We're going for a boat ride."

In less than a minute, the manager returned with the key. "OK, follow me. How much do you know about the Hatteras GT45?"

"Not much. I'm looking for a fishing boat we can take out after tuna and swordfish. I am also looking for a boat with an extended cruising range that sleeps three or four."

"Well, you're in luck. This model sleeps four comfortably and maybe up to six or seven. Let me tell you about the boat while we walk. It's just under forty-five feet in length, with a beam of sixteen and a half feet. It has a four-foot draft and two 850-horsepower diesel engines with a fuel capacity of eight hundred gallons. Best of all, the engines have less than thirty hours on them. The doctor liked to entertain while tied up to the dock. I'll tell you, he threw some wild parties on that boat with some of the most beautiful women on the East Coast. Here we are."

Jack looked down at Winston. "OK, buddy, let's go for a ride." He pulled on the leash in an attempt to get Winston to jump into the back of the boat. But nothing doing; Winston dug in his front paws and wouldn't budge. Jack lifted the dog into the boat.

"All right, let's start her up."

As soon as the twin diesels kicked in, Winston started trembling uncontrollably. Jack yelled to the manager over the roar of the engines, "You can turn it off. The dog is freaked out, and I don't want to stress him."

The manager disappointedly turned off the engines. "Does that mean you're not interested in the boat?"

"Not at all. I'm very interested. Let's go back to the office, and we'll talk price."

Winston's legs were still wobbly when Jack placed him down on the dock. He hooked up the leash, and Winston slowly followed the pair back to the office.

"Let's go into my office. You can bring the dog."

Jack and Winston followed the manager into the office. He motioned to a chair next to his desk. "Please, have a seat. Does your dog need any water? I've got a dog bowl in the back room."

"That would be great. I think he's still a little traumatized."

"I'll be right back." The manager returned within seconds with a bowl of water and a dog bone. Winston gulped down the water but ignored the bone.

Jack leaned in over the desk. "How much are you asking for the boat?"

"Well, first let me give you some background. As I previously indicated, the engines have less than thirty hours on them. The original owner paid $399,500 for the boat in 2003. The bank is listing it at $349,500."

"I'll give you $325,000 cash, pending a mechanical inspection, which I will schedule and pay for."

"I'm going to level with you. As I told you earlier, I'm the bank's agent on this sale, and, as such, I get an eight percent commission on the sale. So here's my offer. If you pay the asking price, I'll throw in a free slip for a year."

"If you throw in an additional smaller slip for my Zodiac Pro, we've got a deal—pending the mechanical inspection, of course."

"You have a Zodiac Pro?"

Jack smiled. "Not yet, but soon. Do we have a deal?"

The manager stood up and offered Jack his hand. "We have a deal."

"I'll have a man out to inspect the boat by the end of the week. If everything checks out, you can draw up the papers, and I'll have a cashier's check for you on Saturday." Jack stood up and gave a gentle tug on Winston's leash. "Let's go home, buddy. You've had a tough morning."

CHAPTER EIGHTEEN

Jack opened the door and smiled.

"Now what?" he asked himself. At the bottom of the stairs, Kate's beat-up Jeep Wrangler and Chief Johnson's police cruiser sat headlight to headlight a foot apart with their engines running. Both Kate and the chief were leaning back against their front fenders, arms and legs crossed, in silence. Jack walked halfway down the steps and sat down. "I know what Kate's doing here, but I'm a little puzzled about you, Chief."

Johnson stood up and uncrossed his arms. "That's simple enough. I came over to pick you up. Dr. Watson has finished his autopsy and asked us to come by this morning—and yes, that's his real name."

"Us? I'm still confused. Why does he want to see me?"

"I told him you found the body, and he specifically asked me to bring you along. Something about a book."

"A book?"

"Don't ask me. He just said he'd like to meet you. That's all I know."

"Can it wait? Kate and I were just going out for breakfast."

Johnson nodded. "We can do breakfast."

"We?" Jack asked.

Johnson looked hurt by Jack's question. "Doesn't it make more sense for me to drive you to the morgue and back? That way, after we've finished breakfast, Kate can get on with her day."

Jack looked at Kate quizzically. "Are you OK with that?"

Kate smiled and shrugged. "Sure, but we'll have to go somewhere other than Royal Treat. Somewhere we can get in and out of a little faster. I would suggest Java Beach on Baltimore Avenue."

Johnson tossed his keys from his left hand to his right. "Sounds good. I'll meet you there."

Kate pulled up to the curb. Johnson was already there, eyeing a young couple sitting at a table near the sidewalk.

Jack looked around the place. "It seems all the tables are taken. We'll either have to wait or go someplace else."

"Not so fast." Johnson walked over to the young couple he'd been eyeing. "Excuse me, have you two ordered yet?"

The young boy looked up. "Oh no, we're not eating. We're just waiting for some friends."

Johnson pulled his ticket pad out of his breast pocket. "That's loitering. Looks like I'll have to write you two up."

The boy jumped up. "That's not necessary. We were just leaving. Come on, Sally, let's get out of here."

The girl got up, and the two walked rapidly down the street.

Johnson turned to Kate and Jack. "It seems a table has opened up."

Kate laughed. "You seem to have a way with the younger generation, Chief."

Johnson smiled. "Let me escort you to your table."

After several minutes of small talk, Jack turned to Kate. "What's the drill here? Does someone take our order, or do we have to go inside?"

"Usually, Ralph comes out and takes the orders. However, it looks like he's overloaded this morning. I think we'll have to order inside."

Kate started to get up. Jack held up his hand. "Stay here. I'll get this."

"But I am supposed to be taking you to breakfast."

"Let's just say I'll take a rain check on Royal Treat. What would you like?"

"I'll have the fruit-and-yogurt bowl and a medium black coffee."

"How about you, Chief?" Jack asked.

"I'll have two glazed donuts and a medium black coffee…with cream and two sugars."

Jack laughed. "Really?"

"What? I like glazed donuts."

Jack doubted if Johnson even saw the irony in it.

The man behind the counter looked like he was having one hell of a morning, and it was only seven thirty.

"You must be Ralph. Kate said to say hello."

"Kate Simpson?"

"That's the one."

"Please apologize to her for me. I would have been out to take her order, but my assistant failed to show this morning. She probably got drunk last night or hooked up. In any event, I'll be looking for a new assistant. Anyway, what can I get you?"

"We'll have one fruit-and-yogurt bowl and a medium black coffee. One all-American with eggs scrambled, bacon with wheat toast, and a medium black coffee. Also, two glazed donuts and a medium coffee with cream and two sugars."

Ralph laughed. "I take it you're dining with the chief?"

"You know your clientele."

"Give me about twenty minutes, and I'll bring it out myself. It's always a pleasure to see Kate."

Jack sat back down. "You were right, he's jammed. However, just so he can say hello to Kate, he is going to bring our order out personally." Jack looked around. "It's an eclectic crowd. What's their story?" Jack nodded toward a couple sitting in the far corner. The man was black, had dreadlocks, and was wearing a burlap tunic. He wore several necklaces and was holding a four-foot-long wooden rod with a fist-sized egg-shaped crystal on top. The woman was white and looked like a witch, with a thin face and long pointed nose and chin. She was wearing a black robe.

"I call him mojo man," Johnson replied. "He claims to be a Haitian voodoo priest, if there is such a thing. He and his wife prey upon the young tourists. They'll sit there for hours nursing a coffee, hoping to get their hooks in a couple of gullible twenty-somethings. They pretend to tell their fortunes. His real name is Willie Jackson. He's a two-bit felon from south Philly. When he's not fleecing the tourists, he buses tables at Blackbeard's Pub. She's a short-order cook at Chicken Jimmy's in Lewes. Ralph hates them. He's tried to get rid of them for years, but they know their rights."

"How about the guy directly behind me sitting next to the window?" Jack asked.

Johnson turned to look. "Oh, that's Captain Eddie. He helps Ralph clean up after the morning rush and does odd jobs for several of the shop owners in town. He's homeless but well liked and has never caused any trouble. In fact, the couple who own the grocery store down the street cleared out a storage room as a place for him to sleep at night. In exchange, he stocks shelves for them after the store closes. They allow him to take whatever food he wants as long as he writes down what he eats. He has a microwave and hotplate in the storeroom. On occasion, some of the restaurant owners in town provide meals for him. Ralph tells me Eddie is a Vietnam veteran. He thinks he might be suffering from PTSD."

"Good morning, Kate. Good to see you too, Chief." Ralph walked out carrying a large tray with their order.

Ralph put the tray on the table, and Kate got up to give him a hug. "Sorry I haven't been around lately. I promise I'll be a more regular customer. I understand you've met my new neighbor."

Ralph nodded at Jack. "Sorry I can't stay and visit, but I've got to get back in there. This has been a tough morning. Tell Timmy I said hello."

"We'll be by this weekend, I promise."

Johnson finished the last bite of his second glazed donut and leaned back in his chair with a satisfied grin on his face. He stretched his arms over his head and leaned forward with his elbows on the table. "Kate, I've done a little research on our new friend here," he said, nodding toward Jack. "I must say, I'm both incredibly impressed and a bit angry. First, I'll bet you didn't know that our friend is a highly decorated Navy SEAL. He served three combat tours, one in Iraq, where he was awarded a Bronze Star for valor and received a Purple Heart for wounds received in combat. In Afghanistan, he was awarded a Silver Star and a second Bronze Star for valor. He also received two more Purple Hearts—not exactly an underachiever."

Kate looked at Jack questioningly. Jack shrugged and furrowed his brow.

The chief leaned back in his chair again and crossed his arms. "That brings me to the part where I'm a bit angry. Dr. Scanlon didn't tell us that he is the assistant director of the Federal Bureau of Investigation for forensic science and testing."

"First, don't call me doctor. I have a PhD. I took several classes and wrote a dissertation; I don't put mangled bodies back together again."

Johnson looked apologetic. "I'm sorry. I sense I touched a nerve."

"It's not that. I just got so sick of watching those geek professors running around campus, always referring to each other as 'doctor this' and 'doctor that.' 'Dr. Smith, are you going to the dean's garden party on Saturday?' 'No, Dr. Jones,

I'm taking Dr. Johnson to the opera.' After three combat tours, watching real doctors putting young boys' mangled bodies back together, I promised I would never refer to myself as doctor. So please, it's either Jack or Scanlon."

"Fair enough." Johnson glanced at his watch. "Are you ready? We shouldn't keep the good—I mean the real doctor waiting."

Kate stood up and grabbed Jack's left forearm. "Could I speak with you a minute?"

J. R. pushed his chair in. "I'll get the car and pick you up out front."

Kate walked with Jack to the sidewalk. "I'm sorry about this morning. I planned to take you out for a nice breakfast to make up for yesterday morning."

"Kate, you have nothing to make up for, except my aching muscles."

Kate laughed. "Tomorrow night, I'm making Timmy's favorite dinner, lasagna. I'd like you to join us if you're not busy."

"That would be great. I accept. What time, and what can I bring?"

"Let's say five thirty for cocktails, and you don't have to bring anything."

J. R. pulled up to the curb and tapped the horn.

Jack smiled. "That's my chauffeur. See you tomorrow night."

"Oh, what about our run tomorrow morning? Are you recovered enough to give it another try?"

Jack groaned. "See you at seven."

CHAPTER NINETEEN

Johnson turned right onto Rehoboth Avenue. It was after nine, and the street was jammed with tourists scrambling to find a parking space and delivery trucks blocking a lane of traffic. Hundreds of tourists were going to and coming from the beach and boardwalk. Restaurants were still serving breakfast as patrons lined up outside waiting for a table.

"I can't believe how crowded this town is in the summer," Jack said.

"Believe it or not, it's pretty much like this from Memorial Day weekend until after Halloween. The town has organized several weekend events in September and October. There's the Elvis Festival, Greyhound Weekend, the Jazz Festival, the Film Festival, and Marathon Weekend, just to name a few. Add to that, the weather in September and October is the best all year, except for the occasional tropical storm."

Jack took it all in as they inched along Rehoboth Avenue toward Route 1 North. "You know you have a siren you could use to get around all this traffic?"

"I never use the siren unless I'm responding to an emergency," J. R. responded tersely.

They pulled onto Route 1 and crawled past the outlets and strip malls for several minutes. To break the silence, Jack finally asked, "So what does the J. R. stand for?"

"It stands for Junior." J. R. sounded annoyed but continued, "My idiot father named me Junior, Junior Johnson."

"Are your parents still alive?"

"My mother died of cancer, and I don't know about my father. I kicked his sorry ass out of our house years ago."

Jack decided he had asked enough questions.

J. R. looked over at Jack. "I suspect that sounds a little strange to you, but he was an abusive father and husband. We lived in Bethlehem, Pennsylvania, when I was growing up. Both my father and mother worked in the steel mill. He was a shift foreman, and my mother worked as a clerk in the accounting department. The abuse, particularly toward my mother, escalated when I was in high school. My father got paid every Friday, and his first stop on the way home was always McGregor's Tavern.

"This one Friday night I was doing homework and studying when I heard screaming coming from the kitchen. Just as I got to the kitchen, I saw my father punch my mother in the face. She dropped to her knees, and I could see blood running out of the corner of her mouth. I yelled at him to leave her alone. He laughed and said if I didn't go back to my room, he'd give me a beating I'd never forget. I was sixteen at the time and in the best shape of my life. I weighed 190 pounds and was the starting center linebacker on the varsity football team. I stood my ground, and he started to come at me. Long story short, I kicked the shit out of him and threw him out of the house. I told him if he ever came around again, I'd kill him. That was the last we ever saw of him. We were told he worked another week at the mill, quit, and moved out of town."

Jack shook his head in disbelief. "What about your mother and you? How did you get along without his income?"

"It was tough at first. I told her I would drop out of school and get a job, but she made me promise that I would work as hard as I could and finish school. She said she'd take care of the rest. She got a second job as a cook at the hospital. I quit the football team and got a job after school and on Saturdays stocking shelves at the local hardware store. We did pretty well without the old man. After paying the mortgage payment, groceries, and the bills each month, we treated ourselves to dinner at one of the local restaurants—nothing fancy, just good food and a chance to relax."

"So did you keep your promise to her about finishing high school?"

"Not only did I keep my promise, going into my senior year, I was only a half a percentage point away from being first in my class. There was this nerd kid who was ahead of me, but in our senior year we had to take two semesters of physical education, which counted toward our grade point average. I aced both semesters, and the nerd got Ds. Therefore, if I continued to get straight As in my other courses, I would be the class valedictorian."

"Your mother must have been proud."

J. R. hesitated for a few seconds before he responded. "In late April, I came home after school to find my mother curled up on the couch in the family room. She was coughing uncontrollably, holding a bloody handkerchief in her right hand. She was coughing up blood. I'd noticed over the past few months her cough had gotten worse. We both thought she was having trouble getting over a chest cold. I convinced her to let me take her to the emergency room. I told her she might have pneumonia.

"The doctor suggested tests and a chest X-ray and recommended that she stay in the hospital overnight. He wanted to start her on antibiotics. The next morning, I went to the hospital to pick her up. Her doctor asked me to call her husband and have him come to the hospital. I explained the situation, and he told me to follow him. We went to my mother's room. She was smiling and sitting up in bed. He asked me to sit down, and I knew then that the news wasn't going to be good. He told us that he originally suspected pneumonia, but after a needle biopsy and several tests, he was certain that it was lung cancer. I asked about treatment. He bluntly told us that it was stage four and that it had spread to other vital organs. I was devastated. My mother very calmly asked him how much time she had left. He told her that she likely had no more than six to eight weeks."

J. R. paused and took a deep breath. "She asked me to promise her that I would see to it that she died in her own home. She promised me that she would not miss my graduation. The next few weeks before graduation were a series of peaks and valleys. On graduation day, she was seated in a wheelchair in the front row. She had the hairdresser come to the house to do her hair, and she was wearing her best dress. On the way to the ceremony, I stopped at the florist to get a bouquet of red roses. As I was called upon to give the valedictorian's speech, I placed the bouquet of roses on the table behind the dais. Everyone thought they were my gift to the principal. After the speech, I picked up the roses and walked down the steps to my mother and placed the roses across her lap. There wasn't a dry eye in the place.

"The next morning, my mother was as peaceful as I'd ever seen her. She asked me to go get my diploma so she could see it again. I sat on the couch, and she lay down across my lap and ran her fingers over the embossed writing on the diploma. She leaned back against me, closed her eyes, and was gone."

"What did you do, just out of high school with no family?"

"I went down to the army recruiting office and enlisted. In the few weeks I had before reporting, I sold the house and everything else we had except for the car. I said goodbye to my friends and reported to Fort Bragg, North Carolina, for basic training. The army became my new home and family. After basic, I was assigned to an infantry company at Bragg. In those days, you took a battery of aptitude tests in basic. One of the tests was, for lack of a better description, basic intelligence. A score of 100 was average intelligence. Above and below, well, you get the picture.

"The average score of the corporals and below in the company was around 78, with the mean around 72. My score was 138, so I was selected as the company clerk. All things considered, a pretty cushy job—no KP, no guard duty. I also doubled as the company commander's driver. He took a liking to me, and after I was promoted to specialist fourth class, he nominated me to attend the Noncommissioned Officer Academy, commonly referred to in those days as 'shake and bake.' The course lasted four months. There were about two hundred E-4s and E-5s in each class, and if you graduated in the top ten of your graduating class, you were automatically promoted to E-6 staff sergeant. I finished second in my class. After graduation, I was assigned to the US Army Military Police School for basic training. For the next twenty-two years, I served in various posts as an MP. Unlike you, I never saw combat and never served in a combat zone."

"You've lived a tough life."

"I wouldn't say that, not at all. I've been very lucky."

"How did you get to be the police chief in Rehoboth?"

"After I left the army, I decided to take a few months and see some of the country. One night toward the end of my travels, I ended up in a motel in Annapolis. The next morning, I picked up a newspaper and came across a job announcement for chief of police in Rehoboth Beach, Delaware. I called, got an interview, and was offered the job. Finally—we've arrived. This is the regional medical center for Sussex County."

J. R. pulled into the emergency entrance and turned off the ignition.

Jack pointed to the sign on the concrete pillar in front of the car reading, "No Parking—Emergency Vehicles Only."

"What? This is a police car."

"But technically it's not an 'emergency vehicle.'"

J. R. leaned forward and pushed the red triangular button on the dash. The emergency flashers began to blink. "Feel better?"

CHAPTER TWENTY

Jack followed Johnson into the lobby of the medical center. A large circular four-foot-high check-in counter dominated the center of the spacious sunlit atrium. Suspended from the ceiling over the counter, a six-foot-wide sign read "Information—Check-In" in bold black letters. As Johnson approached the counter, an attractive elderly woman stood up from a chair behind the counter.

"Good morning, Chief. It's about time you got here. Dr. Watson has been pestering me about your whereabouts for the past hour and a half."

Johnson smiled at her. "You look radiant this morning, Agnes. Is that a new dress?"

"It is." Agnes's face lit up with joy. "I bought it last Saturday, and today is the first chance I've had to wear it. Thank you for noticing."

"How are the grandchildren?"

"They're a handful. I think I'm getting too old for this babysitting stuff."

Johnson laughed. "Nonsense, you love it."

"OK, enough of the small talk. You and your friend better get down to the morgue before the doc drives me crazy."

Agnes picked up the phone, punched four numbers, and waited. "Dr. Watson, this is Agnes. Chief Johnson and his friend are here. I'll send them right down."

Johnson pushed the down button on the elevator wall bank. The mortuary was on the second basement level. Dr. Watson greeted them at the door with a big welcoming smile on his face. "Dr. Scanlon, it's a pleasure to meet you."

J. R. glanced sideways at Jack, wondering how he would react to being called "doctor."

Jack smiled, extended his hand, and said, "Please call me Jack."

Watson shook Jack's hand vigorously and responded, "Only if you call me Mark."

"Nice to see you too, Doc," Johnson interjected sarcastically. "Now, if we can interrupt this lovefest for a moment, what do you have to show us?"

"It took you forever to get here, and now you're in a hurry. Besides, I have a favor to ask of Jack." Watson turned back toward Jack. "I suppose you've been in dozens of morgues over the course of your career with the FBI."

Jack shrugged. "Not so much as you'd think."

"Well then, let me show you around. Follow me."

The room was fairly large, about eight hundred square feet. Eight stainless-steel cold chambers lined the left side of the far wall. Next to the cold chambers was a scrub station. In the center of the room were a pedestal autopsy table and a dissection table. Over both tables hung pull-down surgical lights. Attached to the autopsy table was an additional surgical light with magnification. A surgical saw sat on a tray table with a selection of surgical instruments, and a weighing scale hung from the ceiling.

"This is very impressive. Thank you for the tour." Jack walked back toward J. R., who was leaning impatiently against Watson's desk. "Oh, you mentioned a favor."

"Yes, but before that, let me give you some background about myself."

J. R. stood up. "Doc, how long is this going to take? You realize that the criminal element in Rehoboth will wreak havoc with the town once they realize I'm away."

"Cool your jets, J. R.." Watson continued, addressing Jack. "Where was I when we were so rudely interrupted? Oh yes, I was about to give you some background. I have a general medical practice in Georgetown. Knock on wood, all of my patients are alive and breathing, as opposed to my patients here. I knew nothing about being a medical examiner. Sussex County doesn't have the budget for a full-time ME, so I drew the short straw. I took courses, did research, and bought a few texts. The most helpful text was yours, *Forensic Science, Pathology, and Standard Methods*." Watson walked over to his desk and pulled a book off the top shelf of the credenza's bookshelf. "I'd be honored if you would sign it for me."

"I'd be happy to." Jack took the book and a pen off the desk and wrote a short note and signed the book.

"Doc, can we get on with this?" J. R. implored.

Watson motioned them over to the autopsy table and pulled back the white sheet covering the young girl's body. "I'm ruling this a homicide. She died of blunt force trauma. There was no water in her lungs, so she was dead before she entered the water. I want you both to take a look at her neck and the back of her skull. Tell me what you see."

Jack pulled down the magnification light for a closer look. He stepped aside to allow J. R. a better angle. J. R. waved him off.

Watson walked over to a video console attached to the wall and turned on the monitor. "This is an X-ray of the back of her cranium. Look carefully at the damage to the occipital bone. What do you see?"

J. R. just shrugged. "I'll leave the forensics to the two of you."

"Jack?" Watson asked.

"A couple of things. First, the fracture pattern is unusual. It looks like she was struck with something with a rounded head but with some elasticity to it. I'm at a loss as to what that might be. Second, based upon the bruising on her neck and the blow to the back of her head, I'm pretty sure her assailant was left-handed."

"I agree," Watson added.

"Were you able to get any usable prints?" J. R. asked.

"Better than that. I've already identified her. Her name is Anna Campbell."

"So she was in the system?"

Watson leaned back against his desk. "In a manner of speaking. Her parents had her fingerprinted as a child. It was somewhat common in the late '80s and early '90s. There were a rash of child abductions, and some states initiated a voluntary program for fingerprinting children. So she popped in the Automated Fingerprint Identification System. She's from Martinsburg, West Virginia."

"That's pretty good detective work, Doc," J. R. said admiringly.

"I contacted her parents this morning. As you can imagine, they're devastated. It was her habit to call them every Sunday evening. When she didn't call Sunday night, they started to get worried. They wanted to come down to make arrangements to have her body transported back to West Virginia. I convinced them not to. I'll have the body sent to Singleton's Funeral Home in town. I know Ned will do a good job preparing her to be sent home." Watson turned and picked up a Post-it note off the desk blotter. "Here's her local address. I've already notified the state and local authorities." Watson took a deep breath and walked over to his desk.

"Doc, is there something you're not telling us?" Jack asked.

Watson picked up a manila folder off the desk and handed it to Jack.

"Turn to page two and read number five under findings," Watson instructed.

Jack read the finding, looked up, horrified, and handed the folder to J. R..

He read the section of the autopsy report that Jack pointed out. "What are you saying, Doc?" J. R. asked. "I can't believe what I'm reading."

"Anna was sexually assaulted postmortem. It's called necrophilia. This guy isn't just a murderer; he's a monster. I've been doing this job for over ten years now, and in all that time, I've never seen anything this heinous."

"Were you able to obtain a DNA sample?" Jack asked.

"No, I'm afraid the length of time she was in the water negated that possibility."

"Was there any trace evidence? You know, hairs on her clothing or, if she struggled with her attacker, skin cells under her fingernails?" Jack questioned.

"I know I don't have your experience or the resources of the FBI, but I consider myself quite competent and thorough in conducting an autopsy."

"Doc, I'm sorry, that was uncalled for, and I apologize. I guess I'm just grasping at straws at this point."

"I understand, and you're more than welcome to examine the body yourself. I'm getting to be an old man, and it's possible I missed something," Watson humbly said.

"That won't be necessary, and again, I was out of line," Jack humbly responded.

J. R. tried to defuse the situation but only made it worse. "You didn't say anything about this to her parents, did you?"

"What, do you think I'm a moron?"

Now it was Jack's turn to mollify Watson. "Doc, can I get a copy of the autopsy report? We might be able to use it in our investigation."

It wasn't lost on J. R. that, given the recent revelations, it appeared that Jack was now all in.

"I thought you might ask. Take that one. The original is in the safe, and I hope to see you again soon under better circumstances."

CHAPTER TWENTY-ONE

J. R. pulled up behind the Lewes Police Department squad car. Two Delaware state trooper cars were parked on the other side of the street.

Anna Campbell lived on the second floor of a two-bedroom garden apartment complex just off Kings Highway in Lewes. According to her parents, she shared the apartment with her high school sweetheart.

Jack and J. R. climbed the stairs to apartment 203. The door was open. J. R. recognized Sergeant Holmes of the state police and Lewes chief of police Jeff Conrad walking into a room off the hallway.

Holmes turned toward the open door. "Morning, J. R.. You were my next call. If I understand correctly, this is the apartment of the girl who washed up on your beach Sunday night."

"Close enough," J. R. replied.

"We got here about twenty minutes ago. Doc Watson told us he learned from her parents that the victim lived here with her boyfriend. According to the mail on the table, his name is Billy West. We haven't found much else, but you're welcome to look around."

Conrad poked his head out of one of the rooms. "I thought I heard your voice out here." He walked across the room and shook J. R.'s hand. "This is your case. Just let us know if there is anything we can do to help."

"Thanks, Jeff, what have you found so far?"

"Not much. Follow me. This is the victim's bedroom. As you can see, she was a neat freak, nothing out of place. Her boyfriend, not so much."

J. R. and Jack followed Conrad to the room across the hall. "This appears to be his room. Sort of an old-fashioned arrangement, don't you think?"

J. R. looked at him quizzically.

"You know, separate rooms."

"Maybe he snores." J. R. carefully perused the room. A pair of jeans hung over the back of a chair in the corner, and socks and underwear adorned the closet floor. "Any idea of his current whereabouts?"

"I can answer that," Sergeant Holmes interjected. "I just got off the phone with Delmarva Power, where Mr. West is employed as a lineman. He's in South Carolina helping get power restored after the recent tornadoes. He's been there for two weeks. I explained what happened to his girlfriend, and they said they would contact him immediately. I gave them my number. I'll contact you when I hear from him. I think we're done here. J. R., you take care, and if I can help in any way, call me."

"If there's nothing else, J. R., I'll head back to the station. Just lock the door behind you, and when you're through, drop off the keys at the front desk," Conrad instructed.

"Thanks, Jeff. Let's catch up soon over a couple of beers."

Jack held up an envelope as they walked to the car.

"What's that?"

"It's a paycheck stub from Anna's place of employment. I found it among the bills on the table in the kitchen. I wasn't sure how cooperative your buddies were going to be, so I stuffed it in my pocket."

"Hmmm, that's a good one, an FBI agent tampering with evidence. So where does she work?"

"According to the pay stub, a place called the Roadhouse."

J. R. laughed. "Sounds like a great excuse to have lunch—best burgers in Delaware. I know the bartender. Let's go."

"So what's so funny about this place?"

"The Roadhouse is probably the best steak restaurant on the Delmarva Peninsula. However, after eight o'clock on Thursday through Saturday evenings, it's a titty bar. It's a whole different clientele on those nights."

"I take it you've been there a few times?"

"What can I say? I like a good steak now and then."

Jack followed J. R. to the bar at the rear of the restaurant.

"Good afternoon, Sherry," J. R. said.

The girl arranging liquor bottles behind the bar turned toward the voice. "Good morning, Chief. What brings you here so early?"

"Is the boss in?"

"I think he's in his office."

"Would you please tell him we'd like to see him? Also, we'd like to order lunch."

"Grab a table. I'll be back in five minutes to take your order."

Sherry returned in less than a minute. "He says he'll be out to see you in about ten minutes. He's on the phone with a vendor. Are you both ready to order?" She pointed to Jack. "What would you like, handsome?"

Jack smiled. "I'll have the Philly cheese steak with hot peppers and onions and a draft Dogfish Head 60 Minute IPA."

"Usual for you, Chief—bacon cheeseburger and a draft Budweiser?"

"Better make that an iced tea. I'm still on duty."

Jack noticed a rather portly, unshaven man emerge from a hallway at the rear of the restaurant. He nodded to J. R.. "I think the owner is on his way."

Vinny Puglisi was in his late forties but looked much older. Rumor had it that Vinny was a member of a prominent crime family from Philadelphia and had been temporarily exiled to lower slower Delaware for "certain indiscretions" with the wife of a made member of the family.

"Afternoon, J. R.. What can I do for you?" Puglisi asked.

"It's Chief Johnson," J. R. replied.

Vinny laughed. "Oh, does this mean I need a lawyer?"

"I don't know. Do you?"

Vinny's smile instantly disappeared. "Let's drop the bullshit. What do you want with me, and more importantly, aren't you out of your jurisdiction?"

"We're here to inquire about one of your employees, Anna Campbell."

Vinny crossed his arms. "Well, if you see Ms. Campbell, you can tell her for me she's fired. She ran out of here last Friday a little after noon and hasn't showed up since."

J. R. leaned back in his chair. "She's dead."

"Dead? How? You don't think I had anything to do with it, do you?"

"I don't know. We're just here to follow the trail. The last time she was seen alive was when she left here last Friday. At least that's the story you're telling us. So why don't you pull up a chair and tell us everything you know?"

Sherry had been surreptitiously listening in on the conversation. She now moved down the bar closer to their table under the pretext of fixing one of the taps.

Vinny pulled a chair up to the table, pointing to Jack. "So who's your friend?"

J. R. smiled. "His name is Jack Scanlon, and he's with the FBI." He could instantly see that Jack was not happy with that revelation.

"FBI. What, you think I had something to do with her murder?"

J. R. leaned across the table. "Who said anything about murder? I said she was dead. I didn't say anything about how she died, did I?"

Vinny shifted uncomfortably in his chair. "Look, you're here with an FBI agent asking about Anna Campbell. You tell me she's dead. What do you expect me to think—she died of old age? I'll tell you everything I know about last Friday, and it's not much. I was sitting with a customer over there in the corner booth. Anna was waiting on a customer a few tables away. Suddenly, she started shouting at the man. I got up to see what was going on. She stormed up to me and started shouting something about not having to take it anymore. She ripped off her apron, threw it in the booth over there, and ran out. That's all I know, honest. Now, can I get back to work?"

"Sure, thanks for your help. If you think of anything else, please give me a call."

Vinny stormed off as Sherry approached the table with their lunch.

"Let's see, I have a Philly cheese steak and an IPA for your friend and a bacon cheeseburger and an iced tea for you." Sherry leaned closer to J. R. and whispered, "Did I hear you say that Anna was murdered?"

"We didn't stay that, but, yes, she was." J. R. took a bite of his burger.

Sherry pulled up a chair and sat down. "Anna was the sweetest girl I've ever known. Everybody here loved her."

"What more can you tell us about her?"

"Well, she started working here last September. Initially, she worked from 6:00 p.m. until midnight. She was going to the local community college during the day. About three months ago, she asked Vinny to change her hours so that she wouldn't have to work the weekends after 8:00 p.m. She told the other girls that the customers were getting a little too free with their hands, if you know what I mean."

J. R. nodded knowingly.

"Something else was bothering her about working here."

Jack finally chimed in. "What was that?"

"I don't know for sure. She told some of the other girls that she suspected that something illegal was going on here, but she was vague about what it was."

J. R. put down what was left of his burger, wiped his mouth, and asked, "Is there anything else you can think of that might help us? Did she tell you what she suspected? And what about her boyfriend?"

"You mean Billy? No way. He's a great guy, and they were madly in love with each other. He was very protective of Anna. When he wasn't working, he'd be in here sometimes looking out for her. Besides, I'm pretty sure he is out of town on business. He'll be devastated when he hears. As far as what she suspected, she was very vague."

"How was she around the other waitresses?"

"She didn't socialize much. She was very pleasant and outgoing at work, but outside of work, none of us ever saw her, and she never went on any of Vinny's 'picnic' outings."

"Picnic outings?" Jack asked.

"Vinny owns a boat at the marina in Lewes. We're closed on Mondays, so Vinny invites a few of the girls to join him for lunch and a ride on his boat. I went once, but never again. Keep in mind, some of the girls that work here on weekends are strippers. It seems Vinny expects the girls to reward him, if you know what I mean."

Jack nodded. "Unfortunately, I think I do."

"I've probably said too much already. I need this job. Where else would a person like me, with no education or training, make this kind of money? I keep my head down and go about my business."

J. R. reached across the table and patted her arm. "Thanks, Sherry. This helps a lot. You ready to go, partner?" he asked Jack. "I think we ought to check out the marina. Let's go out the back."

"Why did you tell Vinny I was FBI?"

"I wanted to put the fear of God in him, and I think it worked. He was pretty smug when we first started asking him questions. That all disappeared when I told him you worked for the bureau. Are we good?"

"We're good."

J. R. started the engine, but Jack grabbed his arm.

"Turn it off," Jack commanded. "Do you see what I see?"

"Yeah, it's one of my patrol cars pulling up to the back entrance."

The door of the patrol car opened, and a uniformed officer stepped out. "Isn't that one of your deputies?" Jack asked. "I wonder what he's doing here."

"It's Deputy Crockett, and I haven't a clue."

Crockett walked around to the rear of the patrol car, opened the trunk, and pulled out a leather briefcase. He walked up a short flight of stairs, opened the door, and walked inside.

"I don't think he saw us. Let's just sit here and see what happens."

"Have you ever seen him here before?" Jack asked.

"No. I come here, on average, once or twice a week. He's never been here when I'm here. In the evenings, one of the two of us is on duty. He could be a frequent customer, and I wouldn't know it."

"Here he comes, and he's still carrying a briefcase, but it's a different briefcase from the one he took in."

Crockett walked down the steps, opened the driver's side door, and tossed the briefcase on the front passenger seat. He started the engine and drove off, apparently without noticing J. R.'s cruiser parked fifty yards away.

"Should we follow him?"

"No, I'll deal with him later." J. R. keyed his mic. "Eagle's Nest, this is Hobo Six, over."

A barely audible response soon followed. "Hobo Six, this is Eagle's Nest, over."

"This is Hobo Six. Sara, have Crockett check in with me after his shift ends, over."

"Wilco, out" came the reply.

"Let's visit the marina and Vinny's boat. That's more important right now than determining what Crockett was up to."

CHAPTER TWENTY-TWO

The marina office was nothing more than a house trailer on a cinder-block platform at the end of a parking lot paved with crushed seashells. J. R. pulled up to the handicap ramp leading up to the front door. An "open" sign hung in the window. J. R. and Jack walked up the ramp, opened the door, and walked in.

A young man, no more than high school age, stood up from behind the desk in the corner.

"Can I help you? I'm Jimmy, the marina manager's assistant."

J. R. approached the boy and held out his hand. "Good afternoon, Jimmy, I'm Rehoboth Beach Police chief J. R. Johnson. We'd like to talk to the marina manager if that's possible."

The boy shook J. R.'s hand. "The manager is down at the machine shop working on an outboard motor. Would you like me to take you down there?"

"That's not necessary. Just point us in the right direction."

J. R. led the way down the dock toward the machine shop. At the end of the dock, a ramp to the right led along the boat launch ramp to the shop entrance.

A man was bent over a vintage Evinrude outboard motor.

"Excuse me, would you tell me where I can find the marina manager?" J. R. inquired.

The man stood up and wiped his hands off on a rag hanging over the engine mount. "Yes, I'm the manager. What can I do for you?"

"We're here to see Mr. Puglisi's boat."

"Do you have a warrant?"

J. R. smiled. "Now, why would we need a warrant?"

"You need a warrant to search a boat, just like you need a warrant to search someone's house."

Again, J. R. smiled. "Are you a lawyer, or do you just watch a lot of cop shows? Besides, who said anything about searching Mr. Puglisi's boat?"

"You don't have any jurisdiction around here." He pointed at J. R.'s uniform. "You're a Rehoboth cop."

"You see this gentleman with me? He's an FBI agent, and he would be more than happy to examine the marina's financials for the past three years. Do you think that's what the marina's owners would want?"

"All right, all right, follow me." The manager angrily tossed the grease rag on the floor and stalked out of the shop past J. R. and Jack.

The three men walked halfway down the dock when the manager turned to his right and pointed. "That's Puglisi's boat."

Jack looked at the name on the stern—*Happy Endings*. He turned toward J. R.. "Your friend Vinny is a pig."

"No argument, and he's not my friend."

"I'm going up to the office. Do whatever you like; just don't tell me about it. If you have any questions, you know where to find me." The manager turned and stalked off.

J. R. climbed into the boat. The boat was a twenty-eight-foot cabin cruiser with an inboard engine.

"What are you doing?"

"The man said, 'Do whatever you like,' and I'd like to have a look around. Are you going to join me?"

Jack shrugged and climbed into the boat.

"Come over here." J. R. had moved toward the rear right corner of the boat. "What does this look like to you?"

"It looks like blood. I know what you're thinking, but it could just as well be fish blood. Besides, you will need a warrant to get it tested, and without probable cause, you'll never get that warrant."

"You really are a Debby Downer, Scanlon. Let's go talk to our new friend."

"By the way, you've got to stop using my position with the FBI to coerce people into doing what you want."

"I always say, if you've got it, flaunt it."

"You're incorrigible."

"I know. Isn't that what you love most about me?"

The manager sat on a folding chair outside his office door. When he saw them approaching, he got up, flicked his cigarette over the railing, and walked down the ramp to the parked police cruiser. "Did you find what you were looking for?"

"We weren't looking for anything in particular, just looking around. Do you mind answering some questions?" J. R. asked.

"Do I have any choice?"

"Of course you do. You don't have to answer any questions. Just don't let it come back and bite you in the ass."

"Go ahead, shoot. What do you want to know?"

"How often does Vinny—Mr. Puglisi—take his boat out?"

"That's easy. Every Monday during the season. But you already know that. He leaves the dock around eleven thirty and returns before three. Again, you already know that as well."

J. R. laughed. "Well, here is a question I don't know the answer to. Who else takes his boat out?"

The manager hesitated and looked around, as if to see who else might be listening. "Until last Friday, no one else has ever taken his boat out. I was just getting ready to head home and a white van pulled into the marina. Three men got out. One was white; the other two were Mexicans."

"Mexicans? How do you know they were Mexicans?" Jack asked.

"I don't, but they were speaking Spanish. So I assumed they were Mexicans."

"Do you know that there are over twenty-five countries that speak predominantly Spanish? That's

133

approximately seven percent of the world's population, or 450 million people," Jack stated incredulously.

"All right, I get the picture. There was one Caucasian and two Spanish-speaking males."

"What did they do?" J. R. asked.

"They took fishing gear, a large ice chest, and a sizable duffel bag to the boat. It took two of them to carry the duffel bag."

"How long were they gone?"

"I don't know for sure. I waited until they left; that was a little before 8:00 p.m. Don't know when they returned. I went home and didn't get back here until Saturday morning around nine. The boat was back in its slip when I got here. But I do know how many gallons they used. I filled it up that afternoon, and it took thirty-four gallons. That boat at twenty knots can go approximately two miles per gallon. So you do the math."

J. R. nodded. "Thanks, you've been very helpful." As they approached the squad car, J. R. asked Jack, "So what do you think?"

"I think that the white guy and the two 'Mexicans' dumped Anna's body somewhere out in the Atlantic and Vinny knew all about it. Problem is there's no evidence to prove it, and we don't have probable cause to search the boat."

"What now?"

"I don't know, but I do know somebody is going to slip up if we keep the pressure on." Jack looked at his watch. "Shortly, you have an appointment with your deputy, so we'd better get back."

"I know it's been a long day, but would you mind sitting in on my meeting with Crockett?"

"Sure, I've got no place to go and a long time to get there."

Crockett knocked on the door, and J. R. waved him in. J. R. pointed to a chair next to Jack. "Have a seat." Pointing to Jack, J. R. said, "This is Jack Scanlon, a friend of mine."

Crockett nodded. "Nice to meet you." Turning toward J. R., he asked, "So, Chief, what can I do for you?"

"Where were you around noon today?"

Crockett shifted uncomfortably in his chair. "I was out on patrol."

"Is the Roadhouse in our patrol jurisdiction?"

Crockett looked down. "It was my lunch hour, and I had a debt to repay."

"Debt?"

Crockett explained, "Yes. When I joined the force, I didn't have much money. Certainly not enough to get an apartment or motel room. I pretty much lived out of my car, and the Roadhouse became my home away from home when I wasn't on duty. That's where I met the owner, Vinny Puglisi. He owns some apartments in Lewes. He offered me a place to rent and lent me some cash until I could get on my feet. It took me a while to save up enough to repay him. That's what I was doing there this afternoon."

"OK, but in the future, use your personal vehicle for those errands."

"Got it, Chief. It won't happen again."

"Your shift's over, so get home and enjoy your evening."

After Crockett was out of earshot, J. R. asked, "Any thoughts?"

"I'll give him one thing: he's quick on his feet. Other than that, I think he's lying through his teeth. Let's say on the high side, Vinny lent him $5,000. Could he have saved that much from what he makes here in five months to pay him back?"

"Possible, but doubtful."

"So he either had another source of income or the amount Vinny lent him was considerably less."

"What are you getting at?"

"If I lent you, say, $2,000, how would you pay me back?"

"I'd either write you a check or get the money from the bank in hundred-dollar bills."

"Exactly. Would either of those require a briefcase?"

"No. See why I keep you around? Speaking of which, I'd better get you home. Just in case you have another date tonight."

"Cute."

CHAPTER TWENTY-THREE

Kate was just putting the finishing touches on the lasagna when Timmy came racing down the hall and into the kitchen.

"Is he here yet?" Timmy looked up at the clock over the refrigerator. "It's 5:38 p.m.; you said he'd be here at five thirty."

"He'll be here. He's probably taking Winston for a walk or feeding him. Is your homework done?"

"I've got to finish up the report on my science experiment."

"Go finish up your report and come back and help me set the table. By that time, I'm sure Jack will be here."

Timmy executed a flawless about-face and raced back to his room.

A chime sounded from the oven behind Kate, indicating that it had reached the desired temperature. Kate opened the oven door, picked up the large baking dish, and placed it on the middle rack. She set the timer for an hour and fifteen minutes, estimating that they should be able to sit down to dinner a little after 7:00 p.m. She walked over to the bay window overlooking Jack's deck just as he stepped out onto the deck.

What in the world is he carrying, she wondered. He had satchels over both shoulders and several rolled-up papers under his left arm. Kate's curiosity was getting the better of her as she walked toward the sliding glass door. She opened the door just as Jack stepped onto the deck. "I thought I said you didn't have to bring anything." Waving her arm horizontally, she asked, "So what is all this?"

"Let's go inside and I'll explain." Jack followed Kate into the kitchen and placed the two satchels on the center island. "OK, this is red wine. I have two bottles of Meiomi Pinot Noir for before dinner, two bottles of Santa Cristina Sangiovese for dinner. Are we still having lasagna?"

"It's in the oven as we speak, but that's a lot of wine. What are the other two bottles?"

"That's for after dinner. It's two bottles of Caymus, my favorite Cabernet Sauvignon."

Kate shook her head. "Six bottles of wine for two adults. Don't you think that's a little excessive for one night's dinner?"

"I didn't expect us to drink six bottles of wine. I just thought I'd bring enough for you to have later or in the event that you had invited other guests."

"What's all the rest of this stuff?"

Jack turned as Tim came running into the kitchen.

"Hi, Jack."

"It's Mr. Scanlon to you," Kate scolded.

Jack high-fived Tim and turned to address Kate's previous question. "The other satchel contains drafting tools: rulers, dividers, a protractor, pencils, et cetera. The rolled-up papers are four maps of the Delaware coastline from various years dating back to 1705. I thought Tim and I could estimate what the coastline looked like when the *La Concepción* sank in 1677."

"But wouldn't the coastline be the same today as it was back then?" Tim asked.

"As you'll see from the earlier maps, it's changed dramatically. Let me give you a couple of examples. Have you ever heard of the Cape Henlopen Lighthouse?"

Tim looked questioningly at his mother. "Mom and I have bicycled all over Cape Henlopen, and I've hiked it. I've never seen a lighthouse."

"That's because it fell into the ocean in 1926. The British built a seventy-foot-tall lighthouse on the cape in 1765 to aid navigation. It was constructed on a bluff, almost five hundred yards from the ocean. Can you imagine the amount of beach erosion that took place over 175 years to cause the lighthouse to fall into the ocean? Second example is Rehoboth Bay. Early maps show the bay widely opened to the ocean. It served as a large harbor of refuge for sailing ships during Atlantic storms. Today, except for the Indian River inlet, it's closed to the ocean and considerably shallower than it was in the early 1700s due to silting."

"Ah, so that's the other harbor referenced in the ship's log," Tim surmised.

"Exactly!"

Fascinated by Jack's knowledge of the Delmarva Peninsula, Kate pulled up a stool.

Jack continued, "So if we're going to be able to accurately estimate where *La Concepción* sank, we will need to know what the coast looked like in 1677."

"How do we do that?" Tim asked.

Jack turned to Kate. "Is there some place we can use for a drawing board?"

"We're going to have dinner at the dining room table after I get it set. So you can't use that. How about the island here in the kitchen?"

"Perfect. Tim, I'm going to have you get started while I help your mother set the table. First, tape the most recent map to the granite top of the island." Jack handed Tim the map and a roll of masking tape. "Second, tape this tracing paper over the map and start tracing the Delaware coastline with this pencil. While you're doing that, I'll help your mother with dinner."

Jack turned to Kate. "What can I do to help?"

"The most important thing you can do is pour us two glasses of wine." She handed Jack the wine opener.

"Not necessary. The Meiomi has a screw top. Where do you keep the wineglasses?"

"They're in the top shelf in the cabinet to the left of the refrigerator."

Jack took down two glasses and poured a generous serving in each. "What's next?"

"Help me set the table, and then we can sit down and talk for a few minutes. The salad is made. The bread goes in the oven in about forty-five minutes, and the lasagna should be ready ten minutes later."

Kate led Jack into the family room. "Thank you for humoring Timmy about this treasure thing. He really admires you, and I'm grateful."

"Kate, I'm not humoring Tim. I believe he's really onto something here. I read all of the research he's done, and it's impressive, particularly for someone his age."

"Then why hasn't anyone ever heard of or mentioned a Spanish galleon sinking off the coast of Delaware?"

"Unfortunately, I can't answer that. In any event, it should be a great summer project to keep him busy. Speaking of which, later in the week I want to show you and Tim a new purchase I made."

Kate checked her watch as she walked to the kitchen with Jack in tow. "The lasagna will be ready in twenty minutes, but it will have to sit for another fifteen minutes. I'll put the bread in the oven, and we'll be ready to eat a little after seven. If you'd put the salad bowl on the table, I'd appreciate it."

Jack walked over to see how Tim was doing.

Tim put the pencil down and looked up. "How am I doing so far, and what's next?"

Jack leaned in over the tracing paper. "You're doing great, and dinner will be ready soon." Jack reached into the satchel and pulled out a red pencil. "In the meantime, trace the outline of Rehoboth Bay with this pencil. After dinner, we'll get into the tougher work."

"Kate, that dinner was spectacular. I love a meaty lasagna, and that was the best I've ever had. You've got to give me the recipe."

"You make lasagna?"

"Oh yeah, no. My repertoire includes charcoal-grilled steaks and baked potatoes, and I cook a mean breakfast. Tim and I will clear the table and do the dishes. After that, I'll open the Caymus, and if you'll excuse me for about a half an hour, I'll help Tim get started with phase two of the mapping project."

Jack got two new wineglasses out of the cabinet. He poured a glass for Kate and handed it to her.

Kate smiled. "I'll be in the family room reading. Join me when you're finished."

Jack joined Tim, who had just finished tracing the shoreline of Rehoboth Bay.

"The next step is going to be a little tricky. None of the four maps are the same scale, so we're going to have to create a ratio using two known reference points that would have existed back in the early 1700s. Once we establish that ratio, we can apply it to the measurements we make. I suggest that we use the distance between St. Peter's Episcopal Church in Lewes and North Beach in Dewey to establish the ratio. The graveyard in front of the church has been there since the mid-1600s, and North Beach is unlikely to have changed much either. Now we'll take the protractor and place the center on North Beach with zero degrees facing due north."

Jack handed a pencil to Tim. "Mark each of the three remaining maps from zero to 180 degrees in ten-degree increments. Also, mark the center point at North Beach. Good, now take the ruler and draw radial lines from the center point through the ten-degree increment marks. So what do you think we're going to do next?"

Tim looked up from the map. "I think we're going to measure and do the same thing to the remaining two maps. Then we'll measure the distance along the radius lines from North Beach to the coastline, apply the ratio, and plot the coastline for each of the maps."

Jack raised his hand and high-fived Tim. "I couldn't have described the process better myself. I'm a little surprised. Have you had any of this in school—I mean ratios, degrees, and radius?"

"We've learned how to do ratios, but none of the other stuff."

Kate realized that she had read five pages of her book and couldn't remember any of it. She was more intent on watching and listening to what Timmy and Jack were doing. She hadn't seen Timmy laugh so hard in years, and Jack was almost childlike interacting with him. She placed the book on the coffee table, leaned back into the couch, and pulled her legs up. She felt a warm feeling course through her body. She barely knew this man, but she hadn't been this happy in years. Kate looked at her watch and decided it was already after Timmy's bedtime. She reluctantly got up and walked to the kitchen. "I hate to break this up, but it's past your bedtime, young man, and tomorrow's a school day."

Tim started to protest, but Jack interrupted him. "One more thing before you go to bed. Do you remember telling me that you read an article about a man finding gold coins on the beach south of Dewey?"

"Yes, it was in an issue of *Delaware Today* about six months ago. I've still got the magazine. Do you want me to get it for you?"

"Please. I'd like to take a look at it."

Tim got up and ran back down the hall to his room. In less than two minutes, he was back with the magazine. He handed the magazine to Jack. "The article starts on page twenty-three."

Jack quickly scanned the article. "I've got an idea. Let's see if we can arrange to meet with this guy and see the coins he found. Kate, are you and Tim free this Saturday?"

Kate shook her head in confusion. "I guess so, but why?"

"It says in this article that the coins this guy found were gold doubloons. If we can get a look at them, we might be able to tell whether or not they are from the same era."

Kate smirked. "You mean whether they came from a Spanish galleon sunk off the Delaware coast."

"Exactly."

CHAPTER TWENTY-FOUR

Jack refilled the wineglasses and followed Kate into the family room. Kate returned to the couch and again lay back and pulled up her legs. She pointed to the chair across from her, and Jack sat down.

"You know he prefers to be called Tim."

"I know, he's growing up faster than I care to admit. I guess continuing to call him Timmy is my way of holding back the hands of time. He's all I have, Jack, and it won't be long before he's off to college."

"I understand."

Without warning the skies opened up.

"It's pouring. I don't remember this being in the forecast," Jack said

A distant rumble of thunder prompted Jack to check the weather app on his phone. The map showed a vast swath of red and orange from the Delmarva coast back to Annapolis moving slowly to the east. "Look at this, Kate. I think we're in for a big storm."

Kate got up. "I'll need your help. With the utilities aboveground, we lose power here constantly." A nearby lightning strike accentuated Kate's forewarning as the lights flickered and went out. Within seconds, they came back on.

Jack followed Kate into the kitchen. "How can I help?"

Kate opened the pantry. "There are several candles, flashlights, and hurricane lamps in here. If you could begin taking them out, I'll take a flashlight to Timmy's room."

Jack began taking the candles and hurricane lamps out of the pantry and arranging them on the island in the kitchen.

Kate soon returned. "Thank you. Let's wait this out in the family room. If you can help arrange and light the candles, we can refill our glasses and relax." Jack followed Kate with an armful of candles into the family room just as the power went out again.

Jack walked back with two newly refilled glasses of wine. He handed one to Kate and walked over to the window overlooking his deck. "I can't even see my house it's raining so hard."

A flash of lightning suddenly lit up the room. "Will Winston be all right?" Kate asked.

"He'll be fine. His hearing isn't all that good. I would bet you that he's curled up on his bed in the kitchen sound asleep."

"By the looks of that weather map you showed me, we could be here awhile. Won't he have to go out?"

"Winston has a bladder the size of a basketball. In any event, I took him out just before I came over tonight. He should be good for the duration of the storm."

Jack picked up his wineglass from the table and sat back down.

Neither spoke for several minutes. Kate noticed that Jack was staring into his glass with his head down. She was about to ask if he was all right when he looked up and spoke.

"She died of ovarian cancer."

Kate sat up and placed her wineglass on the coffee table. "Who?" she asked.

"My wife, Nancy. The other night on the beach you were surprised when I told you that I was a widower, and I thought you should know."

"I'm really sorry." Kate didn't know what else to say.

Jack sat back in the chair. "A mutual friend introduced us, and I guess it was love at first sight for the both of us. We got married six months later. She was twenty-nine and working for a senator on Capitol Hill, and I was working for the FBI as the head of a testing laboratory at Quantico. From day one, we both knew we wanted to have children, but it wasn't happening. After a couple of years of trying, we decided to try fertility treatments, but Nancy was starting to experience severe lower abdominal pain and vaginal bleeding. She went to her gynecologist for a checkup. That's when we got the bad news."

Kate felt uncomfortable hearing the details but sensed it was cathartic for Jack. She took a sip of wine and leaned back into the corner of the couch.

Jack continued, "We were told that the cancer was in the advanced stages, but that, given her age, the surgery and chemotherapy should be successful. The surgery went well, but the weeks of chemotherapy were hellish. The drug was injected directly into her abdomen. After the chemo, we were given an optimistic prognosis. We celebrated with dinner at Morton's and a much too expensive bottle of wine. The euphoria didn't last long. Three months later the cancer was back, but this time it had spread to the liver and pancreas. They recommended a more aggressive chemotherapy treatment. Nancy emphatically said no. We argued, but she was adamant. We both understood—with no further treatment, it was a death sentence. I was heartbroken and lost. One night I came home from work. She was sitting in the chair with a book open in her lap. Her eyes were closed, and she had a look of satisfaction on her face. I tried to shake her awake, but she was gone. I was devastated that I couldn't be with her in her final hours on earth."

Kate wiped a tear away and this time gulped down a mouthful of wine.

"I didn't handle it well. I crawled into a bottle of bourbon, several actually. I was functional at work, but when I got home it was back into the bottle. Most mornings I would wake up lying on the bed fully dressed or on the couch. I barely ate, and over the course of several months, I lost over twenty pounds. My friends tried to help, but I drove them away. I was in a downward spiral until one Saturday about two years ago. I needed to repair the toilet in the master bathroom, so I got dressed and went down to the local hardware store. The hardware store was in a small strip mall. Next to the hardware store was a pet store and grooming salon. As I walked toward the hardware store, a young girl walking a dog approached me. She asked me if I would be interested in adopting a wonderful dog who desperately needed a good home. I thanked her but told her I wasn't interested. I got what I needed in the hardware store and headed back to the car. For some unexplained reason, I threw the parts in the back seat and walked over to the pet store. When I entered, the same young girl asked if I would like to see the dog she told me about earlier. I nodded yes and sat down in an overstuffed couch against the far wall."

Kate started to get up with her empty glass.

"Can I get you a refill?" Jack asked as he reached for her glass.

Kate nodded.

When Jack returned with glasses and wine bottle in hand, Kate said, "I assume the dog in question was Winston."

"Yes. The girl brought him out. He ran across the room, jumped up, and put his front paws around my waist. I was told that his owners had moved out in the middle of the night and left two dogs chained up in the backyard. It was during the hottest part of July. Two days later, a neighbor heard a sort of moaning sound coming from the backyard next door and went over to investigate. He found the two dogs. One, a golden retriever, was dead, and the other, Winston, was barely alive. Not knowing what else to do, he took the dog to the pet store. This young girl took him home and nursed him back to health. It took her several months, and he wasn't completely recovered when I got him. She already had two dogs of her own, so her husband wouldn't let her keep him. Four hundred dollars' worth of pet supplies later, Winston and I headed home."

"There should be a special place in hell for anyone who would do such a thing to an animal, any animal. Was his name Winston, or did you give him that name?"

"I asked the girl what his name was, and she really didn't know. She said the neighbor who brought him in thought it was Boomer or something like that. I told her, 'From now on he's Winston.'"

"That's a sad but wonderful rescue story."

"Actually, Kate, Winston rescued me. When we got home, I walked over to the bar to pour myself a bourbon. I turned around to a very disapproving glare from my new friend. I poured the glass into the sink and threw the bottle in the trash. Now, I have a beer occasionally and, like tonight, a fair amount of wine every now and then, but no more hard liquor."

Kate got up and walked over and opened the sliding glass door. "It looks like the storm has passed. Would you like another glass of wine?"

"I think I may have already exceeded my limit. Kate, this was a wonderful evening, and I'm sorry to have dumped my past on you. I don't know what got into me."

"It's not a problem. I'm flattered that you thought enough of me to share a very personal and painful part of your life. Not to change the subject, but are you going to run with me tomorrow?"

"Given the amount of wine I consumed tonight, that will be a game-time decision. If I don't see you tomorrow, I will run with you on Saturday. Good night, and again, thank you for a great dinner and evening."

CHAPTER TWENTY-FIVE

Jack poured a cup of coffee, picked up the copy of *Delaware Today* Tim had loaned him, and headed out to the deck with Winston trailing behind. He opened the magazine to page twenty-three and began reading. He pulled a pen out of his pocket and began taking notes on the back of his paper napkin.

The treasure hunter's name was Ronnie Wilhite. According to the article, he worked as a municipal employee for the town of Ocean City, Maryland. Jack returned to the kitchen, opened a bottom drawer, and pulled out the Delmarva phone directory. He grabbed his cell phone and walked back outside, opened the directory, and started thumbing through the Ws. There was no Wilhite listed, much less a Ronnie Willhite. He thought for a minute and then turned to the yellow pages.

He called the general number for Ocean City and got a recording announcing the various extensions and which numbers to push to be connected. He finally pushed zero, and after the second ring, a woman's voice asked how she could direct his call.

"Good morning, ma'am. I'm trying to get in contact with Ronnie Wilhite. I believe he works for the city."

"Mr. Wilhite works for our roads and highways division, but he's currently out on a job. Can I take a message?"

"Yes, please tell him that Dewey Bratcher called. I'm the editor of *Treasure Hunters* magazine, and I'd like to talk to him about a story we'd like to do on him. My number is (619) 555-0750."

"That's exciting. I'll be sure to get him the message as soon as possible."

"Thank you, and have a great day."

Jack looked down at Winston curled up under the table. "Come on, buddy. Let's go back inside. It's getting a little hot out here, and I need to get back to work on the manual that I'm getting so handsomely paid to write."

Jack had set up an office in one of the spare bedrooms on the second floor overlooking the ocean. He pulled a yellow notepad out of the center desk drawer, opened his laptop, and began to write. After a few hours, he was feeling pretty confident that he could complete the manuals he was asked to produce in five or six months but was determined to slow-play it for the full eighteen-month sabbatical.

He looked at the clock on the desk and was surprised to see that he had been working for almost four hours. Just to make sure, he picked up his cell phone to confirm the time. He had no sooner placed the phone back on the desk when it began to ring. The number was a 302 area code.

Jack answered the phone. "Hello, this is—" He quickly checked himself, realizing this could be Wilhite. "Who, may I ask, is calling?"

"This is Ronnie Wilhite returning your call."

"Yes, Mr. Wilhite, thank you for getting back to me. I'm Dewey Bratcher, the editor of *Treasure Hunters* magazine. One of my reporters read an article about you in *Delaware Today* and thought it would be interesting for us to do a more in-depth article about your recent finds."

"I've read most of the magazines about treasure hunting, and I've never heard of *Treasure Hunters* magazine."

"That's probably because we're relatively new. We launched the magazine in January of this year, but already we have a readership of almost twenty-five thousand. The public interest in treasure hunting has really taken off. That's why we're so interested in doing an article on your find."

"Do I get paid for this article?"

"Absolutely."

"Yeah, how much?"

"Well, that depends on a number of things. If it's just an article with no pictures, you'd get $500. If there are pictures, you'd receive $500 plus $100 for each picture used in the article. If we use your article as our featured article, with a cover photo, you'll receive $2,000. The best part is I'm authorized to pay you a retainer fee up front of $250. How does that sound?"

"It sounds reasonable. When and where do you want to meet?"

"We'll come to you. How does Saturday at ten work for you?"

"I'm off on Saturday, so that works for me."

"Great, here's what we'd like to do. We'd like to take some action pictures of you at the location where you found the coins, pictures of your finds, and a couple of potential magazine cover photos. In addition, my reporter would like to interview you about your hobby."

"Well, there is one problem. The coins and other stuff are in my safe deposit box at the bank."

Jack sensed a reluctance to have the coins photographed. "That shouldn't be a problem. The banks are open until noon on Saturdays. We can photograph the coins at the bank."

"Well, I'm not all that sure that will work for me."

"Look, I sense your reluctance has to do with our being a new magazine. I can assure you that we are on the up and up." Winston raised his head and gave Jack a sideward glance. "Let me sweeten the pot. I'm so sure that your story and pictures will be our featured article and cover photo, I'm going to bring you a check for $500 as an advance. Do we have a deal?"

"Can you make that cash?"

"I can."

"Then we have a deal. I'll see you at ten on Saturday."

"Where do you live?"

"Oh yeah, I live off Route 26 in Bethany Beach, Delaware. Where are you coming from?"

"We'll fly into Philly on Friday and drive down. We're staying with friends in Rehoboth overnight."

"All right, you'll take Route 1 south into Bethany Beach. Turn right onto Route 26 and drive a mile and a half to Sweetwater Lane on your right. I live at the end of the drive. Oh, and by the way, this time of year you should expect a forty-five-minute drive."

"Thanks, Mr. Wilhite. We'll see you on Saturday."

Jack leaned back in the chair and sighed. "Come on, Winston. After that call, I could use a beer."

CHAPTER TWENTY-SIX

Jack pulled up in front of Kate's house promptly at nine in his blue Jeep Grand Cherokee. Kate and Tim were not-so-patiently waiting.

Jack looked at his watch and shook his head. "I'm not late!"

"All right, tell me again what this charade is all about," Kate said.

"The 'charade,' as you so derisively refer to it, is an effort to get a close look at the two gold coins Mr. Wilhite found."

"Didn't the *Delaware Today* article have a picture of the coins?"

"It did, but you couldn't make out any detail from the picture."

"OK, so explain the details of this ruse that Timmy and I are aiding and abetting you in."

"I think 'abetting' is a little strong. Abetting indicates that you are aiding me in a crime or doing something wrong. Anyway, we will be posing as reporters and photographers from a magazine interested in doing a feature article on Mr. Wilhite and his hobby." Jack reached into his pocket and pulled out a plastic-coated name tag and handed it to Kate. Kate took the name tag and, without looking at it, stuffed it in her jean jacket pocket.

"Do I get one?" Tim asked.

"No, you play the role of Kate's dutiful son."

"Wow, that's original. How long did it take you to think that up?"

"Easy, boy, I thought you were on my side." Jack picked up the Nikon camera off the console and handed it back to Tim. "You're going to play the role of the photographer. Satisfied?"

Jack turned right onto Route 26. "If you'd both keep an eye out for Sweetwater Lane, I'll keep track of the distance. He said it would be a mile and a half from the intersection, on the right." Jack drove almost three miles without anyone seeing a sign for Sweetwater Lane.

"Let's go back to the intersection and start over. On the way back, keep your eye out for anything that remotely looks like a road."

Kate tapped Jack's arm. "I see something that could be a road. Make a U-turn, pull into the right lane, and go slowly." They drove for about a hundred yards before Kate spotted a narrow gravel path leading off to the right. "This has to be it. Turn here."

Jack turned right onto the gravel path. It wasn't much wider than the SUV and lined on both sides with tall grasses.

"Looks a little swampy. Somehow I don't think this is it."

Suddenly, the path widened, and they pulled up to a mobile home with a rusted-out Toyota Corolla parked next to the entrance.

"I guess I was wrong. It looks like we have arrived. Put on your name tag, and I'll go knock on the door."

Jack turned off the car, got out, and approached the door to the mobile home. He knocked three or four times before a man dressed in jeans and a wifebeater opened the door.

Jack said, "Hi, I'm Dewey Bratcher, and I'm looking for Mr. Wilhite."

"You found him." Wilhite wiped his right hand on the front of his jeans and held it out.

Jack shook his hand and motioned over his shoulder for Kate and Tim to come join him. "I'd like to introduce you to my staff." Jack pointed to Kate. "This here is Ruby Sue LaRue. She's our reporter, and this is her son, Bubba, who works for us as a part-time photographer." In shock, Kate finally looked at her name tag.

"Did you bring the money?" Wilhite asked.

"I did, but we have some business to transact first."

Wilhite shrugged. "Come on in while I get a shirt on."

Jack held the door open for Kate. She glared and reluctantly stepped inside. To the left, dirty dishes, pots, and pans were stacked up in the sink. A pizza box with two slices inside and a beer can sat on the kitchen table across from the sink. To the right, a threadbare couch was overflowing with papers and magazines. More disgusting was the strong odor of cat urine that permeated the trailer. Kate couldn't wait to get back outside.

Wilhite had exchanged his shirt for a short-sleeved Bethany Beach T-shirt that said "The beatings will continue until morale improves" under a skull and crossbones on the back.

Jack sensed that Wilhite was still suspicious and might pull the plug at any moment. Jack glanced toward the couch and noticed a metal detector leaning next to it. He turned to Wilhite and asked, "Is that the Vulcan 5000?"

Wilhite puffed out his chest and proudly replied, "It's the 3500, but they're virtually the same metal detector, only less expensive."

"Do you mind if I see it?"

Wilhite picked it up and handed it to Jack.

Jack examined the metal detector admiringly. "This is a beauty. Did you find the coins with this?"

"No, I bought it with the money I got from the *Delaware Today* article."

Jack felt confident that Wilhite's suspicions had evaporated. "I suppose we should get to the bank before it closes."

Wilhite held the door as they exited the trailer. Kate took a couple of deep breaths and started to walk to the Jeep.

Jack stopped. "I suppose it would make more sense to take two cars. We have a tight connection in Philly this afternoon." Jack motioned to Wilhite. "Ruby Sue can ride with you and conduct the interview, and I'll—" Kate spun around and shot Jack a look that said it all. "On second thought, maybe the three of us will follow you to the bank."

Traffic was awful, and empty parking spaces on the street were nonexistent. Fortunately, the bank had its own parking lot. Jack, Kate, and Tim followed Wilhite into the bank, where an attractive young girl greeted them. "Good afternoon, Mr. Wilhite. My name is Sally. How can I assist you this morning?" Jack wondered how the young lady knew his name. Given what Jack supposed to be his financial situation, it seemed unlikely that he was a regular customer.

"I'd like to get into my safe deposit box."

"If you have your key, let's go over to the desk and sign in."

Sally pulled out a drawer holding several index cards. She pulled out one from the rear of the box and walked over to the desk where Wilhite was signing in. She compared the signatures and replaced the card in the drawer.

"Come with me." She punched a code into the keypad on the vault door and ushered them into the vault. "Your safety deposit box is number 947. Is that the number on your key?"

Wilhite nodded yes, and Sally led him down a row to the end of the aisle. "Here we are. I will place my key in the lock on the right, and you insert your key in the lock on the left. Now, we'll both turn our keys a quarter turn to the right." Sally opened the box, grasped its handle, slid the box out, and handed it to Wilhite. "There is a cubicle at the other end of the aisle where you can open the box. I'll be at the sign-in desk when you wish to return the box."

Wilhite opened the box and slid it across the table to Jack. Jack and Tim moved closer to see its contents. Inside the box were three rusted pieces of metal and two smaller objects wrapped in white cotton cloth. "What are we looking at here?" Jack asked.

Wilhite picked the rusted metal pieces out of the box and arranged them on the table. "This is the trigger mechanism and lock plate from an arquebus."

"Arquebus?" Tim asked.

Wilhite smiled. "It's a type of portable gun or short musket supported on a tripod or forked rest. They were commonly used from the fifteenth to the seventeenth century and were not very accurate or dependable."

Jack pointed to the rusted object on the right. "What's that?"

"Hard to tell. I've done considerable research, and I think it's either the hilt of a broadsword or an *espada ancha*."

Tim's eyes widened. "That sounds Spanish."

Wilhite shook his head. "I just don't know. It could be Spanish or Italian. There's just not enough detail to accurately identify it. But it is from some type of sword."

"It's Spanish," Jack interjected.

Tim picked up the Nikon and photographed the rusted metal pieces, close up and from every conceivable angle. "How about the coins?"

Wilhite unwrapped the two coins and placed them on the table.

"May I?" Tim asked.

Wilhite nodded, and Tim picked up one of the coins. "Wow, this one is in remarkably good condition. Is there anything around that we can use as a dark background to photograph the coins?"

Jack looked around the cubicle. "How about the blotter on the desk over there?"

"That's perfect, and the desk lamp should provide some extra light." Tim placed the coins on the blotter and began taking photographs of both sides of each coin.

After Tim had finished, Jack stood up from the desk and extended his hand to Wilhite.

"Mr. Wilhite, I want to thank you for agreeing to be interviewed for our article and allowing us to photograph your finds. In addition, I am very impressed with your knowledge of the sword and musket parts you found. Thank you. So let's get these artifacts back in the vault and take some pictures of you in action."

Kate poked Jack in the arm as they reached the parking lot. "I think I'll ride to Treasure Beach with Mr. Wilhite. I have several interview questions to ask him. Is that all right with you, Mr. Wilhite?"

Wilhite shrugged and opened the door for Kate to get in.

Jack looked at Tim and shrugged as well. "What do you think got into her?"

Wilhite pulled the metal detector out of the trunk and pointed to the path between the dunes leading to the beach. They walked south along the beach for about two hundred yards before Wilhite stopped. "This is where I found the coins."

"All right, we'll go about fifty yards farther down the beach. If you would walk toward us as if you were using the metal detector, Tim will take several photos of you at work."

Wilhite walked slowly along the beach waving the metal detector from side to side until he reached them. "Did you get all the pictures you need?"

Jack took the camera from Tim and scrolled through the photographs. "Just one more. Follow me." Jack headed back toward the parking lot and climbed up to the top of the dunes. He approached a fallen tree with Wilhite in tow. "Bubba, come over here with the camera."

Tim shook his head, and Kate rolled her eyes. Jack turned toward Wilhite.

"Put your left leg up on this tree trunk. Good, now put the metal detector across your left thigh and gaze wistfully out to sea."

Tim clicked away.

"Did you get that?" Jack asked.

Tim nodded.

"I guess we're done here." Jack reached into his pocket and pulled out a wad of hundred-dollar bills. He handed the bills to Wilhite. "As we agreed, and I added a little bonus. We will be back in touch when the article is finished. Thank you again, and have a great summer."

CHAPTER TWENTY-SEVEN

Jack pulled out of the parking lot and headed north on Route 1. He turned toward Kate.

"I'm confused. What happened back at the bank with you wanting to ride here with Wilhite?"

"I acted like an ass back at the trailer, and I think he picked up on it. It was just my way of saying I'm sorry. He's really a nice guy, and he's certainly quite knowledge-able about his hobby. Now, don't *you* feel sorry for deceiving him like this?"

"He got handsomely paid for the two hours he had to put up with us."

"How much did you give him?"

"How does $500 an hour sound?"

"My god, you paid him a thousand dollars? How would you like to do a bogus article on me?"

At the first opportunity, Jack made a U-turn to head back south on Route 1.

Kate looked puzzled. "Where are we going?"

"Don't you remember I told you I had something to show you and Tim?"

"Vaguely. So what is it?"

"It's a surprise."

Jack turned right into the marina and RV park and followed the road back to the marina parking lot. "I'll just be a few minutes."

The same surly young woman sat behind the counter doing her nails.

"Good afternoon. Is Mr. Russo in?" Jack asked.

Without getting up, the girl yelled over her right shoulder, "Tony, there's someone here to see you."

Jack mused to himself, *It's either difficult to get good help around here, or they've got something going on.*

"Mr. Scanlon, it's good to see you again. Your mechanic was here on Thursday and spent several hours looking the boat over. He didn't say anything, but I got the impression that it passed with flying colors."

"He sent me a report indicating that the Hatteras is in excellent condition. Therefore, here is a certified check for the amount we agreed upon."

Russo examined the check, folded it, and stuffed it into his pants pocket. He pulled a box from under the counter and handed it to Jack. The box was clearly from the boat builder, with a full-length picture on the top of the Hatteras GT45 racing across the water on a calm, sparkling ocean. "The box contains two sets of keys, one each to the ignition and the cabin. It also has the title, your licenses, a bill of sale, and the owner's manuals. Is there anything else we can do for you?"

"No, that should do it."

"Here's my card. If you need anything pertaining to the boat or the marina, don't hesitate to call me. Are you taking her out today?"

"No, just showing it to a couple of friends."

Jack returned to the car with a big smile on his face. "Are you ready to see the surprise?"

"Did you buy a boat?" Kate asked.

"Wow, way to ruin a surprise."

"I hated to burst your bubble, but it's not really a surprise at a marina. Not to mention the box under your arm with a picture of the boat on the cover. I'm not Sherlock Holmes, but really."

"All right, follow me." Jack led them down the dock and stopped at slip forty-two. "This is it."

Kate stepped back a couple of feet to take it all in. "My god, it's not a boat. It's the frigging *Titanic*. Oops, sorry, that was a bad comparison. I mean it's big."

Tim climbed into the boat. "Can we take it for a ride?"

Jack and Kate climbed in as well. "Not today, but let me show you around. In a couple of weeks, some of my navy buddies are coming down for a fishing trip, and you and your mom are more than welcome to join us. Now, let's get home and have a closer look at the photos of the gold coins."

Tim leaned in over the Jeep's console. "It's almost one, and I'm getting a little hungry. So if it's all right with you, Ruby Sue, can we stop at McDonald's?"

Jack couldn't stifle a laugh as Kate turned toward Tim. "Only if it's the last time you ever call me Ruby Sue."

Jack smiled at Kate. "I've got a better idea. Let's stop at Grotto for pizza. Lunch is on me. It's the least I can do for creating Ruby Sue and Bubba."

Jack pulled up in front of Kate's. "Tim, would you hand me the camera?" He turned the camera upside down and took out the memory card. "I'll make some copies of the photos of the coins and be back in twenty minutes."

"I've done some research on Spanish gold coins," Tim said.

"Of course you have."

"I'll get the folder." Tim slammed the car door and ran up the front steps.

"Kate, I'm sorry about that Ruby Sue and Bubba thing. It was too cute by half. I know it upset you, and I apologize."

"It didn't upset me. It surprised me. I should have looked at it before we got there. In retrospect, it was kind of funny. But I figure you owe me, and I intend to collect. I've been invited to a dinner party at a friend's house in Henlopen Estates on Wednesday evening. Would you be my escort?"

"I'd be honored."

Kate hesitated. "In all honesty, I was asked if I could get you to come. It seems the neighborhood is curious about their handsome new neighbor. Under the circumstances, if you don't want to go, I truly understand."

"No, Kate, it will be fun. What do you wear to this sort of party?"

"I don't know who they have invited, but I would expect to see the men dressed in everything from aloha shirts to sports jackets."

Kate opened the car door. "Thanks, and I'll see you in twenty minutes."

Tim sat at the dining room table, waiting impatiently for Jack to arrive. "You know, Mom, he's not the most on-time person I've ever met. It's been almost a half hour."

Kate sighed. "He'll be here. If you don't learn to exercise some patience, young man, life is going to be very frustrating for you." Just as she finished, the front door-bell rang. "Would you get that, Timmy?"

Jack knocked on the door, opened it, and walked into the foyer. "Sorry I'm late. The photo printer was acting up, but wait until you see the photos. You might make a great photographer someday." Jack spread the photos out on the table. "What do you think?"

Tim studied the photos for several seconds, opened his folder on Spanish coins, and pulled out several sheets of notes. "Let's start with this side. The cross is the crusader's cross, and the coat of arms is the House of Hapsburg, which ruled Spain from 1515 to 1700. So at least we're in the right time frame." Tim picked up the photo of the coin's reverse. Both coins were nearly identical. "This side will tell us the rest of the story. "The *C* in the upper left means the coin was minted in Cuzco, Peru.

Look at the bottom of each coin. The numbers seven and seven appear on this one, and seven and six on the other. According to my notes, this one on the left was minted in 1677 and the one on the right in 1676."

"Why not 1576 and '77?" Jack asked.

Kate sat mesmerized, listening to her son analyze the coins' origin. "I hope you spend as much time on your schoolwork as you do on this project."

"Mom, I'm getting straight As. There is no higher grade."

Jack interrupted, "All right, back to the coins and my last question."

Tim shuffled through a stack of papers, pulled out a sheet, and handed it to Jack. "See the letter R on the left center reverse of each coin?"

Jack nodded.

"That's the mint master's mark, or the initial of his last name. Whose name is on the list as the mint master at Cuzco in 1676 and '77?"

Jack's finger traced down the list of names and dates. "From 1665 until 1687, it was Emilio Rodriquez. Also, there were no coins minted in Cuzco in the 1570s." Jack laughed and high-fived Tim. "You did it. You proved, at least to me, that these coins came from the *La Concepción.*"

Kate got up. "This calls for a celebration." Pointing to Jack, she asked, "What can I get you?"

"I'll have a Budweiser."

Tim raised his hand. "I'll have a beer too."

"Two beers and one root beer coming up."

Kate returned with three bottles and sat down next to Jack. "What's next?"

"The hard part—locating the *La Concepción*."

"On another note, we're having tacos and salad for dinner tonight. Would you like to join us?"

"I can't. I have a date."

"Oh." Kate tried to hide her surprise. "Anyone I know?"

Jack was enjoying this a little too much. "Actually, yes, you're responsible for us getting together."

"I haven't introduced you to anyone."

"I'm having dinner with J. R.."

Kate hoped Jack didn't notice her sigh of relief. "So it's a bromance?"

"Very funny. You were right. He's a good guy, and we've gotten to respect each other. By the way, I'm sorry, I should have told you this earlier. Long story short, the girl on the beach was Anna Campbell. She worked at the Roadhouse as a waitress, and the coroner confirmed that she was murdered. That's all I can tell you now. J. R. and I are working on a theory about her murder. That's what tonight is all about. I'll tell you more as soon as I can."

CHAPTER TWENTY-EIGHT

J. R. approached the bar with Jack in tow. "Good afternoon, Sherry."

The bartender looked up from the paperwork and inventory she was completing and glanced at her watch. "It's not even five o'clock yet. Are you and your friend here for the blue-plate special?"

"Actually, we'd like to eat and get out of here before the lechers arrive."

"Why don't you grab a booth, and I'll be with you in a minute to take your order."

"Looks like we have our choice of seating."

The restaurant was almost completely devoid of customers. The lunch crowd was long gone, and the dinner patrons had yet to arrive.

A man and woman sat at the bar, looking very much like they had been overserved.

Sherry approached the booth with pen and pad in hand and pointed at Jack. "Move over, handsome." She squeezed into the booth and playfully snuggled up next to Jack. She elbowed Jack in the ribs. "Don't look so frightened. I don't bite." Sherry slid away from Jack and leaned across the table to address J. R.. "Anything more on Anna's murder?"

"You know I can't discuss the case with you."

"I know. I just can't get over the fact that someone would kill such an innocent and wonderful girl. The girls that work here are very shaken up about this."

"Is your boss here?" J. R. asked.

"He's in his office. Do you want me to tell him you're here?"

"No, I'm sure he'll surface before we leave."

"OK, then what can I get you? You first, handsome."

"I'll have the New York strip with a baked potato and the asparagus side. Oh, I'll also have the nine-ounce La Crema Pinot Noir."

"How would you like your steak?"

"Medium rare."

"J. R.?"

"I'll have a bacon cheeseburger, fries, and a Budweiser."

Sherry had started to walk away when Jack added, "You can bring me the check."

J. R. motioned for Sherry to return to the table. "I'd like to change my order. I'd like the twelve-ounce filet medium, fries, creamed spinach, and a nine-ounce cabernet."

Jack smiled and shook his head. "You sure know how to optimize an opportunity."

"I'll buy lunch next week."

Puglisi walked out to the corner of the bar, yawned, and stretched his arms up over his head. He summoned Sherry, who was serving a customer at the other end of the bar. "Give me a glass of Maker's Mark on the rocks." He had started to take a sip when he noticed J. R. and Jack sitting in a booth at the other end of the restaurant. Vinny tossed down his drink and slammed the glass on the bar.

"Your friend is heading our way," Jack said.

J. R. took another bite of his steak and reached for his wineglass.

"What are you and your FBI friend doing here?" Vinny asked.

J. R. splayed his arms out across the table. "What does it look like we're doing? We are enjoying a quiet and relaxing dinner. That is until you showed up."

Vinny turned to Jack. "You're spending a lot of time around here. Did the FBI open a new field office in Sussex County?"

"No, not yet. I'm investigating several leads regarding criminal activity in the area. Unfortunately, I'm not at liberty to say much more than that."

"Vinny, you're looking a little pale. Maybe you ought to take tomorrow off and take your boat out. You know, soak up some rays." J. R. grinned and took another sip of wine.

"I don't own a boat."

"Vinny, Vinny, Vinny, we were admiring your boat just the other day."

"All right, so I own a boat. A lot of people around here own boats. What about it?"

"Nothing, I just thought you'd take better care of it."

"What are you talking about?"

"We noticed a fair amount of blood on the rear starboard portion of the deck—most likely fish blood. It was probably those three men who took your boat out last Friday evening."

Vinny looked like someone had punched him in the gut, but he recovered nicely. "I lent the boat to a few of my friends from Philly. They were going out after tuna."

Jack couldn't let that go unanswered. "My understanding is to get tuna you have to go out about sixty miles into the Atlantic."

"That's right. So what?"

"I'm a little confused. If you go out sixty miles, fish for tuna, and return, I would expect that you'd use a lot more than thirty-four gallons of fuel."

"Who told you they only used thirty-four gallons?"

"The marina manager told us he filled it up for you the next day and it took thirty-four gallons."

J. R. was sitting back in the booth, sipping his wine and enjoying the interplay between Vinny and Jack.

"Well, he was wrong, or you just misunderstood him."

"I guess you got a good deal, because he only charged you for the thirty-four gallons."

"I've got to get back to work. Don't let the door hit you in the ass on the way out."

J. R. spoke up. "Is that any way to talk to your regular customers?"

"Screw you, J. R.. If you want to talk to me again, call my lawyer."

"I didn't want to talk to you *this* time. Have a nice evening, Vinny."

As J. R. and Jack walked past the end of the bar, Sherry handed Jack a folded piece of paper.

As they approached the car, J. R. said, "Tell me that's not what I think it is."

"Oh, it's what you think it is." Jack opened the folded paper and showed it to J. R..

"So?" J. R. asked.

"So what?"

"I'm just saying she'd probably show you one hell of an evening."

"You're incorrigible."

J. R. stopped abruptly. "I've got a hunch. Before you drop me off, let's swing by the marina in Lewes."

Jack pulled into the marina parking lot.

"Drive over to where Vinny's boat is docked," J. R. instructed.

Jack pulled up as close to the boat as possible, turned off the engine, and got out.

"Just as I thought." J. R. walked onto the dock and signaled the manager to turn off the power washer. "Excuse me, what are you doing?"

The manager walked to the port side of the deck. "What does it look like I'm doing?"

"Let me guess. Mr. Puglisi called and asked you to clean up his boat as soon as possible. Is that about right?"

"He called about a half an hour ago and said he would be taking some customers out this evening and wanted it cleaned up and the deck power-washed ASAP. He said he'd pay me $1,000 if I got it done by seven."

"Thanks, sorry to bother you."

"How did you know?" Jack asked.

"Like I said, just a hunch. I think the noose is starting to tighten around Vinny's fat neck."

"Still, all we have is circumstantial evidence. We can't even get a warrant to search the boat with what we have now."

"Patience, young one. Vinny is going to screw up, and I intend to be there when he does. Would you drop me off at the station? It's beach week, and we're getting a number of complaints from neighbors about drunken parties."

"No problem."

Jack pulled into the police station parking lot as J. R.'s phone began to ring.

"This is Chief Johnson."

It was Crockett. "Chief, someone just called in a stabbing incident on Baltimore Avenue next to the Iguana Grill. An ambulance is on the way."

J. R. motioned to Jack. "Park the car over there. We can get there faster on foot."

"What's going on?" Jack asked.

"There's been a stabbing. Let's go."

CHAPTER TWENTY-NINE

Jack and J. R. raced down Baltimore Avenue to the scene of the stabbing. Jack was surprised that J. R. could move that fast given his age and size. They stopped at the alley between the Iguana Grill and the adjacent avenue shops just as the ambulance pulled up. Jack followed J. R. twenty yards down the alley where a man in an army field jacket was slumped against the wall. He held both hands against his stomach, but Jack could see the blood seeping between his fingers.

"Oh my god, it's Captain Eddie!" J. R. screamed. "Get the EMTs down here ASAP." J. R. took a knee next to Eddie. "Eddie, can you hear me?"

Eddie nodded.

"You're going to be all right; the ambulance is here. Can you tell me who did this to you?"

Eddie painfully moaned and shook his head.

A crowd had started to gather in the alley.

"I can answer that."

A middle-aged couple approached J. R. and Jack.

"OK, you two stay here. Jack, will you move the rest of these people back to the street so we can get the EMTs in here?"

Jack turned around, spread out both his arms, and started herding the crowd out of the alley.

J. R. stood up and backed out of the way as the EMTs approached and began treating Eddie. He turned to the couple. "Tell me what you saw."

The man spoke first. "We were standing at the end of the alley reading the restaurant's menu when these two teenage boys stopped. The taller pointed at the man sitting on the ground and said, 'Let's have some fun.' The shorter of the two held back as his friend approached the homeless man. The man was holding something small in his left hand, and the boy seemed to want it. The homeless man turned away, and the boy kicked him in the side. The man stood up, and they started to struggle. After about thirty seconds of pushing and shoving, the boy pulled out a rather big knife and stabbed the man three or four times in the stomach."

"Anything else?" J. R. asked.

The woman stepped forward. "Yes, the boy came back down the alley holding up some sort of medal and laughing. A woman who saw the man bleeding started screaming and yelling for help. The boys took off running through the passageway between the shops toward Rehoboth Avenue."

Another officer approached the scene. J. R. turned to address the couple. "Would you mind going back to the station with this officer so we can get your statement down in writing? Also, I forgot, can you give us a description of the two and what they were wearing?"

"They both had on blue Bradford Academy sweatshirts," the woman offered.

The EMTs had Eddie on a stretcher and were moving him to the ambulance. J. R. approached and asked, "How is he doing?"

"I'll be honest with you. He's lost a lot of blood. It's touch and go."

"Do me a favor. Treat him as if he was your own father."

Jack approached the ambulance as it started to pull away and asked J. R., "What do you think? Will he make it?"

"Don't know. The EMT said he lost a lot of blood. What I do know is we need to find these two creeps before someone else gets hurt. I hate beach week, but this is well beyond anything that has ever happened in the past."

J. R.'s phone rang. He looked up at Jack. "It's Sara. This can't be good." He touched the speaker option and held the phone between him and Jack. "What's up, Sara? I have Mr. Scanlon with me."

"Chief, you need to get to the Purple Parrot now. There's some sort of hostage situation going on. I've sent Crockett over to assess the situation."

"Thanks, Sara, we're on our way. Follow me, we can cut through the shopping area. It's on the other side of Rehoboth Avenue."

Crockett stood outside talking to a boy about five foot seven, wearing a blue Bradford Academy sweatshirt.

"What's the situation?" J. R. asked.

"There's a white male inside holding a woman with a knife to her throat." Crockett pointed to the boy next to him. "He says it's his friend from school."

"He's crazy drunk," the boy blurted out.

J. R. turned to Crockett. "Put the cuffs on him and put him in a cell back at the station."

"What?"

"Do what I said. Scanlon and I will handle this."

"So how do you propose we handle this?" Jack asked.

"Don't know. I've never had any training in hostage negotiations, but I know we can't wait for a hostage negotiator to show up. I seriously doubt if there is one within fifty miles of here."

"I had some training at the FBI Academy, but that was several years ago."

"Sounds like you're it."

"Wait!" J. R. shouted as they started to walk up the stairs. "I think I need to deputize you if we're going to do this legally."

"Forget it. Remember, I'm a federal agent."

The bar was empty except for the bartender and a young man holding a woman at knifepoint. The other customers had exited out the back when the altercation began. J. R. started to reach for his gun, but Jack grabbed his arm.

"That's just going to make matters worse."

Jack started to approach the boy.

"Don't come any closer or I'll kill her," the boy screamed.

"Let's just take this down a notch or two. What started all this?" Jack asked.

The boy pointed accusingly at the bartender. "I ordered a beer, and he wouldn't serve me. He said he was going to call the police. So I grabbed her and pulled out my knife."

"Well, it sounds like we can settle this quite easily. Let the woman go, put down the knife, and I'll buy you a beer and all is forgiven," Jack said.

The boy laughed nervously. "Do you think I'm stupid? I know that you know what happened on Baltimore Avenue and you think it was me."

Jack took another step closer. "Look, the man you got into a fight with is going to be all right. We'll charge you with fighting in public. It's a misdemeanor. You'll pay a fine and be on your way."

"You really do think I'm stupid. I stabbed him three times."

The boy tightened his grip on the woman and pulled the knife closer to her neck. To her credit, the woman remained relatively calm.

J. R. screamed at the bartender, "For Christ's sake, Smitty, give the kid a beer!"

"But he's underage."

"It wouldn't be the first time you served an underage customer. *Do it!*"

Smitty pulled a cold mug out of the cooler, filled the glass, and slid it across the bar toward the kid.

Jack pulled a barstool toward him and sat down. "I'm going to sit, and we can talk while you drink your beer. I think we both want to come up with a win-win solution to all this."

"I'm not letting her go."

"I understand. Hold the knife in your other hand. She's not going anywhere."

The boy shifted the knife to his left hand, pulled the girl closer, and lifted the mug. He took a couple of mouthfuls and set it back down on the bar.

"Let's get serious. You assaulted a man tonight. That's a serious matter. Do you want to make it worse by adding kidnapping to that charge? Let the girl go. I'll be your hostage until we can work something out."

The boy thought for a minute and pointed to the bartender. "What about him? I don't know what he has behind the bar."

Jack turned to the bartender. "Scram, get out of here." The bartender didn't waste any time heading for the rear exit. "Now, how about letting the girl go?"

Jack stood up with his hands in the air and moved toward the boy at the corner of the bar. The boy loosened his grip on the girl, and Jack pulled her away. "They'll take care of you outside. *Go.*"

"Turn around and back up toward me," the boy demanded.

Jack slowly did as the boy instructed. He slowly lowered both hands to his shoulders as he continued to back up. Suddenly, he grabbed the beer mug with his right hand, spun, and smashed the mug against the right side of the boy's face. He fell to the floor, dazed and bleeding.

J. R. rushed in, turned the boy on his stomach, and cuffed his hands behind his back. "I'd offer to buy you a beer, but that will have to wait. Let's get him out of here. Help me get him on his feet."

The boy was groggy and was struggling to stay on his feet.

"Wait a minute. Check his pockets," Jack said.

J. R. reached into the boy's right pants pocket and pulled out a military medal. The medal was a blue ribbon with a small red and white stripe on both edges. A bronze cross with an eagle in the center hung from the ribbon.

Jack examined the medal. "It's the Army Distinguished Service Cross, second only to the Congressional Medal of Honor. If it's Eddie's, he's a bona fide American hero."

"Let's get this piece of trash booked, printed, and in a cell."

Outside, Crockett waited in his cruiser with the lights flashing. J. R. pulled a folded piece of paper out of his shirt pocket and propped the boy up against the rear of the car. He began to read from the paper. "You have the right to remain silent. Anything you say can and will be used against you in a court of law. You have the right to an attorney and have him present with you while you are being questioned. If you cannot afford an attorney, one will be provided for you, before any questioning if you wish. You can decide at any time to exercise the rights and not answer any questions or make any statements. Do you understand each of these rights I have explained to you?" The boy nodded his head. "Yes or no?" J. R. asked. "I need a verbal response."

"Yes," the boy responded.

J. R. opened the right rear door and shoved the boy inside. "Take him back to the station and book him.

Scanlon and I will walk back. Oh, and be sure to confiscate their belts and shoelaces."

After Crockett pulled away, J. R. turned to Jack. "You know, Scanlon, my life was a lot less complicated before you showed up in town. Just saying."

Crockett stood at the desk next to Sara.

"We have signed written statements from three eyewitnesses to the attack on Captain Eddie and one from the other boy. How do you want to charge them, Chief?"

"Charge the accomplice with aiding and abetting an assault on an unarmed citizen. Charge the perpetrator with felonious assault, hostage taking, attempted kidnapping, and attempted murder."

"May I make a suggestion?" Jack asked. "It may sound, to a judge, that you're overcharging the defendant."

J. R. turned back to Crockett. "OK, drop the attempted murder charge for now. Also, keep them as far apart as possible."

"I've got them at opposite ends of the cellblock," Crockett replied.

"Good. I'm going home."

"Come on, I'll drive you," Jack offered.

"No, you get home. I'll take one of the squad cars. I need to be back here early in the morning. Get on with your date, and tell Kate I said hello."

Jack shook his head. "You just don't give up, do you?"

CHAPTER THIRTY

Jack walked into the police station a little after ten, carrying three coffee cups. He handed one to J. R. and one to Sara. "Ralph said to say hello."

"Don't I get one?" Crockett asked as he walked in from the cellblock.

"Didn't know you were on duty. Sorry, maybe next time."

"I'm heading out on patrol. Anything you want me to check on, Chief?"

"Actually, yes. Swing by the house at 1632 North Dover Avenue and make sure those high school kids have vacated the place. If not, call for backup and throw them out."

"Anything new with the two in the back?" Jack asked.

"Yeah, the one who attacked Eddie is Jason Broderick. His father is a high-priced K Street lawyer in Washington, DC. He called him early this morning. The father should be here before noon. The other boy is Richard Dean. He also called his parents. Both boys will be arraigned on Monday morning. I've alerted the Sussex County Department of Corrections in Georgetown that we would be transferring them there this afternoon.

"Oh, I stopped by the hospital to check on Eddie. He's out of surgery, and his doctor says the prognosis is good for his recovery, but he's not out of the woods yet. They're worried about infection. They had to repair a tear in his large intestine. Once he's stabilized, they will likely transfer him to the VA hospital in Philly," J. R. said.

"I've taken care of that. He will remain at the medical center until he's released."

"You're something else, Scanlon." J. R. took a sip of his coffee. "Oh, by the way, I'll need a sworn statement from you, and you should plan on accompanying me to the arraignment on Monday in case the judge has any questions. Are you available?"

"Let me check my calendar," Jack replied sarcastically. "Of course I'm available."

"Just asking."

J. R. was preparing to take Jack's statement when a rather tall man in a three-piece suit burst through the front door. "Who's in charge around here?" the man asked.

J. R. stood up from behind the desk. "I am, and you are?" He already suspected who the man was.

"I'm Mason Broderick, and I'm here to pick up my boy. Just let me know how much the fine is, and I'll write the check."

Mason and Jason, how cute, Jack thought.

J. R. walked out from behind the desk and approached the man. "Well, I'm sorry, Mr. Broderick. That won't be possible. Your son and his friend will be confined until their arraignment Monday morning in Georgetown."

"What's he being charged with?" the father asked.

"At this point in time, your son is being charged with felonious assault, hostage taking, and attempted kidnapping. If the victim dies, then it's a whole different ballgame."

"He got in a fight with a bum, nothing more and nothing less."

Jack was livid. "This 'bum,' as you refer to him, is a highly decorated war hero who was viciously attacked and stabbed by your son."

"And who the hell are you?" Broderick angrily asked.

Jack defiantly walked toward him. "I'm with the FBI, and we're looking into this as a possible hate crime."

J. R. couldn't believe what he was hearing.

Broderick stepped forward and jabbed a finger into Jack's chest. "Well, do you know who I am?"

Jack was about to answer him but thought it would only escalate things.

"I'm the managing partner of Williams, Scott, and Parkman, one of the most prestigious law firms in Washington, DC. I'll have both of your jobs and own this town before I'm through. Now, I want to see my son."

J. R. was enjoying the interplay but decided to interject himself. "Unfortunately, you won't be able to see him before the arraignment. He's on suicide watch."

"Suicide? That's ridiculous. I'm his lawyer, and I demand to see him. He has a right to an attorney."

J. R. scratched his chin. "I thought you were a labor lawyer."

"How did you know that?" Broderick asked.

"I make it my business to know. In any event, I'm sorry. You won't be allowed to see your son until his arraignment."

Jack stepped forward. "I think you should leave. If you'll leave your card, the chief will advise you of the time and location of your son's arraignment." He looked down and noticed the man's clenched fists. Suddenly, the father attacked Jack, connecting with a punch to the left side of Jack's face.

"I'm sick of this bullshit!" the father screamed.

J. R. grabbed the father's arm, twisted it behind his back, and cuffed him. "Jimmy, put the two boys in the same cell, and put the father in a cell at the other end of the cellblock. I want one of our deputies to remain in the cellblock and make sure they don't communicate until we take the boys to Georgetown this afternoon."

"Yes, Chief." The deputy grabbed the keys and disappeared into the cellblock.

J. R. turned to Jack. "Come here, let me take a look at your face."

"I'm fine. I shouldn't have let my guard down. I really didn't expect him to do anything that stupid."

"That's really going to leave a mark. Especially his ring imprint in your cheek." J. R. leaned in toward Jack. "Let me see where he went to college."

Jack pushed his hand away. "You can really be an asshole sometimes."

Sara sat at her desk in shock. She had never seen anything like what had transpired over the past ten minutes.

Jack looked up at the camera in the corner mounted near the ceiling. "Does that work?" Jack asked, pointing to the camera.

"Of course it works," J. R. replied indignantly.

"Can I get a copy of the last half hour's recording?"

J. R. turned to Jimmy, who had just returned from the cellblock. "Can you get Mr. Scanlon a copy of the tape?"

"Give me twenty minutes." Jimmy turned and disappeared into a room behind Sara's desk.

"What are you going to do with the tape?" J. R. asked.

"I have a friend who works as a news anchor at one of the local TV stations in DC. I think she'll be very interested in this tape and the attack on Eddie. I also sent her some background on Eddie."

"Background?"

"I did some research last night into the story behind Eddie's DSC award. His full name is Edward R. Williamson from Chicago. In 1969, he was a platoon leader in Alpha Company, Second Battalion, Third Brigade, of the First Infantry Division. His company was conducting a search-and-destroy mission fifteen kilometers northwest of Phuoc Vinh in III Corps when they were surrounded by a North Vietnamese Army battalion. A company's commanding officer was the first one killed in the initial engagement, and Eddie took over command of the company. He organized an orderly withdrawal and called in artillery and directed Cobra gunships over the NVA position. Long story short, his company suffered four KIAs and twenty-six wounded. Trust me, that's an incredibly small number of casualties for a battle of that magnitude. It's a credit to Eddie's quick thinking and leadership. Over three hundred of the approximately eight hundred NVA soldiers were killed and an unknown number of enemy wounded. His brigade commander recommended Eddie for the Medal of Honor, but it was downgraded by the Pentagon to the DSC. I gave all of this to my friend."

"That's incredible. Sort of makes you look like a slacker, Scanlon."

"Incidentally, as his son's attorney, Broderick had every right to consult with his son before arraignment."

J. R. nodded. "I know that. I'm a little surprised that Broderick didn't know that. Probably doesn't come up much in labor law."

By noon, a sizable crowd had gathered outside the station. The local news in Philadelphia and Baltimore aired extensive coverage of the attack on Eddie on the morning newscasts. Channel 4 from Wilmington and Channel 17 from Philadelphia already had cameras and reporters set up at both the front and rear entrances to the station.

"I've never done a perp walk before. You want to assist me?" J. R. asked.

"Can't. The last thing I need is my face all over the evening news. The brass back in Washington would go ballistic."

J. R. turned to Crockett, who was just finishing the last of his bacon-and-egg croissant. "Bring the two boys out. I want their hands and feet shackled. Bring them down the far hallway so that the father doesn't see them."

Crockett disappeared into the cellblock.

"Once we're gone and the cameras leave, you can slip out the back exit. The arraignment is set for ten tomorrow morning. I'll pick you up at eight."

Crockett led the two boys into the front lobby. The two were dressed in orange jumpsuits provided by the Sussex County Department of Corrections. Their hands and ankles were chained together. Dean looked terrified while Broderick shuffled in, head held high, with an obnoxious smirk on his face. Jack wondered how long that smirk would last once he was introduced to the general inmate population at the DOC. He watched from the window as J. R. and Crockett led the two boys to the white van marked "Sussex County Department of Corrections" on its side. They were ushered to seats on opposite sides of the van, and a guard with a shotgun sat facing them. J. R. got in the front passenger side, and the van pulled away. Crockett followed in an unmarked car.

CHAPTER THIRTY-ONE

The Sussex County courthouse was a stately brick building at 1 The Circle in Georgetown. The entrance portico featured eight ionic columns supporting a thirty-foot-by-sixteen-foot gabled roof structure. The central front tower was topped with a twenty-foot-high white cupola with a copper weathervane on top.

It was 9:50 a.m. when Jack and J. R. entered the courtroom and took seats in the second row behind the county prosecutor's table. The bailiff stood next to the bench, checking his watch. Suddenly, the door to his right opened, and a corrections officer led Mason Broderick to the table across from the prosecutor's. He was wearing the suit he'd had on Sunday morning and was looking remarkably put together after his night in jail.

"All rise. Court is now in session, the Honorable Judge William Hoffman presiding," the bailiff announced.

A bespectacled man in his sixties wearing a black robe entered the courtroom from a door to the right of the bench. He took his seat and reached for the gavel. He turned to the clerk.

"Please announce the first case."

"Mr. Mason Broderick, you are charged with assaulting a law enforcement officer in the conduct of his duties."

The judge looked out at Broderick. "Is your attorney present, Mr. Broderick?"

"I will be representing myself, Your Honor."

Judge Hoffman smiled and rubbed his chin with his left thumb and index finger. "I suppose I don't have to remind you of the old adage about a lawyer representing himself?"

"I'm aware but am most confident in my ability to represent myself."

J. R. elbowed Jack in the ribs. "What did he mean by that?"

Jack explained, "The adage is 'A lawyer who represents himself has a fool for a client.'"

"It's my understanding that you are also representing your son and another boy in their arraignments later this morning. Is that correct?" the judge asked.

"I will be representing my son. Mr. Dean has retained independent counsel."

"Smart boy," the judge replied. "All right then, Mr. Broderick, how do you plead?"

"Not guilty, Your Honor."

The clerk handed the judge a calendar book. "I am setting bail at $50,000. Your trial date is scheduled for October 3 at 10:00 a.m. The officer will take you to the cashier to arrange bail. You are dismissed, Mr. Broderick, until October 3. Next case."

A corrections officer led in Richard Dean. A young man in a blue suit met him at the defendant's table.

The clerk again rose from her seat in front of the bench to read the charges. "Richard Dean, you are charged with aiding and abetting in the commission of a felony."

"Your Honor, I'm Spencer Davidson, representing the accused."

"How does your client plead?"

"Guilty, Your Honor."

The judge looked startled. "Mr. Dean, I've read the incident report and the witness statements. Are you sure that you want to plead guilty?"

"Your Honor, my client just wants this all to be over."

"All right, I will accept your plea. I am reducing the charge to a misdemeanor, failing to report the commission of a crime. I therefore sentence you to six months' probation. You're free to go, Mr. Dean."

"Thank you, Your Honor," Davidson responded and rapidly led his client out of the courtroom.

"Next case," the judge ordered.

An officer led in Jason Broderick, still shackled and wearing an orange DOC jumpsuit. He had the same smug look on his face as he had yesterday afternoon. His defiant demeanor was not lost on the judge. Mason Broderick followed his son to the defendants' table.

The clerk stood to read the charges. "Jason Broderick, you are charged with felonious assault, hostage taking, and attempted kidnapping."

"How does your client plead, Mr. Broderick?" Judge Hoffman asked.

Broderick and his son stood. "Not guilty, Your Honor."

The judge opened his calendar and turned a few pages. "Given the seriousness of the charges, I am ordering you remanded to the Sussex County correctional facility pending trial. I am setting an initial trial date for October 28. Does that afford you enough time to prepare your case, Mr. Broderick?"

Mason Broderick was visibly shaken. His hands trembled as he rose to address the judge.

"This is outrageous. I protest your decision. My son will be entering Duke University as a freshman in September."

The judge leaned forward and glared out at Broderick. "Bailiff, have the defendant returned to his cell. As for you, Mr. Broderick, unless you want to be held in contempt of court, tone it down. I'll also see to it that Duke University is notified as to your son's status. Court dismissed." The judge slammed the gavel down, rose from his chair, and disappeared through a door behind the bench.

"Wow, remand; I didn't see that coming," Jack said to J. R. as they exited the courthouse.

"It makes sense, given the seriousness of the charges. In addition, I think Mason Broderick really pissed off Judge Hoffman."

As J. R. and Jack exited the courthouse, Broderick ran up behind them. "You two are going to pay dearly for what you've done to my son. This isn't over."

"Your son did it to himself, and he got what he deserved. Beat it before I arrest you for harassment," J. R. replied.

J. R. turned toward Jack. "Let's go. I've got some paperwork to finish, and I'm guessing you've got better things to do than hang around here any longer."

Jack turned to Broderick. "I'd recommend you watch the Washington, DC, local newscast tonight on Channel 11." As an afterthought Jack said, "Oh, and if I were you, I wouldn't buy any new suits."

Broderick just stood there with a questioning look on his face as Jack and J. R. walked away.

It was six o'clock. Jack grabbed a beer from the refrigerator and turned the channel to the Washington, DC, local newscast. He turned up the volume and took a sip of his beer.

"This is Amanda Breen, bringing you tonight's local news from our nation's capital. Earlier today, Washington attorney Mason Broderick was arraigned in Georgetown, Delaware. He is charged with assaulting a federal law enforcement official in Rehoboth Beach, Delaware, after his son was arrested for viciously attacking a homeless veteran and taking a woman hostage. Following is footage of the attack by Mr. Broderick on the federal agent." A fifteen-second clip of the assault on Jack played on the screen. "We now take you to Casey Roberts."

"Thank you, Amanda. I'm standing on K Street outside the law offices of Williams, Scott, and Parkman, where I understand the partners have been meeting ever since learning this morning of the incident in Rehoboth Beach yesterday morning. I was just handed this press release from the firm. I haven't had a chance to read it. It's very short, if you'll allow me. It reads, in part, 'After careful deliberation regarding the actions of Mr. Mason Broderick at the Rehoboth Police Department on Sunday morning, the partners have unanimously voted to revoke Mr. Broderick's partnership and place him on indefinite leave until his case is resolved.'"

"Thank you, Casey. We will have more on this story at eleven."

Jack turned off the television, grabbed Winston's leash, and headed for the beach.

CHAPTER THIRTY-TWO

Jack rang the doorbell and stepped back. He wasn't sure how to dress, so he had decided to go for the more business casual look. He wore khaki dress slacks, a pale blue button-down shirt, and a navy-blue blazer.

When Kate answered the door, Jack almost fell over backward. "Wow, you led me to believe this was sort of a casual resort affair."

Kate stood in the entrance dressed in a strapless red satin knee-length cocktail dress with a gold clutch purse and four-inch Jimmy Choo heels.

"I'm sorry. I found this dress in the back of my closet and I thought, why not? I haven't worn it since…well, in a long time."

"I'll tell you why not—we look like Lady and the Tramp. Give me twenty minutes."

Jack raced back to the house and tore into two of the unpacked wardrobe boxes in the family room. He finally found his tuxedo still wrapped as he had last received it back from the cleaners. He rooted around the bottom of the box until he found his newest pair of black dress shoes. After examining himself in the mirror, he decided

During a lull between the entrée and dessert, the judge turned toward Kate.

"Kate, would you bring us up to speed on the plans for the new Sussex County Women's Center?"

Kate put down her wineglass. "It's coming along as well as can be expected, given the circumstances. The site and building plans have been approved. The architect did a magnificent job on the design; however, we still face a significant hurdle." Kate lowered her head. "To be honest with you, Judge, I'm just not sure it will ever get built. We're having a difficult time coming up with the necessary funding."

The judge looked incredulous. "That's difficult to believe. The county and the state have more than enough money to build the women's center."

"That's just it, Judge—they don't. I've been to the legislature. There's just no slack in this year's budget, and remember, we're not just talking about the Sussex County Women's Center. There are two others planned as well. One is scheduled to be built in Kent County next year, and one in New Castle County the year after. The structure alone will take over $2 million to build. That doesn't include furnishings, equipment, and everything else needed to make the facility fully functional. The state and county have committed a total of $1 million. The foundation is responsible for raising the remainder, which I estimate to be at least $1.25 million. I am looking to raise that amount through charitable contributions. A little over a week ago, I met with the CEO of Goodwin Industries. I was hoping to get a contribution in the amount of $500,000 as the center's founding sponsor."

"Are you talking about DiLano?" the judge asked.

"Yes, that's who I met with."

"Be careful of him, Kate. He's as sleazy as they come."

"Well, I don't know about sleazy, but he's certainly crafty. In no uncertain terms, he wanted the contract to build not only the Sussex County facility, but the ones planned for New Castle and Kent Counties as well. I told him we couldn't do sole-source contracts. Rather than saying Goodwin wouldn't be a sponsor, he offered me a nearly impossible option. He offered a $500,000 contribution if I could raise another $500,000 by July 1."

Dr. DuBois leaned forward. "I realize it's only a little over three weeks, but that doesn't sound like that difficult a task. Several times over my career at Sloan Kettering, I've been called on to raise larger sums than that through contributions."

Kate had to bite her tongue. "With all due respect, Doctor, we're comparing apples and oranges. I've shaken virtually every money tree in the county, and to date, I've only been able to come up with $89,000."

The judge sat up and puffed out his chest. "Well, Kate, let's see if we can up that amount tonight. Agnes and I will commit to a contribution of $10,000, and I'm sure that Dr. DuBois will match that amount."

DuBois stared over the upper rim of his glasses at the judge. "You're awfully generous with my money, John." He turned to Kate. "Is a contribution to the foundation tax deductible?"

"Yes, Doctor."

"In that case, you can count on $10,000 from Debbie and me. Oh, by the way, does that get us some kind of a plaque?"

Kate laughed. "Absolutely!"

The judge leaned forward in his chair. "I'll also contribute an additional $5,000 on behalf of my son."

Henry slammed his napkin on the table. "I can make my own contributions. I don't need your charity!" he rudely shouted.

An uncomfortable silence hung over the room for several seconds. Judge MacIntyre barely missed a beat. "That leaves Jack and Jeremy."

Jack spoke first. "I will certainly try to match your generous gift."

The judge smiled and turned toward Jeremy. "With the fund being as successful as it is, you surely can add to the pot."

Jeremy shifted uncomfortably in his wheelchair. "I'll check with my accountant, but I'm sure I can contribute as well."

"You see, Kate, that wasn't so hard. You just need to attend more dinner parties." The judge spotted the waitstaff entering the dining room. "Ah, I see that dessert is about to be served. After dessert, I would invite the gentlemen to join me in the library for brandy and cigars."

Kate frowned and looked down the table at Jack. Jack simply tilted his head to the right and shrugged as if to say, *When in Rome.*

The library was a rectangular room, at least one thousand square feet. The wood-paneled walls were exquisite, with floor-to-ceiling handcrafted bookcases lining two walls. A billiards table sat at the far end of the room. At the opposite end sat the judge's mahogany desk. A half a dozen leather chairs were spread out strategically around the room.

Dr. DuBois pushed Jeremy's wheelchair into the library and wheeled him over next to the judge's desk. "Jeremy, what do you hear from your uncle? You know he is one of my best friends here, and I haven't heard a word from him since he left for Florida."

"I talked to him about ten days ago. He's having a hard time of it. I suggested he contact hospice to help care for Gloria, but he wouldn't hear of it. I'll call him this week and tell him you were asking for him."

"I thought his sister's name was Elizabeth."

"No, it's Gloria," Jeremy replied.

"I must be mistaken. Thank you, and please ask him to call me."

The judge ceremoniously lifted a bottle off the credenza behind the desk and held it up for all to see. "This, gentlemen, is a bottle of Louis XIII cognac. How many glasses do we need?"

All hands went up except Jack's.

"Jack?" the judge asked.

Jack knew that the bottle of cognac the judge was serving cost over $3,000. "I'm sorry, Judge. While I'd love to, these days I only drink beer and wine."

"I'll have the bartender bring you a new glass of cabernet." The judge handed Jack a box of cigars. Jack took one and passed the box to Jeremy.

"Doesn't your wife object to the smell of cigars in the house?" Jeremy asked the judge.

"She does, so I installed a state-of-the-art ventilation system in this room. I'm too old to go outside to smoke my cigars in the winter."

Once everyone had settled in, the judge turned to Jeremy. "Jeremy, how much would you estimate I currently have in my account?"

"I can give you an accurate number in the morning."

"I'm just looking for an estimate."

"OK, well, you invested $2 million in the fund in February."

Dr. DuBois's eyes opened wide in astonishment.

Jeremy continued. "That's a little over five months. Conservatively, I would guess you've made around twelve percent. That would put you at around $2.25 million."

Dr. DuBois leaned forward in his chair. "Twelve percent in five months—that's a little hard to believe. I've tried to look up your fund, and I can't find any information on it, not even a reference to it."

"Well, Doctor, that's because it's a private fund catering to large investors. Currently, the minimum investment is $500,000 to join the fund. If you'll stop by the house, I'll share with you a perspective and all of the SEC filings and reporting documents. The fund has outpaced the Dow and S&P by a minimum of twelve percent over the last fifteen quarters."

"I still find it hard to believe." Dubois sat back in his chair, took a puff of his cigar, and blew the smoke toward the ceiling.

The judge again turned toward Jeremy. "Getting back to the subject at hand, I'd like to cash out."

Jeremy looked astonished. "Really? The fund is on pace to return close to thirty percent to investors this year. That's a considerable amount of money to give up."

"I know. But my son is embarking on a rather attractive real estate deal, and I'm going to be his silent partner."

Henry jumped to his feet and pointed at his father. "I don't want your money. This is *my* business opportunity, and I don't need or want any silent partners."

The judge pointed back. "Then tell me how are you going to get the initial financing? What, on your good looks?"

"I'll get the financing. Just stay out of my business." Henry walked out and slammed the library's double doors behind him.

"I'm sorry about that, gentlemen. My son can be a little headstrong and impetuous at times. He'll come around."

Jeremy asked, "Does that mean that you no longer need to cash out?"

"On the contrary. Go ahead and cash me out. How long will it take for me to access the funds?"

"If I cash you out tomorrow morning, it will take from five to seven business days. You should have access to your funds a week from Friday."

Jack felt his cell phone vibrate. He pulled it out and surreptitiously looked at the text message: *Rescue me, PLEASE!*

Jack smiled and stood up. "Judge, I'm sorry to be a killjoy, but I'd better get Kate back home. She has a busy day tomorrow, and I have a conference call at the crack of dawn."

"It's almost ten, Judge. I'd better be on my way as well," Jeremy said.

Jack reached his hand across the desk. "Judge, I can't thank you enough for this evening and introducing me to your friends and neighbors."

Judge MacIntyre vigorously shook Jack's hand and said, "Take good care of Kate. She's a keeper. I only wish I was forty years younger."

Jack didn't know how to respond.

Jack and Kate walked down the stairs as Jeremy came around the front of the house from the handicapped ramp on the side.

"Jeremy, it was great meeting you tonight. I'll be in touch with you about the fund. Can we help you get home?" Jack asked.

"Well, I don't need help, but I sure would appreciate the company." Jeremy pointed to the joystick protruding from an aluminum box on the right arm of the wheel-chair. "This thing really moves out."

Jack and Kate walked along, engaging in small talk with Jeremy until they reached his driveway leading to the side of the house.

"Would you like to come in for a drink?" Jeremy asked.

Kate looked anxiously at Jack, hoping he would decline the invitation.

"I think we'd better get home. We have a busy couple of days ahead of us both," Jack explained. "However, we'll take a rain check and talk about investing in the fund."

Jack and Kate said goodbye to Jeremy and walked back up the street to the Jack's car.

Soon after, Jack pulled up in front of Kate's house.

"Would you like to come in for a nightcap?" Kate asked.

"I'd love to, but I need ten minutes to get out of this monkey suit."

"Make it fifteen so I can get out of this dress. I must have been a size smaller when I last wore it. Come to the back door. I should be out of this dress and in the kitchen by then."

Kate had pulled out two cabernet wineglasses from the cabinet when Jack appeared at the sliding glass door. She waved him in. "Do me a favor and open this bottle of wine. I assumed you wanted wine."

Jack picked up the wine opener. "You assumed correctly." He opened the bottle and poured the two glasses a third full.

"Shall we adjourn to the family room?" Kate asked.

"Lead the way."

Jack followed Kate, and they both sat down on the couch.

"What did you think about the party?" Kate asked, hoping to get the lowdown on what had happened in the library.

"It was a nice evening, but it sure was an eclectic group."

"Oh, by the way, I'm really embarrassed that you were pressured to commit to a donation to the foundation. I thought it was insulting to do that to someone new to the neighborhood."

"Speaking of which." Jack pulled a folded piece of paper from his pants pocket.

"No, no, no; that better not be what I think it is."

He handed the paper to Kate, and she unfolded it. "Oh my god, I can't accept this. Jack, I can't accept this. It's a half a million dollars."

"I insist. Look at it this way. Aunt Ellen left me an enormous sum of money, not to mention the house, mortgage free. I've been trying to think of some way to honor her memory. What better way than to help build a center for abused women?"

Kate started to tear up. She got up and walked to the kitchen for a box of tissues.

"Bring back the wine bottle. We need to celebrate."

When Kate sat back down, Jack asked, "Would it be possible to have a plaque put up or name something in her honor?"

"Hell yes. If I have my way, the entire center will be named after her."

"Now, we have to break the news to DiLano and Goodwin Industries that you've raised the matching amount." Jack raised his wineglass. "And I have an idea. Let me think it over and I'll let you know more tomorrow."

CHAPTER THIRTY-THREE

Kate looked at her watch and sat down on the steps next to Jack. "Not bad. We did three and a half miles in twenty-three minutes and forty-eight seconds. I really enjoy having someone to run with—thank you."

Jack leaned forward, resting his forearms on his thighs. "I've got to admit, I wasn't too crazy about it at first. Now, I actually enjoy it." Jack paused a few seconds. "Remember last night I said that I had an idea about how to approach Goodwin Industries about the matching funds? I don't want to do anything without your concurrence."

"I trust your judgment. What do you have in mind?"

Jack explained that he was concerned that Goodwin Industries—more specifically DiLano—would try to renege on his commitment to the foundation. He outlined his plan to Kate, and she wholeheartedly agreed but doubted that they could pull it off in such a short time frame.

~~~

It was five minutes before the scheduled 10:00 a.m. ground-breaking ceremony and no DiLano. All of the other local dignitaries had long since arrived. Jack had contacted the *Cape Gazette* newspaper on Thursday morning and offered to write an article about the foundation's fundraising efforts, Goodwin Industries' matching contribution, and the scheduled ground-breaking ceremony. He was told if he could get the article and any pictures to the paper by noon, they would run it in Friday's edition. In the article, Jack lavished praise on Goodwin Industries and its chief executive officer, Anthony DiLano, and announced that the ground-breaking ceremony was scheduled for Saturday morning at the site of the new women's center in Lewes. Kate wrote and hand-delivered a letter to Goodwin Industries inviting DiLano to participate in Saturday's ceremony and thanking the board of directors for its sponsorship.

Jack looked at his watch. It was time to get started, and it appeared that his gambit had not worked. He picked up the five new shovels that he had purchased at Quillen's hardware store and handed one each to the three dignitaries and Kate. Just as he'd stepped back with the fifth shovel, a black Lincoln Town Car slowly pulled up to the curb. Jack drew a sigh of relief. It was Anthony DiLano, and he didn't look all that happy. He walked toward the assembled group and shook hands with each of the dignitaries and finally Kate. Jack stepped forward and handed DiLano the fifth shovel.

Sussex County Council president Jeffery Lockhart approached the microphone.

"Good morning, ladies and gentlemen, and welcome to the ground-breaking ceremony for Sussex County's new women's center. At this time, I would like to make some introductions. On my far right is Rehoboth Beach mayor Marty Wood. Next to him is Lewes mayor Wilber Cannon. On my far left is Kate Simpson, director of the Sussex County Women's Center and executive director of the Delaware Women's Center Foundation. Last is the chief executive officer of Goodwin Industries, Anthony DiLano. Before we put these new shovels to use, I'd like Ms. Simpson and Mr. DiLano to step forward." Jack also approached the microphone, carrying a six-foot-by-three-foot ceremonial check. The check was made out to the Sussex County Women's Center from Goodwin Industries for $500,000. Jack handed the check to DiLano, smiled, and stepped away.

The *Cape Gazette*'s photographer stepped forward and took several pictures: DiLano presenting the check to Kate, the assembled dignitaries with shovels at the ready, and lastly, a picture of Kate, Lockhart, and DiLano at the microphone.

"Mr. DiLano, would you like to say a few words?" Council President Lockhart asked.

DiLano stepped up to the microphone. "It's my pleasure, on behalf of the board of directors of Goodwin Industries, to present this check for $500,000 to the Sussex County Women's Center."

Kate stepped forward and graciously accepted the check and approached the microphone. "I want to thank Goodwin Industries for stepping forward as our founding sponsor."

The ground-breaking ceremony and pictures took no more than thirty minutes, and the participants and spectators were on their way to enjoy a beautiful but rather hot weekend.

"Kate, would you walk with me to my car?" DiLano asked as the group broke up. "I really didn't think you could pull it off. I guess I underestimated you. If you'll send me the center's account information, I will see to it that the funds are wire-transferred to the account on Monday."

Kate wondered what he would think if he knew that the lion's share of the matching funds came from one donor. "I really appreciate that, Mr. DiLano. This truly is a dream come true for me."

"I think it's probably time that you called me Tony. By the way, when do you intend to publish a request for proposal for the construction of the new center?"

"The schedule is to publish it next Friday, but I will have a copy delivered to your office by midweek."

"Thank you, Kate. I'm glad this all worked out. Have a nice weekend."

Jack didn't quite know what he was going to do with five shovels. He opened the rear hatch of the Jeep and placed the shovels in the back along with the faux check.

"Ready to head home?" Kate asked.

"How about I take you to a celebratory lunch first?"

"Oh, you want to go back to the Roadhouse again?" Kate asked playfully.

"No way. As hot as it's getting, I could use a cold draft beer. How about Dogfish Head on the main drag?"

Kate looked at her watch. "It could be a little difficult getting a table, but let's give it a shot."

"Also, would you and Tim join me on my deck to-morrow morning for breakfast? It's about time I paid you back for that great lasagna dinner."

"We'd love to. What time?"

"Is seven thirty too early?"

"Not at all. We'll be there at seven thirty. Incidentally, you've paid me back five hundred thousand times over."

CHAPTER THIRTY-FOUR

The sun painted a glistening golden trail across the water as Jack walked onto the deck with place mats, silverware, and three glasses of orange juice. It was a beautiful summer morning. A handful of locals and tourists were enjoying an early morning walk on the beach. He placed the tray on the table and turned toward the sound of Kate and Tim walking up the stairs to the deck. As usual, she was early.

"Good morning. I haven't quite finished preparing breakfast."

"Can we help with anything?"

"Thanks, Kate, but I think I've got everything under control. Have a seat, and I'll be back out in about five minutes."

Kate took a few minutes to take in the view before sitting down at the table. Tim was just about to take a sip of orange juice.

"Put the glass down and wait for Jack to join us," Kate scolded.

Jack emerged from the kitchen carrying a large platter with bacon, waffles, a yogurt-and-fruit bowl, and a large carafe of coffee.

"Jack, that was great. I feel like I'm having breakfast at some swank ocean resort." As an afterthought, Kate asked, "Do you have the time?"

Jack looked at his watch. "It's five minutes before eight."

"Follow me." Kate walked to the far end of the deck facing south. "Every Sunday morning at precisely 8:00 a.m., Judge MacIntyre plays the bagpipes on the beach. He's quite good, and the tourists love it."

Moments later MacIntyre appeared dressed in full Scottish regalia, including a tartan kilt, scarf, and tam. He walked purposefully to the jetty halfway between the shoreline and the dunes. He held the bagpipes in his left arm with all three drones placed over his left shoulder and began to inflate the bag.

Kate's smile turned to a look of alarm as MacIntyre fell to his knees and then face first to the sand. "My god, Jack! He's had a heart attack."

Jack vaulted over the railing and dropped fifteen feet to the dunes below. He somersaulted forward and came up running toward the jetty.

Kate handed her cell phone to Tim.

"Call 911, and have them send an ambulance to the Henlopen Estates Beach Club's upper parking area at the north jetty. Tell them it's a heart attack victim." Kate turned and ran to the stairs.

When Jack got to MacIntyre, a few people were starting to approach the prostrate figure on the beach. He motioned the people to step back as he bent down to check for a pulse. Detecting none, he rolled the judge over to administer CPR. He then noticed a dime-sized hole in the center of MacIntyre's white shirt. A crimson stain radiated out from the hole. The judge had been shot!

Kate arrived just as Jack stood up. "Is he all right?" Kate asked breathlessly.

Jack sadly shook his head. "He's dead, Kate. He was shot. I'm pretty sure the bullet pierced his heart."

"I don't believe it. That's impossible. Why?"

"I can't answer that. Listen, I think you need to get to the MacIntyre's house and be with Agnes before she hears what's happened. I'll call Father Francis and have him meet you there. I'll follow you as soon as everything is finished here."

Kate began to cry. Jack pulled her close and gently stroked her hair. "The best thing you can do now is to be with Agnes."

Seemingly out of nowhere, Crockett appeared. "I was investigating a possible break-in across the street when I heard the 911 call. What happened, and how can I help?"

Jack explained what he and Kate had witnessed and that Judge MacIntyre had been shot.

"One very important thing you can do is move this crowd back and cordon off the area."

Crockett promptly started moving the crowd, which continued to grow, back away from the body lying on the beach.

A teenaged boy dressed in a wetsuit and carrying a surfboard ran toward Jack from the ocean. He threw the board down and yelled to Jack, "Hey, mister, I think I saw what happened. He was shot, wasn't he?"

"Yes. What's your name?"

"I'm Evan Thomson, and I think I saw a muzzle flash over there, just before the man collapsed." The boy pointed toward the dunes to the south.

"Don't leave until the police can get your statement. In the meantime, would you get me that white towel hanging over the back of the sand chair over there?" Jack pointed in the direction of the chair, and the boy raced over to retrieve the towel. When he returned, Jack took the towel and respectfully placed it over the judge's face and torso.

A flurry of emergency vehicles with their sirens blaring entered the upper beach club parking area. J. R. came running toward Jack.

"I heard the 911 call. What happened?"

Jack pulled J. R. aside. "It's Judge MacIntyre. He's been shot through the heart." Scanlon motioned for the boy to come over. "This is Evan Thomson. He said he saw a muzzle flash just before the judge went down. He said it came from the dunes over there."

The EMTs approached the judge's body with a stretcher. Jack cringed when he saw them pull a black body bag out of a large equipment satchel. He'd seen black body bags too many times in his time in the service.

J. R. approached the EMTs. "I know you will, but please threat him with all the respect that he deserves."

He then summoned the Thomson boy standing a respectful distance away. "Can you show us approximately where you saw the muzzle flash?"

Jack, J. R., and the boy walked south along the dune line for a little over a hundred yards when the boy stopped. "This is the spot. This is where I saw the muzzle flash."

"Stay here," J. R. instructed the boy. "Mr. Scanlon and I will approach this location from the other side of the dunes."

J. R. motioned Jack to follow him. They walked another thirty yards down the beach to a narrow trail between the dunes that led from the beach to Ocean Drive. About fifty yards down the trail, J. R. turned to his right and parted an opening between the trees. "We can get in through here." He led Jack up to the crest of the dune and looked down at the boy standing on the ocean side of the dune line. "Is this the spot?" he asked the boy.

"Yes, but about five yards to your right, next to the 'Keep Off the Dunes' sign."

Jack lay down on the dune, simulating a prone shooting position facing north. "It's about a 120-yard shot. There's little or no wind, so the only factor the shooter really had to account for was gravity. The shot would not require the skills of a trained sniper. Anyone with a moderate knowledge of marksmanship could have made the shot. The fact that he hit the judge's heart indicates to me a little higher level of expertise, or blind luck." Jack got up and brushed the sand off his clothes.

J. R. was inspecting the area around where the shooter would have lain.

"What are you looking for?"

"The shell casing."

"I doubt you'll find it. He wouldn't have ejected it; there was no need for a second shot. One shot, one kill. This guy was meticulous. There are no shoe prints or disturbed areas. I would wager that he dragged a large pine bough over the area as he retreated to the trail."

"You know, Scanlon, you would have made a pretty good army ranger," J. R. suggested.

"Ranger—hell, remember, I was a Navy SEAL. That's a couple levels above," Jack chided. "Let's head out to the street. Maybe someone saw something."

When they reached the street, J. R. noticed a Delmarva Power truck parked next to a telephone pole about thirty feet away. A utility worker appeared to be repairing the transformer. J. R. flashed his badge and signaled the worker to lower the bucket. The worker swung the bucket arm around and lowered the bucket until he was within shouting distance of J. R..

"Sorry to interrupt you, but did you see anyone come down this trail in the past thirty minutes?"

"Actually, I did. A man in a tan jumpsuit came out to the road carrying what looked like a surfboard case. A car pulled up. He got in, and they headed toward the state park at the end of Ocean Drive."

"What kind of car was it, and did you see who was driving?" J. R. asked.

"It was a red Mercedes or BMW two-door sedan. I didn't get a look at the driver."

"It's basically a dead end that way." J. R. pointed in the direction of the state park. "Did you see them come back this way?"

"I didn't. They could have. I was too busy working on the transformer to notice."

"Thanks. If you think of anything else, would you call the police station and ask for Chief Johnson?" J. R. turned to Jack. "What do you think?"

"There's not much more we can do here. I'll go over to the judge's house and see if I can help Kate out with Mrs. MacIntyre. How about you?"

"I'm going back to the crime scene to check in with Crockett. If there's anything I can do to help you or Kate, call me. On second thought, after I'm done with Crockett, I'll drop by the MacIntyres'. I'd like to ask Mrs. MacIntyre a few questions if she's up to it."

Jack started to walk north along Ocean Drive toward the entrance to Tidewaters when J. R. yelled, "Hold up a minute! Did Crockett arrive at the crime scene before you?"

"No, but he arrived shortly thereafter. He said he was investigating a possible break-in nearby that was called in."

"There was no break-in called in this morning." J. R. scratched his head and walked back toward the trail.

CHAPTER THIRTY-FIVE

As Jack approached the house, Kate opened the door and came down the steps toward him. Jack could see that Kate had been crying. Her eyes were red, and she staggered slightly as she approached him.

"How's she doing?"

"She's devastated. I'm not even sure she completely comprehends what has happened. We've called for the doctor. Hopefully, he can give her something to settle her nerves."

"How are you doing?"

"OK, I guess." Kate started to cry as Jack reached for her. She fell into his arms and started sobbing. After several seconds, she stepped away and wiped the tears from her eyes. "I don't know why this has hit me so hard. It's just that he was always so kind to me. I can't believe this is happening."

"Once you feel up to it, let's go inside."

Kate nodded. "I'm good."

They turned and walked up the steps with Jack's arm around her shoulder.

Agnes sat in a leather wingback chair, staring blankly at the far wall as Jack approached her.

"Mrs. MacIntyre, I am so sorry for your loss."

Agnes nodded slowly but seemed not to recognize who Jack was as he knelt down in front of her. "Has your son been notified?"

She didn't seem to understand the question.

Jack turned around and looked at Kate. She nodded yes. "Father Francis called him. There was no answer. So he left a message on his cell phone."

"Where is Father Francis?" Jack asked.

"He went to the master bedroom to find Agnes's rosary beads."

Just then the doorbell rang, and Kate turned to answer it. "I'll get it," she said as she left the room.

Father Francis reentered the room from the hallway off the master suite. "Good morning, Jack. I'm sorry we must meet again under these circumstances."

"Good morning, Father. It was good of you to drop everything and get over here so quickly. I know Mrs. MacIntyre appreciates you being here in her time of need."

Jack silently chastised himself. He sounded more like the priest than the priest did.

Kate walked into the room with J. R.. He appeared to be very uncomfortable in the presence of Agnes. He offered his condolences and asked Kate if he could borrow Jack for a few minutes. "Is there somewhere we can go where we won't be interrupted?"

Kate pointed to the veranda outside the French doors across the living room. "You won't be disturbed out there."

Jack placed his hand on Kate's shoulder. "Will you be all right for a while?"

"I'll be fine."

Father Francis sat next to Agnes. They both had their heads bowed, reciting the rosary.

J. R. followed Jack to the veranda. He pointed to the two chairs next to the fountain. "Let's sit. I've been racking my brain, trying to think of anyone who would want the judge dead. I thought if we put our heads together, we could come up with a list."

Jack leaned back in his chair. "Wasn't MacIntyre a criminal court judge? That might be a place to start."

"He served on the criminal court in Sussex County for almost thirty years. They didn't call him 'Maximum Mac' for nothing. He seldom, if ever, meted out anything other than the maximum sentence allowed by law."

"Well then, we might want to start with recently released prisoners the judge put away," Jack suggested.

"I'll have to reach out to Sergeant Holmes of the state police for that information. I don't have access to those type of files. I'll call him as soon as I get back to the office. I was going to read him in on this anyway." J. R. leaned forward. "What else? Didn't you tell me something about a heated argument he had with his son the other night?"

"You're not suggesting his son killed him?"

"Why not? It wouldn't be the first time something like that happened."

"I'll admit, he's got a temper. However, he didn't strike me as being capable of that kind of violence. The other night, for example, he blew up at his father, but rather than confronting him any further, he stormed out of the room."

"I would suggest that shooting someone at a distance is a nonconfrontational act. All right, for now, we'll put him on the B-list, but I still want to check him out."

"Do me a favor. If he arrives here before we leave, don't confront him with Mrs. MacIntyre in the room. She won't be able to handle it."

"What do you think I am, Scanlon, some kind of ogre?"

"Is there anyone outside of the judge's milieu that would want to harm him?" Jack asked.

"Milieu?"

"Acquaintances, circle of friends."

"Dr. DuBois might be able to answer that question. They're drinking buddies. However, he and Debbie are attending a wedding in Savannah this weekend and won't be back until next Tuesday. We could ask Mrs. MacIntyre, but I don't think she'd give us much help in the state she's in."

J. R. paused for a minute as if in deep thought. "You know, Jack, I've been doing this job for almost fourteen years. Do you know how many murders I've had to deal with in all that time?"

"Zero," Jack guessed.

"Correct, zero."

"I hope you're not suggesting that my arrival in Rehoboth is cause and effect."

J. R. laughed. "It does make one wonder."

Jack ignored the comment and started to get up. "I don't pretend to know what's going on here, but the judge's murder and Anna's could somehow be related. I guess I'm just thinking out loud. Unless you have something else, let's go in and see how they're doing." Jack preceded J. R. back into the living room.

Henry MacIntyre had arrived and stood dispassionately in the opposite corner of the room from his mother. J. R. glanced at Jack and nodded toward the corner where the son was standing. "He doesn't seem to be all that upset by his father's death. I think we should talk to him sooner rather than later."

Jack walked over to Kate, who was talking with one of the neighbors. The neighbor had just arrived with a platter of sandwiches. It appeared that the news of the judge's death had spread like wildfire through the community. "I'll be outside, if you need me," he said to Kate.

J. R. walked across the room to the son. "Do you have a few minutes to talk to us outside?" Without answering, Henry turned and walked to the front door. Jack was waiting for them on the portico.

J. R. spoke first. "Mr. MacIntyre, first of all, I'm sorry for your loss. This won't take long. I need to ask you a few questions."

Henry folded his arms defiantly, as though he knew what was coming. "All right, shoot."

Jack rolled his eyes. *What an inappropriate response, given the circumstances*, he thought.

"Can you tell us where you were this morning around 8:00 a.m.?"

"What, you think I killed my father?" Henry asked incredulously.

J. R. continued, "I understand that you got into a heated argument with your father the other night."

Henry turned and glared at Jack. "What's he doing here?

"Agent Scanlon is assisting me in the investigation of your father's murder. Now, if you'd be so kind as to answer the question. Where were you this morning?"

Henry hesitated. "I slept in. Didn't get up until nine when Father Francis called."

"Can anyone verify that?"

"No, I live alone. I need to get back inside unless you have any more questions."

"You can go. Sorry to have inconvenienced you." Henry turned the doorknob and had started to step inside when J. R. asked, "Oh, one more thing. Did you ever serve in the military?"

Henry looked confused. "Yes, three years in the army. What of it?"

"Nothing, just wondering."

J. R. turned to Jack. "I'm heading back to the station. Call me if you think of anything."

As J. R. pulled away, another car pulled into the vacant space in front of the house. An elderly gentleman in a tan blazer and slacks got out carrying what appeared to be a black leather medical bag. "Excuse me, I'm Dr. Samuels, here to see Agnes MacIntyre."

"Follow me, Doctor. She's inside," Jack said.

Kate was standing alone next to the couch when Jack approached.

"There's nothing more you can do here. I'm heading home. Why don't you walk back with me? Tim's probably wondering what is going on."

Kate nodded, said something to Father Francis, and followed Jack to the front door.

"What did you talk to Henry about?" Kate asked as they walked down the street toward Ocean Drive.

"J. R. asked him where he was this morning."

Kate looked surprised. "You don't think he had anything to do with his father's death, do you?"

"Personally, I don't. Earlier, I told J. R. about the incident in the judge's library last Wednesday evening. He's just doing his job. I would have asked the same questions if I were in his shoes." Jack stopped and reached out for Kate's hand. "Are you all right?"

"I'm doing better. I just can't make any sense of all this. The judge and Agnes treated me like their daughter. I guess I'm still in shock."

"Why don't you, Tim, and I go out for an early dinner? It's not going to do you any good to sit around the house thinking about all this. Is five too early?"

"No, I think the earlier the better."

CHAPTER THIRTY-SIX

Jack straightened his tie and grabbed the suit jacket off the back of the chair. He was walking to the kitchen when his cell phone rang.

"Jack, it's J. R.. I'm going to swing by in about ten minutes and pick you and Kate up. Parking at the church will be nearly impossible. Father Francis offered to let me park behind the rectory."

"Thanks, I'll call Kate and let her know."

"Already did. See you in ten. OK, by the way, Father Francis asked that the three of us sit with Agnes and her son."

Jack sighed. "Really? I wonder if he ran that idea by her son."

"He said that Mrs. MacIntyre requested it."

As J. R. pulled up in front of the church, Jack wondered if all of Delaware had turned out for the judge's memorial service. Cars approached the church from every direction, scrambling for a place to park. The line of mourners stretched from the front of the church to the street, then down the street and around the corner.

J. R. pulled into the rectory driveway and parked. "Father Francis said we should enter through the door at the rear of the church. He will be in the sacristy with Mrs. MacIntyre and her son."

Jack held the door open as Kate and J. R. entered the sacristy. Father Francis and Mrs. MacIntyre were seated on a small settee. Henry was standing next to his mother. Hearing the door open, Father Francis rose to greet them. He handed each of them a funeral program.

"We have about ten minutes until the Mass is scheduled to begin. Jack, would you peek out the door on your right and see if the church is starting to fill up?"

Jack walked over to the door leading to the altar. He opened it enough to get a good view of the inside of the church. The judge's flag-draped casket was situated at the foot of the altar. He closed the door and returned to join the others. "Father, the church is completely filled. People are standing in the side aisles and at the back. The doors are still open. It appears that people are still trying to enter the church."

Father Francis addressed the group. "The five of you will be seated in the front pew on the right side. Kate, if you and Henry would accompany Mrs. MacIntyre, Jack and J. R. will enter the pew from the aisle on the right side. Jack, could I speak with you for a moment?" Father Francis directed Jack to the far corner of the sacristy. "Is there any more information regarding the judge's shooting?"

"No, Father. The chief is following some leads, but he has nothing solid."

Father Francis put his hand on Jack's shoulder. "You need to get more actively involved. I don't believe J. R. is up to the task of solving a murder. To my knowledge, he's never been faced with a challenge like this. The town is on edge."

"I'll do what I can to help the chief, if asked. However, I think you may be underestimating his abilities."

The choir and the mourners sang the Navy Hymn, "Eternal Father, Strong to Save," as Father Francis led the pallbearers out of the church to the waiting black hearse.

"I didn't realize that the judge was a veteran," J. R. remarked.

"There was a brief mention of it in his obituary. He served three years as a navy seaman from 1957 to 1960."

As the mourners milled around, Jeremy Madison maneuvered his wheelchair through the crowd to where Jack and J. R. were standing. "Good morning, Mr. Scanlon, Chief. I realize this isn't the appropriate time, but I have updated projections on the fund. If you can drop by later this afternoon, I'll share them with you. Again, I'm sorry to bring this up now, but I'm not going to the cemetery, and I will be leaving town tomorrow for about a week."

"That's very kind of you. I think I'm free any time after three this afternoon. Does 4:00 p.m. work for you?" Jack asked.

"Absolutely, and feel free to bring Ms. Simpson along. I'd like to try and convince her that the center's building contributions would be better invested in the fund."

"It appears that Kate is riding with Mrs. MacIntyre to the grave site. I'll get the car, pull around, and pick you up," J. R. said.

Jack pointed toward the street. Cars were coming from every direction in an effort to get in the queue of those waiting to leave for the cemetery. "Given the traffic jam, I think I'll walk with you to the car."

J. R. dropped Jack and Kate off in front of Kate's house. "I'll be heading back to the station."

"Thanks for picking us up, Chief," Kate said.

Jack leaned in the front passenger side window. "I've got a few friends coming in for the weekend, and I'd like to invite you to come over Friday evening for dinner—steaks on the grill."

"I'll trade shifts with Crockett. What time, and what can I bring?"

"No need to bring anything. I've got everything taken care of. How does six work?"

"See you at six."

J. R. pulled away, and Jack turned to Kate. "That invitation extends to you and Tim as well. I'd really like you to meet these guys. I served with them in Iraq and Afghanistan. I also want them to hear about Tim's treasure quest."

"We'll accept only if I can bring the wine."

"Deal—oh, I almost forgot. Jeremy invited you and me over to his house at four to hear his spiel about investing in his fund."

"Why me? I told him last Wednesday that the foundation's investment policy does not allow us to invest in anything remotely risky."

"I suspect that he will attempt to convince you that the fund is without risk. You have the perfect out. Just listen and tell him you'll present it to your board for consideration."

"It's a waste of time, but I'll go with you."

"Maybe not. I'll come by at 3:45 p.m., and we can walk over together."

"Oh, by the way, I'm curious. How do you know Father Francis so well?"

"After I recovered from Nancy's death, I felt there was something still missing in my life. My mother was Catholic, so I was baptized and confirmed in the Catholic Church. However, when I entered high school, Ellen enrolled me in St. Stephens. It's an Episcopalian high school in Alexandria. Ellen chose to worship as an Episcopalian. She called it 'Catholic lite.'"

Kate laughed. "My parents called it Catholic without the guilt."

"Anyway, a day or two after I moved in, I went over to visit Father Francis. I explained that I was brought up Catholic but had drifted away from the church. I asked him what I would have to do to rejoin the church. We met a few nights to go over the Mass and a few other things, and that was it."

"Sorry to be so nosy. I'll see you at 3:45 p.m."

CHAPTER THIRTY-SEVEN

Kate sat on the front steps as Jack walked up the driveway carrying a tote bag. It had been a long and emotional day, but still she wondered what Jack was up to.

"What's in the tote?"

"Three stemless wineglasses and a nice bottle of cabernet."

"Isn't it a little early in the day for that?" Kate looked at her watch as if to emphasize her point.

"There's a method to my madness. We'll just have to see how it plays out. Let's not be late for our appointment." Jack reached for Kate's hand and pulled her to her feet.

Jack pushed the intercom button, stepped back, and waited for an answer.

"Who is it?" the voice on the other end asked.

"It's Kate and Jack," he responded.

"Please come in. The door's unlocked."

Jack held the door open for Kate and followed her into the great room. He turned toward the kitchen as

Jeremy maneuvered his wheelchair around the large leather couch.

"Thank you for coming over on such short notice. I apologize again, but I'm going out of town tomorrow and wanted to share with you the latest projections for the fund. They are very exciting. Please have a seat on the couch, and I'll pull my wheelchair up to the coffee table."

Jack and Kate sat down next to each other on the couch. A large five-foot-by-five-foot coffee table was covered with charts, pamphlets, and financial reports. Jack lifted the tote bag onto the coffee table. "It's been a difficult day for all of us, with the funeral and all. I thought we could share a bottle of wine in memory of Judge MacIntyre while we hear about your fund."

"That's very thoughtful of you. I think it's a fitting tribute to the judge. Do you need a wine opener and glasses?"

"No, I actually brought everything." Jack opened the bottle, poured three glasses, and handed one to Kate and Jeremy. He lifted his glass and said, "Here's to the memory of Judge MacIntyre, his family, and better times."

Jeremy took a sip of wine, put his glass down, and leaned back in his wheelchair.

"Let me share a little background with you about the fund and how it works. When I was in graduate school at Stanford, I developed an algorithm to predict stock market fluctuations as part of my master's thesis. Most predictive models analyze only ten, sometimes twelve, sectors of the economy. Given the amount of economic information provided by the government, businesses, and research, I divided several of the sectors up into subsectors, twenty-four in all. Let's take, for example, the energy sector. I've split the energy sector in two, energy production and energy exploration. They don't always move in tandem. Therefore, lumping them together sometimes gives a distorted picture of how the energy sector is preforming or will perform in the future. Another example is precious metals. While gold and silver tend to move up and down together, platinum and titanium don't always follow suit."

Jack raised his hand. "I have a question. You talked about economic data provided by the government, businesses, and research. Are you talking US, or is worldwide data factored in? You must have some foreign and emerging market stocks represented in the fund."

"From time to time, there are foreign stock holdings in the fund. However, they never exceed five percent of the fund's portfolio. They tend to be primarily in the energy sector, like Royal Dutch Shell. Emerging markets are very speculative. Therefore, the fund focuses solely on established stocks. US stocks are strong and getting stronger, so currently the fund is heavily focused on domestic holdings."

Kate leaned forward. "This is incredibly impressive, but how does the fund manage to exceed the performance of the stock market?"

"Thank you for asking that question. It brings me to the sole reason why the fund outperforms the Dow Industrial Average and the S&P 500." Jeremy cleared several brochures, reports, and papers away from the center of the table, revealing a four-foot-by-four-foot poster board. In the center of the board was a two-foot-by-two-foot square divided in half horizontally and vertically. A diagonal red line ran from the upper left-hand corner to the lower right-hand corner. Several colored dots were scattered inside the four one-foot-by-one-foot squares. Each colored dot had two letters at its center. A numerical scale ran vertically along the left edge of the graph and horizontally along the bottom.

"So what are we looking at?" Jack asked.

"This is the latest printout from the algorithm program. It represents all of the data that I have entered this week. The twenty-four dots represent the economic sectors that I have identified. Each dot has a two-letter designation in its center." Jeremy pointed to a dot in the upper right box. "This one is designated EE for energy exploration." He pointed to another dot closer to the red diagonal line. "This one, designated CS, represents consumer staples."

"What does this tell you?" Kate asked.

"Any dot in the top right-side box is a buy signal. The closer to the top right-hand corner, the stronger the buy recommendation. Conversely, once a sector moves to the left of the diagonal red line, it signals a sell recommendation. If a sector moves to the lower left box, it is a must-sell signal. For example, the red dot in the upper right box labeled EP for energy production signals a strong buy recommendation. It's been in that box for the past two months. Therefore, the fund has purchased thousands of shares of Exxon Mobil and Sunoco." Jeremy pointed to a blue dot in the lower left box marked GS. "That dot represents the gold and silver sector, and it has been there for the past six months. Therefore, we have no gold or silver company stocks currently in the fund. Notice how many dots are in the upper right quadrant. That tells me the market is about to skyrocket."

"Jeremy, do you mind if I use your bathroom?" Kate asked.

"Not at all. It's down the hall, the second door on the left."

"Excuse me, I'll be right back. Don't continue without me." Kate rose and walked hurriedly toward the hallway.

Jack poured another glass of wine for Kate and Jeremy. Jeremy nodded his thanks and took a sip. "This is an excellent cabernet," Jeremy pronounced.

Kate returned in less than five minutes. "Did I miss anything?"

"No, we were just talking about the funeral service." Jeremy reached down and pulled a briefcase onto his lap. "Now let me show you something that will blow your mind. Do you remember the last recession we experienced? It started about four years ago and lasted almost two years." Jeremy pulled out four legal-sized sheets of paper and handed them to Jack. "Please arrange them on the table from left to right chronologically. The dates are in the upper left corner of each sheet."

Each sheet showed a smaller version of the graph on the poster board in the center of the coffee table. Jack placed the four sheets across the bottom of the table. "So what am I looking at?" Jack asked.

Jeremy smirked. "You tell me."

For several minutes, Jack studied the four graphs. "Since they are arranged chronologically from left to right, it shows a majority of the sectors over the four-month period moving from the upper right quadrant, crossing the diagonal red line to the lower left quadrant."

"Give that man a gold star," Jeremy exclaimed proudly.

Jeremy leaned forward and pointed to the graph on Jack's left. "That graph was produced six months before the recession began, and the remaining three represent the succeeding three months. They indicated clearly that the country was heading into a period of recession, months before economists and financial analysts predicted it. With that knowledge, I began selling off almost eighty percent of the fund's portfolio. When the recession hit, markets plunged, and we were invested in treasury certificates. Twenty months later, before the experts recognized that we were coming out of the recession, I was buying up stocks at bargain-basement prices. Bottom line, during a period when the market lost over twenty percent of its value, the fund gained twelve percent." Jeremy leaned back in his wheelchair, crossed his arms, and grinned.

"That is very impressive," Kate declared. "I wish the center could invest in the fund, but we have a policy that prohibits it."

"Well, Kate, policies are made to be changed. I would be happy to put a presentation together for your board and brief them personally. Possibly, they could grant a one-time exception or amend the policy."

Kate tilted her head and gave Jeremy a skeptical look. "I'd be willing to try, but these people are very fiscally conservative. They have a fiduciary responsibility to the foundation, which they take very seriously."

"I'd love the opportunity to talk with them. We could even set up a video conference call. In addition, I could set up the account in such a way that you could withdraw funds as construction is ongoing."

"I promise you, I will try to get you an audience with the board."

"How about you, Jack?"

"Let me say, I am very impressed. However, I would like to consult with my financial adviser and accountant before I commit."

"I understand, and if you want me to talk with them or provide them with additional documents, I'd be happy to oblige."

"We have taken up an awful lot of your time, and I know Kate has an appointment at six, so we'd better be on our way." Jack stood and shook Jeremy's hand.

Jack started to carefully pick up the glasses and empty wine bottle and placed them in the tote bag.

"I could have those glasses washed and returned to you," Jeremy offered.

"That's very kind of you, but I'm just going to toss them in the dishwasher when I get home."

"Well, thank you again for the wine. It was a great way to end an otherwise sad day." Jeremy escorted Kate and Jack to the door. "I hope to hear from the both of you soon."

~~~

Kate and Jack walked about a hundred yards toward Ocean Drive before either spoke. Kate spoke first. "I'm curious, were you as impressed as I was?"

"He checked all the boxes for me."

"But?"

"Universally, if something sounds too good to be true, then it's usually too good to be true."

"I don't disagree, but he was very convincing. Incidentally, I couldn't help noticing how carefully you picked up those wineglasses and placed them in the tote. What, may I ask, are you up to?"

Jack turned in to his driveway, and Kate followed. "Why don't you come in? I'll show you."

Jack placed the tote bag on the kitchen counter, excused himself, and headed for the stairs. "I'll be back in a few minutes. Would you mind getting me a beer out of the fridge? If you prefer wine, the reds are in the rack in the corner, and the whites are in the refrigerator."

Jack soon returned with a stack of white cards in his hand.

"Here's your beer. What are those?" Kate pointed to the stack of cards Jack had placed on the counter.

"They are adhesive fingerprint cards."

Jack carefully took the wineglasses out of the tote bag and placed them on the counter.

"I think I see the method to your madness, but how do you know which glass was Jeremy's?"

"That's easy. I put a small dot with a silver Sharpie on the bottom of the glass he used."

"Wow, you FBI guys are devious little buggers."

Jack carefully turned Jeremy's glass upside down on the counter. He took one of the cards and peeled back the adhesive side. He examined the glass carefully until he found a visible print. He placed the adhesive side against the glass and pressed it to the print using a three-by-five card. He peeled the plastic sheet off the glass and reattached it to its backing. Holding it up to the light, he declared, "I think we have a usable print. But just in case, I think I'll try to find a few others. One of my friends who is coming down this weekend works with me at the FBI. I'll have him run these prints." Jack looked up to see Kate grinning from ear to ear. "What are you grinning at?"

"I thought you were up to something like this."

"And?"

Kate pulled a tissue out of her jacket pocket and unfolded it. "When I went to the bathroom, I pulled some hairs from a hairbrush sitting on the sink. Strange thing though—the hairs are blond and considerably longer than Jeremy's hair." She handed Jack the tissue. "You might want to ask your friend to run a DNA test on the hairs."

After Kate left, Jack walked back inside to feed Winston. He filled the bowl with dog food and placed it on the kitchen floor next to the dog's water dish. He had started to walk out onto the deck when his phone rang. He looked at the number and pressed answer.

"Afternoon, J. R.. What's up?"

"I came up empty on prisoners recently released who the judge put away. Most are still incarcerated, and the one who did get out is working in Cincinnati, Ohio. I talked to his parole officer, and he indicated he hasn't left the state since his release. However, I looked into the judge's son. His military record is very interesting. In basic training, he qualified as expert in every weapon he fired. After basic, he applied for sniper school and was accepted. Halfway through, he was bounced for striking a lieutenant. He got a court-martialed and was found guilty. He was reduced in rank one grade, fined, and spent six months in the stockade."

"That sounds incriminating but doesn't prove anything."

CHAPTER THIRTY-EIGHT

Kate took a sip of her coffee, placed the mug down, and unrolled the construction plans across her desk. She examined each page, carefully making notes in the margins. She was about to take another sip of coffee when the intercom buzzed.

"Ms. Simpson, you have a call on line one."

"Thank you, Julia. Did you get a name?"

"No, he didn't say. I'm sorry, I should have asked."

Kate sighed and pushed the button for line one. "This is Kate Simpson."

"Hi, Kate, it's Dr. Steve Rosenbaum. I have some good news for you. Ms. Ramsey is conscious and talking. She was interviewed by the police last evening, and she identified her assailant. If you'd like to visit her, I know she'd like to see you."

"That's wonderful news. I'll be there in about twenty minutes."

Kate pressed the intercom button. "Is Crystal still upstairs?"

"Yes, ma'am. Her shift doesn't start until three this afternoon."

Kate walked up the stairs to the suite of rooms on the second floor. Crystal was sitting on the couch watching television, still in her pajamas.

"Would you like to accompany me to the hospital to visit Tina?"

Crystal jumped up from the couch. "Is she all right?"

"Dr. Rosenbaum just called. She's conscious and talking and would like to see us."

"Give me five minutes to change." Crystal raced to her room and closed the door.

Kate and Crystal got off the elevator on the second floor and entered the ICU, this time not bothering to stop at the nurses' station.

The nurse behind the desk stood and shouted at Kate, "Can I help you? You can't just go in there without authorization."

Kate recognized the nurse from their last encounter. She stopped and turned. "Why don't you page Dr. Rosenbaum and tell him Kate Simpson is here as requested?"

Crystal stopped outside room 116, which now had the patient identified as Tina Ramsey.

"Ms. Simpson, I'm afraid to go in there. What if she thinks I didn't do enough to protect her? What if she blames me for what happened to her?"

"That's not going to happen, I assure you. She knows there was nothing you could have done."

Kate entered the room as Crystal hung back near the door. Tina was sitting up in bed sipping water from a Styrofoam cup. The bandages had been removed from her head and face, but evidence of bruising still remained around her eyes and throat. Tina looked up and beamed from ear to ear. "Ms. Simpson, thank you for coming to see me. Dr. Rosenbaum told me you were here several days ago when I was, you know, out of it."

Kate walked to the foot of the bed. "I brought someone with me who has been very worried about you." Kate turned and gestured for Crystal to come into the room.

Crystal slowly entered the room. Seeing her, Tina put down the cup and held her arms out wide, beckoning Crystal to come to her. Crystal ran to her arms. The two embraced, and she climbed up next to her on the bed. Tears streamed down both girls' cheeks as they hugged and laughed.

Kate felt a hand on her shoulder and turned to see Steve Rosenbaum standing next to her. She smiled and nodded toward the bed.

"Best therapy in the world. Her condition has improved remarkably in the past week. Isn't it great to be young? I'm confident that she will make a full recovery. If everything continues to go this well, I plan on releasing her next week."

"Where do we go from here?"

"Do you still have a place for her at the center?"

"Absolutely. She can stay with us as long as she likes."

Rosenbaum gestured toward the bed. "That's great, because given what I'm seeing, she will get the kind of the support there that she will need."

Kate smiled. "Crystal was initially worried about how Tina would react. But it looks to me like they have picked up just where they left off."

"Why don't we step outside and let these two get reacquainted?"

Rosenbaum led Kate down the hall to the doctor's lounge.

"We can talk here without being interrupted. I'm the only doctor on shift in the ICU until noon. Would you like a cup of coffee?"

"No, but I will take a bottle of water."

Rosenbaum opened the cooler door, pulled out two bottles of water, and handed one to Kate.

"I sat in on the police interview last night, just to make sure they didn't unnecessarily upset her. She was a trooper. She told them that the former boyfriend was the person who assaulted her and left her unconscious next to the highway. She identified him as Andrew Mann of Pennsauken, New Jersey. They met at a restaurant where he tended bar and she waited on tables. Six months ago, they moved to Lewes and moved in together. She said he lost his first job due to a fight with his supervisor and has been in and out of work ever since. The more he failed, the more he took it out on her. The state police have issued a warrant for his arrest."

"How does that work? Did they say anything about extradition?"

"They didn't discuss extradition. I'm not a lawyer, so I really don't know how it works."

"Well, I am a lawyer, and I don't quite know how it works either. I'm not sure if Delaware even has reciprocity with New Jersey. I believe Sussex County would have to indict him first and then seek an out-of-state warrant. In any event, it's out of our hands." Kate stood up. "Unfortunately, I have to get back to work."

"Does Crystal have to leave also? I think it would do Ms. Ramsey a world of good if she could stay with her for a while. I'll see to it that she gets back to the center."

"I'm fine with that, but she has to be at work by three this afternoon."

"That's not a problem. We'll get her there on time."

Kate preceded Rosenbaum into the room. "Crystal, I have to get back to the office, but Dr. Rosenbaum will see to it that you get to your shift on time. That will give you a couple of more hours to visit, if Tina is up to it."

Tina smiled and gave Kate a thumbs-up.

Kate and Rosenbaum walked down the hall past the nurses' station to the elevator.

"Steve, I can't begin to thank you enough for getting Tina through all this."

"Actually, you can. Let me take you out to dinner Saturday night."

The invitation caught her completely off guard. She hesitated for a few seconds. "That would be great. Where and when should I meet you?"

"I'll pick you up. Does seven work for you?"

"Seven is perfect." Kate pulled a card out of her purse and wrote her address on the back. "See you Saturday night."

CHAPTER THIRTY-NINE

Jack had just put the finishing touches on chapter four of the manual when a horn blared from the driveway. He looked at his watch. It was 2:15 p.m., and he expected that his guests had arrived. He walked down the hall to the front window overlooking the driveway, and sure enough, his comrades in arms were unloading Micah's new Ford Explorer. He had been looking forward to this weekend for weeks. It was the first time all of them could get the same time off.

Jack raced down the front stairs to the driveway and greeted his friends with handshakes and hugs all around. "Looks like you guys are planning to stay for a while. Micah, what's all this?"

"As we discussed last week, dinner tonight is on us. So that cooler contains one dozen twelve-ounce filets, a dozen Idaho baking potatoes, salad, and dessert. Duffy and I brought our dive gear, and the cases contain all our fishing gear. There's also a large fishing cooler, two cases of beer, and twelve bottles of red wine of various types, but mostly cabernet. So where do you want it?" Micah asked.

"Back the Explorer into the garage. Leave the fishing and dive gear in the SUV. We'll need to take at least two vehicles tomorrow morning. There's an elevator at the back of the garage that goes up to the kitchen. Load the food, beer, and wine in the elevator and send it up to the second level." Jack looked at his watch. "I've got cold beer in a cooler on the deck. We can go out on the deck and catch up."

"My god, I can see why you were considering retirement. This place and the views are spectacular," Micah exclaimed.

"How about a swim?" Duffy asked no one in particular.

"I'm in," responded Hardy. "How about the rest of you?"

Pops gave Duffy a thumbs-down.

"I think I'll drink a couple of more beers and do some catching up with Jack," Micah answered. "You kids go frolic in the surf."

Jack wandered over to the far railing where Micah was surveying the beach. "How's your dad doing?"

"It's worse than they let on. He's terminal. He was diagnosed with stage four lung cancer about a month ago. According to his doctor, he's got less than a month. My mother is in no shape to give him the care he needs; we put him in a nursing home with hospice care. Wednesday, I'm flying back out and will stay until…" Micah started to choke up.

Jack placed his hand on Micah's shoulder. "I'm sorry, man. If there's anything I can do, including financial help, I'm here for you."

"Thanks, I really appreciate that. Luckily, they have a great health insurance plan. On that note, I think I'll have another beer. How about you?"

"Absolutely, let me get them. Two Dogfish IPAs coming up."

"Make that three," Pops added.

"Pace yourself, old man," Micah admonished.

Jack had just finished lighting the grill when the front doorbell rang. When he opened the door, he was surprised to see J. R. standing there with his left hand holding the back of Tim's collar and his right hand holding Kate's collar. Tim was doing all he could do to stifle a laugh.

"I found these two prowling around the front of your house. I just wanted you to know before I take them downtown and book them for trespassing," J. R. announced.

"Nice entrance, you three. Come on in and meet the other cast of characters."

Kate smiled and pointed to Tim and J. R.. "It wasn't my idea. It was those two jokers."

J. R. high-fived Tim and followed Jack out to the deck.

"Gentlemen, allow me to introduce you to my neighbors and our chief of police. This is Kate Simpson, my next-door neighbor, and her son, Tim. Tim is in sixth grade, and Kate is the director of the Sussex County Women's Center and the executive director of the Delaware Women's Center

Foundation. The distinguished older gentlemen wearing the aloha shirt and shorts is J. R. Johnson, the chief of the Rehoboth Beach Police Department. Let me get the three of you something to drink before I introduce you to this motley crew." Jack motioned toward his four comrades, each working on at least their third beer.

"I know what Tim wants. How about you and J. R.?"

"I'll have a beer," Kate replied.

"Make that two," J. R. responded.

"Now, let me introduce you to four of my closest friends. The tall rugged-looking one is Micah Cruise. We went through SEAL training together in Coronado and served a tour in Iraq and two tours in Afghanistan with SEAL Team 2. We were both recruited by the FBI and, until recently, Micah headed up the Phoenix office. He's now at Quantico as an instructor. Mark Hardy, or Doc, as we affectionately call him, was assigned to our SEAL team as a corpsman on our last deployment to Afghanistan. He may actually hold a record for the most Purple Hearts received in one tour—five." J. R. let out an audible gasp of amazement and respect. "Mark is currently the chief EMT with Fairfax County Fire and Rescue. Next is Frank Duffy. Duffy was part of SEAL Team 2 on our last deployment and served as the team's weapons and explosives expert. He now serves as part of the president's Secret Service detail. Last is Matt O'Brien, who served as the chief of our SEAL team. While he's only eight years older than Micah and me, we all refer to him as 'Pops.' He currently works as head of security for FBI headquarters. I'm thrilled that you could meet them. They've been a big part of my life for years."

Jack directed everyone toward the bar. "I'll take your drink orders once more and then you are all on you own. After that, Kate and I will prepare dinner while Tim briefs the rest of you on his project. I am convinced that you will all be as impressed as I was with his research, and it's the reason I asked Micah and Duffy to bring their diving gear. If you'll all head into the family room, Kate and I will start cooking."

Kate walked over to the grill where Jack had just finished seasoning the steaks. "They seem like a great bunch of guys."

"They are. We've been through some pretty tough times together and lost a lot of good friends. You experience something like that together, you soon learn who your real friends are. We've trusted each other with our lives. You don't get more committed than that."

Kate nodded and held her beer up as if to say, *Amen to that.*

"OK, the steaks are ready to go on the grill. If you'll take care of the potatoes and salad, I'll set the table and open two or three bottles of wine. It's such a beautiful night. I thought we should eat on the deck."

"I agree." Kate turned and headed toward the kitchen.

Kate returned after about fifteen minutes, handed Jack a glass of cabernet, and sat in the chair next to the grill. "The salad is ready, and the baked potatoes will take another twenty minutes or so."

Jack took a sip of wine. "Perfect. The steaks will need another twenty or thirty minutes also."

Kate looked at the grill. "Those steaks are enormous. I'm not sure that Tim—or I, for that matter—will be able to finish ours."

"That's why God invented leftovers." Jack twirled the tongs around his index finger. "So I hope that you and Tim are still planning to go out fishing with us tomorrow."

Kate hesitated for a second. "That depends. Can you get me back home by five?"

"I suppose so, but why do you have to be back by five?"

"I've got a date tomorrow night, and he's picking me up at seven. I'll need a couple of hours to get ready."

"A date?"

"Yes, a date. What, you don't think I could have a date?"

"It's not that. It's just, well…" Jack nervously tried to respond but couldn't think of a response that wouldn't dig him a deeper hole.

Duffy and Pops unknowingly rescued him.

"Kate, your son is amazing. I can't believe he's only in sixth grade. The research he's done is phenomenal. He had all of us spellbound," Duffy proclaimed. "I'm convinced his research is accurate and there is a sunken Spanish galleon out there."

Jack turned to Pops. "Would you tell the rest of them to come on out? Dinner is about to be served."

Doc placed his wineglass on the table and leaned back in his chair. "That was the best steak dinner I've had in years, maybe ever."

Micah raised his wineglass in a toast. "Here's to Kate and Jack. Morton's would be envious of the dinner the two of you prepared tonight."

Jack gestured to Kate for a response.

Kate raised her wineglass. "It's been a real pleasure to meet all of you, and preparing a salad and taking baked potatoes out of the oven isn't all that challenging. Jack did all the heavy lifting."

Jack held up his hand. "Enough of the accolades. It was a joint effort. Now, let's discuss tomorrow morning. You've heard Tim's research and seen the redrawn map of the coast as we estimate it looked like when *La Concepción* went down in the hurricane. Based upon the logbook entries and Vega's diary, Tim and I have approximated the location of the galleon at the time of the sinking. I would propose that Micah, Duffy, and I make an exploratory dive at that location tomorrow morning at sunrise."

Pops and Kate groaned audibly.

"All of you are well acquainted with zero-dark-thirty. Well, maybe not Kate and Tim. I propose that we leave here at 5:00 a.m. That should give us enough time to get to the dive site shortly after sunrise. The three of us will do a thirty-minute dive, and then we can head out to fish for the rest of the day."

"I'm guessing no run in the morning?" Kate asked Jack.

"No time, unless you want to get up at three. Maybe we can push our run until Sunday morning."

Kate got up from the table. "Given that, Tim and I are off to bed. We'll see you all tomorrow morning."

J. R. stood up and stretched his arms. "Since I have to work tomorrow, I'll help Jack clean up while the rest of you hit the sack. It was great meeting everyone."

Jack followed J. R. and Micah into the kitchen. "Most of the plates are clean. Just rinse them off and put them in the dishwasher. I'll pick up everything else."

Jack walked J. R. to the front door. "I'm sorry you can't join us tomorrow morning, but I hope you can come over tomorrow night. I've ordered a bushel of hard-shell crabs and a keg of Dogfish Head 60 Minute IPA."

"I'll coax Crockett into earning some overtime pay. What can I bring?"

Jack opened the door. "An appetite."

CHAPTER FORTY

Tim looked like he was sleepwalking as he stumbled down the driveway with Kate. Micah was moving the fishing and dive gear around the back of the Explorer to make room for two coolers that Jack and Doc had brought out from the elevator.

Jack turned to Tim. "You can sleep in the back of the Jeep. Climb in." He looked at Kate inquisitively. "What's in the backpack?"

"Aren't you a little nosy this morning? If you must know, I have a bathing suit, a change of clothes, two large thermoses with coffee, and several types of Danish for your buddies. There's also cream and sugar. Satisfied?"

"You seem to be a little cranky this morning. Not enough beauty sleep?"

Kate held up her mug. "I'll be fine after another cup of coffee."

"OK, it's time to hit the road. Micah, you follow me."

Rehoboth Avenue was deserted as Jack headed through town for Route 1. That was not the case as they drove through Dewey Beach. The twenty- and thirty-somethings were stumbling back to their rentals after boozing it up Friday night at the Starboard, Bottle and Cork, and a myriad of other bars along the coastal highway.

"Kate, would you pour me a cup of coffee? I think last night is starting to catch up with me. Better make it black. By the way, how's Tim doing back there?"

Kate peered back between the bucket seats. "He's asleep. He really enjoyed last night with your friends. That's all he could talk about on the way home. Thank you."

"For what?" Jack asked.

"Timmy really looks up to you. You treat him like he's an adult, and he cherishes that feeling."

"You're fortunate. You have raised a wonderful and intelligent young man."

"That may be so, but if you find any treasure or artifacts on your dive this morning, they'll be no living with him."

Jack and Micah pulled into the marina and parked next to the docks.

Jack turned to Kate. "One thing about going out early—you have your choice of prime parking places. It's probably going to take two trips, but the boat is only about forty yards down the dock on the right. Everyone grab something and follow me." Jack headed down the dock, followed by Kate and a still sleepy Tim.

"My god, it's the frigging *Queen Mary*," Pops exclaimed.

"Just load the gear," Jack directed.

"What's in the coolers?" Kate asked.

"Aren't we nosy?"

"Touché."

"If you must know, the blue cooler has beer, soda, water, six Italian subs, four turkey wraps, and six roast beef wraps. The large fishing cooler contains ice in case we get lucky fishing."

"Do you think you've got enough food?" Kate asked facetiously.

"You haven't seen these guys pack it away. Believe me, there won't be much left uneaten."

Micah handed the last bit of diving gear up to Jack.

"That appears to be everything. Let's get underway."

Jack maneuvered the boat out of the slip and headed into the inlet channel. The eastern horizon was starting to glow a bright crimson. It was going to be a spectacular sunrise. There wasn't a cloud to be seen. Jack motioned Tim to come forward.

"When we get through the channel and into the open ocean, I want you to take the conn. Did your grandfather explain to you what 'take the conn' means?"

"I don't think so. If he did, I forgot what it means."

"It's a naval term. It means to take over navigational duties on the bridge of a ship."

"Are you asking me to take over for you driving the boat?"

"Exactly. I have to get into my wetsuit, and I need someone I trust to get us to the dive site. That's you." Jack could easily see the prideful look in Tim's eyes. "Do you remember when we estimated where *La Concepción* went down?"

"Yes."

"Well, I calculated the longitude and latitude of that location and entered it into the boat's computer." Jack pointed to a computer screen on the boat's dash. "See that little boat icon and the red dot at the top of the screen?"

"Is the boat icon us? I mean where we are right now?"

"Yes, and as you can see, it shows us moving through the channel and out to sea. The red dot is the location of the dive site. In about five minutes, we'll be out of the channel. The currents in the channel are a little tricky or I'd turn the conn over to you right now."

Tim waited by Jack's side until the boat was clear of the channel entrance.

Jack hopped down from the captain's chair. "OK, Captain, she's all yours. Just keep her headed for the red dot on the screen. When you start getting closer, ease back on the throttle. I'm going below to change."

Jack picked up his duffel bag and had started to go below when Tim asked, "Will you teach me to scuba dive?"

"You'll have to be a little older, but yes, I will teach you how to scuba dive. That is, with your mother's permission of course."

"How old?"

"Let's say next summer when you're almost thirteen. How does that sound?"

"I can't wait."

The boat was barely moving when Jack looked at the computer screen on the dash. "Great job. Now, cut the engines and drop the front anchor. It's the button on your right under the fuel gauge."

"I'm guessing it's the one labeled 'BOW ANCHOR.'"

"That's correct, smartass."

Tim laughed and did as instructed. Jack moved to the back of the boat and threw the rear anchor and chain into the water. The sun had risen completely out of the water and lit up the eastern sky.

"Tim, see that disc and rope in the corner? Would you bring it over to me?"

The disc was about eighteen inches in diameter and a half an inch thick. It was equally divided into four quadrants, two opposites painted red and the other two white. A weighted metal ball hung from the bottom, and a lanyard was attached to the top center.

Tim handed Jack the disc assembly.

Addressing only Tim, Jack asked, "Do you know what this contraption is?"

Tim shook his head. "Not a clue."

"It's called a Secchi disc. The lanyard is marked in one-foot increments. I'll lower the disc into the water. When we can no longer see the disc, we'll read its depth with the markings on the lanyard. That will tell us what the visibility is at the surface. Because the distance to the bottom is over forty feet, only a small amount of light will penetrate to that depth. Therefore, the visibility on the bottom will be significantly less that at the surface. However, the Secchi disc reading will give us some idea about what we will be dealing with as far as visibility down there is concerned."

Jack continued to slowly lower the disc into the water. "Tell me when you can't see the disc any longer."

Tim watched carefully as the disc disappeared. "I can't see it," Tim soon exclaimed.

"OK, reach down to the surface of the water and put this clip on the lanyard."

Tim lay down on the diving platform of the boat, reached down, and attached the clip as Jack instructed.

"I'll pull it up, and you tell me what it reads."

Tim grabbed the lanyard and looked at the marking just below the clip. "It's a little more than eighteen feet."

Jack turned to Micah and Duffy. "I packed three OrcaTorch dive lights in the duffel. Duffy, would you grab them? I think we're going to need them down there."

Jack pulled three nylon ropes of varying lengths from the duffel. A six-inch carabiner was fastened to each end of the rope. "I think visibility is going to be a problem. I fabricated three ropes for use on the bottom. They are twenty, forty, and sixty feet in length. There's a carabiner on each end. We'll each attach one end to the anchor chain and the other to our dive belts. We'll swim out to the length of the rope and move slowly around the anchor chain in a clockwise direction. That should allow us to cover over fifteen thousand square feet of the bottom. Any questions?"

Hearing none, the three divers began checking their gear. Each diver checked his gear in an orderly sequence—regulator, gauges, air hose, and mask. Duffy was the first to finish his inspection. He took a couple of breaths of air from his mouthpiece and moved to the dive platform to wait for Micah and Jack. The three lowered themselves into the water, Jack gave Tim a thumbs-up, and they disappeared beneath the surface. When they reached the bottom, Jack took a depth reading: the gauge read forty-seven feet. As Jack suspected, the visibility was limited to about eight to ten feet. They turned on their dive lights, attached their ropes to the anchor chain, and swam off to the length of their individual ropes.

Jack, having the shortest rope, also was responsible for the area within a ten-foot radius of the anchor chain. It took almost twenty minutes for all three divers to circumnavigate the anchor. Micah, having the most area to cover, was the last one finished. Jack signaled a thumbs-down, and Duffy responded in kind. Jack could see Micah smiling behind his mask as he raised his hand. He held up a small piece of metal, about six to eight inches long. They turned off their dive lights, and Jack gave the signal to surface.

Tim waited impatiently at the stern of the boat, but suddenly started to get excited as he saw the large number of air bubbles breach the surface of the water, indicating that the divers were on their way up. Duffy was the first one onto the dive platform. Jack followed, and Micah handed him the piece of metal he'd found.

"What's that?" Tim shouted excitedly, pointing to the metal plate.

"We don't know. Let us get our tanks off, and we'll take a closer look at it," Micah responded.

The three handed their tanks up to Pops and threw their fins over the transom and onto the deck above.

Micah handed the rusted metal plate to Jack, who carefully examined it from all angles. Tim watched anxiously.

"I think this is the firing plate off a flintlock rifle. See the small hole here?" Jack pointed to a small hole about an eighth of an inch in diameter near one end of the plate. "The frizzen and cock are missing, but I think this is the pan." He pointed to a small cuplike extension. "If we put this in an acid bath, we might be able to uncover some markings on the plate."

"Is that all you found?" Tim asked disappointedly.

"I'm afraid so," Jack responded. "Remember, this was a shot in the dark. We only covered a small area. I'm still convinced *La Concepción* is down there. We're just going to have to take another approach to finding her."

Jack stood up and ruffled Tim's long red hair. "Don't get discouraged. Let me get out of this wetsuit, and we'll all try to put out heads together. In the meantime, bring up the bow anchor, and I'll have Pops pull up the stern anchor."

CHAPTER FORTY-ONE

Jack appeared out of the cabin, vigorously drying his hair with a beach towel. He moved toward Kate and Micah talking in the corner.

"I could use a beer. How about the two of you?"

"It's not even nine o'clock," Kate scolded.

"I thought you went to college," Jack chided.

"It was a civilized college."

"Count me in on the beers," Micah responded.

Duffy poked his head out of the cabin. "Make that three."

"Kate?" Jack asked.

"Oh, what the hell, but make mine a Coors Light."

Jack dug five beers out of the cooler, tossed one to Pops, and handed three to Duffy to distribute. "Let me get Tim headed in the right direction. Tim, you ready to take the conn again?"

Tim hopped into the captain's chair. "I'm ready. Where to?"

Jack turned on the computer screen and typed in a few numbers. "We'll head south toward Ocean City. The red dot on the screen is our starting point. When you get there, turn the boat around, heading north. We'll troll north-northeast forty-five degrees at five knots."

"Will I get to fish?"

"Once I get the two pilot chairs attached to their mounting plates, you'll be the first one up. We'll fish two at a time so we don't get the lines tangled."

Jack rejoined Micah and Kate. "You two look deep in thought."

"I was just thinking about your promise to Tim to try another approach. Remember that ensign you were dating in Coronado after we completed SEAL training?"

"Of course. Morgan Wagner—she went by Maggie. She introduced Nancy and me. I haven't seen or talked to her since Nancy's funeral. What about her?"

"Wasn't she somehow involved in undersea mapping?"

"When I last talked to her, she was a lieutenant commander, just assigned as the deputy director of the navy's Undersea Mapping and Rescue Command in Norfolk, Virginia. She was one of two deputy directors. Her responsibility was the undersea mapping mission of the command. But that was almost three years ago."

"Do you still have her contact information?"

"I think so. What are you thinking?"

"She may be able to head us in the right direction. To cover the amount of area we're talking about, we'll need some kind of mapping capability. She might know of commercial firms that do that kind of work or equipment that we could rent or purchase ourselves." Micah shrugged. "It's just a thought."

"When we get back, I'll look for her number and give her a call on Monday."

Tim pointed to the computer screen. "Jack, we're at the red dot."

"OK, hop down and pick out one of the fishing poles over there. You get into the pilot chair on the right. I think we'll use a Gamakatsu 6/0 hook and a chunk of squid as bait." Jack attached the hook to the line and handed the rod and reel to Tim. "When I tell you, start letting out your line."

Jack took the controls and maneuvered the boat to a forty-five-degree north-northeast heading. He pushed the throttle slightly forward, and the boat moved slowly ahead. "OK, start letting out your line."

For almost an hour, Jack steered the boat on course. The group had settled in for the afternoon. Kate had changed into a bikini and was sunning herself on a towel on the front top of the cabin. Pops was snoozing below deck while Duffy fished with Tim.

Micah handed Jack another beer and leaned against the console. "Tell me a little more about these murders you're involved with."

"I'm sort of tangentially involved, but that would be a better topic for discussion tonight when J. R. is present. We could use your input, and I have a few favors to ask."

Duffy turned around and shouted, "I think Tim has a fish on the line."

"Would you teach him how to reel it in?" Jack asked Micah.

Micah stood next to Tim. "All right, you're going to reel this baby in by yourself. Let the rod do the work. Work the fish closer and closer to the boat by pulling the rod tip up, then reel in rapidly as you drop the tip down. When the fish gets close to the boat, I'll snag it with the net. Does that make sense?"

Tim nodded and furiously started reeling in the fish.

"Jack, look at this!" Micah shouted. "I'll need the hook. This fish is too big for the net."

Kate heard the shouts and came back to see what all the racket was about.

"I think your son just caught dinner," Jack announced proudly.

Micah pulled the fish up into the boat. "It's a dolphin fish. Looks to be about four feet in length."

"I didn't think dolphin fish were found in waters this far north. Aren't they tropical fish?" Duffy wondered aloud.

"They are. However, this time of year, the Gulf Stream brings warm water up from the tropics. That could explain it. Regardless, this is quite a catch."

"It doesn't look like a dolphin," Tim said.

"It's not. You've probably seen it on the menu as ma-hi-mahi. Let's put it on ice, and when we get home, I'll teach you how to gut and clean it. We'll cut it up and vacuum-seal it. You and your mother will have plenty of mahi-mahi to eat over the next few months. Now it's time for you to turn your chair, rod, and reel over to Micah and return to the conn."

CHAPTER FORTY-TWO

Over the next two hours, Micah, Duffy, Jack, and Pops reeled in two bluefish, two skipjacks, one southern flounder, and one wahoo, plus countless throwbacks. Jack was just about to call it an afternoon when Micah tapped him on the shoulder and pointed off to the port side. "What do you suppose that's all about?"

About a half mile in front of them on the port side of the boat, a freighter sat dead in the water. Pulled up next to the freighter's stern was a fifty-foot fishing boat similar in size and design to a Chesapeake oyster boat. It appeared that cargo was being lowered from the freighter into the smaller boat.

"That's a bit unusual. Ships going into Delaware Bay pick up a river pilot who navigates the ship into the bay. During heavy commercial traffic, ships queue up in the bay to await a dock to unload in Philly. They seldom, if ever, anchor out here. And what are they unloading?"

"If it's something illegal, I seriously doubt that they would be doing it in broad daylight," Duffy speculated.

"Pops, would you mind going below to get a closer look? There's a pair of binoculars on the starboard bunk.

The porthole in the galley is tinted. You can see out, but they can't see you. Try and see what they're up to."

Pops headed below, retrieved the binoculars, and moved to the galley. After a couple of minutes, he moved to the stairs, looked up at Jack. "There are three men on the stern rail with automatic weapons. The banana clips would seem to indicate AK-47s. They have eyes on us, and a parabolic microphone pointed our way. I would suggest if you're going to talk, turn away from the ship. Also, put some music on and turn it up. Make it look like we're on a party cruise. Maybe Kate should start dancing with one of the guys."

Jack turned to Duffy. "Now what do you think about this being something illegal?"

"The AK-47s sealed it for me. I think it's something illegal."

"What about the boat tied up alongside?"

"Let me take another look. I got distracted by the AK-47s." Pops returned within seconds. "They're lowering large packages in nets to the boat. I would estimate that each package is four feet in length, three feet wide, and about a foot thick."

Jack turned to Micah. "This is very suspicious. I propose we cruise about two miles north, turn toward shore, and head south, putting the shoreline between us and the oyster boat. Let's see where she's heading."

Jack yelled down to Pops, "Come up on deck and bring the binoculars. Keep an eye on that freighter. When you see the oyster boat pull away from her, let me know."

Pops moved surreptitiously to the stern of the boat and crouched down in the port-side stern corner of the boat.

"Reel in the lines," Jack ordered. He pushed the throttle slowly forward and the boat slowly picked up speed.

After about ten minutes, Jack turned to port and headed for shore near the northern end of Cape Henlopen. He moved in until he was about five hundred yards offshore. Then he turned south and paralleled the shoreline.

"The oyster boat just emerged from behind the freighter heading toward shore," Pops announced.

"Keep an eye on her. She's slow, so I'm going to try and get ahead of her. She has to be heading to Indian River inlet." Jack pushed the throttle full forward, and the bow lifted up as the boat lurched ahead.

When Jack reached the channel entrance, the oyster boat was at least a thousand yards behind them and heading for the inlet.

Jack turned to address everyone. "When we get to the marina, I'll back the boat into the slip. Micah and I will take the Zodiac into the bay and wait for the oyster boat to come in. Pack as much as you can into the Explorer, and put the rest in the Jeep." Jack tossed Duffy his keys, and Micah did the same. "Leave the keys to the Jeep on top of the front driver's side tire. Kate has to be back to her house by five—it's almost four now. The keys to my house are under the front doormat. In case we're not back in time, I'm expecting a bushel of crabs to be delivered around 5:30 p.m. There's a check on the kitchen counter."

Jack maneuvered the Zodiac out of its slip and into the bay. He headed along the east shore and pulled into a small inlet to await the arrival of the oyster boat. Fortunately, the bay was overflowing with motor and sailboats, Jet Skis, and kite surfers. The Zodiac would hardly look conspicuous. After about twenty minutes, the oyster boat appeared, rounding the channel and heading into the bay. Jack started up the Zodiac and sped north along the eastern edge of the bay toward North Beach.

He turned to Micah. "When we get near North Beach, I'll swing to the west."

Jack watched the oyster boat approach from the entrance to Bald Eagle Creek. "I think he's heading for Love Creek. Once he's out of sight, we'll follow him at a distance."

Jack pushed the throttle forward and slowly approached the entrance to Love Creek. There were several pleasure boats moving in and out of the creek. "Do you see him yet?" Jack asked.

"Yes, he's about two hundred yards in front of us. He's just in front of that Donzi pulling the water-skier."

"I've got him, but we've got a problem," Jack responded. "The creek narrows significantly about three hundred yards ahead of his current location. I'm going to race ahead of him and head under the Love Creek Bridge. Move to the stern and make it look like you're working on something, but keep an eye on him. When I get past the bridge, I'll turn around, and we'll head back slowly."

Jack slowed going under the bridge, moved about one hundred yards up the creek, and spun the Zodiac around in a tight arc. He maneuvered the boat under the bridge and started slowly down the creek. "Do you see him?" he asked.

"No, I lost sight of him when we went under the bridge to turn around. He was moving very slowly. He must have turned in between here and the crab shack on the right side of the creek."

Jack moved slowly down the creek, looking left and right for some sign of the oyster boat.

"What's that?" Micah asked.

"Don't know. It looks like some kind of abandoned warehouse. It appears to have a dock underneath, but there's a metal enclosure obscuring our view. I don't see any movement or evidence that he pulled in here. Let's keep going."

Jack moved up and down the narrow stretch of the creek for almost an hour, examining both shorelines carefully. "It's no use. He simply disappeared."

"Doesn't make sense. He was only out of our sight for less than five minutes, and he certainly didn't get past us."

"There's no sense in hanging around here. Let's head back to the ranch."

CHAPTER FORTY-THREE

Micah stood by the door to Jack's bedroom for about ten minutes before he spoke. "What are you doing?"

Jack sheepishly turned away from the window. "I just want to make sure Kate is all right."

"She is going on a date with a doctor, not a serial killer. What's really the matter?" Micah walked into the room. "A blind man can see you two have feelings for each other. Why don't you just tell her and end this dance you two are doing?"

"Don't be absurd. We're just good friends," Jack stated defensively.

"Fine, have it your way. Just don't be surprised if she finds someone else while you attempt to get your head out of your ass. Let's go. Your guests are waiting for you on the deck."

≈

"Hey, you two, grab a beer. J. R. is teaching us how to eat Maryland crabs," Duffy shouted.

Jack drew two beers from the keg and handed one to Micah. "Look, I'm still having a difficult time getting on with my life after Nancy's death, but it's starting to get a little bit easier every day. I know you're looking out for me, and I appreciate it."

"Come on, let's get some crabs before those gluttons eat them all." Micah playfully put his arm around Jack's neck and squeezed.

Jack looked around the deck. "Where's Doc?"

Duffy, Pops, Micah, and Tim broke into uncontrollable laughter. "The last we saw of him, he looked like a lobster. He's upstairs applying after-sun lotion to virtually his entire body. At last check, he had gone through two bottles," Pops explained. "We may not see him for a while. I told him he should start drinking to numb the pain."

"So what's on the agenda for tomorrow?" Duffy inquired.

"No plans. I thought we could have a leisurely breakfast and spend some time on the beach," Jack offered.

"That might not work so well for Doc," Pops added, and again the table broke into a fit of laughter.

"When everyone's done, please join me in the family room. J. R. and I would like your collective thoughts on the recent murders we're investigating."

Slowly everyone moved into the family room and got comfortable. Jack pulled Tim aside. "What have you heard about these recent murders?"

"I know you and Mom found a dead girl on the beach, and I was with you and Mom when her friend was shot on the beach last Sunday morning. I've also read a couple of articles about them in the papers."

"Do you want me to walk you home?"

"If you don't mind, I'd like to stay until Mom gets home from her date."

"All right, grab another root beer and join us."

"Anyone interested in an after-dinner drink?" Jack inquired.

Before anyone could answer, Doc walked gingerly down the stairs and into the room. Duffy fell off the couch and onto the floor laughing. Pops got up and walked out to the deck to get another beer so Doc wouldn't see him laughing. Tim couldn't contain himself either. Jack and Micah just grinned.

"Very funny," Doc mumbled through swollen lips.

"You look awful. Maybe we should get you to a doctor," Micah seriously offered.

"I'll be fine."

"Well, at least get some water in you before you consume any alcohol," Jack advised.

Without answering, Doc walked slowly out to the deck, got a bottle of water out of the cooler, and poured himself a beer.

"He walks like he just got off his horse after a long trail ride," Micah observed, and again the room broke into a fit of laughter.

After everyone had settled down, Jack and J. R. provided the group with a detailed rundown of everything that had happened regarding the two recent murders.

Micah spoke first. "You both said you don't think you have probable cause to search the boat. I disagree. Do you think the marina manager would provide you with a statement regarding what he saw and was told?"

"We're not his favorite people, but I think it could be arranged," J. R. speculated.

Micah picked up the autopsy folder off the coffee table. "The marina manager's statement and this, particularly the findings, should get you that warrant. In this county, you must have a law-and-order judge you can approach."

Jack looked at J. R.. "I'll bet Judge Hoffman would help us."

"I'll see if we can get an appointment with him Monday morning, and tomorrow we'll go and see our friend at the marina."

Jack walked upstairs to his office and returned carrying a manila envelope. He held up the envelope as he approached Micah. "This has to do with the favor I told you about yesterday. There are two fingerprint cards in the envelope and a few strands of blond hair. I'd like you to run the prints and see what pops, as well as run DNA on the hair."

"The prints are no problem, but I'll have to go to your lab people for the DNA workup," Micah cautioned.

"That shouldn't be a problem. Take them to Jacqueline Nguyen and explain that they're for me. She'll get it done."

Jack walked back to his bedroom and looked out the window toward Kate's house. He noticed a light in the kitchen and a shadow pass by the window. He looked at his watch—9:28 p.m. He turned away and walked back to the family room.

"Tim, I'm pretty sure your mother is home. So say good night to everyone, and I'll walk you over."

Tim went around the room high-fiving everyone until he got to Doc, and he once again started laughing. The rest of the room started laughing as well.

"I'm sorry. Hopefully I'll see you tomorrow on the beach."

Again, the room started laughing.

Tim opened the front door to his house, and Jack followed him inside. Kate was standing at the other end of the kitchen staring down into her glass of wine. She looked up and smiled weakly as Jack entered the room.

"I'm delivering Tim home safe and sound, well fed, and laughed out."

Kate tilted her head to the side questioningly. "Laughed out?"

"It's a long story. I'll let him fill you in."

Kate held up her glass. "Would you like to join me?"

"I'll take a beer if you have one. How was your date?"

Kate opened the refrigerator and handed Jack a Budweiser. She sat down on the stool without answering Jack's last question.

"Are you all right?" Jack asked hesitantly. He could see tears welling up in her eyes.

"It was a disaster. He took me to Zebra's for dinner. We sat on the porch. It started out very romantic, but all he could talk about all night was himself and being a doctor. He is totally narcissistic. He didn't give a shit about me or what I liked, did, or thought. I would have been better off hanging out with you and your friends tonight."

"I'm really sorry, Kate."

"I know I'm not much company tonight. So if you don't mind, I think I'll go to bed."

"I understand." Jack quickly finished his beer, put it in the recycling bin, and said good night. Halfway to the door, he turned. "I know this is usually a *you* question, but are you still up for a run in the morning?"

"You bet I am, and you'd better be ready for the run of your life."

"That's the old Kate I know. I wouldn't have it any other way. See you at seven."

"Let's make it six. I've got tennis with Roberta at nine."

Jack groaned. "Six it is."

CHAPTER FORTY-FOUR

J ack and J. R. sat on a bench outside Judge Hoffman's chambers, awaiting his arrival. J. R. had requested an 8:00 a.m. appointment with the judge's administrative assistant. He looked at his watch. The judge was already ten minutes late, and his administrative assistant had yet to arrive. Mondays were particularly laid back. There were no cases scheduled to be heard, and after all, this was lower, slower Delaware.

Judge Hoffman and Cathy, his assistant, leisurely walked toward them, coffee in hand. The judge had on black shorts and a golf shirt as a not-so-subtle hint as to his afternoon plans.

Cathy unlocked the door, and Judge Hoffman signaled Jack and J. R. to follow him inside. He opened the door to his chambers and instructed them to take a seat.

"What's so important that you got me in here this early?" he asked neither of them in particular.

J. R. leaned forward in his chair. "Judge, we would like to get a warrant to search a boat in the Lewes marina belonging to Vincent Puglisi. He's purported to be a member of the Giovannati crime family out of Philadelphia."

"Unfortunately, I know Vinny. He's a lousy golfer and a cheat. So what has he done now?"

J. R. continued, "We have reason to believe he aided and abetted in the murder and disposal of Anna Campbell's body. Before her murder, she worked for him as a waitress at the Roadhouse restaurant in Lewes."

"Show me your evidence."

J. R. handed the judge a handwritten signed statement from the marina manager.

Judge Hoffman read the statement, placed it down on his desk, and peered over the top rim of his glasses. "You want me to issue a search warrant based on this?" Hoffman picked up the statement and mockingly waved it at them.

"Judge, that's not all." J. R. pointed toward Jack. "We also observed blood in the back of Puglisi's boat."

"Gentlemen, I've been known to stretch the limits from time to time in the interest of justice, but even I can't issue a warrant on this kind of flimsy evidence."

Jack picked up the file folder he'd placed earlier on the chair next to him. "Judge, this is Anna Campbell's autopsy report. I'd like you to read the findings, particularly item number five."

Judge Hoffman opened the folder and scanned the pages. When he got to the summary, he read the findings very carefully. He put the folder down and looked up at Jack. "This is disgusting."

"It's worse that disgusting, Judge. It's abhorrent."

Hoffman pressed the intercom button on his desk phone.

"Yes, Judge?" came the response.

"Cathy, prepare a search warrant for my signature. I'll email you the particulars in a second." The judge turned toward Jack and J. R.. "You've got your search warrant, gentlemen. You can wait in Cathy's office. She'll finish typing it up, I'll sign it, and you'll be off."

J. R. tossed Jack the keys to the squad car. "You drive. I'll call Chief Conrad, read him in, and have him meet us at the boat. It's his jurisdiction, and I want to make sure we do this by the book. I'll have him bring some evidence bags and rubber gloves. Can you think of anything else?"

"No, I think that about covers it."

Jack pulled out of the parking lot and headed through downtown Georgetown toward the Lewis-Georgetown Highway. "This is cool. I've never driven a police car before. Can I use the siren?"

J. R. glanced across at him scornfully. "Touch that siren and I'll break your arm."

Jack laughed and pressed the accelerator to the floor.

"Keep it up and I'll write you a ticket myself. You know, I think you've been hanging around Kate's son too much. You're starting to act like a kid yourself."

Jack eased off the accelerator. "Sorry, just trying in inject a little levity into the situation."

Jack pulled the squad car into the marina parking lot and drove up next to the slip where Vinny's boat was docked. Chief Conrad and a deputy were standing next to the boat. Conrad jumped down to the parking lot and walked over to their car. "Thanks for including me in on this, J. R.."

J. R. got out of the passenger side and shook Conrad's hand. "I wouldn't have it any other way. After all, this is your jurisdiction. I'm at your command. Here's the warrant. Oh, by the way, I expect we'll be seeing Vinny around eleven thirty. He usually takes a few of his girls out for a 'luncheon cruise' around that time. Be prepared for some fireworks."

Conrad pointed toward the boat. "See my deputy over there? When he's off duty, he moonlights as an MMA fighter. I never leave home without him."

J. R. nodded his head and smiled. "You can be assured that we will treat him with the utmost respect. Maybe he should greet Vinny when he arrives."

"Great minds think alike, J. R.. I was just thinking the same thing. By the way, he's fighting Saturday night in Dover. I can get a couple of more tickets if you two want to go with me."

J. R. shot Conrad a thumbs-up. "I don't know about him, but count me in."

"How about you, Jack?" Conrad asked.

"I appreciate the offer, but I'm going to have to take a pass. Prior engagement."

Jack had already begun to search the boat when J. R. and Conrad joined him.

"Look up here." Jack pointed to the underside of the gunwale. "That looks like blood spatter. Do you have any evidence swabs?"

Conrad walked to the other side of the boat and yelled to his deputy, "Andy, bring over the evidence kit. It's in the trunk."

Within minutes, Conrad's deputy appeared with the evidence kit. Conrad opened the box, put on rubber gloves, and handed Jack a pair, and a plastic tube containing a cotton swab. Jack donned the gloves, extracted the cotton swab from the tube, and swabbed a sample of blood from under the gunwale. He carefully placed the swab back in the tube and sealed it shut. With a black Sharpie, he identified the sample.

"J. R., do you still have the Nikon in the patrol car?" Jack asked.

J. R. tossed Conrad's deputy the keys. "Would you please bring me the Nikon camera? It's in the back seat."

The deputy raced off to the parking lot to retrieve the camera.

Jack took several pictures of the blood spatter and then moved to the boat's cabin. Three steps led down to the cabin. Toward the bow was a rather spacious bed that looked like it had recently been slept in. "Do you have a large evidence bag in your kit?" Jack asked Conrad.

"I do, but it's pretty big, like a contractor-sized bag."

"That's perfect. J. R., would you help me carefully get these sheets off the bunk and into the evidence bag?" In the cramped space, J. R. had all he could do to get into position to assist Jack. Together, they succeeded in getting the sheets into the bag. Jack then sealed the bag, labeled it, and handed it back to Chief Conrad.

Between the galley and the bunk was a small shower enclosure. Jack pulled aside the plastic curtain.

"This is odd," he said to no one in particular. "Would you hand me the camera?" J. R. passed the camera to Jack, who took several shots of the inside of the shower. He handed the camera back to J. R., reached down, and carefully picked up the wooden end of a sixteen-ounce rubber mallet lying near the drain. "I'll need a one-gallon evidence bag."

Jack held up the rubber mallet. Conrad dug a smaller bag out of the kit and handed it into the shower. Jack examined the rubber end of the mallet and placed it in the bag. He sealed and labeled the bag and again handed it back to Conrad. He turned to address J. R..

"Do you recall the X-ray of Anna Campbell's skull? I think this could have been the murder weapon."

J. R. heard the uproar first. "I think our boy and his bimbos have arrived. This should be entertaining."

Jack, J. R., and Conrad emerged from the cabin to see Vinny furiously attempting to get past Conrad's deputy. Finally, the deputy had enough. He picked Vinny off the ground and tossed him back toward the black van. He stumbled and fell to the ground. He slowly got up and brushed off his shorts.

Vinny recognized J. R. first. "What are you doing on my boat?" he screamed.

J. R. gleefully pulled the warrant out of his shirt pocket and waved it in the air. "This will explain everything, Vinny." He shouted to the deputy to let Vinny pass. "Make sure the girls remain in the van."

Vinny came waddling toward his boat as fast as his overweight frame would allow. "What do you think you're doing? I'll have both of your badges for this."

"You might want to read this first." J. R. handed Vinny the warrant. "In the interest of time, I'll explain it to you. You're holding a search warrant signed by Judge Hoffman. We believe that your boat was used in the commission of a crime. We submitted evidence to the judge, and he agreed that we had probable cause and issued the warrant to search your boat. We're just finishing gathering evidence. We'll send it to the crime lab, and the state's attorney will take it from there. In the meantime, the boat is a crime scene and therefore off-limits to you and anyone else not officially involved in the investigation."

Vinny looked like he was going to get sick. His shoulders sagged as he handed the search warrant back to J. R..

"Oh, by the way, this might be the appropriate time to contact your attorney. You and the girls have a great day."

J. R. turned to Jack. "Do you have everything you need?"

"Yes, but we need a fingerprint crew down here and deputies to put up crime scene tape."

"No problem. I'll get that done ASAP."

As they walked back to the patrol car, Jack stopped to address Conrad. "I understand that this is your jurisdiction, but where do you send the evidence to be tested and processed?"

"We use a private testing lab in Dover."

Jack thought for a minute. "Have you used them before, and are they competent?"

"We don't get many cases like this. I mean cases that require blood and DNA analysis. I know the state police use them. What are you thinking?"

"Before I answer that, let me ask you another question. How long does it take to get the results back?"

Conrad leaned against the dock's side rail. "As I said before, we don't have much cause to use the lab's services. I think the last time we did was over a year ago, and my recollection is that it took a while."

"Do me a favor, Chief—don't send it to them until you hear from me."

"What are you thinking?" J. R. asked. "Are you thinking the FBI?"

"I am, but I need a nexus between the crime and the FBI's jurisdiction. I'll call Micah and bounce it off him."

Jack opened the driver's side door and climbed behind the wheel.

J. R. stood in front of the car, arms crossed, staring at him. "What do you think you're doing?"

Jack leaned out the window. "I thought you wanted me to drive."

"That was a one-time thing, and even that was poor judgment on my part. Get in the passenger side."

"Sometimes you're no fun, J. R.," Jack said dejectedly.

CHAPTER FORTY-FIVE

Jack typed "Naval Station Norfolk" into the search bar. The website was considerably more sophisticated than he remembered, but it had been several years. He clicked on the drop-down menu labeled "ABOUT" and clicked on the item marked "BASE LOCATER." He didn't recognize any of the commands or offices. He jotted down the number at the bottom of the menu, grabbed his cell phone off the desk, and dialed the number.

"Naval Station Norfolk, this is Chief Petty Officer Daniels. How may I direct your call?"

"Good afternoon, Chief. I'm trying to locate Lieutenant Commander Morgan Wagner. I believe she's with the Undersea Mapping and Rescue Command."

"Sir, I'm sorry, that command no longer exists. During the recent base realignment, the navy consolidated and combined a number of commands. Give me a couple of minutes. I'm going to put you on hold. Don't hang up; I'll be right back."

Jack was treated to a rousing recruitment message while he waited.

"Sir, we have a Commander Morgan Wagner. She's currently the commander of the oceanography division of the Naval Meteorology and Oceanography Command."

"Thank you. That's got to be her."

"Just a moment, and I'll connect you."

Jack heard two clicks, and the phone began to ring.

"Oceanography Division, this is Petty Officer Third Class Morales. How may I assist you?"

"I'm calling for Commander Wagner."

"Sir, who may I say is calling?"

"Please tell her it's Jack Scanlon. She knows me."

"Mr. Scanlon, she's currently in a meeting, but I'll pass her a message."

"That's not necessary. Just have her call me, or I can call her back later, whichever works best."

"She's in a budget meeting, and I know she'd jump at any chance to get out of it. Let me tell her you're on the line. I'm going to put you on hold."

Jack put the phone on speaker and set it down on the desk. While he waited, he searched for Naval Meteorology and Oceanography Command. He clicked on Oceanography Division, and a picture of Maggie appeared on the screen. He read the mission statement, and sure enough, undersea mapping was listed as the division's primary mission.

"Jack Scanlon, it's been a long time. How's life treating you?"

"Maggie, it's good to hear your voice, and congratulations on your promotion. I'm hanging in there, and by the way, Micah Cruise said to say hello."

"Thank you. I put on the silver oak leaves in January. And tell Micah I said hello also. Is he still with the FBI? I haven't seen him since…" Maggie figuratively kicked herself.

Jack knew what she was about to say but didn't miss a beat. "He's still with the bureau but no longer in Phoenix. He's been assigned temporary duty as an instructor at the academy at Quantico."

"Listen, I'd love to talk longer, but I've got to get to another meeting. What can I do for you?"

Jack briefly related the story about the sunken galleon and their recent dive. "We were wondering if there are commercial firms that do undersea mapping or if the necessary equipment and software can be purchased or rented."

"The answer to all of that is yes. I can't believe you've turned into a treasure hunter. Listen, I've got an idea. Give me a couple of hours, and I'll call you back. Are you still at the 0750 number?"

"Yes. Talk to you soon." Jack ended the call and leaned back in his chair. It was already 4:30 p.m. He looked down at Winston. "Let's get you fed, and then how about you and I go out for tacos and beer at Que Pasa? We can sit on the beach."

Jack grabbed a beer from the cooler on the deck. Winston was curled up at his feet, savoring a foot-long rawhide bone, when Jack's phone rang. It was an 804 area code.

"Jack, it's Maggie."

Jack thought she sounded oddly excited.

"I've got a proposition for you that I think you'll like. First let me give you some background. About a month ago, I got a strange request from the State Department, endorsed by the secretary of defense, but not priority one. It was a request to search for a sunken German submarine off the Delaware coast. According to the archives, a World War II German submarine, the U-211, was sunk by a B-25 bomber on February 13, 1945, approximately five thousand yards southeast of the entrance to Delaware Bay. I put it on the back burner, but I'm thinking this is relatively close to the area you want searched. But get this—the submarine is believed to have been transporting Nazi gold to Argentina. The current German government recently learned about it and requested assistance from the US."

"I'm not really following you. What does that have to do with me?"

"I'm proposing that I bring one of our research vessels up to the University of Delaware's marine science facility in Lewes. We can kill two birds with one stone. Officially, I'll be searching for the German sub, but we'll expand the search to cover any area where you estimate your galleon might have gone down. I'll bring a crew of five. All you have to do is take us all out for a nice dinner and drinks. What do you think?"

"Sort of looks like we're both going to be treasure hunters. Can I reimburse the navy?"

"Absolutely not. We'll have to keep this one on the down-low, understood?"

"Got it. Is it possible to bring the young man who researched the sinking, and his mother?"

"How old is the boy?"

"He's eleven."

"No, now he's twelve."

Jack laughed. "I understand."

"It will probably take me a few days to put this whole thing in motion. I'll get back to you when I have a firm date. It will be great to see you again."

"You too, Maggie."

Jack picked up the phone and dialed Kate's number.

"Hi, Kate. Is Tim there?"

"If you're looking for a playdate, he's got to study."

"You are a laugh a minute. Remember I told him that we would find another way to search for *La Concepción*. Well, mission accomplished."

"Hold on. I'll get him for you."

"Tim, I've talked to the navy, and they have to do a subsurface search off the coast of Delaware, and they have agreed to help us find the *La Concepción*."

"I can't believe it. That's great. When?"

"I don't know yet, but I think it will be within a week or so."

"Can I go out on the boat?"

"Absolutely. Both you and your mom can go. However, as far as the navy's concerned, you're twelve. I'll call you as soon as I learn more."

CHAPTER FORTY-SIX

It was a little past 3:30 p.m. when Jack returned home from a frustrating day at the Sussex County Department of Motor Vehicles. He grabbed a bottle of water from the refrigerator and led Winston out onto the deck. Jack had no sooner put the phone down on the table when it rang.

"Jack, it's J. R.. Can you meet me at 639 Bay View Lane in Dewey, unit #312?"

"Sure, I'll be there in twenty minutes. What's up?"

"I think you'd better see for yourself."

Jack pulled into the parking lot. Two Dewey Beach police cars, an ambulance, and J. R.'s patrol car, all with their lights flashing, sat idling in front of the entrance to a four-story condominium. A large crowd had gathered outside.

Jack flashed his credentials to the officer guarding the front entrance, entered the building, and took the elevator to the third floor. As he exited the elevator, a Dewey Beach deputy stopped him from going any farther.

J. R. was standing outside the door to one of the condos when he heard Jack's voice. "Let him by. He's with me," J. R. shouted from the other end of the hall.

"You're not going to believe this," J. R. said as he ushered Jack into the room.

A body sat slumped in a swivel chair next to a spectacular antique plantation desk. A handgun lay on the floor, and there was blood spatter and gray matter on the far wall.

"The gun's a .357 magnum. Do you recognize the victim?" J. R. asked.

"Yes, unfortunately. Henry MacIntyre." Jack walked around the back of the chair, careful not to disturb anything. A handwritten note on plain white paper conspicuously sat in the middle of the desk's blotter.

"Have you read the note?" Jack asked.

J. R. nodded. "I didn't touch it, but I did read it. It appears it was him after all."

Jack leaned over the desk to read the note.

Please forgive me. I don't know what happened to me. I really loved him.

Your son, Henry

"Do you know if Henry MacIntyre was left-handed?"

"Of course not. Why?"

"The note was written by someone left-handed, and the bullet entered his skull on the left side above the ear. This whole thing looks a little too contrived to me. I have no proof, but I'll tell you what I think. I think someone learned we were looking at Henry as a suspect in his father's murder, and they killed him and made it look like a suicide to confirm our suspicion." Jack bent down to examine the gun.

"I've learned better than to question your instincts, but this is a little out there if you ask me."

"Who else besides you and me would know that we were looking into Henry MacIntyre as a suspect?"

"Well, I asked Sara to research his military record. I think patrolman Jimmy Furman and Crockett were also there. Did you mention it to anyone?"

"I told Kate. She was incredulous that we might suspect Henry. I am confident that she wouldn't tell anyone."

Jack pulled his cell phone out of his pocket and dialed Kate's number. "Kate, it's Jack. Do you by chance know if Henry MacIntyre was left-handed?"

"Was?" Kate questioned.

Jack hesitated for a couple of seconds before he answered. "Yes, Kate. He either committed suicide or was murdered. We won't know for sure until the coroner has had a chance to examine the body."

"I don't understand. What is going on, and why the MacIntyres?"

"I can't answer that, but what about my first question? Do you know if he was left-handed?"

"I don't, but hold on a minute. I'll be right back." Kate placed the phone down on the kitchen counter and walked across the foyer to her office, retrieved an envelope, and walked back to the kitchen. "Yesterday, I got a note from Henry thanking me for helping his mother get through his father's murder and the funeral. It was handwritten. I'll take a picture of the note and text it to you.

Call me when you get home. I have something interesting to tell you."

Jack turned to address J. R. as one of the Dewey Beach patrolmen picked up the note from the desk. "What the hell do you think you're doing?"

"I'm examining the note. It's evidence," the patrolman responded indignantly.

"You're contaminating a crime scene. Get your ass out of here," Jack yelled.

"Who the hell do you think you are, talking to me like that? I'm an officer of the Dewey Beach Police Department, and this crime was committed in our jurisdiction."

Blood was rushing to Jack's face and neck as he reached back and pulled his credentials out of his rear pants pocket. He walked over to the patrolman and flashed his badge and ID two inches in front of the startled man's face. "FBI. Follow me."

Jack led the young patrolman out of the room and down the hall where three other officers were talking. "Sergeant, sorry to interrupt, but does this belong to you?" he asked, pointing to the patrolman.

"Yes, sir. What did he do now?"

"He contaminated a crime scene. I would suggest that you send him outside to guard the bicycle rack next to the building. By the way, the condo will need to be dusted for prints."

"They're on their way. They should be here shortly."

Jack walked back into the room and checked his phone to see if Kate's text was received.

"Just before you jumped that poor kid's shit, it looked like you were going to tell me something," J. R. said.

"Yes. Kate just sent me this photo of a thank-you note she received from Henry a couple of days ago." Jack handed the phone to J. R..

J. R. examined the note and looked up at Jack. "I'm no handwriting expert, but if Henry wrote this note, he's right-handed. See how all the letters slant to the right? This doesn't mean it wasn't suicide, but it certainly raises some doubts. If you've collected enough evidence and taken enough pictures, I suggest we get this body to the morgue and get the hell out of here. Do you have any dinner plans?"

"No, what were you thinking?"

"This whole situation is getting out of hand. The mayor and city council are all over my ass, and I just don't have any answers. Maybe we can sit down and put our heads together on this over dinner. My treat this time."

"Where to?" Jack asked.

"How about Chez La Mer?"

"Great. I'll follow you."

CHAPTER FORTY-SEVEN

Nancy greeted J. R. with a smile and a hug as he entered the bar. "It's been a long time, Chief. I've got a couple of great specials tonight. Where would you like to sit?"

"Nancy, this is my friend, Jack Scanlon, and Jack, this is Nancy Reed. She owns this fine establishment." Turning back to Nancy, he asked, "Do you have some-place quiet and private where we can eat?"

"Sure thing. I've got a corner table in the other room. It's early, and no one is in there. I'll fill up this room be-fore I seat anyone over there. Follow me." Nancy grabbed two menus and a wine list from the receptionist's stand.

They had no sooner sat down than a young waiter ap-proached the table. "Can I get you something to drink?"

J. R. picked up the wine menu and perused it for about thirty seconds before handing it to the waiter. "Bring us a bottle of the Napa Cellars Cabernet."

"Excellent choice," the waiter responded and walked away.

After about ten minutes, the waiter returned with the wine and two large cabernet glasses. He opened the bottle and started to pour a small amount in one of the glasses.

"No need for that," J. R. instructed the waiter. "Just pour us two glasses. We'd like to relax for a half an hour or so before ordering if that's all right?"

"No problem. I'll check back in about thirty minutes."

J. R. took a sip of wine and leaned back in his chair. "Jack, I need your help on this. It's summer, the tourists are flocking in, and the mayor and city council are afraid that these murders are going to start giving tourists second thoughts about coming here, not to mention the business owners. If that happens, I'll be looking for another job."

Jack leaned forward. "I don't have any magic answers for you. However, I still believe that all of these murders are somehow connected. OK, let's start with the basics." Jack took a sip of his wine. "There are many motives for murder, but several of them fall into four or five general categories: crimes of passion, revenge, self-defense, those associated with the commission of a crime, and those committed to cover up a crime. So let's ask ourselves, what are we dealing with here? You can throw out revenge, self-defense, and those associated with the commission of a crime. Therefore, we're left with crimes of passion and those committed to cover up a crime."

J. R. scratched his head. "I'm still thinking that revenge could be a motive in Judge MacIntyre's murder."

"All right, I'll give you that for the time being. Let's take each murder one at a time. First, Anna Campbell—I'm thinking either a crime of passion or to cover up a crime. As far as it being a crime of passion, what about unrequited love? Suppose one of her customers became infatuated with Anna, and she spurned his affections? Remember, Sherry told us she complained to the other girls about some of the customers coming on to her. She also told Sherry and the other girls that she thought—and I'm paraphrasing here—something illegal was going on at the Roadhouse. In other words, she knew too much about something illegal and was killed to cover it up. I know I'm doing a lot of speculating here, but bear with me."

J. R. poured himself more wine. "It's better than anything I've got. Let's keep speculating. Who's next?"

"Judge MacIntyre. I think we can safely throw out self-defense and murder associated with the commission of a crime. That leaves crime of passion, revenge, and possibly the cover-up of a crime.

"Lastly, there is Henry's murder. Did Henry hate his father that much?" Jack asked rhetorically. "While I know nothing about their relationship, I don't think so. If not, that leaves revenge or cover-up. I'm having a hard time with both of these, but it has got to be one of them."

J. R. put down his wine. "Hold on a minute. We don't know for a fact that he was murdered."

"Humor me for a moment as I continue my line of thought. We don't know much about his social life, but I doubt it was a crime of passion or revenge. That leaves us with a cover-up." Jack pulled out a pencil and started jotting something down on the tablecloth.

"Wow, hold on there. I've got a notepad. No need ruining the tablecloth." J. R. handed him his notepad.

"I was using a pencil. It would all come out in the wash. But I appreciate the notepad." Jack wrote "Anna,"

"Judge," and "Henry" down the left column of the pad. Next to each name he wrote the likely motive in each case. He showed it to J. R.. "Do you notice a theme?"

"Yes, murder to cover up a crime is a possible motive in all three murders. I think we need another bottle of wine," J. R. suggested. "We'll think better." J. R. gave the waiter a not-so-subtle high sign, lifting the empty wine bottle in the air.

The waiter brought a new wine bottle to the table, opened it, and this time simply filled their glasses. "Are you ready to order, or would you like some more time?"

J. R. spoke first. "I'll have the filet special, medium rare, with the baked potato and a Caesar salad."

"Make mine the same, except medium," Jack said.

"Excellent, gentlemen, your order will be out in about thirty minutes." The waiter turned and walked away.

"If all three murders were committed in order to cover up a crime, what was the crime?"

"In Anna's case, I'm pretty sure it has to do with something illegal she witnessed at the Roadhouse. I think you'll agree that Vinny or someone who works for him probably murdered her and dumped her body in the ocean. The question is, what did she see going on at the Roadhouse?"

J. R. put his salad fork down and wiped his mouth. "I would guess it's either sex, drugs, or gambling. Does that make sense?"

"Yes, but based upon what Sherry told us, do you think that Anna would get all that worked up about sex or gambling, somewhat victimless crimes? A place like the

Roadhouse, you'd expect something like that must be going on in one form or another."

"So you're thinking drugs?" J. R. asked.

Jack nodded and thought for a minute. "I do. While I have nothing concrete to base it upon, I'm convinced that the three murders are related in some way. Having said that, how do drugs intersect with the judge and Henry's murder?"

The waiter approached their table, holding two plates with oven mitts. "Gentlemen, these plates are very hot, so be careful not to touch them. Can I bring you anything else?"

"Could we get a couple of glasses of water?" Jack asked.

"Certainly."

J. R. pushed what was left of his salad aside and picked up his steak knife. "I think we've beaten this to death for now. I suggested we talk about something else, enjoy our dinner, and pick this up later with a nice glass of port."

Jack nodded his agreement. "You're really enjoying your night out on the town. Do you have a DUI get-out-of-jail-free card? More importantly, do you have one for me?"

Seeing that they were done with their entrées, the waiter again approached the table with two dessert menus in hand. "Can I offer you gentlemen dessert?"

J. R. waved him off. "You can bring us two glasses of Graham's Vintage Port, and please bring me the check."

"J. R., let me at least split the check with you. This bill is going to be, with two bottles of expensive wine, well, hefty to say the least."

"Nonsense, this one's on me. Besides, I expect you to pick up the next three or four before I have to pay again." J. R. laughed, raised his wineglass, and tilted it toward Jack.

After they finished their port, Jack looked at his watch. "I've got to go. Kate asked me to give her a call when I get home. She has something or other to tell me."

Nancy gave J. R. a hug and opened the door for them. "It was nice to meet you, Mr. Scanlon. Please come back soon, and bring J. R. with you."

CHAPTER FORTY-EIGHT

Jack handed Kate a glass of wine and ushered her out onto the deck. The setting sun lit up the western horizon with a soft orange glow. A few couples strolled along the beach, but for the most part, the beach was strangely deserted for this time of evening.

"Is Henry really dead?" Kate asked, hoping to hear it was all a sick joke.

"Yes. One of his neighbors heard a shot and called the police. I believe he was murdered. It was clumsily staged to look like a suicide. That's my take, but I could be proven wrong."

"What about Agnes? Has she been notified?"

"The state police are doing the notification. Father Francis and Dr. Samuels were both called and asked to meet them at the house."

Kate started to get up. "I should go over and be with her. It's one thing to lose your husband, but losing your only son? I'm not sure she's strong enough to handle it."

"Kate, I don't think you going over there is a good idea. Father Francis and Dr. Samuels will be with her.

Maybe in the morning. I almost forgot—didn't you say you had something to tell me?"

"Yes, I ran into Bill and Debbie DuBois today at Hickman's butcher shop. Bill told me he went over to visit Jeremy yesterday to get an address in Florida and a phone number where Dr. Finley could be located. He told me that until this past February when Finley left for Florida, they were closer than brothers. Since then, he hasn't heard from him. Toward the end of the month, Bill is speaking at a medical convention in Tampa, and he intends to take that opportunity to visit Dr. Finley. Jeremy told him that Finley was staying at his sister's house in Sarasota. He's very suspicious of Jeremy and this whole story about Finley going to Florida."

"At the MacIntyres' dinner party, when the men adjourned to the judge's library, I got the strong impression that Dr. DuBois didn't trust or care for Jeremy. He is also very suspicious of 'the fund.'"

"Bill also told me he tried to call the number that Jeremy gave him. A Spanish-speaking woman answered the phone. Initially, she didn't seem to know who he was talking about, and then suddenly there was an 'oops' moment. She told him that Dr. Finley had gone out to the pharmacy to fill a prescription for his sister. Bill thought the whole story was phony."

Jack started to speak but suddenly jumped up from his chair. "I just saw a man walk past your window. Is there anyone visiting you?"

"No, Timmy is the only one in the house."

"This person was too tall to be Tim. Is the sliding glass door to the deck unlocked?"

"No, it's locked."

"Come on, we'll have to go in the front." Jack raced to his office and grabbed his service weapon out of the bottom desk drawer and hurried with Kate out the front door.

Kate followed Jack up the front steps. The door was ajar, but there were no signs of forced entry.

Jack turned to Kate and whispered, "You stay outside until I figure out what's going on." He chambered a round and slowly pushed the door open. There was no one in the foyer, and the kitchen appeared to be empty. He turned to his left and slowly approached the hallway leading to the bedrooms. As he entered the hallway, he saw a man standing twenty feet away holding Tim by his left arm. He didn't appear to have a weapon.

Jack raised his weapon and pointed it at the man. "Let the boy go, and get down on your knees with your hands behind your head."

The man continued to hold Tim tightly by the arm. "Who the hell are you?" the man asked.

"I'm the guy who's going to put a nine-millimeter slug in the center of your chest if you don't let the boy go immediately and get down on your knees."

The man released his grip on Tim and slowly knelt on the floor. Tim quickly moved toward Jack.

"Now it's my turn to ask," Jack said. "Who are you, and what are you doing here?"

The man pointed toward Kate and laughed. "Maybe you should ask her."

Jack turned to see Kate standing a few feet behind him.

"He's Aaron Simpson, my worthless ex-husband," Kate responded with more than a touch of venom in her voice.

"That still doesn't explain what you are doing here."

"I'm here to take my son out for dinner. Is that a crime?" the man asked.

Kate stepped forward, and Jack could see the hate in her eyes. "You worthless piece of shit. You haven't bothered to visit Timmy or acknowledge his existence in over three years. What do you really want?"

Jack turned back to Kate. "Calm down. We can sort this all out at the police station. Call 911 and report a break-in and attempted kidnapping at this location. Have them send an officer here immediately. Do you have any rope or cord?"

"No, but I've got some zip ties in the kitchen."

"Good. After you make the call, bring them to me."

Kate returned with a handful of half-inch-wide zip ties. "I asked for J. R., but he's off duty. They're sending over one of his deputies."

Jack turned back to Simpson, who was still kneeling in the hallway. "Put your hands behind your head and interlock your fingers." Jack handed Kate his pistol. "Do you know how to use this?"

"I suspect I just aim at him and pull the trigger. I'll have to admit I've dreamed about an opportunity like this."

Jack shook his head and stepped behind Simpson. He pulled Simpson's left hand behind his back and secured a zip tie tightly around his wrist. He then interlocked another zip tie and secured his right wrist.

"Do you think you could get these ties any tighter?" Simpson asked.

"You'll live."

Kate walked to the door as the sounds of the siren got closer, and the patrol car pulled up to the front steps. Crockett slowly got out of the car and walked up the steps with no particular sense of urgency.

"What do we have here?" Crockett asked as he entered the foyer.

Jack reached down and pulled Simpson to his feet. "This is Ms. Simpson's ex-husband, who broke into her house this evening and attempted to kidnap her son."

"How did he get in?" Crockett asked.

"The sliding door in the back is still locked. So I'm guessing he entered through the front door," Jack replied.

Crockett returned to the front door and examined the locking mechanism. "There are no signs of forced entry. Was the door locked?"

Kate stepped back into the foyer. "Yes, I locked both doors when I left. He must either have a key or some sort of lockpick."

Simpson tried to step forward, but Jack jerked him back. "I came to see my son and take him out to dinner."

"That's a crock of shit." Kate's face was getting red with rage. "It's after ten o'clock, and you haven't bothered to show any interest in Timmy's well-being since our divorce. I'm sure he came here to harm Timmy in some way. Besides that, I have a restraining order in effect."

"All right, everyone calm down. We'll sort this all out at the station." Crockett turned toward Jack. "I can't transport him with his hands tied behind his back. You'll have to undo his hands."

Crockett pulled a set of handcuffs from a leather pouch on the right side of his belt and secured Simpson's hands in front of him. He grabbed him by the left arm and led him to the front door.

Jack followed them out the door and at the top of the stairs, pulled Crockett aside. "Ms. Simpson is pretty upset. Would it be possible for us to give our statements the first thing in the morning?"

"No problem. Enjoy the rest of your evening."

Jack shook his head in disbelief at the comment. He watched as Crockett led Simpson down the stairs to the rear door of the patrol car.

CHAPTER FORTY-NINE

When they reached the right rear door of the patrol car, Simpson turned his head slightly toward Crockett. "Get these goddamn cuffs off me."

"Get into the car and wait until we get out of sight. He's still standing on the top of the steps watching us." Crockett eased Simpson into the back seat and closed the door. As they pulled away from the house, Crockett asked, "Where did you park?"

"It's in the North Shores marina."

Crockett pulled up next to a black BMW with Pennsylvania plates. It was the only car in the parking lot. He helped Simpson out of the back seat and unlocked the cuffs.

Simpson rubbed both wrists vigorously and clenched and opened his fists three or four times. "Someday I'm going to make that bitch and her boyfriend pay for tonight. In the meantime, it's important that you let me know what's going on with the murder investigations. I haven't heard anything from you in over two weeks. I think it's high time that we move this operation to another location. I've rented an abandoned fish processing plant on the eastern shore. I plan to move everything there within the next two weeks, but there are still a few loose ends to tie up."

"Loose ends?" Crockett asked.

"Yes. For one, Vinny has become a liability and he has a big mouth. He'd sell us down the river in a heartbeat if it meant saving his own skin. I can't afford to take that chance."

"Do you want me to take care of him?"

"No, I have someone else in mind."

Crockett leaned back against the trunk of the car and tilted the visor of his hat back. "What about Malone and Pamela?"

"Malone thinks he can still get a couple of million dollars out of Scanlon and my ex-wife's foundation. I told him I'd give him two weeks, and then, money or not, we're out of here."

"OK, I'll keep my eyes and ears open and let you know what they're up to."

Crockett had started to head to the patrol car when Simpson stopped him. "How are you going to explain letting me go?"

"You know, minor domestic dispute—he said, she said."

"Good luck with that. Scanlon's no fool, and I hope you know that he's an FBI agent."

"I know, and I'm no fool either."

"All right, I'll trust that you know what you're doing. Things could get hot for us in the next few days, so be prepared to pick up stakes and move to the warehouse at a moment's notice. Understand?"

"Got it, boss."

CHAPTER FIFTY

Jack walked back into the house. Kate was sitting at the dining room table with her elbows on the edge of the table and her head in her hands. Tim sat beside her with a comforting hand on her shoulder.

"Are you all right?" Jack asked as he pulled up a chair next to her.

Kate sat back. She had clearly been crying. "I don't understand what's going on. I thought all of this mess was behind us. Do you have a few minutes to talk? I'd like to try and explain."

"Kate, you don't have anything to explain to me. You're my friend, and I'll always look out for you."

"Let me get Timmy settled in and I'll be back. There are a couple of bottles of red on the counter next to the pantry. If you'd open one for me, I think I could use a glass after all this."

After about ten minutes, Kate returned. She had put on sweats and no longer looked like she'd been crying. Jack handed her a glass of wine. "I feel a little overdressed."

"You're more than welcome to go home and get into something more comfortable."

Jack laughed. "That's all right. I'm fine."

Kate motioned Jack to the family room. "Thanks for everything you did tonight."

Kate snuggled up on the couch, and Jack settled into the chair next to her. "I consider myself a pretty strong woman, but it hasn't always been that way for me. You may not believe it, but I only had one date in high school and college, and that was to my senior prom. For those eight years, it was soccer, 24-7, 365. In high school, I played varsity for four years and on an elite travel team. We were ranked number three in the nation. Every one of us received college scholarships, mostly to D-1 schools. I accepted a scholarship to Princeton and started for all four years. When I graduated, I was invited to try out for the US national team. I made it to the last cut, and then my soccer career was over. It left a big void. Fortunately, I had applied and been accepted to the University of Pennsylvania Law School."

Jack picked up his glass as if to toast Kate. "I still see a pretty strong woman."

"What I'm trying to say is that I was very naive when it came to men and relationships." Kate sighed. "I met my ex-husband during my second year in law school. He was smart, kind, and charming, and I fell in love with him. Our final year we moved into an apartment together. My parents weren't happy about it, and his parents had no clue about the arrangement. In February, he asked me to marry him, and I accepted. We planned for an October wedding, after graduation and our bar exams. Aaron graduated first in our class and joined his father and grandfather's law firm, Simpson, Simpson, Richardson, and Wetherbee. It was the most prestigious law firm in Philadelphia, and Daddy had great things planned for his son. His father reluctantly invited me to join the firm as well and was relieved when I told him I had accepted a job with the Philadelphia district attorney's office."

Jack thought for a minute. "Did you say your husband's name is Aaron Simpson?"

"Yes, Aaron Stuart Simpson."

Jack laughed. "I'll bet he wasn't big into monogrammed shirts."

Kate gave Jack a puzzled look. "What?"

"Nothing. I'm sorry to interrupt."

"The Simpsons were not at all happy with their precious son marrying a 'commoner.'" At the wedding, they treated my parents like second-class citizens. Dad was still on active duty, a three-star admiral. They told him he couldn't wear his uniform to give me away. He showed them. He arrived wearing the tuxedo they insisted he wear. When everyone was seated, he ducked into a room at the back of the church and changed into his dress whites, medals and all. When we appeared at back of the church to walk down the aisle, there was an audible gasp from the pews on the right side. The Simpsons were furious, but at that point there wasn't much they could do about it." Kate laughed. "He told them the tuxedo they ordered for him didn't fit properly."

"I hope I can meet your father some day and shake his hand."

"Me too. I think the two of you would really hit it off."

"I did a little research and learned the family secret. Aaron's grandfather was dishonorably discharged from the army during World War II, and his father ran off to Canada during the Vietnam War. However, I digress. As a wedding present, they bought a brownstone in the old city for Aaron. Notice I didn't say us. The title was only in his name, and it was about two blocks from Daddy and Mommy's palatial ten-thousand-square-foot town house, where every Sunday afternoon we were obligated to show up formally dressed for dinner. Four months after the wedding, I learned I was pregnant. For the next four years, our lives were relatively happy, despite constant meddling by his parents into everything we did. Aaron was clearly on the fast track to becoming a partner, and many of his contemporaries resented it. He was only twenty-nine but was pushed to perform as if he had years of experience. It all started to fall apart when a $100 million class action lawsuit was filed against the firm's biggest client. Almost everyone agreed that it was a frivolous suit that would likely be dismissed by the lower court. Much to the chagrin of the partners, Daddy put Aaron in charge of defending their client against the suit. It was a disaster. First, Aaron lost the motion to dismiss the case, and an early trial date was set. The case was going so badly that, a week into it, two members of his defense team quit the case and left the firm. The press had a field day, and the partners were sharpening their knives.

"Things got worse and worse at home. To make a long story short, he began to drink heavily. The more

317

he drank, the more abusive he became. On several occasions, he hit me and slapped me around. I put up with it until one night he took his rage out on Timmy. He was only four. On occasion, like all young children, he would throw a tantrum. This particular evening, I was fixing dinner when Timmy started acting up. I tried to get him to settle down, but he was having a meltdown. Aaron started screaming at the both of us, and without warning, he jumped out of his chair and shoved me away. I fell and hit my head on the corner of the cabinet. He grabbed Timmy, shook him, and then backhanded him across the face. I picked him up and ran to the bedroom. Timmy's cheek was bleeding, and there was blood running out of the corner of his mouth.

"That was the final straw. At the time, we had a live-in nanny. She helped me settle Timmy down and attend to his cuts and bruises. The next morning after Aaron left, we packed the car, and the three of us came down to stay with my parents. Two days later, I contacted a lawyer and filed for divorce."

"I guess I'm curious. Didn't your coworkers notice or question how you got your bruises?"

"I'm pretty good with makeup, but I suspect they knew what was going on. One morning my boss asked if I was all right. That's the closest anyone came to questioning what was happening to me."

"Didn't your husband challenge you for custody?"

"He did. My father learned that Maria, our nanny, had taken pictures of me after each time Aaron beat me. She also had pictures of Timmy's beating. He urged her to testify at the custody hearing and show the judge all the pictures she had taken. Marie was reluctant because she was undocumented and was afraid that she would be deported. My father convinced her that he would do everything in his power to prevent her from being sent back to Colombia. The custody hearing was a circus. The Simpsons brought in the big guns, but when the judge saw the photos, he not only granted me full custody, but he also issued a restraining order. Aaron was allowed one supervised visit a month."

"What happened to Maria?"

"She lived with us for a little over a year. My father called in a few favors, and she was granted a work visa until her case could be heard. She applied for asylum, and it was granted. Now she works as a nanny for a family in Bethany Beach. We see her once or twice a month."

Jack looked at his watch. "We'd better call it a night. Do you want me to sleep on the couch?"

"Thank you, but that's not necessary. We'll be fine."

"All right then. I'll pick you up at seven. I almost forgot—one last question. Does your ex-husband have any dealings with the Giovannati crime family out of Philadelphia?"

"I can't say for sure, but after he lost his third job with Streeter and Wilson, he started working for the public defender's office. Rumor had it that he started heavily using drugs and somehow became indebted to Victor Giovannati. That's as much as I've been able to find out."

"The only reason I ask, and this is between you and me, is the FBI is investigating the family, and about a month ago an Aaron Simpson came up on their radar."

"Personally, I hope they toss him in jail and throw away the key."

"Good night, Kate. If you need anything, I'm a phone call away. Otherwise, I'll see you in the morning."

CHAPTER FIFTY-ONE

Kate opened the passenger side door, handed Jack a cup of coffee, and climbed in. "I was thinking. I would like to purchase a handgun for protection. Will you teach me how to shoot?"

Jack thought for a minute. "I saw the look in your eyes last night when I handed you my gun. I suspected that if he had given you even the slightest justification, you would have pulled the trigger. Are you sure about this?"

"I was a little worked up last night. I'm actually very rational and restrained in stressful situations."

"If you say so."

"I do. So will you help me?"

"I know a gun dealer in Milton. I use their range now and then. If you're free after we give our statements, I'll take you there."

"I don't have anything on my schedule until 3:00 p.m. Thank you."

∼∼

"Good morning, Sara."

"Good morning, Mr. Scanlon, Ms. Simpson. To what do I owe this pleasure?"

"We're here to give our statements concerning the break-in and attempted kidnapping at Kate's home last evening. Officer Crockett responded to the 911 call and took the man in."

"I wasn't on duty last night, but I can tell you we don't have anyone in custody. I checked the cellblock when I arrived this morning. I think you need to talk to the chief. I'll tell him you're here."

Jack looked at Kate and shook his head. "I don't get it. He couldn't have been arraigned and posted bail already. What the hell's going on?"

Jack tapped lightly on the doorjamb.

"Come in, Jack. Good morning, Kate. You have a way of brightening up my day. However, I must admit, I am a little confused. Sara tells me you're here to give a statement about a break-in and attempted kidnapping at Kate's house last night, and you think the perpetrator is here in custody. I can assure you we have no one in custody. If we did, I would have had an arrest report on my desk when I came in this morning."

"We're a little confused as well."

"I apologize. Please have a seat. Let's start from the beginning. Tell me what happened."

Jack pulled the chair closer to J. R.'s desk. "We were sitting on my deck last night around nine thirty when I noticed a man inside Kate's house. Since Tim was the only one supposed to be there, we went over to investigate. The front door was ajar, and Kate's ex-husband was leading Tim down the hallway toward the front entrance. I ordered him to kneel and restrained his hands with zip ties. Kate called 911, and Crockett responded to the call."

"I'm a little confused. This guy simply knelt and let you zip-tie his hands?"

"Actually, I was holding him at gunpoint."

"Ah, small detail. Couldn't this have just been an innocent misunderstanding?"

"No, Kate has an active restraining order. Her ex isn't supposed to be within one hundred yards of her house without her permission."

"So what happened after Crockett arrived?"

"He checked the front entrance and verified that there was no evidence of forced entry. He asked us a few questions, cuffed Simpson, and led him to his patrol car."

"Did he read him his Miranda rights?"

"No, at least not while I was in earshot."

J. R. pushed the intercom on his phone. "Sara, would you tell Crockett I want to see him ASAP?"

"He's not on duty until eight. As soon as he checks in, I'll tell him."

"Good morning, Chief. Sara said you wanted to see me."

"Yes. Come in and have a seat."

Crockett entered the office and glared at Scanlon and Kate. "I think I know what this is all about, but you need to hear my side of the story."

"All right, have a seat and let's hear it."

"You already know that I responded to their 911 call last night. When I arrived, Ms. Simpson was holding the alleged perpetrator at gunpoint. I did a cursory investigation and escorted the perp to the squad car. He told me that he hadn't seen his son in several months and just wanted to take him out for dinner. I decided it was a 'he said, she said' situation and drove him to his car. In my opinion, it would have been harassment to have charged him with breaking and entering, much less kidnapping. In retrospect, I would have been more justified in arresting Scanlon for assault with a deadly weapon at a minimum."

Kate had heard enough. She jumped up and pointed at Crockett. "You moron, I told you I have an active restraining order. That alone should have given you a clue as to what was going on."

J. R. interrupted, "Kate, I don't think name-calling is going to get us anywhere. Let's all settle down. First of all, Crockett, letting him go was not your call to make. Proper procedure would have been to read him his rights, bring him in for processing, and let the court system sort it all out. Once again, you have shown poor judgment. This is your second strike. One more and you're out of here, understood?"

Crockett stood up as if to leave. "I understand that Scanlon calls the shots around here."

J. R. slowly pushed back his chair and stood. "I've had enough out of you. Until you're sitting behind this desk, you'll do as I say. Now, prepare a BOLO with Simpson's description. You can likely get a picture of him off the internet. What kind of car was he driving?"

"Ah, I'm not sure. It was dark. I think it was a black Toyota sedan."

"What about the license plates?

"Again, I didn't get a good look."

"That's great police work." J. R. shook his head in disbelief. "That's enough. Get out of here."

Crockett exited the room, slamming the door behind him.

J. R. turned toward Kate. "I'm sorry about all this. If you need me to have a patrol car monitor you house, I will provide one."

"Thank you, but that won't be necessary. I'm having a security system installed this afternoon."

Jack sat back in his chair for a moment as if in deep thought. "Something is off about all this. Would you speak to your boss like that if you had any intentions of retaining your job for any length of time? Crockett's not an idiot or a moron." He turned slightly toward Kate. She rolled her eyes in response. "I can't put my finger on it, but something here just doesn't add up."

"Well, when you figure it out, let me know. Now, if you will excuse me, I have an appointment with the mayor." J. R. stood up and grabbed his hat off the credenza. "How about the three of us have coffee tomorrow morning at Java Beach, say seven thirty? Maybe if we sleep on it overnight, we can make some sense out of all this."

Kate shook J. R.'s hand. "It's a date."

CHAPTER FIFTY-TWO

Jack turned right onto Rehoboth Avenue. "You still want to purchase a handgun?"

"Yes. I know you think it's a bad idea, but I think, under the circumstances, I'd feel more secure owning one and knowing how to use it. Will you help me?"

"I don't necessarily think it's a bad idea. I just want to make sure you aren't overreacting to last night. Do you have any experience with guns?"

"My father had a .22 revolver. Sort of a western-style gun. When I was twelve, he took me out back of our house and taught me how to use it. From time to time, he would take a bag full of empty beer cans and we'd go out in the country and target shoot. Other than that, it's been years since I last shot a gun. So I think a refresher course is in order."

"It will take us about twenty minutes to get to Milton, if traffic cooperates."

Kate turned in her seat to face Jack. "I'm curious. I got the impression back there that you think my ex and Crockett are somehow involved in all that's going on around here."

Jack took a few seconds to respond. "I've said all along that I think the three murders are somehow connected. I still believe that. Crockett's actions last night and his explanation this morning just don't make sense, but I can't explain why. A few weeks ago, J. R. and I saw Crockett take a briefcase into the back entrance of the Roadhouse and come out with a different briefcase. When J. R. confronted him about it, he said he was just paying back a loan from Puglisi. That made no sense either. We suspect that Puglisi had some involvement in Anna Campbell's murder. We searched his boat and took blood samples and sent several other items off to be tested. I'm convinced they'll come back positive for Anna's blood. There are a few other disturbing issues about her murder that I won't go into right now. Getting back to Crockett, remember when the judge was shot?"

"Of course I do," Kate replied incredulously.

"Sorry, I know you do. When you and I got to the judge, which couldn't have taken more than two or three minutes, Crockett magically appeared out of nowhere. Remember, he said he was investigating a reported break-in in North Shores and heard the 911 call. J. R. said later that there was no reported break-in called in that morning."

"Are you saying you think Crockett shot Judge McIntyre?"

"No, he wouldn't have had the time to take the shot, clean up the area, and get to the scene of the murder. But he could have assisted the shooter. I suspect Crockett is involved in these murders in some manner, but I have absolutely no proof. It's frustrating as hell."

Jack turned right off Route 1 onto a dirt road. About a mile down the road, he pulled into a gravel parking lot in front of a large Quonset hut building. Kate could hear gunshots as she exited the car.

"What's that?"

"He has two firing ranges on the property. You're hearing shots from the rifle range out back. The smaller building to the right is a pistol range. Let's see if we can find a handgun for you."

Kate entered the building first and was shocked at the number of firearms on display. Mounted on the wall behind the counter were over a hundred hunting rifles, semiautomatic weapons, and, surprisingly, machine guns. The counter had glass case after glass case filled with every make and model of handgun imaginable. An older man sat on a stool behind the counter reading a copy of *Guns and Ammo* magazine. When he saw the couple walk in, he put the magazine on the counter and stood up to greet them.

"Good morning. How can I help you?"

"You may not remember me. I come in every couple of weeks to use your pistol range."

"Oh yes, you're that FBI fellow. I never forget a face—names not so much. What can I do for you?"

"The lady is interested in purchasing a handgun for personal protection. We're not exactly sure what we're looking for and thought you could help us out."

"I'd be glad to. Sweetheart, please follow me down to the other end of the counter."

Jack could see Kate bristle. He grabbed her arm. "Relax, he's an old man. I'm sure he didn't mean anything by it."

Kate pulled her arm away and walked defiantly to the end of the counter. In the sweetest voice she could muster, she said, "You can call me Kate."

The old man smiled. "Well, thank you. I'm Charlie."

Kate turned to Jack and stuck out her tongue playfully.

Charlie pulled out three handguns and placed them on the counter. He picked up the first one and handed it to Kate. "This is a Colt .357 Magnum. It will stop an elephant, but you might break your wrist firing it. Most men have a hard time handling it. It would not be my recommendation."

Kate handed it back. "It's very heavy. I think I need something lighter and more compact."

He handed her the second one. "This is a Smith and Wesson .38-caliber snub-nosed revolver. Personally, I think you'd be better off with a semiautomatic handgun, and I would recommend this one." He handed her the third gun. "This is the Walther PPS nine-millimeter. It's a little over six inches long and made of a lightweight polymer."

Kate examined the gun carefully. "I like it. Can I try it out?"

"Sure." The man reached behind him. "Here's a box of nine-millimeter shells and three targets. The range is in the building out the door and to your left. Everything else you'll need is already at the range."

Kate gave Jack a playful shove. "All right, boss. Time to teach me the basics."

Jack wasn't amused. "We're not playing anymore. Handling a firearm is a serious business." Jack directed her to one of the firing lanes and placed the box of shells on the counter. "First thing to remember is to always keep the gun pointing up and down range.

"Studies show that most intruders are first confronted by the homeowner at a distance of between twenty-five to thirty feet. I'm going to attach the target to the pulley and run it out to twenty-five feet."

Jack grabbed two headsets off the far wall and handed one to Kate. He picked up the gun and ejected the magazine. He loaded six rounds into the magazine and placed the gun back on the counter. "I'll demonstrate how to hold the gun in the standing position, and I'll fire six rounds at the target." Jack showed Kate how to stand and hold the gun with two hands. He fired six rounds in rapid succession, ejected the magazine, checked the chamber, and placed the gun on the counter. He reeled in the target and removed it from the frame.

Kate looked at the target. "That's impressive—four rounds center mass and one in the neck." She glanced down at the bottom of the target at the sixth bullet hole. "And, well, let's just say he isn't going to have any more children."

Jack failed to see the humor. "I wasn't aiming. I just wanted to demonstrate the proper stance. Now it's your turn. Load six rounds into the magazine. Press the rounds down and slightly back." He waited patiently as Kate slowly inserted the six rounds. "Good. Now insert the magazine. Push it in with the palm of your hand until you hear a click, and place the gun back on the counter."

Jack checked the handgun. "Now, pick up the gun, pull back the slide, and chamber a round with your left hand. Now brace the gun with your left hand like so." Jack simulated holding a gun with both hands. "Do you see the oblong circle in the center of the target?" Kate nodded. "I want you to fire six rounds into the center of the target when you're ready."

Kate nodded again and began to fire. When she finished firing, she ejected the magazine and placed the gun on the counter.

"I realize you loaded six rounds and fired six rounds, but it's always a good idea to make sure the chamber is clear. Let's see how you did." Jack reeled in the target and stared at it in amazement. "You know, Kate, you're a goddammed show-off."

The six rounds were in the center of the inner ring and could have been easily covered with the bottom of a soda can.

Feigning innocence, Kate asked, "Is that good?"

Jack sighed. "I don't know anyone in the bureau who could match it. I thought you said you hadn't fired a gun in almost twenty years."

"That's right, I haven't. As you already know, my father taught me to shoot, and I was pretty good. He entered me in some competitions at the base when I was in my teens, and I won them all."

"Well, you haven't lost your touch. Shall we go in and complete the purchase?"

Kate picked up the gun, inserted the empty magazine, and grabbed the box of cartridges off the counter.

Jack threw his target in the trash. He rolled up Kate's target and placed it under his left arm.

"How did it go?" Charlie asked.

Kate placed the gun on the display counter. "It's perfect. I'll take it."

"There's something you should see, Charlie." Jack unrolled the target and placed in on the counter.

Charlie stared at the target in amazement. "Nice shooting. Is this yours?"

"No, that's Kate's target, shot at twenty-five feet."

Charlie turned and picked out a black Sharpie from a can full of pens and pencils next to the cash register. He turned the target around and wrote the date, the make and model of the gun, and the target distance on Kate's target. He turned it around and asked Kate to sign it.

"Congratulations. You're our newest member of the Wall of Fame."

"What does that mean?"

Charlie handed Kate four pushpins. "If you'll turn around, you will see several targets attached to the far wall. They represent the absolute best target shooting at this range over the twelve years we've been in operation."

Kate turned to see over a dozen targets pinned to the cork-lined wall behind her.

"Now, if you would do us the honor of attaching your target to the wall, we can get on with the paperwork required for your purchase."

Kate proudly walked to the far wall and attached her target with the four pushpins. She walked back to the counter with a huge smile on her face.

332

"We have some paperwork to fill out for the background check, and as long as you're not a felon, you can pick up your gun on Thursday afternoon or Friday. Here is my card. You should call first."

Kate still couldn't stop smiling as they walked to Jack's car.

"May I take the newest member of the Wall of Fame to lunch?"

"I can't. I remembered on the drive over here that I have another important appointment today. I don't know if you remember me telling you about the terrible beating that Tina Ramsey received from her boyfriend. Well, today she is being released from the hospital. Crystal is picking her up and bringing her back to the center. I want to be there when she arrives. Crystal moved into a two-bedroom apartment last week and has invited Tina to be her roommate. I bought Tina a bedroom set, which will be delivered on Thursday. In the meantime, both Tina and Crystal will be staying at the center. Also, Walmart is giving Tina her job back with back pay, and she starts on Monday. They also kept her health insurance active and have agreed to pick up any additional expenses. There aren't many employers who would go the extra mile like they have." Kate thought for a minute. "I will, however, take a rain check on lunch."

Jack pulled into Kate's assigned parking place at the center. "I was just wondering—what's happening with the boyfriend who attacked Tina?"

"As far as I know, he is in jail awaiting trial. I suspect, unless he cuts a deal with the district attorney, Tina, Crystal, Dr. Rosenbaum, and I will be called to testify at his trial. Let's just hope he takes a deal and saves Tina the trauma of living that night all over again."

"By the way, how are you going to get home tonight?"

"I'll just take a cab."

"Right, good luck finding a cab in Rehoboth. I think they're nonexistent. However, I've been wanting to try this restaurant in Lewes called Gilligan's. Let me pick you up and take you to dinner."

"Can I bring Timmy along?" Kate asked.

Jack grinned. "Of course. Call him and tell him I'll pick him up at 4:30 p.m."

CHAPTER FIFTY-THREE

Jack had just turned off the light and climbed into bed when his cell phone rang. He groped for the phone as he reached up to turn on the lamp.

"Hello," he mumbled into the phone.

"Jack, it's Maggie. I'm sorry to call you so late, but I just got the approval for our project, the search for the German submarine I told you about. I thought you'd like to know. I will be bringing the research ship and its crew up to the University of Delaware's Marine Science Center campus on Sunday afternoon. As we discussed, I have expanded the project search area to include the likely location of your sunken galleon."

"That's fantastic, Maggie. You and your crew are more than welcome to stay at my place Sunday and Monday night."

"Thank you, but that won't be necessary. The navy has a contract with the University of Delaware, so we'll be staying on campus. I would like you, your neighbor, and her son to meet us in the Garrett B. Lyons Hall, room 103, at 0800 on Monday. I have plotted the grid search pattern and estimate that to complete the search, it will take a little over six hours. If we arrive at our launch point by 0930, we should be back at the Marine Science Center before 1700. The ship has a fully equipped galley, so lunch will be on me, and, if you recall, dinner will be on you."

"I remember. How many are in your crew?"

"Including me, we carry a crew of six."

"I will make dinner reservation tomorrow as soon as they open. Thanks again, Maggie. I know one young man who is going to be extremely excited when I tell him the news. We'll see you Monday morning."

Jack parked in the visitor lot across from Lyons Hall. Lyons Hall was a stately four-story ivy-covered brick building near the Rehoboth-Lewes Canal. Kate, Tim, and Jack walked up the concrete steps to the front entrance and into the marble foyer. Jack casually pointed to the sign on the far wall indicating that rooms 101–105 were down the corridor to the right. His excitement more than evident, Tim hurried down the corridor to room 103. He held the door open for Kate and Jack and followed them into a medium-sized classroom. Maggie stood at the front of the room next to the dais talking to her crew. She was dressed in her navy whites summer uniform with three rows of awards and service ribbons. The ship's crew members stood at ease along the side wall, dressed in the navy's blue-and-black camo uniform. She turned as she heard Jack and his neighbors enter the room. Maggie walked back to greet them.

Bay. All right, Tim, I have a trivia question for you. I understand your grandfather is a retired navy admiral. According to the navy, what is the difference between a ship and a boat?"

Tim proudly stood up. "Any vessel over one hundred feet in length from bow to stern is a ship. Those vessels under one hundred feet are boats."

He was so proud and confident that Maggie felt bad correcting him. "That definition probably works, and it's also a popular misconception. But according to the US Naval Institute, a boat is small enough to be carried aboard a larger vessel, and a vessel large enough to carry a smaller one is a ship. In other words, you can put a boat on a ship, but you can't put a ship on a boat. Your definition is more definitive and could be more accurate, but I can envision a one-hundred-foot vessel being transported aboard an aircraft carrier." Maggie shook her head. "Actually, I'm sorry I asked that question at all."

Maggie advanced to the next slide, which showed a map of the Delaware coastline with several small red dots. "We will start our mapping at point alpha, which is fifteen hundred yards off the northern tip of Cape Henlopen. At this point, navigation will be controlled by the computer. We will parallel the Delaware shoreline for approximately twenty-five miles south-southeast to Fenwick Island. From there we will turn and parallel our original course north-northwest to point delta. I think you can see the pattern. This grid search will give us coverage of almost 125 square miles of ocean. When we're finished, we will return to the Marine Science Center and enter the data into the university's computer. If we've done everything correctly, the computer will print out a multibeam image of the ocean bottom. If there are wrecks down there, we should be able to accurately locate them. Now, if you'll follow Master Chief Pierce, we'll board the vessel."

CHAPTER FIFTY-FOUR

Maggie turned to Tim. "I'm sorry, Tim, but navy regulations require all minors wear a life jacket at all times aboard ship."

Tim shrugged. "No problem, Commander. It will be all worth it if we find the *La Concepción*."

When they reached point alpha, Maggie turned over navigational control of the ship to Master Chief Pierce.

"Navigation of the ship will now be controlled by the onboard computer. The GPS coordinates of the course corrections have been entered into the computer. Master Chief Pierce will assume the conn to ensure we do not ram any clueless recreational boaters. Now, if you follow me to the chartroom, we will begin the grid search."

Maggie led Kate, Jack, and Tim to the chartroom behind the bridge. On the far wall, a thirty-two-inch computer screen was beginning to show computer-generated images of the ocean bottom. "This is likely to get a little monotonous and boring unless we pass over something of significance, like your Spanish galleon. I'm going to leave you in Chief Martinez's capable hands for a few minutes while I attend to some necessary paperwork."

Chief Martinez took considerable pride in explaining to Tim and Jack how the multibeam echo sounder worked and what they were seeing on the screen. He showed great patience in answering the myriad of questions that Tim asked.

After about twenty minutes, Maggie returned to the chartroom to find Tim and Jack still glued to the computer screen. Kate stood in the corner looking like she'd like to be anywhere else.

Maggie approached Kate and asked, "Would you be interested in joining me for a cup of coffee?"

"I would love to."

"Great. Follow me to the galley. It's on the lower level."

Maggie poured coffee into two white ceramic mugs printed with the navy seal and the words "USS *Cam Ranh Bay*" underneath. She handed one to Kate. "There's cream and sugar on the counter to your left."

"Thanks, but I take mine black."

"Wow, tactical coffee. I'm impressed. I've never been able to do that." Maggie poured a little cream and a teaspoon of sugar into her mug and stirred. "Unless you're anxious to get back to the chartroom, I suggest we take our coffee to the fantail and relax. I have a couple of comfortable chairs back there. We can enjoy this beautiful morning while the boys search for their treasure."

Maggie led Kate to two wicker fan chairs on the fantail of the ship. "These are not regulation, but sometimes I need a break from the boredom of these mapping missions."

TOM DONNELLY

Kate nodded. "I know what you mean. I had no idea that this was going to take over six hours. I don't know what I was thinking, but Timmy was so excited about today, I felt I needed to support him." Kate held up her coffee mug. "Thanks for the diversion. This is very pleasant." They sat in silence for several minutes enjoying the morning sun before Kate's curiosity got the better of her. "Are you married, Maggie?"

Maggie was somewhat taken aback by the question. "No, you know what they say. If the navy wanted you to have a husband, they would have issued you one."

Kate laughed. "I never heard that one."

Maggie paused for a moment. "You know, Kate, I always pictured myself with a family, and the closer I get to retirement, the more I dwell on it. Unfortunately, I think I'm getting a little beyond the biological power curve, and I just haven't found the right man."

"There's always adoption. God knows there are millions of children in the world looking for a good home and someone to love them."

"You're right, Kate. Maybe there is hope for me after all."

Kate decided to play a wild card. "You know Jack is available, and he's a great guy." She could see the comment caught Maggie a little off guard.

"You may not know this, but Jack and I dated years ago. We just weren't a good fit."

"People change. I'm sure Jack is not the same person you dated all those years ago."

"Don't get me wrong, Jack is a great guy. If I didn't think so, I would never have introduced him to Nancy, and unfortunately, I still don't think he's gotten over her death."

Maggie glanced at her watch. "Let's head to the ship's mess. It's almost noon, and Petty Officer Connors has prepared a special lunch for us."

Kate looked at the printed menu in disbelief. Crab cake sandwich with Old Bay french fries and a Caesar salad were followed by pineapple upside-down cake. The meal turned out to be as good as anything you could find in any restaurant in southern Delaware.

After lunch, Kate sought out Petty Officer Conners. "Thank you for that wonderful lunch. If I ever decide to open a restaurant, you'll be my first call."

"Well, ma'am, you'll have to wait another eleven or twelve years. I'm halfway through my second reenlistment, and my fiancé and I plan to make the navy a career. We are getting married next June."

"Congratulations. He's a lucky man. If the way to a man's heart is through his stomach, I'd say you've got that covered."

Kate decided to head back to the chartroom to support Timmy and give Jack a much-needed break. She tapped Jack on the shoulder as he stared at the computer screen. "I'm here to see how the search is coming along. Why don't you go outside and get some fresh air?"

"Thanks, Kate. I could use a break to walk off that lunch. Chief Martinez tells us we're running ahead of schedule. We have five more legs to run before we head back to the Marine Science Center." Jack nodded toward Tim staring at the screen. "He's starting to get a little disappointed that we haven't found anything yet. You might want to provide some moral support."

Kate winked at Jack and walked over and put her arm around Timmy's shoulder. "How's it going, sport?"

"Not very well. We've almost completed the search, and nothing has shown up on the screen."

Chief Martinez heard the exchange and walked over to Tim and Kate. "Don't get discouraged. Just because you haven't seen anything on the screen doesn't mean that the echo sounder hasn't detected something on the ocean floor. We won't know definitively until we get back and enter the data into the university's computer."

CHAPTER FIFTY-FIVE

It was 1610 when the USS *Cam Ranh Bay* docked at the Marine Science Center. Kate, Jack, Tim, and the crew followed Maggie down the gangplank, along the dock, and into the university's computer center. The facility was amazing. Massive computers lined three walls, and the room was kept necessarily cool. In the middle of the room sat a twelve-by-twenty-four-foot machine.

Tim turned to Chief Martinez. "What does that machine do?"

"It's the largest printer you'll probably ever see." Martinez sat down at one of the computers and inserted a thumb drive. He pulled out the keyboard and typed in several lines of text that Tim couldn't decipher.

"What does that mean?"

"The gibberish I just typed into the computer tells it to begin to process the data on the thumb drive. It will take about fifteen minutes to complete. Once that happens, I will instruct the computer to print the data. The massive machine in the center of the room will begin printing a high-resolution map of our search area. That should take another twenty minutes." Martinez could sense that Tim's impatience was beginning to resurface. "Tim, would you do me a favor?" Go down the hall to room 118. It's a storage room. There is a blue cooler on wheels in the corner. Would you bring the cooler back here please?"

After about ten minutes, Tim returned, pulling the heavy cooler. Martinez turned to Maggie. "Commander, I know that 'officially' alcohol is not allowed on US Navy vessels. However, it's my understanding that the university has no such prohibition. With your permission, I have a cooler full of soft drinks and Dogfish Head 60 Minute IPAs for those so inclined."

Maggie nodded her approval, and Martinez took orders and handed out the requested beverages.

They all turned as the printer began to print the map of the search grid. Maggie joined the others gathered around the printer table. The map slowly emerged from the printer showing the ocean bottom in various shades of green, orange, yellow, and red. Another five minutes passed before Maggie excitedly pointed to the upper edge of the map. "Tim, tell me what that looks like to you."

Tim starred at the image. "It looks like some sort of ship lying on its side. Is it the submarine you were searching for?"

Maggie was grinning from ear to ear, and Jack returned her smile.

"Congratulations, Commander. Mission accomplished—you found your German U-boat."

The crew exploded with cheers and slaps on the back all around.

Tim starred disappointedly at the completed map. Maggie walked around the table and put a reassuring arm around his shoulder. "Why so glum, chum?"

"I was sure we would find the *La Concepción*, but we didn't," Tim replied.

"Are you sure of that?" Maggie asked.

"I don't see anything anywhere on the map that looks like a ship."

"Let me ask you a question. If you built a ship like a galleon and launched it down the slipway into the ocean, what would happen?"

Everyone listened curiously as Maggie quizzed Tim. Jack knew she was up to something but couldn't imagine where she was going with this.

Tim thought for a minute. "I guess the ship would be ready for the crew to board."

"Actually, Tim, the ship would probably capsize. Ships require ballast to become stable in the water. In the era of the wooden sailing ships, they used large stones or boulders to provide ballast. Come with me." Maggie led Tim around the table to the lower right-hand corner of the map. Maggie pointed to a spot on the map. "What do you think that is?"

Tim studied the map intently. "It looks like some sort of mound."

"Exactly. When the wood of a sunken ship rots away, the only thing that is left is a pile of ballast stones. After over three hundred years, the only thing that would be left of *La Concepción* would be the ballast and some metal fittings. I would be willing to wager you that

that pile of stones is all that is left of your Spanish galleon. Congratulations, Tim. You found *La Concepción*." Maggie turned to Martinez. "Can you give me the GPS coordinates of this location?"

In less than thirty seconds, Martinez provided Maggie with the coordinates. She handed Tim a slip of paper. "Your treasure is located at 38.566434–74.951923."

Tim surprised Maggie by hugging her. He raised both hands in triumph and raced around the room give all of the crew members high fives.

Jack gave Maggie a big hug and a kiss on the cheek, none of which was lost on Kate.

Jack turned to Kate. "Would you mind driving Tim and the crew in my Jeep over to the restaurant? Maggie and I have some business to attend to; we'll join you in about twenty minutes."

Without answering, Kate took the keys and walked out of the room, followed by Timmy and the crew.

"What was that all about?" Maggie asked. "We don't have any business to conduct."

"I know. I just wanted some time to privately thank you for everything you've done for Tim. In case you missed it, he's on cloud nine. His feet haven't touched the ground since you pointed out that pile of ballast stones to him."

"Well, thank you, but I got as much enjoyment out of it as he did. While I've got you alone, I think we need to talk about something that has been bothering me."

Jack looked apprehensively at Maggie. "What do you mean?"

"Jack Scanlon, you've got your head up your ass. That woman is madly in love with you."

"You mean Kate? That's absurd. We're just good friends, and besides—"

"Stop, that's enough. I know what you're going to say, and I can assure you that Nancy wouldn't want you to live like this. It's been almost five years, and you have mourned long enough. If you don't think that Nancy would want you to be happy and get on with your life, you didn't know her like I did."

"I think you're misreading this whole thing," Jack countered.

"Bullshit. I know when a woman is in love. Kate is in love with you, but at some point, she is going to have to move on with her life. If she does, you are going to have missed out on an opportunity to be truly happy. I'm telling you this because I care for you, as do all of your friends. We've all been worried about you for a long time. Enough said. If I've overstepped by bounds, I'm sorry."

Jack sat in silence for several minutes.

Maggie finally broke the uncomfortable silence. "We'd better get over to the restaurant. I'll call the shuttle."

CHAPTER FIFTY-SIX

Kate's heart sank as Jack and Maggie walked arm in arm into the room. Jack pulled out the chair for Maggie and sat down next to her.

The party seemed to be in full swing when Jack and Maggie arrived. The crew were engaged in an animated conversation, and Kate sat quietly next to Tim, nursing a glass of red wine.

"I see that Tommy has taken good care of everyone," Jack said to no one in particular. Jack had requested Tommy as their waiter for the evening.

"Mr. Scanlon, it's good to see you again. What can I get for you and your guest?" Tommy took their order and disappeared into the bar area.

Jack ordered after-dinner drinks and an assortment of desserts for the table. Everyone seemed to be relaxed and enjoying themselves, except for Kate, who was uncharacteristically quiet and withdrawn. Jack was about to ask her if everything was all right but decided that she was simply tired and somewhat bored after almost eight hours searching for a German U-boat and a young boy's dream. He turned instead to Maggie. "I'm curious. What happens now that you've located the U-boat?"

"I'll turn in my report and our findings to the secretary of the navy through channels. Then it's up to the State Department and the lawyers to figure out the next steps." Maggie turned to Jack. "Let me ask you the same question. What are you going to do next?"

"I haven't given that much thought yet, but I suppose I would try and get Micah, Doc, Frank, and Pops to help me do an exploratory dive on the GPS location you gave us."

Maggie reached under the table and pulled a pen and small notepad out of her canvas tote bag. "Let me make a couple of suggestions. First, marine salvage law can be very complex. In general, anyone who recovers cargo lost at sea is entitled to financial compensation. That's the good news. The bad news is the state of Delaware, the federal government, or possibly even Spain could make a claim to whatever you find. I would suggest you read up on the *Atocha*. Several years ago, a salvage enterprise discovered the Spanish galleon *Atocha* off the Florida Keys and salvaged an enormous treasure of gold and silver. The state of Florida claimed the treasure, and the case went all the way to the US Supreme Court. All I'm suggesting is that you get legal advice from a firm experienced in maritime salvage law before you go off half cocked. Here are the names and contact information for two highly qualified firms." Maggie ripped a page out of her notebook and handed it to Jack.

"Thanks. Anything else?" Jack asked.

"Come to think of it, yes. Marine salvage is a tough job. Five guys and a boat might not hack it. You may need professional help." Maggie could see that Jack was hurt by her irreverent comment. "Let's say you find an unopened chest and try to raise it. In all likelihood, the wood would simply disintegrate. A professional salvage company would know how to raise the chest without damaging it. That's all I'm trying to say. I can provide you with names and numbers if you need them."

Maggie looked across the table at Tim and glanced down at her watch. "It looks like Tim is about to fall asleep, and I'm not far behind him."

Jack stood and helped Maggie with her chair. "It's been a long day, but I can't thank you and your crew enough for such an exciting afternoon. I'll take you and your crew back to the campus and come back and pick up Kate and Tim."

"That won't be necessary. Chief Martinez has already called the university's shuttle, and they are on their way. On behalf of the crew, I want to thank you and Kate for a spectacular dinner and a wonderful evening." Maggie reached out and gave Jack a hug. "Don't be a stranger, Scanlon, and Kate, I hope to see you and Tim in the near future."

CHAPTER FIFTY-SEVEN

Tim was curled up asleep in the back seat, and they were nearly home before anyone spoke.

"A penny for your thoughts?" Kate asked.

"What?"

"You haven't said a word since we left the restaurant. Is everything OK?"

"I'm sorry. I've got a lot on my mind."

"I understand. Maggie left you with a lot to think about."

Jack turned into Kate's driveway. "Actually, I haven't given that much thought since after dinner."

Kate said good night and had started to get out of the car when Jack reached across and grabbed her arm.

"Kate, I think we need to talk. J. R. should have brought Winston back by now, but I'll need to take him out again. Can you meet me on the beach in about twenty minutes?"

The knot in Kate's stomach tightened, and she felt as if she was having a hard time catching her breath. "Of course. Let me change into something more comfortable and check on Timmy."

ÝÝÝ

Jack waited on the beach for what seemed like an eternity. His heart was pounding, and he was having a hard time catching his breath. He took a couple of deep breaths that seemed to be calming. The night was hot and humid, which only added to his discomfort. The ocean was still, with gentle waves lapping at the shoreline. A few couples strolled along the beach in the fading twilight.

Kate tried to act nonchalant, but her heart was racing and her legs felt a little unsteady.

"So what's up?"

Jack didn't know where to start. "It's a nice night. Let's just walk down the beach." Jack's mouth was as dry as he could ever remember.

Kate tried to start a conversation as lightning flashed in the western horizon. "It looks like heat lightning. I haven't seen that in a while."

"Actually, Kate, there is no such thing as heat lightning. It's either a storm approaching or a distant thunderstorm reflecting off the dust particles in the atmosphere. At least that's what we were told in SEAL training."

They had walked almost a half mile before Jack stopped and turned toward her. Kate felt like she was going to faint. Her mind went numb. She felt as if her legs were going to give out.

Jack reached out for her hand. "Kate, I think…" He hesitated for a second. "No, I know that I'm madly, head over heels in love with you."

Kate's legs finally gave out, and she dropped to her knees in the sand.

Jack knelt facing her. "Kate, I understand if you don't feel the same."

Kate struggled to catch her breath. "I've been in love with you since the night you showed up with all those silly maps."

"Silly maps? Those maps helped us locate Tim's sunken galleon."

Kate threw her arms around his neck. "Jack, just shut up and kiss me."

Kate's heart was still racing, and tears welled up in her eyes and slowly slid down her cheeks.

"Why are you crying?"

"They're tears of happiness. It's been a long time since I've felt like this, and I don't want this feeling to end."

Jack kissed her again, this time with a passion he hadn't felt in years. A few raindrops started to fall. "It looks like we're going to get a storm after all." He helped Kate to her feet, put his arm around her shoulder, and pulled her close. "We'd better get back to the house before it really starts to rain."

They had gone no more than a hundred yards when the skies opened up. It was raining so hard they could barely see ten feet in front of them. They carefully climbed over the slippery rock jetty and raced for the stairs to Jack's deck. Kate beat him across the deck to the protection of the awning. She collapsed laughing against the sliding glass door.

Jack reached behind her neck, pulled her close, and kissed her. "Even soaked to the skin, you are beautiful."

Kate returned his kiss. "I have to check on Timmy. Can you come over?"

"Give me about twenty minutes to get out of these wet clothes."

"I'll leave the sliding door open." She kissed him one more time and raced across the deck and down the stairs.

Jack closed and locked the sliding glass door. Over a dozen candles were spread out around the family room. He thought the power had gone out until he saw the digital microwave clock. He loved the open floor plan and intended to make similar renovations to his house. He turned as Kate walked into the room barefooted and dressed in black sweatpants and a Princeton Soccer T-shirt.

Jack smiled. "Very sexy."

"I was going for comfortable."

"In that case, you nailed it."

"I thought we could cuddle on the couch and talk. I'm still trying to process everything."

Jack lay down on the couch and patted the cushion next to him. Kate curled up next to him, and Jack pulled her close and kissed her on the forehead.

"Wow, have we already regressed to a kiss on the forehead?"

Jack pulled her close and kissed her. "Is that better?"

"Yes, much better."

"What did you want to talk about?"

"Well, where do we go from here? Do we tell our friends that we're a couple or what?"

"I really don't think we have to. J. R. has been convinced for weeks that we are already a couple, and my

SEAL buddies knew I was in love with you before I realized it."

"Can I tell Roberta?"

"Of course. She's your best friend."

"You know that she'll tell Dave."

"Kate, if it wasn't pouring outside, I'd go out on the deck and shout it to the world. I haven't been this happy in many years."

"I don't think we should tell Timmy until we think this out. He idolizes you, and I'm not so sure he will be all that happy with having to share your attention. In any event, we have a couple of weeks to sort that all out. On Friday, I'm taking him to Camp Accohannock on the eastern shore. It's near Centreville, Maryland, on the Chester River. He's been going there for the past two years and loves it."

Jack sat up and thought for a minute.

"What's wrong?"

"Nothing. Can you take next Monday off?"

"I guess so. I'll have to juggle a few things. Why?"

"I am supposed to check in with the deputy director periodically and brief him on my progress. I thought we could both drive Tim to camp and continue on to Washington for a long weekend. You told me when you lived in Northern Virginia, you never got to see much of the capital. We could do some sightseeing, check out a few of my favorite restaurants, and maybe catch a play at the Kennedy Center or Ford's Theatre. What do you think?"

"It sounds amazing. I'll start packing tomorrow."

"I can get passes for the House and Senate gallery and arrange for a tour of the Capitol. I'll call Duffy in the morning and see if he can arrange a private tour of the White House for us."

Kate pulled Jack back down on the couch. "Let's snuggle, but you'll have to leave before Timmy wakes up." She ran her fingers up his chest. "You know, I thought you were going to tell me that you and Maggie had decided to rekindle your relationship."

"Kate, Maggie and I never had a relationship, at least not a sexual one. We dated years ago and soon realized that we were not compatible in that sense. I have always thought of Maggie as the little sister I never had. Don't get me wrong, I think the world of Maggie and always will."

Kate put her head on his chest and closed her eyes.

CHAPTER FIFTY-EIGHT

Malone tossed the brandy glass into the fireplace. His frustration again came bubbling to the surface. He had been cooped up in Finley's house for almost six months. Except for an occasional amorous visit from Pamela and a handful of cocktail and dinner party invitations, he remained housebound. He felt it was almost like being in prison.

He was heading for the veranda when his cell phone rang. He picked it up, knowing who was calling. "Hello."

"It's Aaron."

"I know. What's up, boss?"

"I want you to shut things down and move to the warehouse. Things are starting to get hot around here. I'm moving the entire operation to the eastern shore. I've rented an abandoned fish processing plant. The location will make it easier to distribute the product."

"What about shipments from Mexico?" Malone asked.

"We'll just have to make alternate arrangements. We've got enough product for a month or two. That will give us the time we need to arrange for the shipments to be rerouted."

"I've got a couple of fish on the line," Malone responded. "What do you want me to do about them?"

"If you mean Scanlon and my ex-wife, forget it. They're either on to you or very suspicious."

Malone detected a hint of irritation in Simpson's voice. "All right, give me three or four days to clean things up around here, and I'll head for the warehouse."

"Make it sooner rather than later." Simpson ended the call, and Malone sat staring at his phone.

Sherry was tabulating the night's receipts and closing up the bar when she heard her phone ring. She walked to the other end of the bar, grabbed her backpack from under the counter, and pulled out her phone.

"Hello, this is Sherry."

"It's Aaron. Remember our recent discussion about Vinny?"

Sherry's body tensed. "Yes."

"Well, it's time to execute our plan. Understand?"

"Yes. Do you mean tonight?"

"Yes. Are there any problems on your end?"

"No. No problems."

"Good. Once you're done, put the signs on the front and back doors and close up. Get everything you need and meet me at the warehouse as soon as possible."

Sherry hung up without responding. This was more than she had bargained for, but she was in too deep to turn back. She put her backpack on the bar, unzipped one of the side pockets, and pulled out a vial of clear liquid. She pulled out a silver-plated tray from one of the cabinets and grabbed two brandy glasses off the shelf behind the bar. Sherry opened the vial and poured an equal amount of the liquid in both glasses. She then swirled the glasses in her hand one by one, coating each glass with the liquid. She grabbed an unopened bottle of Maker's Mark off the shelf and placed it in the center of the tray. She then placed a glass on each side of the bottle. She leaned back against the counter and took a deep breath.

Sherry knocked on the office door, opened it, and walked in. "I've finished sorting the night's receipts. I'll bring in the cash and send the credit card charges to the accountant."

Pointing to the tray suspiciously, Vinny asked, "What's this all about?"

"It's been a long day. I thought you and I could use a drink before closing up. I hope you don't mind me joining you."

Vinny waved her in. "Put the tray on the desk."

Sherry ran a knife around the rim of the distinctive faux candle-wax seal. She poured two fingers in each glass and handed one to Vinny.

"I'll take the other glass if you don't mind," Vinny said suspiciously.

Sherry shrugged. "No problem." She handed Vinny the other glass and sat down in the chair in front of his desk. She put her glass down and faked the beginning of a sneezing fit.

Vinny lifted his glass, tipped it toward Sherry, said, "Salut," and took a swig of the poisonous liquid. He sat back in his chair and stared at Sherry as if to say, "Why?"

Vinny grabbed the edge of the desk with both hands. His body stiffened and convulsed. Sherry watched with a twinge of sympathy as Vinny's eyes rolled back in his head and white foam seeped from the corner of his mouth. After a few seconds, his body went limp. His chair spun backward and across the room as Vinny's body fell to the concrete floor.

Sherry placed the bottle and both glasses on the tray and returned to the bar. She wiped down the bourbon bottle and placed it back on the shelf. She rinsed out both glasses and put them in the dishwasher.

Sherry grabbed her backpack and returned to Vinny's office. Vinny could never remember the combination to the safe, regardless of the fact that it was only four numbers. She knew he kept the combination written on a three-by-five card in the top unlocked drawer of the desk. She opened the drawer and, without much searching, found the combination.

A large framed picture of Vinny's boat hung on the wall, concealing the safe. She removed the frame and spun the dial to the right several times, stopping at forty-seven. She followed the directions on the card until she finally heard the tumblers fall into place. Pulling down on the handle, the safe opened. She stepped back in amazement at the contents in the safe. It contained a .38 revolver and stacks and stacks of hundred-dollar bills. She estimated that it contained at least a quarter of a million dollars.

Sherry pulled her gym clothes out of the backpack and started stuffing it with stacks of hundreds.

Surprisingly, all of the money fit, with a little room to spare. She tightly rolled her gym clothes, placing them on top of the money, and tucked the .38 revolver in a side pocket. She closed the safe and hung the framed picture back on the wall.

She returned to the bar and retrieved two large cardboard signs from behind the beer cooler. The signs were identical. They indicated that the restaurant and bar were closed until further notice by the Sussex County Department of Health and Safety and displayed an official-looking seal of the department.

Sherry taped the signs to the front and rear entrances to the restaurant and returned to the bar. She tossed the credit card receipts in the beer cooler, stuffed the cash in her jeans, picked up her backpack, and headed for the front door.

She closed and locked the front door, turned to leave, and, startled, jumped back against the door. "Jesus, J. R., you scared the shit out of me." She bent over with her hands on her knees to catch her breath.

"Sorry to startle you like that. I thought you were open until after midnight. I just came by to have a little chat with Vinny."

Sherry stepped aside to allow J. R. to read the sign on the door. "The county health department dropped by this afternoon for a surprise inspection. They claimed to have found several serious health code violations and ordered Vinny to close the restaurant and bar immediately. Vinny thinks that he was set up. In any event, the Roadhouse is closed until further notice."

"So where is Vinny?" J. R. asked.

"He called his boss in Philly to report what happened, and they requested his presence. Actually, it was more of an order than a request. They have had Vinny on a short leash for some time. I thought it was only a matter of time before they canned him, or worse."

"I thought I saw his car out back."

"You did. I called him a town car to take him up and back. He was in no condition to drive. He had been drinking all afternoon, and it only got worse when the health department inspectors arrived."

"When do you expect him back?"

"I don't know for sure, but I suspect he will be back no later than tomorrow afternoon."

"If you see him before I do, please tell him I need to talk to him about his whereabouts on the night that Anna disappeared."

"I will. Is that all you wanted?"

"Yes. Can I walk you to your car?"

"Sure. Thanks, J. R.. You are a true gentleman."

"Let me carry the backpack for you. It looks heavy."

Sherry felt the sweat run down her neck. "Thanks, but I can manage. I'm a big, strong girl."

As they walked to Sherry's car, J. R. noticed the barrel of a handgun sticking out of the side pocket of her backpack. "Do you carry that for protection?"

"What?"

"The handgun in the side pocket of your backpack—do you carry that for protection?"

"Ah, yes. I have a concealed carry permit for it. Leaving this place late at night, you never know who you'll run into."

Sherry opened her car door. "Thanks for walking me to my car. I hope to see you again soon if the Roadhouse ever reopens."

"Have a nice evening." J. R. tilted his hat back as he watched Sherry pull out of the parking lot.

CHAPTER FIFTY-NINE

Tim sat on the front porch steps next to a military-style backpack as Jack pulled up in his Jeep. Jack turned off the engine, walked to the back of the Jeep, and opened the rear liftgate. "Good morning. Where is your suitcase?"

Tim lifted his backpack and handed it to Jack.

"That's it? You're going to camp for two weeks with what's in your backpack? Don't you think your clothes are going to get a little ripe?"

"I doubt it. They have laundry service every Wednesday and Saturday. They give you a mesh laundry bag with a brass tag that has your cabin and bunk number on it. They pick up the laundry on Wednesday and Saturday mornings and have it back to you in the late afternoon. Oh, by the way, only dorks bring a suitcase to camp."

"Sorry, I stand corrected. I've never been to camp, unless you count SEAL training and Iraq and Afghanistan as camp. But then we didn't have to bring much. They provided us with everything we needed."

"You mean you never went to camp when you were my age?"

"Never, but my father took my brother and me on weekend camping trips when we were young." Jack looked around and up at the front door. "Incidentally, where is your mother?"

Tim laughed. "The last time I saw her, she was in her room packing. She had two large suitcases on the floor and one of those makeup things. There were dresses spread all over the bed. She picked out four pair of shoes, not counting her running shoes."

"You've got to be kidding me. We're only going away for a few days," Jack said, exasperated.

Tim pointed to Jack's Jeep Grand Cherokee. "If you're going to travel with my mom, you're going to need a bigger car."

Jack sighed and sat down on the steps next to Tim. *No need getting off on the wrong foot. Just suck it up*, he thought to himself.

Kate struggled to the front door with two medium-sized suitcases, a backpack, and a makeup case. Jack turned as he heard the door open. He ran up the stairs to help Kate with her luggage. "Let me carry those." Jack picked up the two suitcases and started down the stairs. "What do you have in here, gold bars?"

"No," Kate responded indignantly. "You said we would be going out to dinner two or three nights and possibly to a play. In addition, you said we may be going to the White House. You can't expect me to wear the same thing day after day."

He could, but he realized that it was a guy thing and there was no upside to responding. "I guess that makes sense." Through all his huffing and puffing, he hadn't noticed how beautiful Kate looked. When Tim turned to get in the back seat, Jack kissed Kate gently on the cheek.

When they got onto Route 1, Jack asked Tim about camp. "So are you excited to get back to camp?"

"I've been looking forward to this for almost a year," Tim said excitedly. "This year I'm in the senior cabin."

"What does that mean?"

"The camp is divided up by age groups, seven- and eight-, nine- and ten-, and eleven- and twelve-year-olds. There are three eight-man cabins for each age group, with an equal number of ages in each cabin. For example, this year I will be in a cabin with three other eleven-year-olds and four twelve-year-olds. The different age groups learn and do different things. The younger group learns to swim, goes on hikes, and does crafts. The older group learns how to sail, competes in orienteering, and is taught survival skills. Do you know what orienteering is?"

"I think so. It's sort of a navigation sport."

"It will be my first year competing. I've watched it before. They give you a map and a compass, and you must navigate your way through eight checkpoints in the fastest time possible. I can't wait to try it."

"I almost wish I could go to camp with you. Do they have a geezer age group? You know, I went through survival training with the SEALs. What sort of things do you learn in their survival training?"

"This will be my first year doing it, so I've only heard stories. Oh, there is a great story from last year. On the final Tuesday, the 'graduating' twelve-year-olds have to go into the woods and find food and drink for their own supper that night. Usually guys come back with berries, roots, water, and apples. Last year, this one guy came back with a snake that he had killed. He skinned and gutted it, boiled the carcass, and ate it for dinner. It was disgusting. He was sick the next day. I suspect he'll grow up to be a marine."

Jack and Kate erupted in laughter. Tim settled back in his seat and rummaged through his backpack for his iPod and earphones.

"That sounds like a pretty exclusive camp. There must be a waiting list a mile long. How did you get Tim in?"

"You're right. There is a huge waiting list. Some boys never get into the camp. Some parents sign their boys up shortly after they are born. I'm not proud of it, but I pulled some strings. Dr. Dubois and Debbie are two of the camp's major benefactors, and Bill is on the board. Both of their boys went there. If fact, they are the ones who told me about the camp. So I asked Bill if he would write a letter of recommendation for us to send in with Timmy's application, and surprise, surprise, Timmy was accepted the first year."

"I wouldn't know, but it seems to pay to have friends in high places."

"Like I said, not proud of it, but, as you know, I'd do anything for Timmy."

Jack slowly pulled into the parking lot that also doubled as the camp's soccer field. Several "dorks" were pulling their Rollaboard suitcases across the grassy field. The Jeep hadn't come to a complete stop before Tim opened the back door. As Jack and Kate got out to say goodbye, they heard a boy near the cabins yell out Timmy's name.

"Tim, over here. We're in the same cabin," shouted the boy.

Tim grabbed his backpack out of the back of the Jeep and ran across the field toward the cabin and his beckoning friend. Kate looked crestfallen as Timmy raced away.

"He didn't even say goodbye," she muttered to herself.

Jack put his arm around her shoulder. "At least you know he's going to enjoy the next two weeks."

Suddenly Timmy stopped, turned around, and waved goodbye to Kate and Jack.

"See? He didn't forget to say goodbye after all. It's not the hug you were expecting, but just take comfort in how happy he is."

CHAPTER SIXTY

Jack pulled under the Italian Renaissance–style portico to the front entrance of the historic Hay-Adams Hotel. The hotel was named for John Hay, who served as personal secretary to President Abraham Lincoln, and Henry Adams, descendant of Presidents John Adams and John Quincy Adams. It was the most elegant hotel in the nation's capital and had played host to such luminaries as Charles Lindbergh, Amelia Earhart, Mark Twain, President Theodore Roosevelt, and many others.

Kate sat agog in the passenger side as the doorman approached the car. "This place is spectacular."

"You haven't seen anything yet." Jack rolled down his window as the doorman approached.

"Good afternoon, sir and madam. Are you checking in?"

"Yes," Jack replied. He stepped out of the car and walked around to the passenger side to open the door for Kate. "Yes, we're checking in for three nights. The name is Scanlon."

The doorman pulled a sheet of paper from his vest pocket and perused the list. "Ah yes, Mr. and Mrs.

Scanlon, welcome to the Hay-Adams. Your room is ready. If you would please check in at the front desk, I'll see to it that your luggage is immediately delivered to your room."

Jack handed the doorman a twenty-dollar bill, took Kate's hand, and escorted her into the lobby. As they approached the front desk, a beautiful young girl in a well-tailored gray suit greeted them with a packet of information in a blue folder with "The Hay-Adams" embossed in gold leaf across the front. "Welcome to the Hay-Adams, Mr. and Mrs. Scanlon. I have you staying in the presidential suite for three nights."

Kate was starting to feel overwhelmed, first by being referred to as Mrs. Scanlon and then by learning that they would be staying in the hotel's presidential suite for their romantic getaway.

Jack took the packet of information and the keys to the suite from the desk clerk. The young girl signaled the bellman and escorted Kate and Jack to the elevators. "Robert will see you to your room. Your luggage should already be there. If you need anything during your stay, please call the front desk. My name is Angela."

Jack opened the door, and Kate gasped in astonishment. The suite was enormous, with a large master bedroom and bath, a dining room that sat six, and a small library with an antique writing desk. The sitting room opened to a rooftop balcony overlooking Lafayette Square and the White House.

"This is bigger than most people's homes. I've never seen anything like it," Kate said in amazement.

Jack held her close and kissed her. "I just wanted to do something special for you." Jack looked at his watch. "Now, however, I've got to run an errand. I should be back in an hour. We have a 6:30 p.m. dinner reservation at the Occidental Restaurant. It's only a fifteen-minute walk from here. If you need anything or would like to visit the spa, just call the front desk."

"I think I'll just relax with a glass of wine on the balcony and take it all in."

A distinguished-looking woman, approximately in her mid- to late sixties, approached as Jack entered the store. "Good afternoon, and welcome to the Tiny Jewel Box. How can I help you?"

"I'm looking for an engagement ring."

"Congratulations. If you'll follow me to the other end of the display case, I'm sure we will be able to find a spectacular ring that will fit your budget."

Jack shrugged. "Congratulations may be a little premature. She hasn't said yes yet."

The woman sensed that Jack was a little anxious. She smiled warmly. "I'm sure she will. However, in the unlikely event that she doesn't, you can return the ring for a full refund."

Jack took a deep breath, wishing that she had stopped after saying, "I'm sure she will."

"How much do you know about diamonds?" she asked.

"I'm afraid not much."

"Do you have time for a short tutorial?"

Jack didn't know why, but he instinctively looked at his watch. "Yes, thank you. I'd appreciate that."

"Diamonds are graded according to what we call the four Cs: cut, color, clarity, and carat weight. Arguably, the most important of these is cut, because it has the greatest influence on a diamond's brilliance or sparkle." She pulled a small chart off the shelf behind the display counter. It showed three diamond shapes. "The diagram on the left shows a diamond whose shape is too shallow, and the one on the right shows one that is too deep. The one in the center is the perfect shape because it most effectively reflects the light."

"Sounds a little like the Goldilocks story," Jack interjected. "Sorry for interrupting."

"No problem. I understand you might be a little nervous about all this." She continued without missing a beat. "Very few diamonds fall into the ideal shape. The second most important feature is color. In this case, the less color, the higher the diamond's grade. The color scale runs from D through Z. The highest color grade is D."

Jack looked surprised. "D is the highest color grade? What happened to A, B, and C?"

"Yes, I'm not exactly sure why, but color is graded from a grade of Z, the lowest, to a grade of D, the highest. If you're still curious, I'll try to find out why D is the highest grade."

Jack laughed and waved her off. "That's OK. It is what it is. I can always Google it if it keeps me awake at night."

"I apologize. I forgot to introduce myself. I'm Margaret Barrett, the store manager. My friends call me Peggy."

"I'm Jack Scanlon—actually it's John. My friends call me Jack."

"All right, back to the tutorial. The least important factor in evaluating a diamond is clarity."

"Ah, why's that?" Jack asked. "I would think that it would be the most important."

"Most people do. However, imperfections in commercial diamonds are so small that they often can't be seen without the use of high magnification. The final factor is the weight of the diamond, called carat weight. This is the most misunderstood characteristic. Weight does not mean size. A large percentage of diamond buyers think that the higher the carat weight, the better the diamond. In actuality, a half-carat diamond that is colorless with an ideal cut and few flaws may be of considerably more value than a two-carat diamond. So that's Diamonds 101 in a nutshell. Any questions?"

"No, thank you. You've covered it quite well."

"Shall we look at some engagement rings?" she asked. "I'll show you several, but we can get you anything you would like. It just may take us a few days."

"I'll need something today."

"I understand." She unlocked and opened the display case and placed two black velvet trays on the top of the case.

"What's the nicest ring you have?"

Peggy picked up a ring and placed it on a small velvet pillow. "This is the finest diamond engagement ring we currently have in stock. It is a 4.01 carat colorless D diamond. It is rated a VS1 on the clarity scale, which is rated between very good and ideal."

"How much is it?"

She picked up a small white tag attached to the ring and turned it over. "This one is $53,000, but we have very nice rings for a fraction of the cost."

Jack didn't flinch. "I did some research and know that the Tiny Jewel Box has an outstanding reputation." Jack pointed to the ring on the black velvet pillow. "May I?"

"Of course."

Jack picked up the ring and carefully examined it. "I'll take this one," Jack said, handing the ring back to her.

Peggy was a little surprised by what she considered an impulsive buy. She leaned back against the counter. "Tell me a little bit about your future fiancée."

Jack was a little taken aback and uncomfortable by the store manager's query. "I'm not sure where to start. Her name is Kate, and she's two years younger than me. She's divorced, with a young son we both adore. She's a lawyer who works helping abused and battered women. I'm not sure what else to tell you."

"The only reason I ask is I'm not sure how many women would be comfortable wearing a $53,000 ring on a regular basis. Personally, I'd be afraid of losing the ring or having the diamond come loose from the setting at some point."

"I would certainly insure it," Jacked responded somewhat crisply.

"Enough said. I'll write up the sales receipt and be right back."

Jack handed her an American Express platinum card.

After what seemed to Jack like an inordinate amount of time but was actually less than five minutes, she returned. She handed Jack the credit card receipt and the ring in a fancy small box.

Jack signed the receipt and thanked her.

"Don't forget, you can return it if she is not satisfied or would like to see something else. If I'm not here, ask for my son, Matthew."

"Thank you. I appreciate all your help and the tutorial."

CHAPTER SIXTY-ONE

As the waiter approached, Kate reached across the table and placed her hand over Jack's. "I still can't believe all of this is real. I'm afraid I am going to wake up to find out this was a dream. Ever since we arrived, I've felt like I'm in a fairy tale. You certainly know how to impress a girl."

The waiter cleared his throat in an effort to get the two lovers' attention. "May I bring you a dessert menu?"

Kate turned to Jack. "Would you split the crème brûlée with me?"

"Certainly, and how about a glass of port?" Jack asked her.

"That sounds great."

"Would you bring us two glasses of the Presidential Twenty-Year Tawny Port and one order of the raspberry crème brûlée with two spoons."

Jack kissed Kate's hand. "I'm a little surprised at your choice of entrées and now the dessert. You're usually so calorie conscious."

"There are no calories when you're on vacation or away from home. Besides, I can work it all off sightseeing the next couple of days."

"Speaking of which, the night is still young, and I'd like to show you the National Mall from the Lincoln Memorial at night. It's a sight I never get tired of. Besides, it's a beautiful night for a walk."

Hand in hand, Jack led Kate through a marble arch.

"This is the new World War II Memorial. It honors the men and women who served during the war, including those who supported the war effort from the home front. In my opinion, it's long overdue. We are losing more and more of our World War II veterans every year. I only wish that they all could have seen this."

"It's spectacular, particularly with the sun setting behind it."

"The only problem I have with it is that it looks like it was designed by Albert Speer," Jack lamented.

Kate looked at Jack questioningly. "Albert Speer?"

"He was Hitler's architect."

"Wow, I sure hope no one else thinks that."

"Me too." Jack took Kate's hand. "Let's continue on down the Mall. Have you ever seen the Vietnam Veterans Memorial?"

"No, I've only seen pictures."

"Be forewarned: it's an emotional experience. It's like visiting the *Arizona* Memorial or the Holocaust Museum. It leaves you speechless. I visited it with my father after it was dedicated in 1982. He served two tours in Vietnam and knew several of the men whose names are on the wall. I tried to ask him questions, but he was so choked up that he couldn't talk. He told me months later that several of the men on the wall were in his unit."

Kate reached for Jack's hand as they entered the memorial from the east. "This is very stark and yet so solemn. It's like being at a funeral."

She watched as an older gentleman did an etching of a name on one of the black marble panels. He turned and handed it to the woman standing behind him. She took the rubbing, looked at it, and started sobbing uncontrollably. Kate could feel tears welling up in her eyes as they walked past the couple.

"That sort of thing happens virtually every day. They are over fifty-eight thousand names of soldiers who gave their lives in Vietnam on these marble slabs. The memorial was very controversial when it was first erected, but today most people have accepted it as a fitting tribute to the men who died there." Jack stopped next to a bronze statue of three soldiers in combat gear. "The controversy was so strong that this statue was added in 1984. Oddly enough, it's the first statue of an African American on the National Mall."

Kate squeezed Jack's hand. "I can see that this memorial has special meaning for you."

"I warned you it is an emotional experience. I guess I think a lot about what my father must have seen and been through during his combat tours."

"You must have seen similar horrors during your deployments."

"I think it was very different from Iraq and Afghanistan, particularly their homecoming. They were spit on and called baby killers. If you were stationed in this area, you never went off post with your uniform on."

Jack led Kate along the path south toward the Lincoln Memorial. He stopped in front of another statue depicting three women attending to a wounded soldier, one looking skyward, supposedly for a medevac helicopter.

"This statue was added to the memorial in 1993 to honor the more than 250,000 nurses who served in Vietnam. When people think of the Vietnam War, they rarely think of the nurses who served and helped save so many lives. Now I want to show you my favorite memorial."

Jack took Kate's hand as they walked down the path to the Lincoln Memorial. "I've read almost everything that has been written about President Lincoln. Well, that's a bit of an exaggeration, but I have read a lot and consider him our greatest president. I used to come here regularly. I think it's very moving."

"I agree. Let's climb the steps to the statue."

As they reached the top step, Jack pointed to the columns. "There are thirty-six columns surrounding the memorial, representing the thirty-six states of the Union at the time of President Lincoln's death."

"Have you ever considered being a tour guide? You'd be good at it."

Jack smiled. "Maybe in retirement."

Kate walked to the base of the statue. "It's magnificent."

"It's a very special place, and I wanted you to see it. Many famous speeches have been given on the steps of this memorial, including Martin Luther King's 'I Have a Dream' speech in 1963." Jack reached for Kate's hand again. "The sun has set. Why don't we sit on the steps for a few minutes and enjoy the view? They call Paris the City of Lights, but it can't hold a candle to our nation's capital at night."

Jack walked down a few steps, took off his suit jacket, and placed it on the steps for Kate to sit on. He stood leaning against the south buttress. He could feel his heart pounding as he reached into his pocket for the small velvet-covered box. He took a deep breath, stepped down, and knelt in front of Kate. He slowly opened the box. "Kate Fitzgerald Simpson, will you marry me?"

Kate was so startled she could barely speak. After several agonizing seconds for Jack, she nodded her head and whispered yes.

"This is the most spectacular ring I've ever seen."

Unbeknownst to Kate and Jack, several small groups of tourists had recognized what was happening and, at a respectful distance, stopped to watch. Someone shouted, "Is that a yes?"

Embarrassed, Kate nodded and leaned forward to kiss Jack. Polite applause erupted from several corners of the memorial.

Jack helped Kate to her feet and grabbed his jacket. "I'm so sorry. I hadn't intended this to be so public. Let's head back to the hotel and celebrate."

"I think it was sweet and certainly memorable. You're full of surprises, Mr. Scanlon. I think our life together is going to be extremely exciting. Now, let's grab a taxi. My feet are killing me in these shoes."

CHAPTER SIXTY-TWO

As the elevator doors opened, Kate grabbed Jack's hand and whisked him down the hall to the suite. Jack impatiently searched his pockets for the room key. Kate held up her key and inserted it into the lock.

"Isn't his where I'm supposed to carry you across the threshold?" Jack asked.

"Actually, that's a wedding night thing."

Jack opened the door with a gentlemanly flair. Kate bowed slightly and entered the foyer. She kicked off her shoes and uttered a soft sigh of relief. Jack took off his tie and hung his suit jacket over the chair next to the desk. Jack kicked off his shoes as well. "Why do women wear shoes that hurt their feet?"

"I don't know. Fashion, I suppose. I think by know you know I'm not a girly girl, but I wanted to look nice for our special evening. Only I had no idea how special the evening would really be. Women will go through a lot of pain for the men they love."

Jack reached for the phone on the desk and started to dial.

"What are you doing?"

"I'm ordering the best bottle of champagne the Hay-Adams has to offer."

"Hang up the phone," Kate ordered emphatically.

"What?"

"I said hang up the phone. I have a different idea of how we're going to celebrate."

Kate slowly unbuttoned her blouse and let it fall to the floor. Jack stood paralyzed as she approached him. He started to fumble with the buttons on his shirt. Kate had a fire in her eyes that he had never seen before. She reached out with both hands and ripped Jack's shirt open. Involuntarily, he started to retreat backward as Kate steered him in the direction of the bedroom. She reached down and unbuckled his belt. His pants fell to the floor. Kate unzipped her skirt and let it fall to the floor as she stepped forward, once again forcing Jack to retreat. She unclasped her bra and flung it to the side, and then she stepped out of her panties and tossed them aside as well.

Jack could retreat no farther as he backed against the foot of the bed. With both hands, Kate forcefully pushed Jack backward onto the bed. She slowly crawled up his torso and straddled his chest. She leaned forward and kissed him gently on the forehead and then passionately on the lips.

She kissed his chest as she slowly slid back down his body. She could feel his erection, and she reached down and guided him into her. Kate sat back and felt as if a bolt of lightning had coursed through her body. She took a deep breath and rocked forward and back a couple of times.

Suddenly, Jack's body stiffened. "Oh my god, Kate, I am so sorry."

Kate leaned forward and placed her index finger against his lips. "Shh, it's all right."

"I'm so embarrassed. It's just that I haven't been with a woman in a long time."

"It's been a long time for me as well." Kate smiled. "I guess we'll just have to practice and practice until we're back in form." Kate sat up. "Now, lie back. I'll be right back."

Jack watched her as she walked to the bathroom. He was awed by her grace and beauty. He couldn't believe how lucky he was to find love again.

Kate returned in seconds with a towel and damp washcloth. She gently washed and dried his genitals, wadded up the towel and washcloth, and tossed them toward the bathroom door. She slid up the bed and kissed him. "Now, let's cuddle."

Kate opened one eye and glanced at the digital clock on the nightstand. Its two-inch red digits read 5:43 a.m. She could see the first light of day starting to illuminate the bedroom. She felt movement on the bed as Jack's hand reached around and cupped her breast. She turned as Jack kissed her on the cheek, and suddenly, she felt a hardness against her buttocks.

It must be time to practice, she thought to herself.

For the next forty-five minutes, they made love in every position known to man, and a couple that were not.

Finally, Jack collapsed next to Kate. "I think we're starting to get the hang of this sex thing."

Kate breathlessly tried to laugh. "That, Mr. Scanlon, was wonderful."

Jack leaned up on one elbow. "I've got an idea. Why don't we put the 'Do Not Disturb' sign on the door and spend the rest of the day practicing?"

"Not on your life. I want to do some sightseeing, and don't forget, Duffy has arranged a private tour of the White House for us at two o'clock. Now, you rest up while I shower, and then I'll order room service."

Jack lay back and closed his eyes.

Kate sat on the foot of the bed for a moment with her hand over her mouth to stifle a laugh. A trail of clothes led from the entrance hall to the foot of the bed. Her bra hung precariously from a lampshade. A bust of Abraham Lincoln sat on the corner of the credenza. Kate's panties hung ignominiously around Honest Abe's neck. Kate giggled. *Mary Todd would not have approved.*

Kate jumped up and ran to the closet. She grabbed a laundry bag and began stuffing the clothes into the bag. If a guest's laundry and dry cleaning were placed outside the front door by 8:00 a.m., the hotel would have it back to them by 4:00 p.m. She peered out the peephole at the hallway. With no one in sight, she quickly opened the door far enough to toss the laundry bag outside.

Kate emerged from the bathroom dressed in a white terry cloth robe with the Hay-Adams logo emblazoned over the left breast pocket. Her hair was wrapped in a white towel atop her head, and she was wearing the fluffy hotel slippers.

Jack rolled onto his side, facing her. "You look like some sort of Mideastern potentate. However, with all the hotel's logo wear you've got on, maybe we should get someone up here to take a picture of you for their promotional brochures."

"You're a laugh a minute, Scanlon. I'm going to order breakfast. What would you like?"

"Bacon," Jack replied emphatically.

"Bacon—just bacon?"

"No. You know, the stuff that goes with it, scrambled eggs, hash browns, toast, juice, and coffee."

"Why don't you hop in the shower while I order room service?" Kate walked away, rolling her eyes and mumbling to herself, "Right, bacon."

Kate picked up the phone and pushed the button marked "Room Service."

It rang twice, and a young woman's voice answered. "Good morning, Mrs. Scanlon. How can I be of service?"

Kate was beginning to get used to being referred to as Mrs. Scanlon and wasn't about to correct her. "I'd like to order breakfast for two."

"Of course. What can I get for you?"

"We would like one fruit-and-yogurt bowl, one all-American breakfast, a medium carafe of coffee, and two small orange juices."

"Excellent." The young girl repeated the order. "We'll have that up to you in about thirty minutes."

Kate hung up the phone and had started to walk back to the bedroom when the door chime rang.

She opened the door to see Micah Cruise standing there dressed in a dark blue suit with a briefcase in his left hand.

"Kate?"

"You look surprised." Kate held up her left hand.

"Well, I see that silly ass finally came to his senses." Micah reached down and hugged Kate. "Congratulations. We've known for weeks that he was in love with you. When did he finally realize it?"

"Earlier this week he told me that he was madly in love with me, and last night he surprised me by asking me to marry him." Kate again held up the ring. "I obviously said yes."

"You think it's big enough?" Micah teased.

"Yes, I know. We're going to exchange it for something a little more practical later this morning. Please don't say anything about it. I think he's a little hurt, and it's become a touchy subject. I'm afraid I teased him about it without considering his feelings. He wanted everything to be so perfect last night that he went a little overboard with the ring. Now, I just ordered breakfast. Would you like to join us?"

"Thank you. I'm starving. I was going to pick up something on the way to the office."

"Great. What would you like?"

"I'll have juice, coffee, and something with bacon."

Kate walked to the desk, picked up the phone, and again pushed the button marked "Room Service."

"Good morning, Mrs. Scanlon. How can I be of service?"

"I'd like to add another all-American breakfast to our previous order. We'll be three for breakfast. Please add another juice, and make that a large carafe of coffee."

The girl again repeated the order. "Excellent, we'll have that up to you shortly."

As Kate hung up the phone, Jack appeared in the opening to the bedroom, dressed in khaki slacks and drying his hair with a white hand towel. "Micah? Oh damn, I forgot about our appointment this morning. I'm sorry."

"It seems like you've had a few other things on your mind. Congratulations."

"Please make yourself comfortable while Kate and I finish getting dressed." Jack closed the French doors to the bedroom behind them.

CHAPTER SIXTY-THREE

Micah leaned back in his chair. "That was outstanding. Sure beats the breakfast burrito from Miguel's food truck on 10th Street. I've got a ten o'clock appointment with the deputy director, so why don't we go over the results of the testing you asked us to perform?"

Kate cleared the table and poured coffee for Micah and Jack.

Micah opened his briefcase and pulled out a stack of papers and photos. "Let's start with the fingerprints and hair samples you gave me." He slid a photo across the table to Kate and Jack. "Do you know the man in the photo?"

Jack picked up the photo, examined it, and handed it to Kate. "It looks like a young Jeremy Madison." Kate nodded in agreement.

"The prints you gave me belong to that man. His real name is Gerald Malone. He did three years in the Alabama State Penitentiary for fraud and embezzlement, and he's currently wanted in Louisiana for multiple felonies."

Micah shuffled through a stack of papers and pulled out the photo of a woman. He slid the photo across the table. "The hair samples belong to that woman. Do you know her?"

Jack showed the photo to Kate. "Yes, we know her. Her name is Pamela Quinn. She's a real estate agent in Rehoboth Beach."

Micah laughed. "Well, you're close. Her first name is Pamela, but her last name is Malone. She's Gerald Malone's biological sister. Allow me to give you a little background on these two." Micah again shuffled through his stack of papers and pulled out a yellow legal pad. "They ran away from home, allegedly due to parental abuse. They stole a car and went on a minor crime spree through Florida, Georgia, and Alabama until they were apprehended outside of Mobile. They were both convicted. However, since she was a minor at the time, she was sent to a youth facility. They hooked up again after he got out of prison and allegedly swindled a few wealthy old ladies in Louisville, Kentucky, out of several hundred thousand dollars. After that they simply fell off the grid. That was almost eight years ago."

Jack scratched his head. "What you're telling us is hard to believe. We met with this guy to discuss an investment fund he manages. He's a very bright guy, and Pamela, from all accounts, is an excellent Realtor."

Micah tapped his pen on the legal pad for emphasis. "I didn't say they weren't smart. Simply to evade the law as long as they have takes considerable talent. They're survivors."

Micah pulled several papers from the stack to his left. "That brings me to the crime scene evidence that the

Lewes Police Department and J. R. requested us to process. I contacted the medical examiner, and he provided us with a sample of Anna Campbell's blood. It was an exact match with the blood found on the sheets. That's not all. There were semen stains on the sheets. We ran the DNA through the national database, and it matched this charmer." Micah slid another photo across the table to Jack.

Jack and Kate examined the photo and looked back at Micah in shock.

"That's Deputy Crockett," Kate exclaimed.

"Deputy? What the hell are you talking about?" Micah asked disbelievingly.

"He's J. R.'s number two. He has been with the Rehoboth Beach Police Department for a little over six months."

"What the hell? Doesn't J. R. do a background check on prospective applicants?"

"I'm sure he does," Jack responded defensively. "Somehow Crockett must have fallen through the cracks."

Micah leaned back in his chair. "Let me tell you something about this scum ball. He makes Malone look like a choir boy. He was charged with raping seven different women in Slidell, Louisiana. At trial, somehow the police evidence went missing, and he got off on a technicality. A month later, he was arrested, tried, and convicted of assaulting a woman in Alabama. He was sentenced to serve five years in the Alabama State Penitentiary. Guess who his cellmate was?"

"I'm guessing that would be Gerald Malone," Kate chimed in.

"Give that lady a gold star. Oh, and there is something I forgot to tell you. The evidence also included a rubber hammer. We ran the prints on it, and there were no matches in the system. So if that was the murder weapon, then Crockett didn't deliver the fatal blow or was wearing gloves. In other words, he might have had an accomplice or accomplices."

"I'm trying to wrap my head around all this and how it fits in with the three murders," Jack replied. "Clearly, Crockett killed or abetted in the killing of Anna Campbell. Anna was most likely killed because of something she knew about illegal activity at the Roadhouse. I'm also pretty sure that Puglisi ordered the killing. I've said from the start that I thought all three murders were connected. Now, I'm not so sure. How does Anna's murder and what was going on at the Roadhouse have anything to do with the MacIntyre murders? I now think we have two separate crimes."

Jack's train of thought was interrupted by the ringing of Kate's cell phone.

Kate stood up and started to walk toward the bedroom. "Sorry, I've got to take this. It's Timmy's camp calling."

Jack turned back to Micah. "Have you notified J. R. about Crockett?"

"No. I didn't know until just now that he was J. R.'s deputy."

"I'll call him, and maybe Kate and I should go back."

"You're not going back with this hurricane coming, are you?"

"What hurricane?"

"Do you two live in a bubble? There's a major Category 3 hurricane coming up the East Coast. It's predicted to hit somewhere between Virginia Beach and Cape May sometime late Sunday evening. Turn on the news."

Kate returned to the table. "That was Timmy's camp counselor. There is a hurricane coming up the coast, and they're shutting down the camp until it passes. We have to pick him up before noon tomorrow."

"Micah just told me about the hurricane. They are about to give an update on the storm." Jack turned up the volume on the TV.

"This is a News 9 alert. We now take you to the National Hurricane Center in Atlanta for the 8:00 a.m. update. Good morning, Dr. Sperry, and thank you for joining us. What can you tell us about Hurricane Jennifer?"

"Good morning, Jackie, and thank you for having me on. Jennifer has just been downgraded to a strong Category 2 storm with winds of up to 110 miles per hour. Make no mistake, this is still an extremely dangerous storm. Jennifer is currently located 280 miles north-northeast of the Bahama Islands, moving in a northwesterly direction at nine miles per hour, and is expected to pick up speed over the next several hours. This map shows the projected track of several models. All of the models except one have the storm following the US coastline from Cape Hatteras all the way up the New Jersey coast and then swinging eastward toward Boston. The one model that has us scratching our heads is the European model. It is typically the most accurate. The European model has Jennifer making landfall near Newport News, entering the Chesapeake Bay, and moving north toward Baltimore. At this point in time, we think that the European model is an anomaly and are focusing on the other five. However, we'll revisit it after the next round of projections. It's too early to predict landfall. If the storm stays offshore and hugs the coast, we will be looking at a significant storm surge event that will cause considerable property damage and flooding. I'll have more information for you after the 3:00 p.m. update."

"Thank you, Dr. Sperry. We will check in with you later this afternoon."

Jack turned off the TV and returned to the table. "We can pick up Tim in the morning. Given what Micah has told us, I think we need to get back to Rehoboth. I'm sure they will have shelters set up either at Cape Henlopen High School or the convention center. I'll call J. R. and give him an update. Tonight, however, I have arranged for a small dinner party to celebrate our engagement. I've reserved the Wine Room at the Monocle Restaurant on Capitol Hill for 6:00 p.m. Micah, I would appreciate it if you would contact Doc, Duffy, and Pops and invite them to join us."

"Absolutely, I've got you covered. I'll see you at six."

"Thanks for all the hard work. I owe you one."

"Indeed you do." Micah held his outstretched arms to Kate. "Congratulations again. I couldn't be happier for the two of you. I suspect I—correct that, we—will drink several toasts to the happy couple tonight with friends."

As Micah left, Jack turned to Kate. "I don't know about you, but my head is spinning. I'm going to call J. R., and then we're going to forget about all this until after the dinner tonight."

Kate kissed him on the cheek. "Agreed."

CHAPTER SIXTY-FOUR

Jack stepped into his loafers, straightened his tie, and grabbed his sports coat off the back of the dining room chair. He turned toward Kate as she walked into the living room. "Are you ready to go?"

Kate motioned him toward the couch. "Let's talk. You went to a great deal of effort to pick out this ring for me, and I love you for it. We don't need to exchange it. It's beautiful."

Jack turned toward Kate and kissed her on the cheek. "I mistakenly thought that the bigger and more expensive the engagement ring, the more you would understand how very much I love you. I understand now that was very childish of me. However, I want you to have a ring that you will wear every day without the fear that you'll somehow lose the diamond or damage the ring."

"It wasn't childish. It was sweet, and I love you for it."

Jack stood up and helped Kate off the couch. "Let's go to the jewelry store and look at what they have." Kate started to object. "Kate, just humor me."

"Where to?" the taxi driver asked.

"We're going to the Tiny Jewel Box on Connecticut Avenue."

"Have you talked to J. R. yet?" Kate asked.

"Yes, I talked to him while you were getting ready. It was a fairly short call. He was scrambling getting ready for the storm. The mayor issued an emergency evacuation order, and they have opened several shelters."

"Did you tell him what Micah found?"

"I did. He didn't seem to believe the part about Crockett. He said he talked to the deputy police chief in Slidell, and he assured him that Crockett served honorably for several years at the department and was an excellent officer. He thinks it's a case of mistaken identity. I told him we'd be back before noon and that we should confront Jeremy Maddox, Malone, or whatever his name is as soon as possible. Sara is managing the operations at the convention center. That's where you and Tim should go when we get back. Maybe you can lend Sara a hand and check in on Winston."

Peggy Barrett looked up and smiled knowingly as Kate and Jack walked into the store. She was assisting a customer and held her index finger up to indicate that she would be with them shortly. A young couple with their arms around each other were looking at wedding rings.

After almost twenty minutes, Peggy approached Kate and Jack, shaking her head. "I'm so sorry for the delay. The gentlemen I was helping is celebrating his fiftieth wedding anniversary, and he wanted to get something special for his wife." She extended her hand. "You must be Kate, and you obviously said yes. Congratulations. I would also guess that you're looking for a ring that is, shall we say, a little less ostentatious."

Jack looked to the heavens, and Kate smiled sheepishly. "I love the ring. It's beautiful, and Jack picked it out for me. It's just that I want to wear my engagement ring every day, and I'm not sure I would be comfortable wearing this one."

Peggy nodded understandingly. "I understand perfectly. Follow me. We have an excellent collection of engagement rings." Peggy unlocked the display case and pulled out two trays containing over a hundred diamond engagement rings.

Kate took several minutes examining a variety of rings. "May I see these two?"

Peggy placed the two rings on a small black velvet pillow. "Excellent choice, Kate. Try them on."

Kate tried each of them on. "I think I like this one, and it actually fits perfectly. What do you think, Jack?"

"I think it's simple, stylish, and it's you."

Kate handed Peggy the ring. "We'll take it, and if it's all right, I'll wear it."

Peggy smiled and handed it back. "Certainly, and just so you know, it's a two-carat diamond solitaire in fourteen-karat white gold. I think it's a bargain at $2,795. I'll write this all up for you." She turned toward Jack. "Unless you want to pick out wedding rings and a special wedding gift for your future bride, I will be writing you a huge check for the difference."

Jack looked at his watch. "Sure, let's do it all. We've got time."

For the next hour, they looked through several catalogs of wedding rings. Finally, Kate found the one she wanted, and Jack selected a simple eighteen-karat gold band.

Peggy pulled Jack aside. "Kate, will you excuse us for a moment?" She led Jack to the far corner of the store. "I have the perfect wedding gift for Kate." She opened the glass case and pulled out an ornate black box and placed it on the counter. "Go ahead. Open it."

Jack opened the box, revealing the most exquisite necklace he had ever seen. The tag indicated that it was a halo pendant featuring a pear-shaped pink sapphire framed by pear and marquise diamonds in eighteen-karat white gold. "It's spectacular. I'll take it."

"Don't you want to know how much it costs?"

"Not really. Can you gift wrap it for me?"

Peggy laughed. "For that price, I'll hand deliver it to her on your wedding day."

"Now I'm curious. How much does it cost?" Jack asked.

"It's $25,000, and I'm sure it will appraise much higher."

Jack shook his head. "Has anyone ever told you you're pretty good at sales?"

Jack carried a gift-wrapped box as he and Peggy rejoined Kate.

"What's in the box?" Kate asked.

"It's my wedding present to you, and you can open it on the morning of our wedding day."

"Well, if there is nothing else I can help you with, I'll be writing you a very large check, or would you like me to credit your American Express card?"

Jack pulled out his card and handed it to her. "If you'll credit my card, you'll save me a trip to the bank."

Kate looked puzzled. "You just purchased an engagement ring, a wedding gift for me, we picked out our wedding rings, and you're getting a 'very large' refund. How much did you pay for the original ring?"

Jack looked at Peggy and shook his head, but it was too late.

"The 4.01 carat ring was $53,000," Peggy announced.

Kate's jaw dropped, and for once she found herself speechless.

CHAPTER SIXTY-FIVE

Kate sat silently looking out the window as the taxi sped up Pennsylvania Avenue.

"Is everything all right? You've barely said a word since we got back to the hotel."

Kate turned and reached out for Jack's hand. "Since we're getting married, I guess I'm worried about all the money you've been spending. First the boat, and then the overly generous donation to the women's center, and now the wedding ring. It all seems so extravagant."

Jack patted her hand. "Not to worry. The boat was my midlife crisis, and the donation to the women's center was a tribute to my aunt. The engagement ring and wedding gift were for the woman who I love more than anything else in the world." Jack noticed the driver pretend to gag. "I'm actually very responsible financially. My aunt Ellen left me very well off."

"I thought you told me she and your mother came from a poor family," Kate questioned.

"They did, but Aunt Ellen lifted herself up. She worked her way through college. After college, she started her own advertising and public relations firm. Before she sold it, she had over forty employees and represented the campaigns of more than sixty congressmen and senators. She also had advertising accounts with several Forbes 500 companies, and add to that she was a genius when it came to investing. I know you've heard of Apple and Microsoft. She invested tens of thousands of dollars in them when they were just start-ups, and that's just to name a few."

"If you don't mind me asking, how much did she leave you?" Kate asked.

"Not at all. Depending on current market fluctuations, between $38 and $42 million." Jack saw the driver's eyebrows rise.

"Driver, the Monocle, this is it on the right." He helped Kate out of the taxi and handed the driver a hundred-dollar bill.

"Is that all you can spare, Daddy Warbucks?" the driver asked sarcastically.

Jack smiled. "No, not at all." Jack took back the hundred-dollar bill and handed the driver a ten.

The driver wadded up the ten-dollar bill, threw it at Jack, and sped away.

Jack opened the front door to the Monocle and was immediately greeted by the maître d'.

"Kate, I'd like to introduce you to Nick Selimos. He is the premier maître d' in all of Washington, DC. Even some of his more arrogant and pompous clientele love him."

Nick reached for Kate's hand and gently kissed it. "So who is this beautiful creature?"

"This is my fiancée. Kate Simpson."

"It's a pleasure to meet you, Kate. I've never seen Jack with a female companion. I was beginning to think he was… you know. Not that there is anything wrong with that."

"Nick, I think you'd better quit while you're ahead."

Kate laughed. "I guarantee you, he's not."

Nick led Jack and Kate toward the stairs. "Your posse arrived almost an hour ago. I suspect by now they are several drinks ahead of you. Be careful, Kate. They can be an unruly bunch."

Kate smiled. "I wouldn't have it any other way."

"I like her, Jack. She's a keeper. Enjoy your evening."

Jack noticed the owner walking toward them. "Jack Scanlon, I thought you dropped off the face of the earth. We haven't seen you in three or four months."

Jack turned to Kate. "Let me introduce you to John Valanos. He's the owner of this fine establishment. John's parents opened the Monocle in 1960. When they retired, John and his wife, Vasiliki, took over the restaurant. John, I'd like to introduce you to my fiancée, Kate Simpson."

"Kate, it's a pleasure to meet you."

"The reason you haven't seen me lately is I recently began an eighteen-month sabbatical. I've been living in Rehoboth Beach since mid-May. But rest assured, whenever I'm back in DC, I will be dining at the Monocle."

John took Kate by the arm. "Let me escort you to our Wine Room. You'll find your friends have already started an impressive bar tab."

Micah's face lit up when Jack and Kate entered the room. "Where have you two been? As you can see, we were forced to start without you."

Jack looked at his watch. "I said the reservation was at six. It's now 6:10."

"Oops, I thought you said the reservation was at five."

Duffy and O'Brien laughed. Doc just rolled his eyes and took another sip of his wine.

"I just want to know if we can hug the bride-to-be?" he asked.

Kate didn't hesitate. She walked around the table, hugging first Doc, then Pops, Duffy, and finally Micah.

Micah filled two wineglasses and handed them to Kate and Jack. "Now, if we can all remain standing, I would like to propose a toast. Here's to Kate and Jack, a couple that all of us knew weeks ago were meant for each other. May the best of your past be the worst of your future, and we hope that we can be around to share some of it with you. Now let's eat."

Jack picked up the menu. "Kate and I are honored that you could take time out of your busy schedules on such short notice to help us celebrate our engagement. You all are very special to us. By the way, I strongly recommend the New York strip."

Kate started to protest. "We had steak last night. Oh, what the hell. Let's make it New York strips all around."

CHAPTER SIXTY-SIX

Jack suddenly sat bolt upright in bed. Kate rolled over, rubbed her eyes, and glanced at the clock on the night-stand. It was 5:48 a.m.

"What's wrong?"

"I know what happened, and I was right. All three murders are connected." Jack threw off the covers. "We need to get back to Rehoboth as soon as possible. Why don't you shower while I order breakfast?"

Kate reminded him, "We can't pick up Timmy before nine. Tell me what you think happened."

"We don't have time now. I'll explain it all on the drive. If we leave here by eight, we should get to the camp a little after nine. After I order breakfast, I'll start packing."

Jack showered and dressed in record time. He entered the sitting room as the waiter exited after setting breakfast on the dining room table.

Kate was pouring coffee as Jack approached the table. "Have a seat. Breakfast just got here. You can tell me your theory of the murders over breakfast. I'm too curious to wait any longer."

Jack sat down and took a sip of orange juice. "I believe that Malone, a.k.a. Jeremy, was running an elaborate Ponzi scheme, and the money was used to finance their drug operation."

"Whose drug operation?" Kate asked.

"Well, we know that Malone, Pamela, and Crockett are involved, but I don't think they're connected enough to pull this kind of sophisticated operation off by themselves. There is someone higher up involved. I'm just not sure who just yet."

"I'm still confused about the Ponzi scheme. I understand that he was bilking the Henlopen Estates residents. But what happens when someone wants to pull out their investment?"

"As far as we know, no one did until Judge McIntyre informed Jeremy after the party that he wanted to close out his account of over $2 million. Therefore, if they eliminated the judge, his estate would be tied up in probate, giving them more time."

"Are you saying that Jeremy killed Judge McIntyre?"

"I didn't think so at first because of the invalid act, but I do now."

"Act? You mean he's not paralyzed?"

"I don't think so. But if he's not, he sure puts on a convincing act."

"I still have a thousand questions. Like how does this tie into Anna Campbell's death?" Kate asked.

"I think the Roadhouse was used to distribute drugs. Remember, I told you that J. R. and I saw Crockett entering the Roadhouse one afternoon carrying a briefcase and then come out minutes later carrying a different briefcase. I think the briefcase he carried in contained drugs, and the one he carried out contained money. I also think Anna saw and knew too much, and they needed to eliminate her. Does that make sense?"

"So far, yes, it does. What about Vinny? How is he involved?"

"I believe Vinny was freelancing. He is simply a conduit, selling drugs for Malone and company. Don't forget Vinny works for the boys in Philly. Granted, they're involved in almost everything that is illegal in the tristate area, but my contacts in the bureau tell me they draw the line at drugs."

Kate poured herself another cup of coffee. "What about Henry McIntyre?"

"Henry was murdered to throw us off the track. They wanted us to believe that he committed suicide because he was remorseful for killing his father. His apartment was crudely staged, but it planted some doubt and bought them some extra time."

Kate glanced at the clock above the writing desk. "I know I have more questions, but we'd better get on the road."

The traffic was much worse than Jack expected, and he focused his full attention on the road. He crossed over the beltway on Route 50 before he spoke. "Do you think we should tell Tim about our engagement?"

"Why not? He may be only twelve, but he's not stupid. He knows we went away for a weekend together. I would wager he knows we are more than friends by now."

"I don't disagree, but I think he considers me a friend, and he might think marrying his mother would change all that."

"Make that best friend. He considers you his best friend," Kate added. "You have nothing to worry about. He idolizes you."

Jack continued to ponder how they would broach the subject of the engagement to Tim. Before he knew it, he was turning onto Maryland State Route 213 toward Centreville. He had grossly underestimated the traffic and the time it would take to get to Centreville. It was now close to 10:00 a.m.

Jack pulled into the parking lot and turned off the SUV. He took Kate's hand as they walked toward the cabins.

Kate playfully poked Jack in the arm. "Don't you think walking hand in hand might announce our new relationship before we break it to him?"

Jack let go of her hand. "You're right."

"I think this is his cabin." Kate climbed the two steps and peeked inside.

Timmy was sitting on his bunk with his head in his hands. In appeared to Kate that everyone else had already departed. "Good morning, sport. Are you ready to go?"

Timmy looked up, and Kate could see that he had been crying.

"This whole thing is stupid. The storm is not going to come close to us. They have ruined the two weeks for us. Everyone is upset."

Kate picked up Timmy's backpack. "They're operating out of an abundance of caution. We'll bring you back as soon as the storm passes and they say it's safe."

Timmy smiled at Jack and reluctantly followed them to the car with his head down.

Jack pulled onto Route 404 before anyone spoke.

Kate checked an email on her phone and turned to Timmy, still sulking in the back seat.

"I have some good news for you. The camp just announced that they will tentatively reopen on Wednesday and extend the session for an additional week. If all goes well, we will drive you back Wednesday morning. How does that sound, Mr. Sourpuss?"

Tim leaned forward between the front seats. "Can I read the email?"

Kate handed him her phone. He read the email, threw his hands in the air, and settled back in his seat.

"That's great. I can't wait to get back."

Kate leaned over and whispered to Jack. "Maybe this is a good time to tell him."

Jack took a deep breath and looked in the rearview mirror at Tim. "I think you know that I'm very fond of you and your mother."

Kate sighed and shook her head.

Jack tried again. "What I'm trying to say is I really like your mother."

"Jesus," Kate exclaimed as she turned toward Timmy. "Jack asked me to marry him, and I said yes." Kate turned back, folded her arms, and stared at Jack.

After several minutes of uncomfortable silence, Tim was the first to speak. "Jack, will we still be friends?"

"Absolutely, you'll still be my best friend." Jack knew that Tim was still trying to wrap his head around the future with Jack as his father. "I'd also like to ask you to be my best man at the wedding."

"What's a best man?" Tim asked.

"Well, the best man stands next to the groom at the wedding. He is also in charge of the wedding rings. When the minister asks for the rings, you hand them to him. And, most frightening of all, you have to compose a toast to the bride and groom."

"When and where is the wedding?"

Jack turned toward Kate. "Actually, we haven't set a date yet. Weddings take a lot of planning."

Kate chimed in. "It will be a small wedding with only close friends and family. I suspect we will probably try to reserve a small room at Rehoboth Beach Country Club."

"Why not have the wedding at the house?" Tim questioned.

"That's an option," Kate replied. "You see, there's a lot of issues to consider."

They had just passed Denton when Kate suggested, "Why don't you call J. R. and tell him we are on our way?"

Jack picked up his phone and punched in J. R.'s number on speed dial. It rang twice before J. R. answered.

"J. R., it's Jack and Kate. We're about an hour out. We should be there around noon."

"The state police are blocking all of the roads into Rehoboth. I'll alert them that you are coming. Just show them your credentials, and they'll let you past."

"Kate and Tim are with me. We plan on dropping our things off at Kate's house, and Kate and Tim will go to the convention center to shelter. I'll call you when we get there. Where is Crockett?"

"He didn't show up for work this morning. It looks like you were right about him."

"It sounds like they're on the run. See you in an hour."

CHAPTER SIXTY-SEVEN

Jack dialed J. R. as he and Tim schlepped Kate's luggage up the stairs.

"We're back. Can you meet me at Finley's house in about twenty minutes?"

"I'll try. We're pretty slammed with the evacuation and preparations for the storm."

"I understand. I'll wait for you. Call me if there's a problem."

"Kate, I'd like you and Tim to shelter at the convention center, and I'm guessing Sara can use all the help she can get setting up. I'm meeting J. R. at Finley's house to confront Malone."

"Let me drop off Timmy at the convention center, and I'll come with you."

"Please, no, I want you and Tim out of harm's way," Jack said emphatically.

He kissed Kate goodbye and raced down the stairs.

~~~

Jack pulled into the driveway, got out of the car, and walked into the ground level, which was underneath the house. On the right was a cinder-block utility enclosure. He looked for an entrance, to no avail. On closer inspection, he could see that at one point an entrance did exist but had been bricked over. He turned around and walked to the elevator. A sledgehammer rested against the elevator shaft housing. Two badly mangled wheelchairs were thrown into the corner. Jack turned as the sound of J. R.'s patrol car pulled into the driveway.

"Any sign of Malone?"

"No." Jack pointed to the corner. "I think that indicates he's gone and not coming back. Let's try to find a way inside. There used to be an entrance to the utility room, but it's been closed."

"I guess we'll have to go in through the front."

Jack followed J. R. around to the front of the house and up the front stairs. J. R. turned the doorknob, and the door opened.

"This is the police. If there is anyone here, come out with your hands up."

There was no response. Regardless, J. R. pulled out his service weapon, a Heckler & Koch nine-millimeter. "Do you have your service weapon with you?"

"Yes."

"Good. You take the kitchen, and I'll head down the hall toward the back of the house."

It took ten minutes to check all the rooms and closets.

"Let's try to find a way into the utility room. Given the layout, I suspect it's somewhere in the kitchen," Jack suggested.

"I think I found it." J. R. pulled a pocket door open, exposing a hidden panel. He searched for a way to open the panel. After several minutes of trying, he raised his right leg and kicked it in. The shattered wooden panel gave way to a steep staircase leading to the utility room. J. R. stepped over the shattered panel and started down the stairs.

"Be careful. These stairs are very steep."

Jack grabbed the handrail and inched his way down the steps. J. R. turned on the lights. The room was large, with a workbench and several cabinets lining the far wall. A white chest freezer was in the northeast corner. Jack started opening the cabinets.

He pulled a rifle out of one of the cabinets and held it up. "How about this?"

"Looks like military issue," J. R. responded.

"More to the point, it's a M40A5 sniper rifle, which fires a 7.62 NATO round. The same type of round that killed the judge." Jack opened another cabinet. "Look at this."

J. R. leaned over Jack's right shoulder. "What's so strange about a bunch of old clothes and that junk?"

"That junk is theatrical makeup, and those clothes are most likely costumes. I suspect Malone was going around town in disguise." Jack pulled out a jacket. The jacket had a Grotto Pizza logo over the right breast pocket. He pulled out a white work shirt. It had a Delmarva Power patch on the right sleeve.

Jack handed the shirt to J. R.. "You don't suppose that Malone was the guy in the bucket truck the day the judge was killed? He certainly steered us in the wrong direction."

"It makes sense and would indicate that Malone did shoot the judge." He threw the jacket on the workbench and turned around to examine the rest of the room. He leaned back against the workbench for a moment, contemplating the freezer. "Who do you know that has a padlock on their freezer?"

"No one I know." Jack grabbed a crowbar hanging on the pegboard. "Let's find out why." He wedged the claw behind the clasp and, with one forceful pull, broke the lock away. Jack lifted the lid, turned toward J. R., and pointed inside. "Dr. Finley, I presume."

J. R. stepped closer and looked inside. "Jesus, that's him, the poor bastard."

"That's not the half of it. Look at the lid." Jack examined the bloody scratch marks. "He tried to claw his way out."

J. R. held his hand up and pulled out his gun. "Quiet, I think someone is upstairs." They had moved to the foot of the stairs when a voice called out.

"Jack, are you here? It's Kate."

"We're in the basement. Be careful of the stairs—they're very steep."

Kate worked her way carefully down the stairs.

"I thought I asked you to stay at the convention center with Tim and to help Sara out."

"You did, but Sara has everything under control. When I left, she and Tim were just setting up the last few cots. I thought I could be more help here." Kate pointed to the table. "Where did you get the rifle?"

"It's a military sniper rifle. We believe it's the rifle that killed the judge."

Kate turned around and noticed the lid of the freezer. "What's with the freezer being open?" Kate had started toward the freezer when Jack grabbed her arm.

"It's better you don't look. It's Dr. Finley. His body was locked in the freezer."

"My god, these people are monsters."

Jack gently took Kate's hand. "Let's get you back to the convention center."

"Good idea, and I need to get back to work," J. R. added.

They were headed down the front steps when J. R.'s phone chimed.

"It's Sara. I'd better take this. Sara, is everything all right?"

"No. Is Jack with you?"

"Yes. What's up?"

"Kate has been in a terrible car accident. She's been rushed to the emergency room in critical condition."

"Kate who?"

"Kate Simpson."

"What are you talking about? That's impossible. Kate is standing right next to me."

For several seconds there was silence on the other end of the phone.

"Oh my god, what have I done?"

"Sara…Sara, do you hear me?" There was no answer.

"Something is wrong. We need to get back to the convention center. Sara called to tell me that you were in a car accident and rushed to the hospital in critical condition."

Jack grabbed Kate's arm. "Come on. We'll take my car."

Sara sat at the reception desk with her head in her hands as Jack, J. R., and Kate rushed through the front entrance. Sara looked up; she had obviously been crying. She stood up and blurted out something that made no sense.

"Sara, calm down and start from the beginning. What happened?" J. R. asked.

Kate interrupted Sara as she started to speak. "Where's Timmy?"

"He's gone, Kate. He left with your ex-husband. The man stormed in and asked where Tim was. He said he was his father and that you had been in a serious car accident and were rushed to Cape Henlopen Regional Medical Center in critical condition. I asked to see his ID. He showed me a driver's license with his picture that identified him as Aaron Simpson. Tim was setting up the last of the cots when I called for him. He confirmed that the man was his father, but he was very standoffish. He told Tim about the accident, and Tim agreed to go with him to the hospital. Kate, I am so sorry."

"When did they leave?" Jack asked.

Sara looked at her watch. "They left about twenty minutes ago."

Jack walked off and leaned against the wall as J. R. and Kate continued to question Sara.

Kate grabbed Jack's arm. "Let's go. We've got to follow them."

"Follow them where?" Jack asked. "Given the ten minutes we've been here, he has a half-hour head start on us."

J. R. joined them. "What are you doing over here?"

"I'm thinking."

"Thinking?"

"Yes, and I am convinced I know where he's taking Tim." Jack turned to Kate. "I told you that there was someone else running this operation. It's your ex. He is the brains behind all of this, and Crockett releasing him after he attempted to abduct Tim makes a lot more sense now. Remember I told you about Micah and me following the oyster boat up Love Creek and how we lost it after we turned around under the bridge. Well, there is only one place the boat could have gone. It went into the dock under the old warehouse. By the time Micah and I returned, the boat was well hidden. I believe they're using the warehouse as a base for their drug operation. Given recent events, they are most likely packing up to move to another location. Can you meet me there?" Jack asked J. R..

"I'll try, but my first responsibility is to the town and preparing for this storm, which, if you haven't noticed, is upon us."

"I'm going to come in from the bay. It will take me over an hour to get into position."

"Are you crazy? The bay will be treacherous in this storm."

"It's nothing that the Zodiac can't handle."

Jack raced out the door and headed for his Jeep.

"Wait, I'm going with you," Kate shouted.

"No, you're not. It's too dangerous."

"That's my son out there, and I'm most certainly going with you."

Jack shook his head. "All right, but you're going to do as I say, understood?"

"Understood."

CHAPTER SIXTY-EIGHT

County tax records disclosed that the warehouse was built in early 1942 on land purchased by the Thompson Metallurgical Company. From 1942 until the end of World War II, the company produced the nose ring for the navy's F4U Corsair fighter plane. The nose rings were shipped by barge to Norfolk, where the fighter planes were being assembled and shipped to the Pacific Theater. In 1954, the Nebraska Tractor Supply Corporation purchased the warehouse to produce tractor-driven plows. The company went out of business in the late sixties, and the property was seized by the county for delinquent taxes.

The warehouse was fifty feet wide by one hundred and fifty feet long and in need of major repair. The support columns and beams were badly rusted, and several of the windows were cracked or broken. The north end of the building was cantilevered over Love Creek, supported by thirty-two wooden pilings. A large dock had been constructed under the building with access to Love Creek. On the south end of the building, a concrete loading dock could accommodate three large semis at a time.

Two-thirds of the main floor was on a reinforced concrete slab, while the north end was hardwood flooring supported by the pilings and joists. A threadbare Oriental rug covered the wooden floor, along with two overstuffed couches and an eclectic assortment of chairs. At some point, a second floor had been added at the south end for an office and sleeping quarters.

Malone drove the van through the front gate and came to a sliding stop next to the loading docks.

Crockett looked down from the loading dock and hailed Malone as he got out of the van. "Up here."

Rain bands were now moving across the bay from the east, indicating that the storm was still offshore and just to the south of Rehoboth Bay.

Malone clawed his way to the stairs as the rain intensified. "Who's here?"

"Sherry is upstairs packing, and Pamela is wandering around here somewhere. Sammy and Martinez are on their way. They should arrive late this afternoon or early evening, depending on the storm. How about Simpson?"

"No sign of him," Crockett replied.

"Walk with me. I've got something I want to propose for your consideration. Follow me to the back of the warehouse. I don't want anyone to overhear this."

Crocket followed Malone to the north end of the warehouse. "So what's up?"

"What I'm proposing must remain between the two of us, no one else—not even Pamela, and particularly not Sherry."

"Agreed."

"I was thinking, why do we need Simpson? We do all the dirty work. Why should he get a cut of the action?"

"I suppose it's because he has the contacts with the suppliers and worked out the payment arrangements."

"Yes, but I'm confident that they will do business with us. What do they care about Simpson? They're only concerned about the money."

"So what are you proposing?"

"I say we eliminate him. There is no better time than now, while we are moving the operation."

"Wow, you mean kill him? I've got to think this through."

"Don't take too long. If we're going to do this, it needs to get done tonight."

Simpson covered his head with a poncho as he approached the side door to the warehouse.

Crockett saw him coming and raced down the hallway to intercept him. "Boss, I need to talk to you in private."

"Where is Malone?"

"He's down at the dock, gassing up the boat like you asked."

"Follow me outside. I need you to help me with something."

Crockett followed Simpson out to his car. The rain had diminished as the most recent squall line passed through.

"There's no one around. What's so important that we need to talk in private?" Simpson asked.

Crockett took a deep breath. "Malone approached me about an hour ago. He wants you eliminated. He thinks we can run the operation without you."

Simpson leaned against the car and thought for a minute. "Thanks, Crockett. I won't forget this. I'll take care of Malone when the time comes. Let me know if you hear anything else. In the meantime, play along with him. Now, if you'd help me with another matter." Simpson opened the car door and popped the trunk.

Crockett lifted the trunk lid. "Who's the kid, and what's he doing here?"

"He's our insurance. Take him inside, and tie him to a chair. Don't forget to gag him as well. There is a roll of duct tape in the top drawer of the workbench."

Simpson failed to tell him that the boy was his son. Crockett began to wonder if he had done the right thing, telling Simpson about Malone's plan, but it was too late now. The die was cast.

Malone had started up the stairs to the main level when he saw Simpson staring down at him. "Hi, boss. We've been worried about you. I filled the boat with gas as you asked."

"That's excellent. Come on up, and fill me in on the move." Simpson put his arm around Malone's shoulder and led him to the couch.

Malone stared at the boy tied to the chair, with duct tape across his mouth. "What's with the kid?"

"It's nothing to worry about. He's sort of an insurance policy in case anything goes south on us. Now, fill me in on what's going on."

Malone fidgeted on the couch before he answered.

"What's the matter, Malone? You seem a bit nervous."

"No, I'm just collecting my thoughts."

Simpson smirked and sat back in his chair. "I see. Sorry to have interrupted you."

Malone leaned forward. "Crockett, Pamela, and Sherry are all here. Sammy called about an hour ago. Martinez is renting a twenty-two-foot moving van, and Sammy is driving a white panel van. Sammy estimated that they should arrive around 6:00 p.m., depending on the storm. Everything else is ready. All we have to do now is sit back and wait for the boys to arrive."

"Excellent. Is anyone monitoring the perimeter fence?" Simpson asked.

"Yes, Crockett and Pamela have been making the rounds every half hour."

"Excellent."

CHAPTER SIXTY-NINE

The streets were empty as Jack raced south on Bayard Avenue past Silver Lake and onto the coastal highway. A quarter of a mile later, he came to a screeching halt. The ocean had breached the dunes and was flowing across the road, through the Rusty Rudder parking lot, and into Rehoboth Bay. He put the Jeep in park and got out to find a way through the waves of ocean water surging across the highway. Kate joined him as he began wading into the water.

"I'd estimate that the water level is at least three feet in the center. It's too high to just drive through, and it's a good fifty yards across. The Jeep isn't high enough. We would most likely stall out."

"Can we drive up on the sidewalk or the median?"

"No, the sidewalk is too narrow, and the median has too many signposts to get around." Jack thought for a minute. "I think I've got an idea that might work. We'll back the Jeep up a hundred yards or so. You drive it down to here and turn off the engine. The Jeep will coast into the water, and I'll start pushing it when the water slows

427

down its momentum. When we get through the water, the Jeep should start up again."

"And what if it doesn't?"

"I don't know. Have you ever walked five miles through a raging hurricane?"

Kate waded into the water and looked toward the bay. "I think your plan is too risky, but I've got an idea. Notice how the water fans out in the parking lot farther down the drive? It can't be more than a foot deep there. We can drive across the sidewalk, through the hedge ringing the lot, and into the parking area."

"You're a genius. I don't know why that didn't occur to me."

"Maybe it's because you were more focused on the macho solution rather than on the common-sense solution. Sorry, that was a cheap shot. Let's just say we're a good team."

"Get in. Another band of heavy rain and stronger winds appears to be moving through."

When they pulled back onto the coastal highway, the storm had greatly intensified. Even at full speed, the windshield wipers were a waste of time. He turned them off and slowed to thirty miles per hour. He hugged the yellow center line. By the time they reached the marina, the rain and wind had somewhat abated. Jack grabbed a backpack out of the back seat, took Kate's hand, and raced down the dock to where the Zodiac was moored. He helped Kate into the boat and cast off the stern and bow lines. He opened a compartment on the dash and pulled out a laminated map of Rehoboth Bay. He estimated that once he got adjacent to Burton Island, a course of 320 degrees off magnetic north would take him into the entrance to Love Creek.

Once he got into the bay, the waves were considerable, with the wind gusting to seventy miles per hour out of the north-northeast. The Zodiac was rocking violently. He had two options: proceed at a slower speed and fight the storm, or go at full throttle. At full throttle, the Zodiac would plane out, but any obstacles in the water would be on him too fast to react. Not uncharacteristically, he chose the second option. Kate pulled the rain parka over her head and hugged Jack's waist as the Zodiac sped across the bay. At the speed the Zodiac was going, the rain felt like razor blades cutting into Jack's face.

After about twenty minutes, Jack could see the far shore and the entrance to Love Creek. He eased back on the throttle, and the Zodiac settled into the water. The visibility was about one hundred yards as he hugged the north shore past Robinson Landing. He estimated that the warehouse was about five thousand yards ahead on the south bank. Several empty docks lined the south bank.

"Kate, I'm going to back into one of these empty docks. Can you grab the stern line and jump onto the dock when I cut the engine?"

Kate didn't answer. She simply moved to the back of the boat, grabbed the line, and prepared to jump onto the dock.

Jack grabbed the backpack off the deck. He lifted the bow line and stepped onto the dock. "Let's pull the boat as far back as possible and tie her down. We'll have to go the rest of the way on foot. It's about a mile through the woods."

Once again, the wind and rain intensified. Jack glanced at his watch; it was almost six o'clock. The combination of the hour and the thick cloud cover made navigating through the woods a significant challenge.

They struggled through the woods and underbrush for almost a half hour before they finally arrived at the warehouse.

Kate grabbed Jack's arm. "What if Timmy's not at the warehouse? What if this is a wild goose chase?"

"Calm down, Kate. This was our highest percentage play. If he's not there, remember, this is a kidnapping. The FBI will get involved, and they have significant resources. We'll find him. Trust me on that."

Kate smiled weakly. "I trust you."

Jack held out his arm and crouched down in the bushes. Kate knelt beside him. "We're there. See the fence?"

A twelve-foot-high chain-link fence topped with razor wire ringed the property.

"Let's stay put for a few minutes," Jack said. "They may be patrolling the perimeter."

After several minutes, Jack stood and approached the fence. He unzipped the backpack and pulled out a small wire cutter.

Kate pulled his arm back. "What if the fence is electrified?"

"Do you hear that humming in the distance?"

"Yes."

"I believe that's a small generator. The power is out, and they're using the generator to light the warehouse. A small generator couldn't possibly supply enough power to electrify a fence enclosure of this size. However, just in case I'm wrong…" Jack pulled up his right trouser leg and unsheathed an eight-inch knife strapped to his calf. He gently tapped the chain link with the tip of the knife blade.

"We're good."

He tossed the knife in the backpack and started cutting through the chain links. The small wire cutter was barely adequate for cutting through the quarter-inch-diameter steel fencing. Jack's right forearm ached as he struggled to cut through the links. After about fifteen minutes, he finally had cut an opening large enough to squeeze through.

He threw down the wire cutter, rubbed his aching right arm, and turned to Kate. "I want you to stay here." Kate started to object. "I insist. If Tim is in there, I will get him out."

Kate held up the fencing as Jack slithered under it and pulled the backpack through the opening. He crawled about twenty yards toward a row of hedges bordering the entrance road. The rain and wind again began to intensify. Suddenly he saw a flash of light approaching from his left. A dark figure walked along the fence line. For once the weather was working in their favor. Visibility was limited, and the torrential driving rain would discourage anyone from conducting a thorough search of the perimeter. He looked back toward the opening in the fence. Kate was no longer there. He hoped that she had also seen the light and hidden in the underbrush. Despite the driving rain, Jack recognized Crockett. Jack now suspected that his hunch was correct—Tim was in the warehouse. Crockett stopped near the fence where Jack had cut the opening and shone the flashlight back and forth. Jack exhaled in relief as Crockett moved on. He stood and slowly moved toward the hedgerow. The warehouse was quiet. The light from inside cast a soft glow onto the loading dock. Jack stepped from behind the hedge and had started to approach the loading dock when he saw headlights approaching from the access road. He stepped back as the two vehicles stopped. The driver of the lead vehicle stopped, got out, and unlocked the gate. The metal gate slowly swung open, and the two trucks entered the compound and backed up to the loading dock. The drivers got out, ran up the stairs, and into the warehouse. Jack moved behind the hedge line and waited.

CHAPTER SEVENTY

Simpson paced impatiently back and forth. He took one last drag on his cigarette and flicked it across the room.

"What are trying to do, burn the place down?" Malone asked.

Simpson turned and glared at Malone. "What's it to you, Malone? You're starting to get on my nerves." Instantaneously, his demeanor changed. He didn't want to risk getting Malone suspicious. "Sorry, Malone, I'm just a little on edge. Sammy and the Mexican should have been here hours ago."

"The Mexican's name is Miguel. It's Sammy and Miguel," Malone responded contemptuously.

"I wasn't being disparaging. I'm just not good with names. We've got to get this place packed up and out of here before the cops close in on us."

"Don't worry about that. Johnson and his crew are incompetent, and besides, this hurricane is keeping them plenty busy."

"I'm not worried about the local LEOs. It's that FBI agent that concerns me. He's no dummy."

Simpson looked at his watch. It was already after six. He and Malone suddenly turned as the rear door to the warehouse blew open. Sammy forced the doors closed, and he and Miguel walked across the warehouse toward Simpson.

"Where in hell have you been? You should have been here hours ago," Simpson shouted.

Sammy stepped forward. "In case you haven't noticed, boss, there's a major hurricane raging out there. We've been driving for hours. Most of the roads are underwater, some bridges are out, and the cops have closed all the major roads leading in. We've driven all over the peninsula trying to get here, and right now we'd like a drink and something to eat."

"How long is it going to take you to get everything packed up and loaded?"

"What has to go?"

"All of the drugs and the equipment. Essentially everything, including the personal stuff upstairs."

"Give me about ten minutes and I'll have an answer for you. In the meantime, get us something to eat and drink."

Simpson turned to Malone. "Get Sherry down here and have her prepare something for these two."

Sammy returned after a short tour of the warehouse and upstairs living area. "It will take at least five hours to get everything packed up and loaded."

"Five hours?" Simpson responded incredulously.

"At a minimum."

434

Simpson again looked at his watch. "All right, get cracking."

Sammy glared at him. "After we eat."

Simpson turned on his heels and stormed away. It would be well after midnight before they would be done.

CHAPTER SEVENTY-ONE

Jack opened the backpack and pulled out two tracking devices. The GPS trackers used by the FBI and most law enforcement agencies were small battery-operated devices that could easily be attached to any surface. The device instantaneously recorded the vehicle's speed and location.

Jack stepped from behind the hedgerow and raced the short distance to the loading dock. He ducked under the overhang and attached one tracker inside each vehicle's rear bumper. He listened for movement from the loading dock and, satisfied that no one was near, sprinted back to the hedgerow, knelt, and waited. The warehouse was eerily quiet. He had started to rummage through the backpack when he heard what sounded like someone chambering a round. He turned to confront his would-be attacker.

"Well, well, if it isn't Jack Scanlon. Now what might you be doing out here on a night like this?" Pamela asked mockingly. Jack started to get to his feet. "Don't get up. Stay on your knees. I'm afraid this just isn't your lucky day." Pamela raised the gun and pointed it at Jack's forehead.

A soft voice behind Pamela called, "Oh, Pamela."

She spun around, but it was too late. The nine-millimeter round entered her forehead an inch above the bridge of her nose. She fell backward face up in the mud. Kate stood there in the rain, looking down at Jack.

"You can point that gun in another direction, if you don't mind." Jack rose to his feet. "I thought I told you to wait at the fence."

"And where would you be now if I had?"

"Good point."

"I saw her moving toward the hedgerow and thought you might need some help. Next time I'll just follow your orders," Kate responded sarcastically.

Jack grabbed Kate's arm and pulled her behind the hedge as two men walked out of the warehouse and onto the loading dock. He couldn't hear what they were saying but recognized them as the drivers of the two vans.

"It looks like they're pulling up stakes. See the car parked next to the side door?"

Kate nodded.

"When they go back inside, let's see if we can get to the right side of the car for a closer look."

Kate followed Jack closely as he ran across the muddy field. They crouched behind the passenger side door and waited.

After several minutes, Jack rose. "You stay here. I'm going to try and get a closer look inside."

Jack moved to the rear of the car and continued to listen. He slowly moved to the side door of the warehouse. He peered inside but saw nothing. He moved along the outer wall and looked inside a broken window and quickly retraced his steps.

"Good news, Tim is inside. Bad news, your ex, Crockett, and Malone are with him. He's tied to a chair and duct-taped. The other two are packing up the place. We're going to need some sort of diversion." He thought for a minute and pulled off his backpack. He pulled out a three-foot-long white cord.

"What's that?" Kate asked.

"It's det cord. I'm going to try and create some sort of explosion out near the loading dock. That should draw them all outside while we get Tim out of the building. We should be able to get to the fence before they realize what's happened."

Jack rolled up the det cord and moved along the wall toward the loading dock. He crawled under the overhang and waited. The drivers were loading equipment into the moving van. Jack surmised that the panel van would likely be used to move the drugs. When the drivers reentered the warehouse, he moved to the left side of the panel van and slowly removed the gas cap. He lowered the det cord into the tank, attached the electric cap, and moved back under the overhang. He waited a few minutes and quickly made his way back to Kate.

Jack pulled his knife and a detonator out of the backpack. "We're going to have to move fast. When I push the detonator, we will need to get into the warehouse quickly and cut Tim loose." He held the detonator up and pushed the button. A huge explosion erupted at the rear of the warehouse. Jack and Kate raced to the side door, entered, and rushed to cut Tim loose. Kate pulled the duct tape away from his mouth while Jack cut through the ropes around his wrists and ankles.

"Let's go!" Jack shouted.

They had taken no more than three steps when Crockett stepped out from behind a partition. "Not so fast, Scanlon. Drop the knife and raise your hands. I sort of figured you'd show up. I saw what you did to Pamela— such a pity. However, I doubt if Malone will be as forgiving as I am." Crockett laughed. "You see, he loved his sister, and in a very perverted way. In fact, it's illegal in most states."

Crockett pointed his gun at Tim. "He'll be the first one to die unless you follow my instructions to the letter. Now, I know at least one of you has a gun. I would advise you to slowly pull it out using only your thumb and index finger."

Both Kate and Jack carefully reached into their waistbands and slowly pulled out their guns.

"Now place them on the floor and back up. You know, Scanlon, blowing up that panel van was not your brightest idea. The boss is really going to be pissed, considering half of our inventory was already loaded. That's a lot of money that just went up in smoke. I'm just glad I'm not you. Now, the three of you, get on your knees."

Simpson was red with rage when he and Malone walked back into the warehouse.

He turned to Malone. "We're going to need another van. See to it that Sammy finds one and gets it back here ASAP. He can take my car. The keys are in the ignition."

Malone turned and walked back out of the warehouse. When Simpson turned back, he saw Crockett holding three individuals at gunpoint. As he moved closer, he recognized Kate, Scanlon, and his son kneeling on the floor.

Crockett spoke first. "I caught these two trying to escape with the kid. That's not all. They killed Pamela. She's outside lying in the mud."

"Does Malone know?" Simpson asked.

"No."

"Good. Don't tell him until I figure out what to do with these two. Hand me the gun. I'll cover them while you tie them to the chairs. Then tie Scanlon and the bitch to the support column in the center of the room. After that, take the kid downstairs. Put him in the boat and tie him up." Simpson settled into the end of the couch, still pointing the gun at Jack and Kate. "You two have cost me a lot of money, not to mention killing one of my staff."

Kate exploded with rage. "How can you do this to your own son? You're a monster."

"He hasn't been my son since our divorce. You saw to that, sweetheart."

"What are you going to do to him?"

"Well, if you must know, tomorrow afternoon, he will be auctioned off to the highest bidder on the dark web. I suspect in a few days he will be living in some Middle Eastern country, doing god knows what. Maybe I can recover some of the money you two blew up today."

Jack and Kate turned as Malone walked back into the warehouse. When he recognized them, he stopped and laughed. "I'm guessing neither of you is going to invest in the fund." He sat down in a chair next to Simpson, crossed his legs, and leaned back. "So it was these two who blew up the van? What are you going to do with them?"

"There's a box on the workbench in the corner. Bring it to me," Simpson instructed.

Malone returned and handed the box to Simpson. He opened the box and pulled out four sticks of what appeared to Jack to be dynamite that were taped together and connected to a timing device. He handed it back to Malone.

"Strap this to the support column above their heads, and make sure they can both see the clock on the timing device. I want them to know how much time they have left on this planet. If the blast doesn't kill them, then the warehouse collapsing on them certainly will." Simpson sneered at Kate. "For their sake, I hope the blast does the trick."

Malone returned and took his seat. He turned to Simpson. "By the way, have you seen Pamela? I haven't seen her in hours."

Kate yelled, "She's dead, asshole. I shot her. She's lying face up in the mud outside."

It took Malone a minute to comprehend what he had just heard. He jumped from his chair, pulled out his gun, and headed for Kate.

Kate screamed as the explosion echoed throughout the warehouse. Malone slumped to the floor with the right side of his face blown away. Simpson stood over him, holding a smoking .357 Magnum revolver.

When Kate caught her breath, she stared up at her ex-husband. "Why?"

"He had outlived his usefulness."

Jack smiled. "It looks like you have a staffing problem."

"Not to worry, Scanlon. I'm sure I'll be able to find qualified replacements."

Scanlon turned as Sherry walked down the stairs to the main level and approached them. "Well, if it isn't Roadhouse Sherry. This night is full of surprises."

"I'm hurt, FBI man. You never called me. I would have taken you for the ride of your lifetime. Your eyes would still be rolling back in your head." Sherry looked down at Kate. "Don't tell me this is what you turned me down for."

"That's enough. Go see if Sammy has returned," Simpson ordered.

Sherry turned defiantly and walked away.

Simpson was fuming. It took several hours before Sammy returned with the replacement van. He walked in and immediately held up his hand.

"Don't start. It wasn't me that blew up the van."

"How long do you think it will take you to get the rest of the equipment and drugs packed up?"

"I should be done by sunup."

Simpson banged his fist on the arm of the couch. "This has been the night from hell."

Jack laughed contemptuously.

"Laugh it up, funny boy. Once we're packed up, you and my ex will have less than an hour to live."

CHAPTER SEVENTY-TWO

Simpson was half asleep on the couch when Sammy and Miguel approached. Sammy kicked his boot. He rolled over and opened one eye. He slowly sat up and rubbed his eyes.

"Is everything packed up and ready to go?"

"We're all set. Sherry will ride with me in the moving van, and Crockett will go with Miguel. I'll leave first, and Miguel will follow thirty minutes later. I don't know what the roads are like, but we plan to take different routes."

Simpson looked at his watch. It was a little after 5:00 a.m., and it was starting to get light.

"All right, take off. I'll take care of these two. I should be able to meet up with you by midafternoon."

Simpson again rubbed his eyes, stretched his arms, and approached Kate and Jack. He reached up and started the timer. "I decided to give you a half hour to say your goodbyes. I suspect we'll hear the explosion from the bay. Au revoir."

Jack looked at Kate. Tears streamed down her cheeks, and her lips quivered as she glanced up at the timer counting down.

"I love you, Kate, and we're going to get out of this." She nodded unconvincingly. "If I can just get to my knife."

He tried to reach for his leg but realized the knife was in his backpack. He looked up at the timer as he heard the boat's engine start up. The timer read 21:47.

"I've got an idea. This chair is pretty flimsy. If I can lift it up and come down hard on it, it should break apart." Jack pushed the chair against the beam and raised up on his toes. It lifted the chair off the floor about three inches. He held it there for a couple of seconds and dropped his full weight on it, but to no avail. He looked at Kate, and she gave him a faint smile.

"I love you too, Jack. The last two months have been the best of my life."

"Don't give up, Kate. I've got another idea. The edge of this beam is rough. Maybe I can use it to cut through these ropes."

Jack glanced up. 18:38. He maneuvered his chair into a position where the ropes binding his wrists were against the edge of the beam. He worked the ropes up and down, but he soon realized that time would run out long before the ropes broke. Several minutes passed as he tried to come up with another plan.

"Jack, look to your right," Kate exclaimed. "I think I saw a flash of light."

Jack turned but saw nothing. "It was probably the headlights from a passing car out on the highway."

"No, there it is again."

Again, Jack turned and saw a beam of light moving up and down just outside the side door to the warehouse. "Help! In here!" he screamed.

The side door slowly opened as J. R. cautiously entered, a revolver in his right hand and a flashlight in his left. He directed the flashlight beam in Jack and Kate's direction. "What the hell?"

Jack glanced up at the bomb taped to the beam, two feet above their heads. "Quick, turn off the timer."

"How?" J. R. carefully inspected the device.

"There's a red button on the side of the timer. Press it in. It should pause the timer."

"Should?" J. R. questioned sharply. He held his breath, reached up, and pushed in the red button. The timer stopped at 2:47. He exhaled, bent down, and untied Kate. "What do you think, Kate? Should we leave him here?"

"You're a funny guy, J. R.. I'd love to stick around and banter with you, but we've got to rescue Tim. They left about twenty minutes ago by boat. We should be able to catch them in the Zodiac if we hurry."

J. R. untied Jack, and they raced for the door. Jack bent down and picked up their guns, handing Kate hers. He started to open the door but hesitated. He returned to the beam they were tied to, reached up, and unfastened the bomb.

"What the hell are you doing?" J. R. asked.

"I'm taking it with us. It may come in handy."

"And what if it accidentally goes off?"

"Then I won't have to listen to any more of your insufferable jokes."

Jack, Kate, and J. R. raced across the muddy field to the opening in the fence. He held up the fencing as Kate slithered under it. He motioned J. R. to follow and pulled up the fencing as far as he could. J. R. crawled on his stomach but could barely fit through the opening.

"Kate, grab his hands and try to pull him through. I'll push from this end." Jack followed him.

They made it to the Zodiac in under ten minutes. J. R. was struggling to catch his breath. He literally rolled off the dock and into the boat. Kate untied the bow and stern lines and jumped in. Jack turned the key, and the motor roared as he pushed the throttle forward. He turned sharply into the creek and raced toward the bay. The storm had passed. The bay was calm as a brilliant sun slowly rose out of the ocean. At full throttle, the Zodiac skimmed across the water.

"There he is!" Kate screamed, pointing to the slow-moving oyster boat approximately three hundred yards off the starboard bow.

"J. R., take the wheel," Jack commanded. "I want you to ram the port-side stern section of the boat. He will have to struggle to gain control of the boat. When you make contact, I will jump in and attempt to get Tim over the side."

Simpson turned as the Zodiac sped toward him. He picked up his gun off the console. J. R. raised his weapon and started to fire as Jack knocked his arm upward. "Don't shoot. You might accidentally hit Tim."

They were twenty yards away from the boat when Jack picked up the bomb and moved to the bow of the Zodiac. As the Zodiac slammed into the port side, Jack leaped into the oyster boat. Simpson continued to fire wildly as he tried to regain control of the boat.

Jack crawled across the deck toward Tim, who was tied up in the corner. He pushed the red button on the side of the timing device and slid the bomb across the deck toward the engine compartment. He untied Tim's hands and feet and pulled the duct tape off his mouth.

"We're going for a swim. When we get to the gunwale, take a deep breath." As Jack picked Tim up off the deck, Simpson turned and fired three more shots. Holding Tim, Jack leaped up, ran to the port side, and rolled over the gunwale into the water.

Kate scanned the water as J. R. eased back on the throttle. "Where are they? I don't see them. They haven't surfaced," she screamed. "They're drowning!"

"There they are." J. R. pointed to the starboard side of the boat, where two heads bobbed in the water. He eased the throttle forward and moved alongside. Jack lifted Tim up as Kate and J. R. grabbed his arms and hoisted him into the boat.

"Are you all right?" Kate asked frantically.

"Yes, but I think Jack was wounded."

J. R. turned as Jack's raised arm sank into the water. He leaned over the side, snatched Jack by the wrist, and lifted him out of the water.

"Kate, can you give me a hand here? He's a load."

Kate moved to the gunwale and seized Jack's right forearm. As they hoisted him over the side, Jack moaned in pain.

"Oh my god, he's been shot," Kate shouted.

"All right, let's get him on the deck," J. R. instructed. "Rip his shirt open and see if you can find the wound." J. R. turned to Tim. "Tim, take the wheel. See the compass on the dashboard?" Tim nodded. "Keep the boat on a heading of 345 degrees. When you get close to the canal entrance, let me know."

Suddenly, they all turned as a massive explosion rocked the bay. About a half a mile away, an orange-and-yellow mushroom cloud rose into the air.

J. R. turned back to Kate, who had pulled Jack's shirt open. A nickel-sized crimson-ringed hole located a half inch below Jack's right pectoral muscle oozed small frothy bubbles.

"Jesus, it's a sucking chest wound."

He turned on hands and knees and scrambled across the deck. He pulled out a large red canvas bag with a white cross on the top and sides. He returned to Jack's side, unzipped the bag, and pulled out a three-inch square gauze dressing in a plastic wrapper. J. R. ripped the gauze in half, wadded it up, and placed it over the wound. He then placed the plastic packaging over the hole in Jack's chest and taped it securely, making sure it was airtight. He rummaged through the first aid bag and pulled out an Ace bandage.

"I'm going to roll him on his left side and slip the bandage under him. Grab it and hand it back to me."

They repeated the procedure two more times. J. R. pulled the bandage taut and secured it with two metal clips. Kate looked at her right hand. It was covered in blood.

"He's been shot in the back." J. R. again rolled him onto his left side and lifted his bloody shirttail. He located the wound, packed it in gauze to stop the bleeding, and taped it.

"We need to get him to the hospital in Lewes," J. R. declared.

Jack squeezed Kate's hand and smiled weakly.

"Don't let him lose consciousness. Slap him silly if you must, but keep him awake," J. R. instructed.

Tim continued to pilot the Zodiac across the bay. J. R. opened a cabinet under the console and pulled out a sat phone. He extended the antenna and punched in ten numbers.

"Cape Henlopen Regional Medical Center, how may I direct your call?"

"Connect me to the emergency room."

"This is the emergency room, Nurse Kelly speaking."

"This is Chief Johnson. I'm bringing in a gunshot victim by boat. Have an ambulance meet us at the town dock. The victim has a sucking chest wound and another bullet lodged in his back near the spine. We'll be there in about ten minutes. Please call Chief Conrad and ask him to meet us there as well. Thank you."

J. R. placed the sat phone back in the cabinet and tapped Tim on the shoulder. "Good job. I'll take over. Navigating the canal at high speed can be tricky. See if you can help your mother."

J. R. pushed the throttle forward as far as it would go. The Zodiac sped down the canal past the Henlopen Estates marina and into the state park. He eased back on the throttle as they approached the old railroad swing bridge. The narrow passage could be difficult to navigate. Fortunately, it was at slack tide, and the Zodiac moved under the bridge without incident.

Conrad and the two EMTs waited on the dock as J. R. eased the boat alongside and turned off the engine.

He turned to Kate. "How's he doing?"

"I'm worried. He conscious but unresponsive."

The two EMTs jumped into the boat. "It's going to take all of us to get him on the board and onto the dock," one of the EMTs announced. He ordered Kate, Tim, and J. R. out of the boat. They eased Jack onto the board and lifted the board up. Conrad and J. R. reached down and hoisted Jack onto the dock. The EMTs placed Jack on the gurney and raced across the dock to the waiting ambulance.

"Kate, you go in the ambulance with Jack. Tim and I will follow with Chief Conrad."

CHAPTER SEVENTY-THREE

A doctor and two nurses waited anxiously as the ambulance pulled up to the emergency room entrance. Kate jumped out of the back as the EMTs lowered the gurney onto the drive-through. The two nurses grabbed the handles on each side and raced through the entrance and down the corridor, followed by the doctor. Kate ran after them with tears running down her mud-streaked cheeks.

As they approached the double doors, the doctor turned and stopped Kate. "I'm sorry, ma'am. You can't go any farther."

"Please, Doctor, I'm his fiancée," Kate pleaded.

"You'll have to stay here. As soon as we get him stabilized, I will be out to give you a status report." The doctor turned and disappeared behind the double doors.

Minutes later J. R. and Tim came running down the hall and into the waiting area. J. R. put an arm around Kate's shoulders as she reached out and pulled Timmy closer. "They won't let me go in there," Kate groaned.

"Kate, it's for the best. They are going to need all the room they can get to work on him. I called Micah on the way over. He's on his way to brief the deputy director.

Let's get you home. You can get cleaned up, and I will get you right back to the hospital."

"I'm not leaving him."

"He's lost a lot of blood. It's going to take them several hours to get him stabilized and ready for surgery."

Kate pushed his arm away and stepped back. "I'm not leaving him!" she shouted emphatically.

"Kate, please, you're covered in mud and blood, and you're scaring the other patients."

She turned to see that every eye in the waiting room was watching her.

A young nurse cautiously approached them. "Excuse me, may I offer another option? The doctor's lounge is just down the hall and has a shower. I can get you a set of scrubs, and we can get your clothes laundered. I'll stand guard at the door while you shower."

Kate smiled with relief. "Thank you."

"Now that that's settled, I'll take Tim home. What can I bring back for you?"

"There's a medium-sized suitcase next to my bed. That has everything I will need. Thank you, J. R., and I'm sorry. Please forgive me."

He bent down and kissed her on the forehead. "No apology necessary. I'll be back as soon as possible."

Kate smiled and followed the young nurse down the hall. "What's your name?"

"It's Jackie, Jackie Merritt."

"Thank you, Jackie. I really appreciate what you're doing for me."

"You look much better," the young nurse exclaimed as Kate stepped into the hallway. "Let's get you back to the waiting room."

Kate was invigorated after the hot shower. It was as if a fog had been lifted and she now felt confident that she would be better able to face whatever challenges lay ahead.

"Can I get you anything else? Some food or something to drink?"

Kate reached out and hugged her. "Jackie, you've been wonderful. I can't thank you enough."

"If you need anything, I'm on duty until noon."

J. R. walked into the waiting room pulling a medium-sized black Rollaboard suitcase. "Is this the right suitcase? It was the only one next to your bed, and Tim thought you might need these." He handed her a pair of black sweats with "Princeton Soccer" in orange lettering on both the top and bottom.

"Thank you, that's it. How's Timmy doing?"

"He's asleep. Sara is with him. She brought him some food, and she is going to stay at your house until I get back. Any word on Jack?"

"Nothing. It's been close to two hours."

Kate noticed the nurses' station jump into action. One nurse was checking charts, another exited the station, and Jackie looked as if she was going to cry. Kate didn't notice the woman striding purposefully down the hall until she was almost in front of them. She was a little over five feet tall and grossly overweight. She wore an orange tent dress and looked like a pumpkin with legs.

She turned to the nurse sitting at the desk. "Where's the Scanlon party?"

"That would be us," Kate announced.

The woman turned sharply and glared at Kate. "I don't know who you are, lady, but you're not getting any special treatment at this hospital."

"Ma'am, I have no idea what you're talking about."

The woman raised her voice another octave as her face turned a bright crimson. "I just got off the phone with some self-important jackass from the FBI. He is insisting that I turn over the entire seventh floor to him and his team to care for one of his agents. I told him to stick his request where the sun don't shine."

J. R. stood up. "Just who the hell are you, lady, and how do you get off blatantly ignoring a bureau request? One of their agents has been shot and is in critical condition."

"I'm the hospital administrator, and this is my hospital. I decide what happens around here, not the FBI."

An imposing figure of a man in a neatly tailored blue suit burst out of the conference room across from the nurses' station. "What the hell is going on out here? This is a hospital."

Kate decided to return serve. "Sir, I'm Kate Simpson. My fiancé, FBI agent Jack Scanlon, was shot taking down a major drug operation controlling the mid-Atlantic region. He was brought here in critical condition. The deputy director of the FBI called your hospital administrator this morning, requesting her assistance in the care and treatment of this agent. Apparently she told him to go shit in his hat, pardon the vulgarity. I recall a similar episode involving a political fundraising organization last year. They also refused to cooperate with the FBI. The bureau, in conjunction with the Internal Revenue Service, initiated a forensic accounting audit of the organization's financials going back several years. They also audited every member of the organization's board of directors. Two of the directors eventually went to jail. I just hope that type of thing doesn't happen to this hospital as a result of your administrator's careless actions."

"Ms. Simpson, I'm Franklin Stein, chairman of the hospital's board of directors. Be assured that your fiancé and the FBI will have everything they need." Stein handed Kate his business card. "If you need anything, please feel free to call my personal number. I am very sorry about this misunderstanding. Trust me, it won't happen again."

The administrator's face now turned from crimson to scarlet. "What do you mean 'misunderstanding'? I'm responsible for the operation of this hospital."

Franklin Stein was clearly not a man to be trifled with. He turned, reached down, and pointed his right index finger into her chest. "I would strongly suggest that you return to your office and await further instructions. I will be meeting with the board of directors later this afternoon, and be assured that your conduct this morning will be our number one agenda item."

Stein reached out and shook Kate's hand as the administrator stormed off down the hall. "Again, anything you need, just call me."

J. R. just stood there shaking his head. "I'm impressed. That was one ballsy move. Was that story about the political fundraising organization true?"

"I don't know. It could have been."

"Wow, you and Jack are going to make a great team."

J. R. pointed to the nurses' station. "You certainly made their day."

The nurses were laughing and high-fiving each other. Jackie smiled at Kate and flashed a thumbs-up. Kate nodded and sat down to continue their wait for more news.

CHAPTER SEVENTY-FOUR

Kate jumped out of her seat as the doctor pressed through the double doors. J. R. had nodded off but quickly sprang to his feet. As the doctor approached, Kate felt as if her heart was in her throat.

"Ma'am, I'm sorry I didn't get a chance to introduce myself earlier. I'm Dr. David Lyons, the hospital's chief of surgery. We have stabilized your fiancé. He has received two pints of blood, and his blood pressure has returned to normal. He's on his way up to surgery as we speak. I will be operating on his chest wound. The bullet in his back is very close to his spine. I'm not comfortable operating that close to his spinal cord. Therefore, I've called a colleague at Johns Hopkins in Baltimore. Dr. Howard Russell is a renowned neurosurgeon. He specializes in spinal cord surgery. He's one of the few people on the planet that I would trust to do the operation. The FBI is flying him here by helicopter. He should arrive within the hour. It appears the entire seventh floor will be at your disposal. It's a much more comfortable place to wait. I'll have one of the nurses take you and the chief up there as soon as possible. Now, if you will excuse me, your fiancé awaits."

Jackie quickly volunteered to take Kate and J. R. to the seventh floor. As the elevator doors opened, Kate couldn't believe her eyes. "Wow, this is amazing."

"It's exclusively reserved for our VIPs. Four years ago, the previous president contracted pneumonia while vacationing in Rehoboth. The Secret Service rushed him here. Your fiancé will be staying in the same room. The room is just down the hall. Please follow me."

The corner room was forty-foot square overlooking Delaware Bay. It also featured an adjoining large bathroom with a roll-in shower. A small galley kitchen with almost every amenity graced the interior wall. A sitting area with a couch, love seat, coffee table, and three overstuffed leather chairs was just inside the sliding entrance doors.

"The queen bed in the far corner is for your use, Kate. When they bring Mr. Scanlon up, his bed will be against that wall." Jackie pointed to an area festooned with monitors, IV stands, and a bedside table. "I'm told, given the attempt on your fiancé's life, our nurses will not be allowed on this floor because they don't have security clearances. The FBI is bringing a nursing staff that has been cleared. However, if you need anything before they get here, just call the nurses' station in the emergency room. As far as they are concerned, you are a rock star. They will get you anything you need. The word has spread all over the hospital about how you took down the administrator this morning. Make yourself at home. I suspect it will be a while before you hear anything."

"Jackie, again, thanks. You've been an angel."

"Kate, I hate to leave you here alone, but I've got to get back to the station. I'll check in on Tim and be back as soon as I can. Is there anything you need before I leave?"

Kate looked around the cavernous room. "Company. Would you call Roberta and explain what has happened and ask her if she can come over and sit with me until Jack is out of surgery?"

"Consider it done. I'll have one of my deputies drive her to the hospital."

Kate and Roberta were sitting on the couch talking when Dr. Lyons knocked on the sliding glass door. She looked at her watch. It was almost 6:00 p.m.

"May I?" Lyons asked, pointing to the chair next to Kate.

"Please join us. This is my best friend, Roberta Robinson. This is Dr. Lyons. He operated on Jack." She turned anxiously. "How is he doing?"

"The operation went as well as could be expected. He'll be in recovery for another hour or so, and then they will bring him up. I don't want you to be alarmed when you see him. He has a drainage tube in his chest and a feeding tube. He also has a catheter. He is sedated, and I don't expect him to regain consciousness for several more hours. When he does, he will be in a great amount of pain. I've ordered a morphine drip. I will be back in the morning to check on him. Do you have any questions for me?"

"What's his prognosis?"

"I'm convinced he will make a full recovery, but it will take several weeks before he's back to normal. Incidentally, the FBI has arrived in force. This floor is locked down, and there are four nurses from Georgetown Hospital on duty at the nurses' station down the hall. Any guests that you are expecting will have to be cleared ahead of time."

It was after 9:00 p.m. when the nurses wheeled Jack's bed into the room and hooked him up to the monitors. Despite Dr. Lyons's warning, Kate was still shocked when she saw him. He looked like a man at least twenty years older. Tears streamed uncontrollably down her cheeks and onto her blouse. She walked to the side of the bed, took his hand in hers, and started to sob.

One of the nurses placed her hand on Kate's shoulder. "Don't be alarmed. He's been through a difficult operation. He will look more like himself once he regains consciousness."

Kate forced a smile and thanked the nurse for her kindness. She pulled a chair next to the bed to begin her all-night vigil.

CHAPTER SEVENTY-FIVE

As the early morning sun illuminated the room, Kate awoke sensing that she was being watched. A distinguished-looking man in a three-piece dark gray suit stood next to the sliding door. He was a ruggedly handsome man in his early to midsixties, and Kate suspected immediately who he was. She started to get up.

"Please, don't get up. May I join you? I'm Jim Rankin, and you must be the Kate I've heard so much about. How's our boy doing?"

Kate motioned Rankin to the couch. "He's doing better than he looks. At least that's what I've been told. He was shot in the chest and the back. The doctors removed both bullets, but he still has a drainage tube in his chest."

"How did this all happen? I sent him on sabbatical to recharge his batteries, not to get shot chasing drug runners."

For the next twenty minutes, Kate related the events leading up to Timmy's kidnapping and his rescue.

"So I understand our boy popped the question."

Kate held out the engagement ring. "It was very romantic. He asked me to marry him on the steps of the

Lincoln Memorial." Kate giggled. "I thought he'd never ask. I fell in love with him shortly after we met."

"So have you set a date?"

"Not yet."

Rankin pulled a small black calendar out of his vest pocket. "Well, let's see. August is no good—I'll be in Europe at a summit and then two weeks of vacation with the grandkids." He turned the page. "Early September is out; we have a bureau-wide leadership meeting in Kansas City. Ahh, Saturday, September 21, is perfect. There's not much time between now and then. My wife has helped plan all our daughters' weddings. I know she would be delighted to help you."

Kate sat back in shock. She knew from Jack that Rankin was a take-charge kind of guy, but this was over the top. "Sir, I think this is a decision that Jack needs to be involved in."

"Kate, when it comes to matters of the heart, Jack can be a procrastinator. You need to take the bull by the horns. Now, where were you thinking you'd be married?"

"Well, I thought we'd have a small wedding at Rehoboth Beach Country Club, just close friends and family."

"Perfect. You'll probably have to make a reservation this week." Rankin started to continue his thought but stopped in midsentence. "Kate, Jack is moving."

Kate leaped off the couch and ran to Jack's bedside. She squeezed his hand, and he squeezed back. Tears of joy welled up in her eyes, and she smiled across the room at Rankin. Jack tried to speak, but his lips were stuck together. Kate took a small sponge stick, dipped it in ice water, and gently rubbed it along his lips. His eyes opened, and a weak smile seemed to appear. He silently mouthed the words *I love you*.

"Look who's here."

Jack slowly turned his head in Rankin's direction and attempted to give him a thumbs-up.

With a soft knock on the door, J. R. announced his arrival, with Micah Cruise and Winston in tow. "Good morning. I see he's awake. I thought I'd bring Winston by to cheer him up."

Jack smiled and tried to reach down to pet Winston, to no avail. J. R. moved him closer and lifted his paws onto the side of the bed. Jack now gently stroked Winston's head.

"We come bearing news, some good and some not so good," J. R. announced. "I'll start. I inspected the storm damage at both of your houses. Kate, you lost about a quarter of your deck. Other than that, your home survived the storm in great shape. Jack's, not so much."

Jack tried to sit up. Kate pushed a button on the side of the bed, elevating his head and back. She then fluffed up the pillows to make him more comfortable. He was now keenly aware of what was going on around him and what J. R. was telling him.

"Your deck is completely gone. The windows on the ocean side are all blown out, and there's considerable water damage inside the house. I have a neighbor, Carl Alesi, who owns the premier home renovation and construction company in Sussex County. He's swamped with work but has agreed to go over, assess the damage, and give you an estimate."

Jack beckoned J. R. closer to the bed. "I don't need an estimate. Tell him to do the work, and I will pay him a fifty percent premium over and above his costs. Also, tell him I would like a more open concept like Kate's main floor."

Micah approached the bed. "I'm afraid my news is much more disturbing. It appears Kate's ex-husband was not killed in the explosion."

"That's impossible," Kate exclaimed. "No one could have survived that explosion. It was massive. I don't believe it."

Micah pulled a laptop out of his briefcase. "This footage is from a surveillance camera in the marina parking lot. It's a little grainy, but it shows a man limping across the lot, dragging his left leg. His left arm hangs limp at his side. The time stamp is approximately twenty-five minutes after the time J. R. said the explosion occurred. Who else could it be?"

The room went deadly silent. Rankin stood up and moved closer to the bed. "Let's assume for a moment that it is Simpson on the surveillance video. Where did he go? He must have required medical care."

"We checked all the hospitals and health clinics on the Delmarva Peninsula. None of them reported treating a patient for that type of injury. We rounded up all the others on the eastern shore. There was no sign of Simpson," Micah reported.

"Maybe he died somewhere of his injuries," Kate offered.

"We thought of that and are still canvassing the area."

"Any more exciting news?" Jack asked sarcastically.

"Yes, we're getting married at Rehoboth Beach Country Club on Saturday, September 21," Kate blurted out.

Jack smiled at Kate. "I have no objection to that, but isn't it rather short notice?"

Rankin stepped forward. "Kate and I have discussed it, and Molly will help with all of the planning. If you're looking for a best man, I'm available."

"Well, sir, I already have a best man."

Rankin's smile faded. "I understand. You and Micah have been through a lot together."

"Actually, sir, my best man is Kate's son, Tim. I'm not sure you're aware of the fact that my father, mother, and brother were killed in a car accident when I was a teenager. My aunt died last year, so I have no family. I would be moved if you and Molly would serve in place of my parents at the wedding."

"It would be our honor."

A soft knock on the wall got everyone's attention.

"Well, I see that there's a party going on, and I wasn't invited. I hope you're not overstimulating my patent." Dr. Lyons looked up at the monitor as he approached the bed. "I see your vital signs are good. I've ordered a morphine drip for the pain."

Jack emphatically shook his head. "No narcotics. I'll take ibuprofen for the pain."

"There isn't enough ibuprofen in Sussex County to manage the pain you're going to experience after the sedative wears off."

"I can handle the pain."

"Have it your way." Dr. Lyons turned to Kate. "Is he always this stubborn?"

"I'm just now finding out that about him."

"Dr. Russell will be up shortly to check on him." Dr. Lyons turned to leave and then hesitated. "Just out of curiosity, who bandaged his chest wound?"

"I did. Why?" J. R. asked defensively.

"Because you saved his life. Where did you learn how to treat a sucking chest wound?"

"The combat medics course at Fort Sam Houston."

"They taught you well."

J. R. turned to Kate. "Hmm, saved his life. That ought to be worth a few steak dinners."

"Once I'm cleared to eat solid food, you can count on free steak dinners for the foreseeable future," Jack confirmed.

J. R. got up and headed for the door. "Oh, I forgot. There's someone who wants to see you."

Several minutes later J. R. returned pushing a man in a wheelchair. It was Eddie Williamson. "I ran into Eddie downstairs. When I told him what happened, he insisted on coming up to see you." J. R. wheeled Eddie up next to the bed.

"I thought you'd be out of here by now," Jack said.

"I would have been, but the stab wound got infected. I want to thank you for all you've done for me. The doctor told me."

"You're welcome, but I had hoped to keep that anonymous. Before this happened, I was planning on visiting you. We've got a couple of more surprises for you. J. R. talked to the president of the Rehoboth branch of Wilmington Trust. He's agreed to hire you on a probationary basis in their commercial loan department. We also rented you an apartment in town, and Carlton's will fit you for three business suits and accessories."

"I don't know what to say. I'll never begin to repay you for all this."

"I saved the best for last. I was able to get in contact with your platoon sergeant from Vietnam. He has reached out to several members of your platoon, and they are petitioning the Department of the Army to reevaluate your DSC award for a possible upgrade to the Medal of Honor. They are adamant that you deserve the upgrade, and after reading the citation and after-action report, I agree."

"I doubt if that's possible."

"I wouldn't be so sure. They recently upgraded Daniel Inouye's DSC to the Medal of Honor."

"Yes, but he's a United States senator, and I'm a…"

"I think the word you're searching for is 'hero.'"

"I'll never be able to repay you. Thank you all."

"Your service has paid all of us back many times over."

CHAPTER SEVENTY-SIX

"Good morning, Mr. Scanlon. You must be a pretty important person to warrant these accommodations and all of this high-powered attention. Are you related to the president or something like that?" Dr. Russell asked.

"No, sir, I'm just a midlevel government employee with a lot of good friends."

"Right. Let's see how you're doing." Dr. Russell moved to the foot of the bed, pulled back the sheet, and lifted Jack's left leg. He took a fountain pen from the breast pocket of his lab coat and ran it from Jack's heel to his toes. His toes reflexively curled. "Did you feel that?"

Jack nodded.

"Excellent." He repeated the procedure with Jack's right foot with the same result. "Well, young man, it appears that the operation was a success. With Dr. Lyons's concurrence, I would like you up and on your feet tomorrow morning, walking. I will have the feeding tube and catheter removed. With assistance, before every meal this week, I want you to walk down to the nurses' station and back. Next week it's down to the elevator and back. With luck, I'll have you out of the hospital and home in ten days. However, you will need in-home care."

"That's no problem, Doc. I'll take some vacation days, and he can stay with me," J. R. offered.

Kate held up her engagement ring. "I'm his fiancée. He'll stay with me. For the most part, I can work from home."

"Excellent. It looks like you have everything covered." Dr. Russell moved to the side of the bed. "Let me guess, Mr. Scanlon. You were in the military and saw some combat. I suspect in either Iraq or Afghanistan."

"Actually both," Jack responded.

"I would also guess you were wounded."

"Yes, three Purple Hearts. Where are you going with this, Doc?"

Russell reached into his lab coat pocket and pulled out a small plastic jar. He held it up and rattled it. "I took these three pieces of shrapnel out of your back. The one with the razor-sharp edge was the closest to your spinal cord. Eventually, it would have migrated closer to your spinal cord and potentially severed it. You're a lucky man, Mr. Scanlon. Did you know they were in your back?"

"No, it happened on my last tour in Afghanistan. I was taken to a field hospital. It was meatball surgery. They patched me up as best as they could and shipped me off to Germany. Thanks for everything, Doc. Dr. Lyons is your second biggest fan, next to me."

"He also owes me a steak dinner at Morton's next week in DC. I think I'll have the forty-eight-ounce porterhouse with an expensive bottle of cab. Take care of yourself, Scanlon, and congratulations on your engagement. You outkicked your coverage on this one."

Rankin stood up and walked to Jack's bedside. "It looks like my work here is done. I think I'll head back to Washington. I'll see you both on September 21, if not earlier, and Kate, I'll have Molly call you next week." He reached out and patted Jack on the head. "Take good care of him, Kate. He's a keeper."

When everyone had left, Jack closed his eyes and drifted off to sleep. Kate lay down on the queen-sized bed, said a silent prayer of thanks, and closed her eyes.

CHAPTER SEVENTY-SEVEN

Three Weeks Later

Duffy, Doc, and Micah carried the diving gear to the boat. Pops and J. R. schlepped the coolers. There was no fishing gear this time. Jack and Tim were on a mission.

"You're not thinking about diving, are you?" Kate asked Jack.

"Of course not. Micah, Doc, and Duffy will do the dive. The rest of us will simply provide moral support. Look at Tim. Have you ever seen him this excited?"

"I just hope this isn't another wild goose chase. He'll be devastated."

"No, he won't. He's matured considerably since the kidnapping. You may not like to admit it, but he's not a young boy anymore. He's a young man."

Kate just sighed and climbed up the gangway and into the boat.

Jack turned back to Tim. "I've programmed the coordinates Maggie gave us into the onboard computer. Once we get into the channel, you take over."

They cruised for twenty minutes before Tim eased back on the throttle. "We're here. It's fifty yards ahead,"

Tim called out to Jack. "I'll drop the bow anchor; you throw out the stern one."

Jack winked at Kate. "See what I mean?"

Tim barked out more orders as the three divers appeared on the deck dressed in wetsuits and diving gear.

"We'll do the same thing we did the last time," Micah directed. He handed out the ropes, and they moved to the fantail. "Wish us luck." Micah pulled down his mask and dropped backward into the water. Doc and Duffy followed his lead.

Visibility was not as good as their last dive. A recent storm had stirred up the bottom. Micah was the first to reach the bottom. He couldn't believe his eyes. Hundreds of gold coins carpeted the ocean floor. They looked at each other in amazement. Each diver carried a small mesh bag, but it was nowhere near adequate enough to bring the treasure to the surface. The ropes were no longer of use. They attached them to the cable line in case they might be needed later. For ten minutes they swam around, filling their mesh bags with gold coins. Micah finally signaled them to surface.

Tim waited, anxiously looking over the side at the emerald-green surface of the ocean. A large grouping of water bubbles began breaking the surface.

"Oh no, they're coming up," Tim exclaimed. "It's too soon. They must not have found anything."

Micah was the first to surface, and the grin on his face told Jack all he needed to know. He placed an arm around Tim's shoulder. "They found it."

Tim looked up in surprise. "Are you sure?"

Jack pointed to Micah. "Just watch."

Micah pulled himself onto the fantail, lifted the mesh bag, and poured its contents onto the deck.

Tim squealed with joy as the coins rolled onto the deck. Doc and Duffy emptied their bags onto the deck as well. Everyone ran around hugging and slapping each other on the back.

Micah took off his mask, tank, and fins and hopped up in the captain's chair. "This is it, Jack. There are hundreds of gold coins scattered all over the ocean floor. Amazingly, there are three large chests still intact, but there is no way we will be able to raise them."

"I don't intend to. I have tentatively contracted with a marine salvage team out of Norfolk. They can be on-site in a couple of days. I also have a lawyer who specializes in marine salvage working on the required permits."

"We've got enough air to make three more dives. Let's get up as much as we can before the salvage team takes over," Micah proposed.

"Agreed. J. R., you and Pops empty the fishing cooler, clean it out, and fill it half up with seawater. We'll put the coins and whatever else they bring up in the cooler."

The three dives netted several hundred gold coins, a gold chain and crucifix, and a lump of silver coins fused together.

When the divers had gotten out of their wetsuits and dried off, Jack passed out beers all around. Jack raised his beer in salute to the divers.

"Everyone on board will share equally in the treasure. However, I propose for your consideration that Tim be allotted two shares. After all, without his research we wouldn't even have known the treasure existed." Everyone raised their bottles in agreement. "Now, let's get back to the house and divide up the treasure. I'll spring for the sushi and beer."

"Tim, I know you're excited, but do you think you can get us back to the marina?" Jack asked.

"Absolutely. If you'll get the stern anchor, I'll start up the engine." Tim settled back in the captain's chair and eased the throttle forward.

Tim smiled contentedly as Kate and Jack approached arm in arm.

"I am very proud of you, Tim. You believed in yourself and stuck to it. Congratulations," Kate declared.

"You called me Tim."

"Yeah, I guess I did. I guess you're not my little boy anymore."

"So now that you've completed your quest, what's next?" Jack asked jokingly.

"Well, interesting that you should ask. Have you ever heard of the Beale treasure?"

Kate rolled her eyes. "Come on, Jack. It's time for another beer."

The two SUVs pulled up to Kate's front door. In their euphoria, no one noticed the black car idling across the street. The left side of the man's face was badly scarred. He glared at Kate and Jack as they walked up the stairs with their arms around each other.

ABOUT THE AUTHOR

The Author and Winston.
The dog is a character in the book named
Winston (a real story).

Tom Donnelly holds a BS and MS in civil engineering from Norwich University and Rensselaer Polytechnic Institute. He served for 10 years as a US Army engineer officer, where he was awarded the Bronze Star in Vietnam. Following military service, Tom became staff director of the Senate Water Resources Subcommittee, where he advised members on natural resources policy and for over 30 years worked as a lobbyist for various water resource organizations. For the past 25 years, Tom has umpired high school baseball and softball. Now retired, he and his wife, Joan, reside in Rehoboth Beach, Delaware.